Carol Goodman grew up on Long Island, attended public school, and started writing at age nine, when her teacher introduced the topic 'Creative Writing'. She wrote a ninety-page, crayon-illustrated epic entitled *The Adventures of the Magical Herd* in which a girl named Carol lives with a herd of magical horses. She knew from that moment that she wanted to be a writer.

During her teens Goodman wrote poetry and was awarded Young Poet of Long Island by Long Island University at the age of 17. She took a break from writing to major in Latin at Vassar College, never realising that her first published novel would be about a Latin teacher, her bestselling and critically acclaimed debut novel, *The Lake of Dead Languages*.

Since its publication, Goodman has been writing full time and her books have been nominated for the IMPAC award twice, the Simon & Schuster/Mary Higgins Clark award, and the Nero Wolfe Award; *The Seduction of Water* won the Hammett Prize in 2003. She lives with her family on Long Island.

Praise for Carol Goodman:

'Hopelessly addictive . . . definitely the season's guilty pleasure' *Time Out*

'Enchants with its fairy-tale motif and sensuous atmospherics' *People*

'Goodman's New England gothic sets up a chilling atmosphere and a gruesome scenario very nicely indeed' *Guardian*

'Embrace your inner goth with this atmospheric shiver fest' *Elle*

'An urban fantasy series with an unusual heroine. Fans of . . . Mercedes Lackey should enjoy this vibrant addition to the urban fantasy genre' *Library Journal*

Other novels by Carol Goodman:

INCUBUS

CAROL GOODMAN

EBURY
PRESS

3 5 7 9 10 8 6 4

Published in the UK in 2011 by Ebury Press, an imprint of Ebury Publishing
A Random House Group Company

The Random House Group Limited Reg. No. 954009

Addresses for companies within the Random House Group
can be found at: www.randomhouse.co.uk

A CIP catalogue record for this book
is available from the British Library

The Random House Group Limited supports The Forest Stewardship Council
(FSC®), the leading international forest certification organisation. Our books
carrying the FSC label are printed on FSC® certified paper. FSC is the only
forest certification scheme endorsed by the leading environmental organisations,
including Greenpeace. Our paper procurement policy can be found at
www.randomhouse.co.uk/environment

Typeset by SX Composing DTP, Rayleigh, Essex
Printed in the UK by CPI Group (UK) Ltd, Croydon, CR0 4YY

ISBN 9780091940188

To buy books by your favourite authors and register for offers visit
www.randomhouse.co.uk

To L.
who holds the key to my heart.

The Dark Stranger
Dahlia LaMotte, unpublished ms.

Best keep your door locked, Miss.

The housekeeper's words came back to me as I readied myself for bed. It seemed a strange warning in a house as isolated as Lion's Keep where our only neighbors were sea and heath. Had there been trouble with one of the servants – perhaps with that impertinent groom with the roving eyes?

Or could it be the Master that Mrs. Eaves was worried about? Haughty, remote William Dougall, who had looked down at me from his horse with such icy condescension – a cold look which had paradoxically lit a spit of fire from my toes to the roots of my hair. Surely not. The great William Dougall wouldn't deign to bother a lowly governess such as myself.

I locked the door all the same, but left the windows open as it was a warm night and the breeze coming off the ocean felt deliciously cool as I slid between the crisp lavender-scented sheets. I blew out my candle . . . and immediately noticed something odd. There was a crack of light at the bottom of the door. Had Mrs. Eaves left a candle burning in the hallway for my benefit? If so, I ought to tell her it wasn't necessary.

I threw the sheets off and swung my legs over the side of the bed, preparing to go investigate, but froze before my toes touched the floor. The bar of light at the bottom of the door had been split in two by a shadow as if someone were standing there. As I stared at the door, seeking some other explanation, the brass knob silently began to turn. I opened my mouth to scream, but no sound came out. My throat was frozen with fear, as were my limbs, powerless to run from whoever was at the door. All I could do was watch as the knob turned . . . and stopped.

The door didn't open. It was locked. The knob paused there as if whoever was turning it was deciding what to do next. Would he break the door down? Would he force his way in and then . . . what then?

But he must have decided that breaking down the door would make too much noise. The knob silently revolved back. The shadow disappeared from beneath the door and the light slowly faded.

I let out a shaky breath, my limbs reduced to quivering jelly now that the moment of crisis was over. Should I go find Mrs. Eaves and tell her what had happened? But tell her what? That I had seen a light, a shadow, a turning knob? Already I mistrusted the evidence of my own senses and I had no wish to look an hysterical child on my first day of service.

So I crept back into bed, pulling the sheets over me, but kept my eyes on the door. What if he had gone to retrieve a key? I lay like that, rigid beneath the crisp sheets, all my attention riveted to the door, for I don't know how long. I was sure I would not sleep, but it had been a long day of weary travel and learning new faces and new duties, and the sound of the waves crashing on the shore below the cliff and the scent of saltwater mingled with honeysuckle from the garden were hypnotically soothing . . .

I must have drifted off because when I came to the room was bright with light. I startled awake, thinking the light in the crack below the door had seeped into the room, but then I saw that the light came not from the door, but from the open window. Moonlight spilled in, white as cream, soaking the sheets and my nightgown . . . I was wet, too, from the heat . . . drenching the whole room except for a pillar of shadow that stood at the window . . .

A pillar shaped like a man.

For the second time that night I opened my mouth to scream, but my throat was as frozen as if the moonlight was a carapace of ice. I could not see the man's features, but I knew it must be William Dougall. I recognized that arrogant bearing, those broad shoulders, the slim agility of his hips as he moved forward . . .

He was moving forward, slowly, gliding across the floor so as not to make a sound. He must think I was still asleep. I must let him go on thinking I was asleep. If he knew I was awake he might become violent.

The master has his moods, Mrs. Eaves had said. Best not to get on the wrong side o' them.

I clenched my eyes shut. Perhaps he had only come to look at me, as he had stared down at me from his mount earlier today. Perhaps I could bear it if he'd only come to look . . .

I felt a tug on the sheet that lay over me, a minute movement as if the breeze had lifted it, but then it began to slide down, dragging across my breasts, tugging the placket of my nightgown . . . which I'd left unbuttoned because of the warmth of the night. The cool air tickled my bare skin and to my acute embarrassment I felt my nipples harden beneath the thin cloth. I could feel his eyes on me, a prickling sensation that made the hairs on my legs stand up . . . my bare legs! My nightgown had ridden up around my hips in my sleep. Cool air licked at my thighs, my calves, and finally, as the sheet slipped away in a soft swoosh that sounded like running water, my toes. I lay, still barely daring to breathe, alert for the slightest sound or movement. If he touched me I would scream. I'd have to. But nothing happened. The breeze played across my skin, teasing the bare places – my breasts, the crook of my arm, the inside of my thigh. At last I couldn't bear it – I risked a peek through slitted eyes . . . and saw nothing. The room was empty.

Had I imagined the shadow at the window? Perhaps I'd tossed the sheet off myself . . . but then I felt something touch the sole of my foot. A breeze warmer than the outside air, warm and moist as breath. The shadow was still there, at the foot of the bed, crouched by my feet, but whether man or dream I could no longer say. The pull it had on me seemed otherworldly. Why else would I lie silent as it breathed on my calf, its breath hot and wet? Why else would I stir only to widen my legs as its breath traveled up my leg? Why else would I close my eyes and give myself over to its rough warmth lapping inch by inch up my thigh? Like a wave lapping at the shore, leaving wet sand as it retreats, and traveling a little further each time it returns. Insinuating itself into the cracks and crevices, wearing away the stony shore. I felt my own stoniness wear away as the warm tongue found its way into my very center and then licked deeper into the depths I didn't know I had . . . deep underwater caverns where the surf rushed and boiled, retreated, lapped again, and filled me. Retreated, lapped again, filled me. I was riding the waves now, born higher and higher. The room was filled with the smell of salt and the roar of the ocean . . . and then the wave dashed me down to the strand.

I opened my eyes and watched the shadow slip away like

a retreating tide leaving me wet and spent as a woman drowned. I knew at last what had happened to me. I'd been visited not by William Dougall – or any other mortal man – but by an incubus. The demon lover of myth.

CHAPTER ONE

"So, Professor McFay, can you tell me how you first became interested in the sex lives of demon lovers?"

The question was a bit jarring, coming as it did from a silver-chignoned matron in pearls and a pink tweed Chanel suit. But I'd gotten used to questions like these. Since I'd written the bestselling book *Sex Lives of the Demon Lovers* (the title adapted from my thesis, *The Demon Lover in Gothic Literature: Vampires, Beasts and Incubi*), I'd been on a round of readings, lectures and, now, job interviews, that focused on the *sex* in the title. I had a feeling, though, that Elizabeth Book, as chair of Fairwick College's folklore department, might genuinely be more interested in the *demon lovers* of the title.

It was the folklore department that had brought me to the interview. It certainly wasn't the college – second tier Fairwick College, enrollment 1600 students, 120 full-time faculty, 30 part-time ("We pride ourselves on our excellent teacher-to-student ratio," Dr. Book had gushed earlier). Or the town: Fairwick, New York, population 4,203, a faded Catskill village shadowed by mountains and bordered by a thousand acres of virgin forest. A great place if your hobbies were snowshoeing and ice fishing, but not if your tastes ran, as mine did, to catching the O'Keeffe show at the Whitney, shopping at Barneys, and dining out at the new Bobby Flay restaurant.

And it wasn't that I hadn't had plenty of other interviews. While most new Ph.Ds had to fight for job offers, because of the publicity surrounding *Sex Lives* I had already had two offers (from tiny colleges in the Midwest that I'd turned down) and serious interest from New York University, my undergraduate alma mater and first choice since I was determined to stay in New York City. Nor was I as financially desperate as many of my friends who had student loans to pay back. A small trust fund left by my parents had paid for college and grad school and I still had a little left over to supplement my teaching income. Still, I wasn't sure about N.Y.U. yet, and Fairwick was worth considering if only for its folklore department. Few colleges had one and I'd been intrigued by the approach the college took, combining anthropology, English and history into one interdisciplinary department. It jived well with my interests – fairy tales and gothic fiction – and it had been refreshing to be interviewed by a committee of cross-discipline professors who were interested in something other than the class I taught on vampires. Not that all of them were fans. An American history professor named Frank Delmarco – a burly guy in a proletarian denim shirt rolled up to show off his muscular hirsute forearms – had asked me if I didn't think I was catering to the "lowest common denominator" by appealing to the popular craze for trashy vampire books.

"I teach Byron, Coleridge and the Brontës in my classes," I'd replied, returning his condescending smile. "I'd hardly call their work *trash*."

I hadn't mentioned that my classes also watched episodes

of *Dark Shadows* and read Anne Rice. Or that my own interest in demon lovers wasn't only scholarly. I was used to academic snobs turning up their noses at my subject area. So I phrased my answer to Elizabeth Book's question carefully now that we were alone in her office.

"I grew up listening to my mother and father telling Scottish fairy tales . . ." I began, but Dean Book interrupted me.

"Is that where you got your unusual name, Cailleach?" She pronounced it correctly – *Kay-lex* – for a change.

"My father was Scottish," I explained. "My mother just loved the stories and culture so much that she went to St Andrews, where she met my father. They were archeologists interested in ancient Celtic customs – that's how I got the name. But my friends call me Callie." What I didn't add was that my parents had died in a plane crash when I was twelve and that I'd gone to live with my grandmother on the Upper West Side of Manhattan. Or that I remembered little of my parents *besides* the fairy tales they told me. Or that throughout my teens I'd been haunted by strange dreams of a shadowy figure.

Instead I launched into the spiel I'd delivered a dozen times before – for my college essay, grad school interviews, the pitch for my book. How listening to my parents telling those old stories had fostered a love of folklore and fairy tale that had, in turn, inspired me to study the appearance of fairies, demons and vampires in Romantic and Gothic literature. I had told the story so many times that it had begun to sound false to my ears. But I knew it was all true – or at least it had been when I first started telling it. I *had* felt a passion for the subject when I first realized that the stories my parents had told me when I was little existed in the outside world – or at least pieces of them did. I'd find traces of their stories in fairy tale collections and Gothic novels – from *The Secret Garden* and *The Princess and the Goblin* to *Jane Eyre* and *Dracula*. Perhaps I'd felt that if I could trace these stories down to their origins I would reclaim the childhood I'd lost when they died and I moved in with my conscientious, but decidedly chilly and austere grandmother. Perhaps, too, I could find a clue to why I had such strange dreams after their deaths. But instead of becoming clearer, the stories my parents had told me had grown fainter . . . as if I'd worn them out with use. I'd become a very competent researcher, earned a doctorate, received awards for my thesis, and published a successful book. The dreams had ended, too, as if I'd exorcised them with all that scholarly research and analysis, which had sort of been the point. Hadn't it? Only with the disappearance of the dreams the initial spark that had spurred my work had also gone out and I was struggling with ideas for my next book.

I sometimes wondered if the storytellers I documented – the shamans sitting around a campfire, the old women spinning wool as they unfurled their tales – ever grew bored with the stories they told and retold.

But the story still worked.

"You're just what we're looking for," Elizabeth Book said when I'd finished.

Was she actually offering me the job here and now? The other universities where I'd interviewed at had waited a seemly ten days to get back to me – and although I'd had two interviews and taught a sample class for N.Y.U., I still wasn't sure if they were going to hire me. If Dean Book was actually offering me a job, her approach was really refreshing – or a little desperate.

"That's very flattering," I began.

Dean Book leaned forward, her long double rope of pearls clicking together, and clasped her hands. "Of course you'll have had other offers with the popularity of your subject. Vampires are all the rage now, aren't they? And I imagine Fairwick College must look rather humble after N.Y.U. and Columbia, but I urge you to consider us. Folklore has been taught at Fairwick since its 'inception' and the department has been nurtured by such prominent folklorists as Matthew Briggs and Angus Fraser. We take the study of legend and myth very seriously . . ." She paused, as if too overcome by emotion to go on. Her eyes drifted toward a framed photograph on her desk and for a moment I thought she might cry. But then she squeezed her hands together, turning her knuckles white, and firmed her mouth. "And I think you would find it an inspiration for your work."

She gave me such a meaningful smile that I felt sure she must know how much trouble I was having with my second book. How for the first time in my life the folklore and fairy tales that had seemed so alive to me felt dull and flat as pasteboard. But of course she couldn't know that and she had already moved on to more practical issues.

"The committee does have to meet this afternoon. You're the last applicant we're interviewing. And just between you and me and the doorpost, by far the best. You should hear from us by tomorrow morning. You're staying at the Hart Brake Inn, correct?"

"Yes," I said, trying not to cringe at the twee name of the B&B. "The owner has been very nice . . ."

"Diana Hart is a dear friend," the dean said. "One of the lovely things about teaching here at Fairwick is the good relationship between town and gown. The townspeople are truly good neighbors."

"That's nice . . ." I was unsure of what else to say. None of the other colleges – and certainly not NYU, which had all of Manhattan to boast of – had bothered to talk about the amenities of the town. "I certainly appreciate you taking the time to consider my application. It's a fine college. Anyone would be proud to teach here."

Dean Book tilted her head and regarded me thoughtfully. Had I sounded too condescending? But then she smiled and stood, holding her hand out. When I placed mine in hers I was surprised at how forcefully she squeezed it. Beneath her pink suit I suspected there beat the heart of a steely-willed administrator.

"I look forward to hearing from you," I told her.

Walking through the campus, past the ivy-covered Gothic library, under ancient leafy trees, I wondered if I could stand to live here. While the campus was pretty, the town was scruffy and down at the heels. The heights of its culinary pretensions were a handful of pizzerias, a Chinese takeout and a Greek diner. The shopping choices were a couple of vintagey-studenty boutiques on Main Street and a mall on the highway. I paused at the edge of the campus to gaze out at the view. From up here the town didn't look too bad, and beyond were forest-covered mountains that would look beautiful in the fall – but by November they would be bare and then snow-covered.

I had to admit I had my heart set on New York City, as did Paul, my boyfriend of eight years. We'd met our sophomore year at N.Y.U. Although he was from Connecticut he was passionate about New York City and we agreed that someday we would live there together. Even when he didn't get into graduate school in the city he had insisted I go to Columbia while he went to U.C.L.A. Our plan was for him to apply to New York City schools when he finished rewriting his doctoral thesis in economics and got his degree next year. Surely he would tell me to hold out for the N.Y.U. offer rather than leave the city now.

But could I really say no to Fairwick if I hadn't gotten a definite yes from N.Y.U.? It would be better if I could find a way to put off my answer to Dean Book. I had until tomorrow morning to think of a delaying tactic.

I continued walking past the high iron gates of the college onto the town road that led to Hart Brake Inn. I could see the blue Victorian house, with its decorative flags and over-spilling flowerboxes, from here. The opposite side of the road was bordered by massive pine trees, the beginning of a huge tract of protected state forest. I paused for a moment at the edge of a narrow trail, peering into the shadows. Even though the day was bright the woods were dark. Vines looped from tree to tree, filling every crevice and twisting into curious shapes. This is where all the stories start, I thought, on the edge of a dark wood. Was this why the dean thought that living here would be an inspiration to me? Because the woods were the natural habitat of fairies and demons? I tried to laugh off the idea . . . but couldn't quite. A wind came up and blew out of the woods toward me, carrying with it the chill scent of pine needles, damp earth and something sweet. Honeysuckle? Peering closer, I saw that the shadowy woods were indeed starred with white and yellow flowers. I closed my eyes and inhaled deeply. The breeze curled around me, tickling the damp at the back of my neck and lifting the ends of my long hair like a hand caressing me. The sensation reminded me of the dreams I'd had as a teenager. A shadowy man would appear at the foot of my bed. The room would fill with the scent of honeysuckle and salt. I'd hear the ocean and be filled with an inchoate longing.

The psychiatrist my grandmother had sent me to said the dreams were an expression of grief for my parents, but I'd always found that hard to believe. The feelings I'd had for the shadow man were not at all *filial*.

Now the invisible hand tugged at me and I stepped forward, off the pavement and onto the dirt path. The heels of my boots sank into the soft, loamy soil.

I opened my eyes, stumbling, as if waking from a dream, and started to turn away . . . That's when I saw the house. It was hidden from the road by a dense, overgrown hedge. Even without the hedge the house would have been hard to see because it blended in so well with its surroundings. It was a Queen Anne Victorian, its clapboard painted a pale yellow that was peeling in so many places it resembled a cleverly camouflaged butterfly. The roof was slate and furred with moss, the decorative cornices, pointed eaves and turret were painted a deep pine green. The honeysuckle from the forest had encroached over the porch railings – or, more likely, the honeysuckle from the house's garden had spread into the woods. The vines and shrubs circling the porch were so thick it looked as though the house were sitting in a nest. I stepped a few feet closer and a breeze stirred a loose vine over the door. It waved to me as though it were beckoning me to come closer.

I looked around to see if there were any signs of habitation, but the driveway was empty, the windows were shuttered, and a green dust, undisturbed by footprints, lay over the porch steps. Such a pretty house to be deserted, I thought. The breeze sighed through the woods as if agreeing. As I got closer I saw that the verge board trim along the pointed eaves was beautifully carved with vines and trumpet-shaped flowers. Above the doorway in the pediment was a wood carving of a man's face, a pagan god of the forest, I thought, from the pinecone wreath resting on his abundant flowing hair. I'd seen a face like it somewhere before . . . perhaps in a book on forest deities . . . The same face appeared in the stained glass fanlight above the front door.

Startled, I realized I'd come all the way up the steps and was standing at the front door, my hand resting on the bronze door knocker, which was carved in the shape of an antlered buck. What was I thinking? Even if no one lived here it was still private property.

I turned to leave. The wind picked up, lifting the green pollen from the porch floor and blowing it into little funnels around my feet as I hurried down the steps, which groaned under my boot heels. The vines that were twisted around the porch columns creaked and strained. A loose trailer snapped against my arm as I reached the ground, startling me so much that I stumbled. I caught my balance, though, and hurried down the front path, slowing only because I saw how slippery it was from the moss growing in between the stones. When I reached the hedge I turned around to look back at the house. It gave one more sigh as the wind stopped, its clapboard walls moaning as if sorry to see me go, and then it settled on its foundation and sat back, staring at me.

CHAPTER TWO

"Who owns the house across the street?" I asked later while having afternoon tea with Diana Hart on the porch. Diana, a slim, copiously freckled woman in her fifties, shifted in her wicker rocker.

"What house?" she asked, her large brown eyes widening. She wore her chestnut brown hair so closely cropped that it accentuated the size of her eyes.

I pointed across the street even though the house wasn't visible. "The one behind the overgrown hedge. A pretty yellow Queen Anne with green trim. It has a very unusual stained glass fanlight over the front door."

"You went up to the door?" Diana asked, setting down her delicate china cup in its matching saucer. Milky tea sloshed over the brim.

"The house looked empty . . ." I started to explain.

"Oh yes, no one's lived there for more than twenty years. Not since Dahlia LaMotte's cousin died."

"Dahlia LaMotte, the novelist?" I asked.

"Oh, you've heard of her?" Diana had her head down while she added more sugar to her tea. I could have sworn she'd already put in two teaspoons, but then she had quite the sweet tooth, as evidenced by the pink frosted Victoria sponge cake and chocolate-chip scones spread out over the wicker table in front of us. "I thought her books had gone out of fashion long ago."

Diana was right about that. Dahlia LaMotte had written a half dozen bodice ripper romances at the turn of the twentieth century – the kind of books in which a young girl loses her parents and then finds herself at the mercy of an overbearing Byronic hero who locks her up in a Gothic tower and makes threats against her virginity until he is reformed by her love and proposes honorable marriage. Obviously influenced by Ann Radcliffe and the Brontës, her books were avidly read in the beginning of the twentieth century, but then fell out of favor. They'd been reprinted in the sixties when authors like Mary Stewart and Victoria Holt made Gothic romance popular again. You could still find copies of those reprints – tattered paperbacks featuring nightgown-clad heroines fleeing a looming castle on their covers – on the internet, but I hadn't had to buy them there. I'd found them hidden behind the "good books" on my grandmother's bookshelves, a dozen books all with the name Emmeline Stoddard written on their flyleaves, and devoured them the summer I was twelve – which was another theory of where the shadow man of my dreams had come from: reading all those steamy Dahlia LaMotte books!

"I'm interested in the intersection of fairy tale and the Gothic imagination," I said primly – a primness ruined by the blood that rose to my cheeks at the memory of a particularly salacious scene in my favorite Dahlia LaMotte book, *The Dark Stranger*. "I knew she lived in upstate New York, but I didn't know she lived here."

"Oh yes, we've had quite a number of famous authors in Fairwick. Dahlia was the daughter of Silas LaMotte, who made his fortune in shipping tea from the Far East. He built Honeysuckle House in 1893 for his wife and daughter. He planted Japanese honeysuckle all around it because his wife, Eugenia, loved the smell of it. Sadly, Eugenia died a few months after they moved into the house and Silas died soon after that. Dahlia lived all alone in Honeysuckle House, writing her novels, until her death in 1934. She left it to a younger cousin, Matilda Lindquist, who lived there alone until her death in 1990."

"Matilda never married?"

"Oh no!" Diana widened her eyes and then looked down, noticed the spilled tea in her saucer, and blotted it with a cloth napkin embroidered with hearts and flowers. "Matilda was a sweet, but rather childlike woman of very little imagination. Really the perfect one to live in Honeysuckle House."

"Why's that?" I asked.

"Just that living alone on the edge of the woods might scare some people if they had active imaginations," she said, pouring herself another cup of tea. She held the pot over my cup and raised a tawny eyebrow. I indicated I'd take another cup, even though I'm more a coffee person than a tea person.

"But Dahlia LaMotte lived there alone," I pointed out. "And she certainly had an imagination."

"Yes," Diana conceded, "but Dahlia *liked* to scare herself. That's how she got the ideas for her books."

"Hmm, that's an interesting notion," I said. "I'd love to see the house. Do you know who owns it now?"

"Some LaMotte relation in Rochester. Dory Browne of Browne Realty holds the key, sees to repairs, and shows it to the occasional house hunter. A lovely gay couple from the city looked at it last year and almost bought it. They would have been perfect for it, but they changed their minds."

"So Dory Browne could show it to me if I wanted to see it?"

Diana looked up from her tea and blinked her long dark lashes. "Are you thinking of buying it?"

I began to protest, but I stopped. Really I only wanted to see the house out of literary curiosity, but if I told Diana that she might not be able to convince Dory Browne to show it to me. "Well, if I get an offer to teach here I'd have to find someplace to live. And I'm tired of living in a cramped little apartment." That part was at least true. My studio apartment in Inwood was the size of a closet.

Diana was studying me carefully. For a moment I was afraid she'd caught me in a lie. But then it turned out that wasn't it at all. "I'll call Dory and ask her to come by tomorrow morning to show you the house. I'm not sure if Honeysuckle House would be right for you," she said. "But I think you might be perfect for *it*."

After consuming Diana's ample tea, I decided that although I was too full for a run, I'd better take a long walk to burn off the scones and clotted cream. I walked down toward Main Street, past Victorian houses, some lovingly restored like the Hart Brake Inn and others in various stages of disintegration or restoration. As I neared Main Street the houses grew larger, but also shabbier. Clearly the town of Fairwick had enjoyed a time of prosperity at the end of the nineteenth century. Faded signs on brick walls advertised long gone businesses: LaMotte Tea Company, Miss Fisk's Haberdashery, and, in giant letters across a huge brick building, the Ulster & Clare Railroad. I vaguely recalled that the town had been an important railroad hub in the late nineteenth century, but then the Ulster & Clare had failed, the trains had stopped coming to Fairwick, and the town began its long slow decline into shabbiness and poverty. It still had elegant bones, though. A Greek Revival library stood in a green park that had once been prettily landscaped. Now the rose bushes were leggy and a strange looking bush with feathery gray blooms – like a giant dust mop – had taken over the paths and flowerbeds. The yards of once stately Victorians were overgrown and crowded with garden statuary. The residents of Fairwick were apparently partial to red-capped gnomes, plastic deer statues, and metal cutouts of winged fairies. No Madonnas, no baby Jesuses, but maybe those came out at Christmas.

Main Street itself was sad and dreary. Half the storefronts were abandoned. The businesses that looked to be flourishing were the tattoo parlor (ubiquitous in college towns, I'd noticed from my recent lecture tours), an old airstream diner, the head shop, and a coffee place called Fair Grounds. At least the latter smelled like it brewed a decent cup of coffee. I bought a soy latte and the *New York Times* and a sandwich in case I got hungry later, although I suspected that Diana's tea would hold me till bedtime.

Walking back uphill to the Inn, I passed Browne Realty. Looking at the listings pasted onto the window I saw that the houses in town were going for even less than I'd imagined. For the price of a one-bedroom apartment in Manhattan I could get a five-bedroom Victorian here. I wondered what Honeysuckle House would sell for.

It started to drizzle then, so I walked faster up the hill. It wasn't raining hard when I reached the inn, so I stopped on the other side of the road and peered through the hedge at Honeysuckle House. The face on the pediment seemed to look back at me. The raindrops streaming down its cheeks looked unnervingly like tears. Suddenly the rain began to fall harder. I crossed the street and sprinted up the steps to the porch, stopping to shake the rain out of my hair and off my jacket so I wouldn't shed water all over Diana's hooked rugs and chintz-upholstered furniture. A thump on the wooden steps behind me made me turn around, sure that someone had followed me up the steps, but no one was there. Nothing was there but the rain, falling so hard now that it looked like a gray moiré curtain that billowed and swelled in the wind. For a moment I saw a shape in the falling water – a face, as if just behind the watery veil, a face I knew, but from where? Before I could place it, the face was gone, blown away in a gust of wind. Only then did I recall where I'd seen that face. It was carved into the pediment of Honeysuckle House.

It was an afterimage, I told myself later when I was lying in the too-soft four-poster bed, listening to the rain that hadn't let up all evening. I'd stared at the face on the pediment long enough that I'd fashioned it out of the falling rain. A face, after all, was the easiest pattern to find in random shapes. And that face – the wide-set dark eyes, the broad brow, the high cheekbones, aquiline nose and full lips – was particularly striking. So striking that I'd even imagined for a moment that it was the face of the shadow man from my adolescent dreams, but that was impossible because I'd never seen his face. He'd always stood on the edge of the darkness, inches from the moonlight that would have revealed his face. I could almost see him now, taking shape behind the veil of my eyelids instead of the scrim of rainwater.

I forced my eyes back open. I was tired, but I'd told Paul I would call him at nine California time so I was struggling to stay awake until midnight. At a quarter to, I called him, hoping he was back from his evening seminar early. He was.

"Hey you," he said. "How was the interview?"

"Good, I guess. I think they're going to offer me the job."

"Really? So soon? That's unusual." I thought I detected a faint note of jealousy – the same edge I'd heard in his voice when I got into Columbia and he didn't and when I'd gotten a publishing contract for my thesis just after his thesis had been turned down by his reading committee. "What are you going to say if they do?"

"I don't know. I can't imagine living here and it seems ridiculous to leave the city when you'll be applying for jobs there next year. I suppose I could just turn it down . . ."

"Hmm . . . better to try to put them off until you have a firm offer from N.Y.U. How far did you say it was from the city? A couple of hours? I could visit weekends."

"It's three hours over mountainous roads," I told him. "It's really the back of beyond. The place where I'm staying is called the Hart Brake Inn." I spelled it for him and he laughed. "And there's a place across the way called Honeysuckle House . . ."

"Let me guess, there are plastic cows everywhere and the town bar's called the Dew Drop Inn."

"Plastic deer," I said, yawning, "and it's the Tumble Inn."

"Yeah, well it does sound pretty unbearable. I bet it's freezing in the winter, too. Still, better not burn your bridges until you've got a firm offer in the city. I'm sure you'll think of a way to keep your options open."

We talked a little more and then said good night. When I turned off my phone a wave of dejection swept over me as random as the gusts of damp air that were coming through the open bedroom window. I supposed it was just the strain of maintaining a long distance relationship – the uncertainly of not knowing when we'd ever manage to be together for longer than the summer or winter vacation. But then we'd known what we were getting into when we agreed, during our senior year of college, that neither of us would compromise our careers for "the relationship." We'd done better than most of our friends and we had a good chance of ending up on the same side of the country next year. Really, it made sense for me to hold out for the job at N.Y.U. If Dean Book offered me the job I'd find some way to hold her off and then I'd call N.Y.U. and tell them I had another offer. Maybe that would propel them into giving me the job.

The decision made, I felt a weight lift off me, a lessening of tension that made a space for sleep to enter. As I began to drift off my last thought was that I should get up and close the window to keep the rain from coming in . . . but I was already too far gone to move.

I couldn't move. I should get up and close the window but I couldn't move an inch. There was a weight settled on my chest, pinning me to the bed, pushing me deep into the soft mattress, which surrounded me in an enveloping embrace. I couldn't move a muscle or draw in a breath. Even my eyelids were pasted shut. I struggled to open them against the light.

Light?

The rain had stopped. Instead of wet gusts of air, moonlight streamed through the windows. It was the moonlight that had pinned me to the bed. I could see it spilling across the wide pine planks, a white shaft carrying on its back the shadows of tree branches that quivered in the breeze, trembling to reach me. I recalled the tangled trees and shrubs surrounding Honeysuckle House and had the confused impression that the moonlight was coming from *there*. There was something wrong with that idea, but I was too tired to figure it out and the moonlight was so bright I couldn't keep my eyes open any longer. They fluttered shut and I saw *him*. The shadow man from my teenage dreams. With him came the scent of honeysuckle and salt air I remembered from those dreams and the longing I'd always felt. He stood on the threshold between shadow and moonlight, where he always hesitated . . .

He stepped forward into the moonlight. It *was* him, the man from the house across the way. I forced my eyes open and he was still there, hovering above me, looking down at me, his face thrown into shadow by the moonlight cascading over his back like a silver cape. I could only see the places the moonlight touched: the plane of one cheekbone as his head tilted sideways, a lock of his hair falling over his brow, the blade of his shoulder. Each piece of him took shape and weight as the moonlight touched it. It was as if he were made of shadow and the moonlight was the knife sculpting him into being, each stroke of the knife giving him form . . . and *weight*.

The moonlight sculpted a rib and I felt his chest press down onto mine, it rounded a hip and it settled onto my pelvis, it carved the length of a muscular leg and it pressed against the length of my legs.

I gasped . . . or tried to. My mouth opened, but I couldn't draw breath because of the weight on my chest. His lips, pearly wet, parted and he blew into my mouth. My lungs expanded beneath his weight. When I exhaled he sucked in my breath and his weight turned from cold marble into warm living flesh. Moving flesh. I felt his chest rise and lower against mine, felt his hips grind into his mine, his strong legs part mine . . . He inhaled a long draft of my breath and I felt him harden against me. He rocked against me, pushing his breath into my lungs just as he pushed himself between my legs and then inside of me. He felt like a wave crashing over me, a moonlit wave that sucked me down below the surf and pulled me out to sea, onto a crest, and then back under again . . . and again and again and again. We rocked to the rhythm of the ocean until I lost all sense of what was me and what was him, until we were the wave cresting, then crashing onto the flat hard sand.

Then I lay panting like a drowning person, slicked in sweat, alone on the bed in a pool of liquid moonlight.

CHAPTER THREE

I awoke the next morning with the bone-melting contentment that follows a night of really good sex – quickly followed by a rush of shame at the realization that the sex had all been inside my own head. I had been embarrassed by the dreams I'd had as a teenager, but they'd never gone this far. The shadow man had always stayed on the threshold between dark and light. He'd never come forward . . . or *come* inside me the way this creature had. I'd never felt sore between my legs . . .

I got up quickly, eager to clear the fuzzy from my head and bloodstream. I didn't have time to languish in erotic daydreams. Dean Book would be calling later this morning and I had to decide what to say to her if she offered me the job. Plus, I wanted to get inside Honeysuckle House before I left. I hadn't spent the whole night wallowing in X-rated fantasies. Sometime in the night I'd had an idea for an essay on Dahlia LaMotte's work, maybe even something longer . . . I'd scribbled something in my notebook, which I always kept beside my bed. I looked at it now.

The threshold, I'd scrawled in great loopy script across a blank page, *between shadow and moonlight*. Now if I could only remember what that meant.

I decided to take a jog to clear my head. One part of my dream that I hadn't imagined was the clearing weather. Crisp, dry, sunlit air poured through the open window where moonlight had spilled last night. When I pulled open the curtains I was greeted with a fresh-washed blue sky. The hedge across the street sparkled in the sun. There were bright flashes of pink and red amidst the branches, long tubular blooms that looked like an exotic strain of honeysuckle. Oddly, though, I noticed that there were no tree branches near my window, nothing that could have cast the shadows I'd seen last night. Even that part had been a dream.

I shrugged off the memory of those ghostly branches and pulled on sweatpants,

T-shirt and sneakers. I padded downstairs as quietly as I could on the creaking wooden steps, even though I was the only guest staying at the inn. I wondered if Diana was up making breakfast, but I didn't hear any noise from the kitchen. I checked my watch . . . 6:15. Breakfast at the Hart Brake Inn was served at 8:30. I had plenty of time for a long run and a shower.

While I stretched out my leg muscles on the porch I thought about possible routes to take. The campus would be a logical choice but somehow I didn't want to run into Dean Book in my jogging clothes. I could head down toward town, but then I'd have to stop for stop signs and traffic. In the city I jogged in Van Cortlandt Park where there were dirt cross-country trails that were kinder on my knee joints.

There *was* a dirt path here, I remembered, that went into the woods behind Honeysuckle House. I didn't know how far it went, but since the woods went on for miles surely the trail would too. I could find out if the woods were as inspiring as Dean Book thought they were.

I crossed the street at an easy lope, slowing at the entrance to the path to adjust my eyes to the woods' diminished light. Even after I'd become accustomed to the light though, I kept the pace slow so I could keep an eye on the unfamiliar terrain to avoid tripping on roots or branches. The surface of the path was fairly smooth, however, and pleasantly springy – as if it had once been a bog. It curved slightly to the north. From the map I'd glanced at yesterday I imagined that the trail circled around the boundary of campus. I decided to run for twenty minutes – about two miles at my current pace – turn back, run another ten minutes and then walk the last mile back to cool down.

For the first mile I rehearsed various polite ways of asking for time to consider a job offer should I receive one from Dean Book. Then my mind went pleasantly blank and I noticed how good the clean mountain air felt moving in and out of my lungs. The ground beneath my feet was so springy my knees hadn't twinged once. I picked up the pace, feeling that little endorphin kick that made getting up at the crack of dawn to run worth it. What a great place to run! If I lived in Honeysuckle House this trail would be right outside my door. I could run here every morning.

But I wasn't going to live in Honeysuckle House. Where had that idea come from? Even if I took the Fairwick job, what would I need with a big old house?

Though it would be nice to finally have room enough for all my books *and* shoes. Every year I had to choose which to put in storage.

I laughed out loud at the idea that I might take a job for adequate storage space. The woods echoed back the sound. The trees were lower here on this part of the path. They weren't even trees anymore, really, more like very tall

overgrown shrubs that sprang over the path and intertwined
to form an arched colonnade, some eight or nine feet above
the ground, decorated with great looping swags of vines and
sprigged with white and yellow flowers which smelled—

I pulled what felt like a gallon of air into my lungs.

—delicious!

The honeysuckle shrubs and vines that Silas LaMotte had
planted around his house had spread over a mile into the
woods! The whole house must smell of them. At night the
breeze from the woods would blow through the open
windows and fill the rooms with their scent.

At the thought of a bedroom filled with moonlight and
honeysuckle, images from last night's dream came flooding
back to me: shadow branches borne across the floor on a
shaft of moonlight, the light carving a man out of those
shadows, the shadow man making love to me like a wave . . .

Of course. The man in my dream was a demon lover. The
demon lover always came in dreams. One of its names was
mare, from which we derived the word *nightmare*.
(Although what I'd experienced last night hadn't felt
anything like a nightmare.)

I had been writing about the demon lover in literature for
years. In truth, I'd started writing about it because of the
dreams. Only the dreams had gone away as I catalogued and
studied the species of incubus and demon lover, vampire
and phantom. Why had the dreams come back now?

It was the house. Honeysuckle House. An abandoned
Queen Anne Victorian, overgrown with shrubs and vines, a
beautiful man's face carved above its door. It was my
glimpse of the house that had conjured the mirage I'd seen
in the rain, and it was that image that had come to me in my
dream. I remembered, too, that in the dream I'd had the

sense that the moonlight was coming from across the street. The house had haunted me. And why not? In Gothic novels the house was always a major character in its own right – the Castle of Otranto, Thornfield Hall, Manderley – and often it was the moment of crossing the threshold of the house that began the heroine's adventure.

A line from Joseph Campbell's *The Hero with a Thousand Faces* occurred to me: "it is only by advancing beyond those bounds . . . that the individual passes, either alive or in death, into a new zone of experience."

That's why I had scrawled that note about thresholds last night. The doorway of the house was the threshold of adventure for the heroine of a Gothic novel, especially for women like Emily Dickinson or Dahlia LaMotte who had totally confined themselves to their houses. It would be interesting to write about the influence living in Honeysuckle House had had on Dahlia LaMotte's work. I ran faster as I spooled out the idea, my feet barely touching the ground. I'd call it *The Threshold between Moonlight and* . . .

One moment I was mid stride, soaring free of the earth, the next I was flat on the ground, face in the dirt, the wind knocked out of me. I gulped for air, but the ground was pressing too hard on my chest. I had the confused notion that the ground itself had risen up to slam into my chest. It was pressing against my chest, my mouth, my nose . . . dragging me down into the darkness. Dimly I felt my fingers clawing at the soft, warm earth. I was sinking . . .

He was rising to meet me, emerging out of the darkness as if rising out of dark water. The face of the man who'd come to me on the moonlight last night. His features were clearer this time, but not because there was more light to see him by (it was very, very dark where he was) but because there was more of him to see. He was *growing*, becoming more solid. As if to reward me for this insight he smiled. His beautiful lips parted and came closer until they touched my lips and pushed them open. His tongue flicked into my mouth – hot and wet. I felt myself go hot and wet between my legs where I was still sore from last night, so overcome with desire I felt myself sinking into that blackness . . . then he breathed into my mouth.

The air seared my lungs, but I gulped greedy mouthfuls of it. With the oxygen came consciousness. I opened my eyes. I was lying on my back, looking up at a tangled canopy of honeysuckle vines. They formed a vaulted green chapel starred with white and yellow flowers. Like a wedding chapel, I found myself thinking dazedly, still panting from the erotic force of that kiss. Or a funeral chapel if I hadn't caught my breath.

I ran my hands over my chest, feeling for broken ribs, but everything seemed to be intact. Then I slowly pushed myself up into a sitting position and wiggled my toes. My right ankle felt a little tender, but otherwise I seemed remarkably unscathed. How had I fallen anyway? I looked around the path behind me for a root or branch that could have tripped me, but the ground was clear. Apparently I'd stumbled over my own two feet.

Abashed at my own clumsiness – and by the direction my imagination seemed to be taking me since last night's dream. I got slowly to my feet, slapping dirt from my sweatpants. I gingerly stretched my arms over my head and then bent down to touch my toes. I was going to be sore from the fall *and* from stopping so abruptly without a cool down, but I seemed to be okay. I wasn't going to be running any more today, though. I'd have to walk back.

I looked at my watch. It was 7:10. I'd run for almost a

whole hour and at a pretty fast pace. Damn, I could be four miles from the Inn! I'd better start walking. I turned to go . . . and turned again. I turned in a circle twice before admitting that I couldn't tell which way I'd come. I examined the dirt path for my own footprints, but somewhere along the way it had gone from soft loam to dirt packed so hard that it didn't show footprints. Surely when I fell though . . . I squatted on the ground and stared at the dirt for an impression of my body. Nothing.

I stood up again – too fast. My head spun. Maybe I'd hit it in the fall and I had a concussion. That would explain the confusion and the hallucination of the face. I couldn't really be lost in the woods, could I?

I took a deep breath, willing myself to be calm. I could figure this out. I'd been heading north. All I had to do was find the sun and I'd know where east was and then I just had to go south. Easy enough. But when I peered into the woods I couldn't see further than a few feet. The honeysuckle shrubs and vines formed a dense underbrush that I couldn't see through to the sky. I was in an enormous thicket.

And I wasn't alone.

Something was moving in the underbrush a few feet off the trail. I could hear it thrashing against the dry branches.

"Hello?" I called . . . and then felt stupid. I pushed a branch down to see better. The branches and vines were so intertwined that when I moved one branch the whole shrubbery creaked and moaned. It was like a wicker basket, I thought, or a nest . . .

Just as I thought the word *nest* my fingers grazed something soft and furry.

I snatched back my hand, imagining I'd found a mouse nest in the branches, but if it was a mouse nest it was a long-abandoned one. Tiny bones fell to the ground at my feet.

The thrashing in the underbrush quickened. Something was trapped. I felt a sickening drop in my stomach. This nasty thicket was sucking the life out of some poor defenseless animal. *As it would you,* an insinuating voice whispered in my ear.

Angry now, I tore at the vines and branches, some of which had thorns, tunneling into the underbrush. The trapped creature thrashed harder at my approach, whether because it sensed help was coming or thought the hunter had arrived, I didn't know. Not knowing made me more frantic to reach it – to free it. An awful apprehension that it might be wounded came over me, mixed with the fear that it might strike at me when I reached it. A logical voice in my brain told me that I was crazy to approach a trapped wild animal, but I didn't seem to be listening to that voice.

I pulled an armful of prickly berry-heavy vine out of the way and something flew past me. It startled me so badly that I plopped down on my rear, but it was only a bird . . . a small black bird that flew a few feet before crashing to the ground. Could this little thing really have caused so much noise? But the thicket was quiet now so I supposed it must have been. It had thrashed so hard that it had injured its wing. I moved toward it to see if it could fly and it turned and looked at me with keen yellow eyes. We stared at each other for a long still moment and then it hopped a few inches away from me, flapped its wings, and took off. At the same moment I noticed that sun was slanting across the path, coming from the hole in the shrubbery on my right.

That was east. The bird had gone north. I looked down the path in the direction it had gone, but it had vanished into the trees. Then I turned around and headed south.

CHAPTER FOUR

It was 8:30 when I got back to the road. I saw Honeysuckle House first. Its shutters and windows were open. White lace curtains billowed in and out of the open windows, fluttering among the honeysuckle vines. The house looked like it was breathing. The realtor must have come over early to air it out before showing it to me. I felt a pang of guilt at making her go to the trouble when I had no intention of buying it.

Or was it a pang of regret?

I should, by all rights, have been more determined than ever to get out of here after my mishap of the morning, but even though I was sore and tired – and *hungry* – I also felt curiously elated. The fall had been painful – but that kiss! When had Paul last – or *ever* – kissed me like that? It had made me feel . . . *alive*. The smells of coffee, eggs and maple syrup coming from across the road nearly made me break into a run – but I restrained myself out of respect for my sore muscles.

Diana Hart's voice called out from the kitchen as soon as I opened the front door. "Is that you, Callie?" She came out of the kitchen, wiping her hands on a red and white checked tea cloth. She was wearing a sweatshirt that read: SHE WHO MUST BE OBEYED. "I was afraid you'd forgotten the breakfast time . . ." She faltered to a stop when she saw me. "Oh my, you look like you had a fall. Are you all right? Do you need some ice?"

"I'm fine," I said. "I went running in the woods . . ."

"In the woods?" The question came from someone who had followed Diana out of the kitchen – a petite woman in her early thirties with a blonde pageboy framing a heart-shaped face and delft-blue eyes. She was wearing a denim jumper, white sailor blouse, and navy and white spectator pumps. She was adorable enough to have walked off one of the Mary Engelbreit plaques that adorned Diana's kitchen and dining room.

"Oh, Dory, you were right! She did go running in the woods . . . Oh sorry!" Diana waved her hands between me and the blonde woman by way of making introductions. "Callie McFay, Dory Browne of Browne Realty. She came by to show you the house and said she thought she saw you heading into the woods earlier. I would have suggested a different route if I'd known you were going running. Those woods . . . well, they can be tricky."

"The woods were fine. I was just clumsy. Do I have time for a quick shower before breakfast?"

"Of course!" Diana exclaimed. I had a feeling that if I had asked Diana to serve breakfast on the roof she would have tried her best to accommodate me.

"I'll be quick," I promised.

I hobbled up the stairs to my room. Soreness from the fall was setting in, but the hot water helped. I took two Advil as well, dressed in a light cotton dress (Dory's prim outfit had made me feel underdressed) and sandals, twisted my wet hair into a sloppy bun, and hurried downstairs. The two women were sitting at the dining room table, their heads together, whispering. A floorboard creaked under my foot as I came into the room and Diana lifted her head, her large brown eyes looking startled.

"There you are, you look worlds better. You sit down and help yourself to some coffee while I go get your breakfast. Dory will keep you company."

I didn't see why I needed company, but I smiled sociably at the realtor and sat down across from her. She poured coffee into my cup and offered me the milk pitcher, which I took, and the sugar bowl, which I declined.

"I brought a couple of other listings," she said, patting a glossy decorative folder that lay by her coffee mug. I noticed that the folder's paisley design matched the pattern on the quilted tote bag hanging from Dory's shoulder. "I've got a darling little Craftsman bungalow just down the block that might be perfect for you."

I should have realized that asking a realtor to show one house in the current housing market was like asking an alcoholic to have an aperitif.

"I don't even know if I have a job yet," I replied. "But the house across the street is so striking . . ."

"Oh yes, Honeysuckle House is one of our grandest old Victorians. The LaMottes were one of the leading Fairwick families back in the days when the railroad made the town an important center of commerce. Silas LaMotte spared no expense in building the house for his wife."

"It's a shame she didn't live to enjoy it for long," I said, taking a sip of my coffee.

"Yes, it *was* a shame," Dory Browne replied, narrowing her piercing blue eyes at me as if I'd just said something original. "I think you might find the bungalow a little more cheerful . . ."

Dory was interrupted in her sales pitch by the appearance of Diana with a plate of French toast smothered in blueberry preserves, a bowl of fresh strawberries, and a basket of assorted muffins and scones. I was accustomed to having half a toasted bagel for breakfast but my run had made me hungry. I took a bite of the French toast and found that it was so tender it nearly melted in my mouth.

"I was just telling Callie that she might find old Mrs. Ramsay's bungalow cozier than Honeysuckle House," Dory said to Diana, who had sat down at the table with us. "Those big old Victorians are hard to keep warm in the winter and some people find all those woods in the back gloomy."

"I thought the woods in the back were beautiful," I said in between mouthfuls of French toast. "I found a thicket of honeysuckle shrubs. I guess they must have spread from the house."

"You made it as far as the thicket?" Diana asked, sounding as surprised as if I'd told her that I'd run all the way to New York City. "Most people don't get that far."

I glanced up from my plate and caught the two women exchanging a meaningful look. Something clearly bothered them about my foray into the forest. "Are the woods privately owned?" I asked. "I didn't see any private property signs. Was I trespassing?"

"The woods belong to the LaMotte estate, but they've always been open to the whole village," Dory answered "It's just that the thicket is so overgrown."

"Yes, I noticed. It's so dense that a bird had gotten stuck in the underbrush. I helped it out."

I was expecting exclamations of surprise and approbation from Diana – who greeted practically every word out of my mouth with cheerful approval and who had such an outstanding collection of ceramic woodland creatures that I figured she must have a soft spot for all wildlife – but instead my announcement was met with silence. Diana had gone pale beneath her freckles and her brown eyes were fixed on Dory's wide blue ones.

"You rescued a bird from the honeysuckle thicket," Dory said slowly and deliberately.

"I guess you could say I rescued it. I suppose it would have gotten out eventually."

"Not once it was trapped in the thicket," Diana said, shaking her head. "The creatures that stray there generally die there."

I recalled the little bones that fell out of the nest and shuddered. "How awful! Can't someone clear it?"

"It would just grow back," Dory said. "But you can see why the spot isn't so popular. Mrs. Ramsay's bungalow, on the other hand, faces a lovely park . . ."

"I want to see Honeysuckle House," I said, putting my napkin on the table. I had polished off the whole plate of French toast and a pumpkin scone as well. "Besides, you've already gone to the trouble of opening all the windows."

Dory Browne stared at me. "What are you talking about?" she asked. "I didn't open any windows."

Diana and Dory were up and heading out of the house before I could rise from the table. I really was sore now and I could only move slowly. By the time I got outside the two women were already across the street at the edge of the hedge, staring up at the house.

"Is everything okay?" I asked. They were looking at the house as if it were on fire.

"Oh yes," Dory answered. "I forgot that I told my

handyman, Brock, to come over earlier to air the place out. Diana?" She turned deliberately to the other woman and spoke slowly. "Perhaps you'd do me a favor and make that phone call we talked about earlier."

"Are you sure you don't want me to go inside with you?" she asked.

"No, we'll be fine. Apparently the house *wants* to be shown." She laughed nervously as she fished out a key from her quilted tote.

Diana squeezed the realtor's arm. "Well, I'm just across the street if you need anything."

I couldn't imagine what the two women were worried about. Mice, maybe? Rotting floorboards? But when we walked up the porch steps I thought the wood seemed firm and in good repair. The wooden face in the pediment gleamed as if it had been washed clean by yesterday's rain. It glowed in the morning light with the complexion of a young person who'd had a good night's sleep. And when Dory opened the front door (with a long iron skeleton key that turned smoothly in the lock) there was no moldy or mousy odor. Instead the air the house huffed out at us smelled like honeysuckle.

Dory held the door open and I stepped through first, into a wide foyer. Light from the stained glass fanlight spilled onto the polished wood floor like a scattering of rose petals strewn for our arrival.

"The floors are oak," Dory said, closing the door behind us. "As well as the banister." She ran her hand over a carved newel post at the foot of a wide flight of stairs. "Silas had the wood milled himself at his shipyards. He liked everything built like a ship. There are pocket doors leading into both parlors." She opened a double door, both sides sliding into the walls with a shooshing noise that echoed loudly in the big, empty house. A draft from the stairs moved at our backs as we entered the dim parlor. Although the shutters were open, the honeysuckle shrubs and vines had grown over the windows blocking out the light. Dory turned a switch and a crystal chandelier sprung into sight high over our heads.

"The ceilings are twelve feet high," Dory informed me. "The chandelier was made in Venice."

"It's beautiful," I said, marveling at the fanciful shapes and colors of the crystal droplets. "Kind of exotic for these parts, isn't it?"

"Silas made his fortune in the shipping business. He brought back treasures from all over the world. The tiles around the hearth—" she gestured to the fireplace "—are Wedgewood from England. The mahogany mantelpiece was brought over from an Italian castle." I walked over to the fireplace and ran my hand over the intricately carved wood. A satyr's face stared out of the center roundel; a procession of Greek gods and goddesses adorned the top frieze.

"The mantelpiece depicts the wedding of Cupid and Psyche," Dory said in her tour guide voice. "The theme is repeated in the dining room frieze . . ." Dory had opened another pocket door that led into a large octagonal room. Plaster figures paraded across the walls beneath swags of pine boughs and acorns. There were built-in china cabinets in each corner.

"And here's the kitchen. I'm afraid it hasn't been modernized since the sixties . . ."

The "modernization" consisted of an Amana refrigerator and gas range, both in the same hideous shade of lime green.

The floor was worn linoleum in a faded checkerboard pattern. "Matilda had this addition built on and spent most of her time back here," Dory said, opening a door onto a mudroom with a washer and dryer and then another door to a rather drab bedroom papered in yellowed, peeling wallpaper with an old iron bed frame painted a matching peeling yellow. "Her arthritis made going up and down the stairs difficult and it was cheaper just to heat the downstairs. She closed off the library . . ."

"The library?" I asked. I was glad to leave Matilda's little apartment behind. It had the atmosphere of a retirement home and, curiously, felt older than the rest of the house even though it was a newer addition.

"Matilda didn't read much, so she had no use for the library. She donated all her aunt's books to Fairwick College and closed off this room."

I wondered if Dahlia LaMotte's books were still in the college library. They might have notes in the margins . . .

My musings were cut short when Dory slid back the doors to the library. This room, which faced east, got the morning light. Streaming through a screen of shrubbery, it turned the room a glassy green, like a forest glade, but instead of being lined with trees the room was lined with floor to ceiling built-in bookcases. There was enough room in here to shelve all the books in my apartment and storage unit and still have spare space to acquire *more* books.

"Is this where Dahlia LaMotte wrote?" I asked.

"No," Dory answered. "Her study was upstairs in the tower room off her bedroom."

A study *and* a library! In my apartment in Inwood I wrote at my kitchen table. I stored files and books in the kitchen cabinets. I imagined what it would feel like to have a proper desk and to wander into my own library to find any book that I needed. No wonder Dahlia LaMotte was prolific – she wrote more than sixty novels – this was the perfect house to write in.

Dory preceded me up the wide oak stairs. Her high-heeled pumps clicked lightly on the bare wood, while my crepe-soled sandals awakened a chorus of creaks and cracks that sounded like a swarm of crickets.

"You wouldn't have to worry about a burglar sneaking up these steps," I said. "They're like an alarm system."

Dory turned to me on the second floor landing. "No," she replied, taking my remark seriously. "You wouldn't have to worry about anyone breaking *in*. Besides, the town is quite safe."

She showed me four small bedrooms – one complete with built-in bed and cabinets exactly like a ship's cabin, which Dory told me had been Silas's bedroom – a linen closet, a bathroom with an enormous claw-foot tub, and then, finally, she opened the last door at the end of the hallway. "The master bedroom," she announced.

The corner room faced the east side of the house. Two large windows overlooked an overgrown garden and the mountains in the distance. The bed would go up against the west wall so you could lie in bed and look out at the mountains. At night you'd see the moon rise. The southeast corner of the room opened into an octagonal turret. A desk had been built across three sides of the turret; on the other three sides were built-in bookshelves below the windows. A straight-backed wooden chair with a needlepoint cushion stood facing the desk. I sat down at it. The desk had been fitted out with dozens of tiny drawers and shelves. I opened one of the drawers and found, to my utter delight, a blue robin's egg.

"I suppose Dahlia LaMotte's papers were given to the library with her books," I said, trying another drawer that turned out to be locked.

"Actually, I believe Matilda moved all her aunt's papers up to the attic."

"The attic?" I asked.

Dory Browne sighed. "I suppose you'll want to see that too."

Having spent most of my life living in apartments I had very little experience with attics. I was picturing a dusty, cobweb-filled space at the top of a rickety ladder, but the room, which we reached by a narrow flight of stairs, was clean and smelled pleasantly of tea. It smelled of tea because Dahlia LaMotte's papers had all been stored in tea crates, each one marked with the insignia of the LaMotte Tea Company and the type of tea inside – Darjeeling, Earl Gray, Lapsang souchong, and other exotic varieties.

"They were left over from her father's warehouses," Dory told me.

There were twelve of them. I opened one gingerly, half-afraid after my experience in the woods that a mouse would jump out at me, but the only thing that came out of the box was the scent of bergamot. Three notebooks, each one bound in the same marbled paper, lay across the top of the chest. I picked up one and saw there was another identical notebook beneath it. I turned to the first page and found Dahlia LaMotte's signature and the dates *August 15, 1901 – September 26, 1901* in a florid, but readable hand. She'd filled up the book quickly.

"Why aren't these in a library?" I asked, thumbing through a few pages. *Started* The Wild Moon *today*, I read on one page; *I had the dream again last night*, I read on another.

"Dahlia's will specified that her papers remain in the house."

"That's odd."

Dory sat down on a tea crate – this one labeled Ceylon – and shrugged. "Dahlia *was* odd. Years of living alone immersed in your own fantasies will do that to a person."

"Does her will stipulate what use can be made of the papers?" I asked.

"Whoever owns the house, owns the papers. As long as they physically remain in the house you can read them, write about them, copy them, and even publish them – although a half-share of the royalties of any published work must go to the estate, which pays for the upkeep of the house."

"I've never heard of anything so strange," I said, running my hands across the worn paper binding of one of the notebooks.

Dory smiled a trifle condescendingly. "You've led a very unstrange life then," she said. Then she sighed again. "I don't suppose you'd be interested in looking at that Craftsman bungalow now?"

I helped Dory close up the house. It was quite a job. The shutters flapped in the wind, rattled their hinges and slammed shut on our fingertips when we least expected it. The four over four, double-sashed windows groaned on their way down like children forced to leave a birthday party before cake was served. While Dory was closing the front door – and telling me that the asking price, which sounded ridiculously low to me, was really too high – she got her thumb stuck in the doorjamb.

"It's like it doesn't want us to leave," I said, looking back at the house from the front lawn. Shuttered, it looked sad and glowering.

"That may well be," Dory snapped, sucking her thumb, "but we can't all have everything we want."

I didn't ask what she meant by that – or why she was so set on *not* making this sale. Instead I added up figures as we walked back to the inn. Aside from the small trust fund left by my parents, I had gotten a nice advance for *Sex Lives*. Paul and I had talked about using it to buy a larger apartment if he got a job in New York City, but with the same money I could buy this house and keep my rent-stabilized Inwood apartment for our pied-a-terre. It could be our country house, even if I didn't get the Fairwick job . . .

I was so immersed in my thoughts that I didn't notice until I came up the inn's steps that Dean Book was waiting for me on the front porch. Diana Hart was there too, sitting in the wicker glider with her arms crossed over her chest and her lips thin with seeming anger. Had the women been arguing? I wondered. But Elizabeth Book, dressed today in an ivory linen shift with a matching cotton sweater draped over her shoulders, looked radiantly pleased.

"Professor McFay," she said, "please come join me. Diana was just going to bring out another pitcher of iced tea."

Diana glared at the dean but got up obediently.

"I really don't need . . ." I began, but Diana had already gone inside, letting the screen door slam behind her. Dory

Browne looked after her but stayed on the porch. I sank down into a wicker rocking chair, suddenly tired out by all the drama of the morning. Elizabeth Book didn't waste any time getting down to business.

"On behalf of the committee, I'd like to offer you the position of assistant professor of English and Folklore," she said. "Of course, I know you may be considering other offers, so if you'd like time . . ."

"That won't be necessary," I replied, suddenly sure of what I wanted – had – to do. "I'd like the job and . . ." I glanced across the street. I couldn't see the house but I could smell it – honeysuckle and salt air as if it stood on a cliff above the sea instead of on a street in a remote mountain town. It was the smell of my dreams. Not that that was the reason I had to do it.

I turned back to Dory Browne. "I'm going to buy Honeysuckle House."

CHAPTER FIVE

When I called Paul from Manhattan that night he took the news that I'd accepted the job at Fairwick surprisingly well.

"I've been asking around and the school has a pretty good reputation. They have an honors program with very generous financial aid that draws some top students from around the country and the world," he told me. I could hear his fingers tapping on his laptop keyboard in the background. He must have been Googling the college and town for hours. "And according to MapQuest it's only three hours from the city. When I can get a job there next year it'll be an easy commute. In the meantime it looks like the closest airport is Newark . . ."

He was less than thrilled when I told him I'd bought a five bedroom Victorian house.

"I thought we were going to use that money to buy a bigger apartment in the city when I moved there," he said, his voice sounding young and wounded. "You could have at least discussed it with me."

I argued that we'd always agreed we should each take the job – or graduate school offer – that was best without worrying about what the other one thought.

"Yes, but a *house*," he said. "That's so . . . permanent."

"Tenure's permanent," I countered. "A house is . . ." I wanted to say that a house could be bought and sold, but I knew already that it wasn't ever going to be easy to sell Honeysuckle House. The very thought of letting the house go already gave me a strange pang. ". . . it's a vacation house. You'll come up on weekends. We'll spend our summers there. You'll see, once you're in the city full time you'll be dying to get out of it like all good New Yorkers."

"You should have at least talked to me first," he said with uncharacteristic hurt. Paul was generally the most easygoing of guys; we hardly ever fought. And we didn't now. Paul got off the phone saying he had papers to grade.

Looking for some girlfriendly support I took the subway to Brooklyn to my friend Annie's bakery to tell her what I'd done. She'd been my best friend since high school and even though she didn't date men herself (she had come out when we were in tenth grade) always had good advice about them. And she'd been after me for years to ditch the long-distance relationship with Paul and go out with someone in the city.

"Sorry, Cal, I'm with Paul here," she told me while squirting yellow icing on a row of sunflower-themed cupcakes. "You acted like a man – all high handed. And I don't buy all this crap about doing what's best for each of you, damn the relationship. That just sounds like neither of you care enough about the relationship to make a sacrifice for it to make it work."

I'd forgotten that since Annie had moved in with her girlfriend, Maxine, she'd gotten a bit sanctimonious about commitment.

"You think I should sacrifice my career and move out to L.A.?" I asked, nabbing one of the half-finished cupcakes.

I had a sudden urge for sugar, which I blamed on all the sweets I'd consumed at the Hart Brake Inn.

"I didn't say that. But if you both really wanted to be together you would have found a way by now, and buying a house for yourself doesn't sound like the kind of thing a person does when she's in love."

Unless she's in love with a man who appears in a dream, I thought but didn't say.

Strangely, it was the same view that my grandmother Adelaide took when I called her up in Santa Fe (where she had retired when I graduated high school) to tell her my news. "Fairwick's a second-tier college with a second-rate staff," she drawled in her starchy New England voice. It was the same voice she had once used when she spoke of my mother's decision to go to college in Scotland ("The women in our family have always gone to Radcliffe or Barnard."), my mother's marriage to my father, my decision to go to N.Y.U., and my choice of scholarly concentration ("Fairy tales are for children!"). When she'd finished belittling my new employer, she asked if this meant I'd broken up with "that boy in California." When I told her no, she said it was only a matter of time; if we were serious about each other we would have managed to live on the same side of the country by now.

Adelaide's and Annie's verdicts haunted me on the way to visit Paul in California. Oddly it was the dream I'd had at the Hart Brake Inn that made me feel like they might have a point, as if I'd been unfaithful to Paul and bought Honeysuckle House so I could be with that moonlight lover. The fact that my knees turned to water every time I remembered the dream seemed to corroborate that theory. When I got to L.A., though, I explained to Paul about the boxes of Dahlia LaMotte's papers in the attic and he began to relent.

"You mean you can write about them – even reproduce them – as long as the originals stay in the house?"

I showed him the codicil to the deed that said so.

"Why didn't you say so in the first place?" he asked, rewarding me with the wry crooked smile that had first warmed me to him in our Sophomore English class. "That's brilliant, Cal. We'll have enough to buy a place in Manhattan when you publish your next book!"

As much as I was relieved that he'd forgiven me, I'd still had the uneasy feeling that my rashness (and the spectral infidelity he didn't know about) had been forgiven because it had been judged profitable. So I spent the two weeks in L.A. feeling a little like a high-priced hooker, trying to convince myself that having erotic fantasies about an imaginary lover was *not* the same as cheating. So what if I recalled the way the moonlight had carved sinuous muscles out of shadow when I looked at Paul? Or that I remembered the touch of those pearly lips when Paul kissed me? It was only a dream – and one I hadn't had again since that night at Hart Brake Inn. And if I cut my trip a day short so I'd have time to settle into the new house before term began, it didn't mean I was longing to be back at Honeysuckle House to see if the dream would come back there. Did it?

If I'd believed in the pathetic fallacy – that the weather in a novel reflected the emotions of the heroine – I'd have had to suspect that my purchase of Honeysuckle House had indeed been dictated by a malevolent force. I drove up to Fairwick in a torrential rainstorm that threatened to blow my new green Honda FIT off the highway. When I got to Fairwick all the houses on my street were dark. The power must be out, I thought, wondering how often *that* happened. I considered going first to the Hart Brake Inn and asking Diana for a room – or at least a flashlight and candles – but when I drove up in front of Honeysuckle House I knew I couldn't wait any longer to claim it as my own. Even the wind seemed to be pushing me up the front steps (there was that pathetic fallacy again!), urging me to the front door. I glanced up at the fanlight, but the face was dark and somehow brooding with no light shining through the stained glass. Like the lover in my dreams before the moonlight awakened him. I had a feeling that *he* was somewhere in the shadowy house, waiting for the sound of my key to awaken him. I now held the big old-fashioned key that Dory had sent me in the mail wrapped in brown paper and twine, poised centimeters from the lock. It felt heavy in my hand, weighted with all the questionable decisions I'd made over the last month.

I'd passed up a possible career in Manhattan – the center of my known universe – for a job in a second-tier college in a podunk town where I knew no one. I'd bought a hundred-year-old house which, despite its sterling inspection report, was likely to require maintenance that I, a lifetime apartment dweller, couldn't even begin to imagine. Although I'd planned to keep the Inwood apartment I'd sublet it at the last minute when my TA admitted she didn't have anywhere to live, so now if I decided to go back to the city I'd have no place to stay. Worst of all, I'd put stress on a eight-year relationship with a decent man whom I believed I was in love with. And all because of a dream that reminded me of some fantasy lover from my imagination.

I should turn around right now, get in my car, drive back to New York City, tell Dory Browne to put the house on the market, and take adjunct teaching jobs until I could reapply for next year at a college within commuting distance of Manhattan. Yes, that's what I should do, only . . .

Something clicked. Something metal.

I looked down at my hand and saw that the key was now in the lock. How had *that* happened? I pulled the key out and held it half an inch in front of the lock. It quivered in the air. Was my hand shaking? Or . . . I touched the key to the keyhole, which I noticed now was surrounded by an iron plate shaped like a rooster. I felt a tug at my hand as the key leapt forward and slid smoothly into the lock.

Damn! I stared at it for a full minute until the idea clicked in my head with the same resolute sound the key had made when it slid into the lock. The lock must be magnetic. It seemed like pretty sophisticated technology for a nineteenth century house, but then I remembered what Dory Browne had said about Silas LaMotte: he liked everything ship-shape, he'd built this house to last, and, according to the inspector I'd hired, it was in pristine condition. "A little paint and some caulking and you're good to go," he'd told me, recommending his cousin Brock Olsen for the repairs. Dory had let Brock in last week and offered to oversee the work. I had nothing to worry about. It hadn't been crazy to buy the house, but it would be crazy to walk away from it now.

I turned the key. The tumblers turned smoothly in the lock and the door opened silently on well-oiled hinges, not at all like the creaking doors of Gothic romance. Nor was I greeted with cobwebs and dank miasmas. The house smelled like fresh paint and varnish. A clean, practical smell that vanquished the ridiculous notion that I'd bought the house because of a dream.

It was, after all, a beautiful house. As I stood on the threshold a bit of moonlight struggled through the clouds and skidded across the newly varnished floors like a stone skipping across a pond. I stepped inside with the wind coming in on my heels, ruffling the lace curtains in the parlor and trembling the glass in the windows. The house creaked like a ship in a storm – maybe that's how Silas LaMotte had built it. I even thought I could smell a whiff of sea air beneath the paint and varnish, but when I closed the door the house seemed to settle. The storm was clearing, letting in enough moonlight to make the new white paint glow like polished marble and casting a distorted reflection of the fanlight onto the foyer floor – the face of the pagan god elongated and distorted so that he seemed to be smirking.

I shivered at the thought . . . but also because I was damp and tired from the long drive. I needed a hot bath (assuming the hot water heater worked without electricty) and bed (assuming the bed I'd ordered had come and been set up). The movers were coming early in the morning. Once I'd had a good night's sleep and filled the house with my books and furniture it wouldn't feel so strange . . . or echo so hollowly.

I climbed the stairs, my footsteps sounding loud as firecrackers in the empty house. I recalled what I'd said to Dory Browne about not having to worry about burglars and her reply: "No, you wouldn't have to worry about anyone breaking *in*." Why had she emphasized *in* as if there were something dangerous already lurking in the house?

I was afraid that the upstairs hallway would be

completely dark, but the moonlight had found its way here too, through the windows of the smaller bedrooms, the doors of which had been propped open. Only the door at the end of the hallway to the master bedroom was closed.

I made my way down the hallway feeling peculiarly *watched*. Looking down I spied the shadow of a mouse at my feet. I screamed and jumped a good two feet before realizing the shadow belonged to a cast-iron doorstop shaped like a mouse holding its little paws out.

Cursing Diana Hart's love of animal tchotchkes (I suspected she was responsible for the mice doorstops), I turned the knob of my bedroom door, but it wouldn't budge. It must have swung shut when the paint was still wet and had dried stuck. I leaned my shoulder against the door, cursing softly under my breath. *Open up, damn it, I'm tired . . .* the door swung open so suddenly I stumbled into the room. An angry gust of wind snapped the curtains at the window and ruffled the linens of the bed.

The bed.

I'd asked Dory Browne to accept delivery on the bed I'd ordered from Anthropologie and I'd hoped that the workman had assembled it, but I half expected to be sleeping on a bare mattress on the floor. But not only had someone assembled the pine four poster frame, but someone had also made it up with crisp white sheets, plump pillows, and a lofty feather-filled duvet. All of it white in the moonlight. It looked like it was meant for a bride – not for sweaty me in my scruffy shorts and T-shirt.

I should take a bath, I thought, but I was suddenly too exhausted. I walked toward the bed . . . and stubbed my toe on something hard. Cursing, I groped on the floor and picked up something heavy and cold. Holding it up in the moonlight, I saw it was one of the cast-iron mice. It must have fallen there when the wind slammed the door shut before I arrived. It had a splash of white paint on its chest – probably from when Brock painted the room – and it was missing the tip of its tail. Another glance on the floor revealed the missing appendage. I picked that up lest I impale my foot on it later and held it up in front of the mouse's little whiskered face.

"Wounded in the line of duty, eh?" I said. "It's all right, soldier. I'm giving you the night off." I put the mouse doorstop outside in the hall with the rest of its companions and closed the door. Then I peeled off my sweaty clothes and crawled into the white virginal bed, sinking into its deep, pillowy embrace and into an even deeper sleep.

But not for long.

Someone was tapping at the window. I got up and walked across the dark room toward the lighted window. Moonlight was banked up against the glass like water pressing against a dam, but it wasn't coming in. I was standing in the dark, on the threshold between shadow and moonlight, where *he* always waited for me. And someone was knocking. I walked closer to the window and saw that there was something metal hanging from the window frame, a round medallion with spokes like a wheel and three dangling keys. Although it was made of some kind of dark metal, it reminded me of a dream catcher. It was tapping against the glass, propelled by the wind whistling through a crack in the window frame. If I didn't take it down it would break the glass. I grabbed it and pulled, snapping the ribbon that held it. Instantly a crack appeared in one of the windowpanes, splintering the glass into a million jagged shards. They fell to the floor at my feet and the moonlight rushed in with the wind – a wind that smelled like honeysuckle and salt – and circled around me like an angry riptide. It slammed me up against the window, my back hitting the glass and shattering the rest of the panes. The moonlight was so bright I was blinded. I closed my eyes against it, but it was still there beneath my eyelids, still there pressing me up against the windowpane, a cold, hard surge that pushed my hips up onto the window ledge and spread my legs and poured into me . . . I grasped the window frame for balance and cut my hand on broken glass. I gasped and my mouth filled up with saltwater. I tried to push back but that only made the surge come again . . . and again, sucking me down into the riptide.

I'd heard somewhere that if you're drowning you should relax and let the current take you. I did that now and the current turned warm and carried me down into the darkness, like a lover carrying me to bed, down into the darkness where *he* lived.

CHAPTER SIX

The sound of the moving truck in the driveway woke me up the next morning. I lay for a moment, sprawled in a tangle of sheets, trying to remember where I was. Hadn't I drowned? But that was only a dream. As I scrambled into my discarded clothes from last night, though, I noticed the broken glass on the floor and a long jagged cut on my hand. I gingerly approached the window and saw that there among the broken glass was the metal wind chime. I stared at it for a moment, recalling the violence of my dream, but then a knock on the front door startled me out of my reverie. The sound of the wind chime hitting the window must have woken me up and I'd gone to the window to close it. That's when I must have cut my hand. The wind and the broken glass must have mixed in with my dream and created the rest out of all my pent-up longing for the fantasy lover to come back. That was the only explanation, I told myself hurrying down the stairs, the only one that made sense.

It didn't take long for the two men and two women from Green Move (the eco-friendly moving company run by Annie's partner, Maxine) to unpack the contents of my Inwood apartment and the boxes from my storage unit. When they finished, the house still looked empty. I invited them to share the basket of sandwiches that had arrived courtesy of Deena's Deli ("We're Deli-ghted you're our new neighbor!!!"). We sat on the front porch enjoying the cool breeze that came out of the woods.

"The summers are great up here," one of the women told me. "My partner and I have a place in Margaretville about forty minutes east. But the winters . . ."

The woman, whose name was Yvonne, proceeded to tell me about a couple who'd moved up here year round and gone a little stir crazy, but then, she assured me, they'd always had "issues." I laughed off the idea that I was worried about going stir crazy in the country and they all agreed that it was different because I was teaching at the college. When they left the house felt quiet and even emptier than before they had come with my meager belongings.

Before I could wonder if the first sign of going stir crazy was having strange erotic dreams, I threw myself into unpacking, figuring that the surest way to ward off melancholy was to make the house feel like my home. I hung framed prints and photographs in the library and parlor and unpacked my mismatched collection of mugs and dishes into the built-in china cabinets. It would be fun, I told myself, to find odds and ends in antiques stores to fill the house up.

After dinner – a pizza delivered courtesy of Mama Esta's Pizzeria and a bottle of Shiraz from a local vineyard – I took a long overdue soak in the claw foot tub, pouring in the rose-scented bath oil that had come in a welcome basket from a store called Res Botanica ("May your new home be sweet!"). Then I put on a loose nightshirt and started unpacking my files and office supplies into the desk in the tower office while sipping a glass of wine. It was fun opening up all the little desk drawers. In addition to the robin's egg I had found the first day I saw the house, I found a glossy black seedpod shaped like a horned goat's head, a china doll's head with one blue eye scratched out, and a bird's nest. Only one drawer was locked. I looked for a key in the other drawers, but didn't find one.

I left all the objects where they were and added my own collection of stones and shells, as well as pens and pencils, tape, stapler, a dagger-shaped letter opener I'd gotten as a souvenir at a Scottish castle, file cards, and notebooks. I unpacked the reference books I liked to have near me while I was writing – the abridged Oxford English Dictionary (a gift from my grandmother when I graduated college), the Penguin Dictionary of Symbols, Roget's Thesaurus, *The Golden Bough*, *From the Beast to the Blonde*, Gilbert and Gubar's *The Madwoman in the Attic,* and half a dozen other books on fairy tales and folklore. On one shelf I put my favorite novels, from *The Mysteries of Udolpho* and *Jane Eyre* through *Rebecca* and Dahlia LaMotte's *The Dark Stranger*. When I'd placed my pens in my Oxford University mug (a souvenir from my junior year abroad) and emptied a handful of paperclips into a chipped Sèvres teacup, which was the last remnant (according to my grandmother) of my great-great-grandmother's wedding china, I finally felt at home.

I sat back and looked up, meeting my own eyes in my reflection in the darkened windowpane. I'd tied my hair up in a loose knot for my bath, but tendrils had escaped and curled around my face; my auburn hair looked black against my white skin. My nightshirt, I noticed, was rather transparent. For a moment I imagined what I'd look like to someone looking in from outside – a maiden trapped in a tower like on the cover of one of Dahlia LaMotte's Gothic romances. I had started to laugh at the idea – before long I'd be running in my diaphanous nightgown towards a cliff with a castle looming in the background – when a flicker of white out in the back garden caught my attention. Just because my bedroom faced the woods didn't mean no one could be out there. Although classes didn't start until next week freshmen had started arriving for orientation and it wouldn't take them long to figure out that the woods were a good place to get high and drink.

I pulled a Columbia sweatshirt over my nightshirt and leaned forward. There *was* something on the lawn just at the edge of the woods, a white shape that swayed in the breeze. For a moment I was sure it was a man in a white shirt and dark pants standing on the edge of the woods, looking up at my window. I could make out a pale face and dark eyes . . . and then the eyes widened and spread, devouring the rest of his face—I had the impression of eyes widening so far to see that they dissolved the rest of him— and then I saw that it was an illusion. The white shape was a plume of mist rising from the ground and dispersing on the breeze.

Great, now I was becoming like one of the heroines of the books I wrote about, jumping at noises and imagining faces in the mist. Violet Gray in *The Dark Stranger* imagining phantom lovers in the moonlight – like the one I'd dreamt about last night. Only the dream I'd had last night hadn't been of a romantic shadow lover. The flood of moonlight that had rushed into me had been an elemental force – urgent and impatient.

Because of how long you've waited for the shadow lover,

a voice inside my head whispered. *Because of how long you've made him wait.*

"That's ridiculous," I said aloud as I closed and locked the window. It was just being in a strange house, that's all. And the house was already ceasing to feel strange.

Still, it took me a long time to fall asleep that night. I lay awake listening to the creaks and taps the old house made settling on its foundation and watching the moonlight cast jagged shadows as it shone through the broken glass in the window, unwilling to relax my guard against whatever might form out of the moonlight and shadow, afraid of a repeat of last night's violent dream.

When I finally fell asleep, though, the dream that was waiting for me was completely different. Shadows stole softly across the floor, skirting the sharp blades of moonlight as if they were actually made of glass. The shadows slipped into my bed and wrapped themselves around me, murmuring words that I couldn't understand but which sounded like the drone of the surf inside a seashell. The sound poured into my ears like warm oil and spread a feeling of contentment throughout my body. It was like being massaged all over at once. The shadows were everywhere, like a warm bath with fingers and lips, sucking on my mouth, my nipples, and between my legs. As if they were feeding on me and growing stronger with every orgasm they gave me.

I woke up the next morning feeling strangely refreshed, not sore at all from the heavy lifting I'd done the day before. I unpacked a dozen boxes before breakfast and then decided I might as well use all this energy to move into my campus office. The campus as I drove through it was relatively quiet except for the freshmen here for orientation. They were instantly recognizable from the way they walked in tight-knit clumps of fours and sixes, as if the bucolic ivy-covered campus were a dangerous wilderness that could only be broached by group expedition. I remembered how in my first week at N.Y.U. all the kids from out of town traveled together in packs. A city kid, I'd been disdainful of their timidity and dependence, and stayed mostly to myself or socialized with city friends from high school. As a result, I hadn't made a lot of new friends at college and then I met Paul and I spent most of my time with him or in the library. I supposed it had paid off when I got into Columbia (where the easy camaraderie of college had given way to the competition of grad school), but now watching these kids laughing and jostling up against one another under the stately autumn-colored trees I felt like I might have missed something.

I parked in front of Fraser Hall, a four-storied half-timbered faux Tudor building which held the folklore department offices. It was named for Angus Fraser, a famous folklorist who had founded the Royal Order of Folklorists at the turn of the last century, written dozens of book on Celtic folklore, and taught at Fairwick over a hundred years ago. My office was on the top floor and, I soon discovered, there was no elevator. On my second trip hauling boxes up the steep, winding stairs a pair of brawny arms relieved me of my burden.

"You sound like you're going to expire of consumption at any moment." I recognized Frank Delmarco, the American History professor who had sneered at the inclusion of vampire books in my curriculum during my interview. Now he was apparently critiquing my stair-climbing capacity.

"I'm . . . fine . . ." I huffed. "I've been . . . doing . . . a . . . lot of un . . . packing."

"Yeah, I heard you bought the old LaMotte house. Isn't that a little big for just one person alone?"

For a split second I almost told him I *wasn't* alone in the house. I felt my face go red recalling what company I'd found in my dreams. Luckily, Comrade Delmarco (today he was wearing a red T-shirt with pictures of Marx and Lenin wearing party hats that read JOIN THE COMMUNIST PARTY) would just think I was embarrassed to be hogging a big house to myself.

"I may rent out one of the rooms," I said, although I had no plans to and I instantly didn't like the idea of anyone else in the house.

"Really? That's a good idea . . ." he began, but I cut him off.

"You know, it's funny that someone who disapproves of 'catering to the common denominator' would be a socialist."

"A socialist? I'm not a socialist!" he sputtered, dumping one of my boxes on the floor of my new office. "Do you have more boxes?"

"Yes, but please don't put yourself to any trouble on my account." I turned and headed down the stairs. He followed.

"No problem. We socialists like to help out our comrades. Geez, even if I were a socialist, I don't see what despising commercial vampire dreck has to do with anything—"

"Dreck? What a snob! Have you ever read Anne Rice?"

"No."

"Stephenie Meyer?"

"God, no!"

"Charlaine Harris?"

"Who?"

We continued arguing as he helped me bring up all my books and files. It took three trips, at the end of which we were both breathing hard and drenched with sweat.

"Sheesh, it's hot," he said, wiping the sweat off his brow with a red bandana. "Would you like a beer?"

"At ten in the morning?" I asked.

"Now who's the snob?" he asked, throwing his hands up and walking out of my office.

I unpacked my books and files in a snit of annoyance that turned gradually into an insatiable urge for a beer and then into regret for not having thanked Frank Delmarco for helping me carry up all those boxes. I went out into the hall to find his office. I followed the sound of laughter around the corner and saw, through an open doorway, the profile of a young, pretty girl sitting in an office chair next to a large desk. All I could see of the man behind the desk was a pair of Timberland hiking boots propped up on a stack of books, but I recognized Frank Delmarco from his booming laugh. The girl joined in his laughter, tossing her waist length shiny hair over her shoulder and crossing her very long, very bare legs. I suddenly felt like I'd had enough socializing with my new colleagues for the day and decided to go home.

When I stopped back in my office to lock up, though, I found I had a visitor. A student – or maybe a student's kid sister, she looked that young – was perched on the edge of the straight-backed chair next to my desk, her shoulders hunched over, her medium-length hair – which was the color of weak, milky tea – obscuring her face. When I walked into the room she flinched and looked up. Her eyes were huge and the same milky tea color as her hair.

"Oh, excuse me, Professor McFay, I hope you don't mind me coming in . . . The door was open and it was drafty in the hallway."

It was eighty degrees in the hallway but this girl looked as if she could be blown away by a summer breeze. The reason her eyes looked so big, I saw now, was that her face was so thin.

"No problem," I said, not sounding as if I meant it. I was tired and wanted to go home. "Office hours haven't really begun yet . . ."

"Oh, I am so sorry!" She jumped up from her chair. She was wearing a soft blue peasant blouse that flapped around her rail-thin chest. This girl wasn't just thin, she was undernourished. Anorexia? I wondered. "It's just I come late to school and have not made the registration."

I noticed her accent now. Eastern European, I thought. "It's okay, please, sit down. I just wasn't expecting any students today, but I'm new here and I don't know the routine yet."

"Me, too. I am new, too!" She smiled. Her teeth had clearly not had the benefit of American dentistry, and the smile failed to brighten the pastiness of her skin. "I am . . . how do you say? Change student?"

"Exchange student," I corrected her as gently as I could. She looked as if she might crumble under the slightest rough handling.

"*Ex*change student," she repeated dutifully. Then she wrinkled her brow in confusion. "But that cannot be correct. Exchange means to trade one thing for another, no?"

I nodded in agreement.

"But I do not think Fairwick College will be sending an

American student back where I am coming from." She said this with such stolid gravity that I felt a little chill.

"Where exactly *do* you come from?" I asked.

She shook her head, making her lank hair whisk against her thin shoulders. I noticed the ends of her hair were split and damp – as if she'd been chewing them. "The borders change so often I hardly know anymore."

When I'd walked into the room I had thought she looked younger than the average college student, but now, talking about her country, she suddenly looked much older. Where could she be from, I wondered? Bosnia? Chechnya? Serbia? But if she didn't want to say which war-torn corner of Eastern Europe she came from, who was I to pry?

"What can I do to help?" I asked instead.

She gave me a snaggle-toothed smile and relaxed her shoulders. "I would like to take your class Vampires and the Gothic Imagination," she said very carefully, as if she had rehearsed this bit. "But it is full." She frowned. Then smiled again (she was beginning to seem a little manic). "You are a very popular teacher! Everybody wants to take your class!"

"It's my first semester here," I reminded her. "So, it's not because of me. The class is popular because vampires and the supernatural are popular right now. Is that why you want to take the class – because you liked the *Twilight* books?"

"I don't know what this *Twilight* is," she said. "I read the description of your class. It says that the heroine of the Gothic novel confronts evil – within and without – and survives it. That is what I would like to know – how one survives a confrontation with evil."

The girl was leaning forward, her hands clasped in her lap, her pale tea-colored eyes wide and glassy. Her pupils were dilated, the black swimming over the light irises as if something dark were rising up inside her. For a moment, looking into them, I thought I caught a glimpse of the horrors they had seen. A wave of cold, like a current in the ocean, passed over me and I shivered.

"Of course you can take the class," I said, wishing there was something more I could do for this girl. "Do you have something for me to sign?"

After I signed Mara Marinca's add slip I decided I had to go home to take a nap. All the energy I'd woken up with had drained away. Moving boxes up all those steps had really worn me out. I felt as if I'd had that beer Frank Delmarco had offered – several, in fact.

On my way out of the building, though, I ran into a woman struggling on the stairs with two boxes. The boxes were uncovered and filled with newspapers and magazines that kept slipping out so that she had to stop every few steps and restack them. The boxes themselves looked as if they were coming apart at the seams.

"Here," I said, taking pity on her predicament, "let me help you with those."

"Omigod, you're a lifesaver sent from heaven!" she declaimed dramatically, casting her big blue eyes upward. She was dressed for dramatic gestures – in a sweeping bell-sleeved kimono and a long flowing skirt – not for moving. Her wispy blonde hair was pinned up in a clip that fell out twice before we made it up to her office with the collapsing boxes.

"Thank you so so much!" she said, spilling the contents of her box onto a pile of more newspapers and magazines spread out on her office floor. "I've been collecting all the journals and magazines that have reviewed my book this year and haven't had a second to organize them all."

"Wow," I said, looking appreciatively at the pile. *The New Yorker*, *People*, and *Vanity Fair* were mixed in with literary journals like *The Hudson Review* and *Blueline* and writing magazines like *Poets & Writers* and *The Writer's Chronicle*. I looked up from the pile to a stack of books on her desk: multiple copies of *Phoenix – Coming up from the Ashes*.

"You're Phoenix," I said, feeling a little odd using the single name, but like Cher or Sting, that's all she went by. "I've read about your memoir." So had most of literate America. A harrowing tale of growing up with child abuse and incest in a dirt-poor Appalachian hollow, *Phoenix* had been featured on dozens of talk shows and gotten a rave review from a *New York Times* critic who was better known for excoriating her subjects.

"Oh, have you?" she asked, batting her eyelashes. I heard the Southern accent now and remembered she was from North Carolina. "Everybody's been so sweet. It's very gratifying, you know, when you write something as hard to write as my book was and then people are affected by it. Some of the messages I get on my website just make me bawl like a baby!"

"I guess your honesty about your own travails encourages your readers to open up about their own hardships," I said, thinking that while *Sex Lives* had gotten me a fair amount of publicity it at least hadn't gotten me a string of confessional Emails.

"Exactly!" Phoenix nodded her head eagerly. "You must be a writer, too, to understand that."

I admitted I was and introduced myself. She claimed to

have heard of my book, but not to have had a chance to read
it since she'd been so busy touring for her book this year.
She demanded I get a copy of my book from my office so
we could exchange signed copies ("The truth will set you
free!" she wrote, drawing a little picture of a plumed bird on
fire beside her signature) and that I make a date with her to
"get good and plastered" the coming weekend before
classes started. She was teaching a writing seminar. "I just
know once I get involved with my students I won't have a
minute for myself – that's just the way I am!"

I left her introducing herself to Frank Delmarco ("A big
strong man like you wouldn't mind carrying up a few teeny-
weeny boxes for me, would you?") and made my escape. I
was now really and truly exhausted. I was so tired that when
I let myself into my house I couldn't face one more flight of
stairs. I collapsed on the couch in the library, not even
bothering to draw the blinds against the late afternoon sun,
and fell into a deep sleep.

I must have slept for several hours because when I woke
up the room was nearly dark. The last of the sun bathed the
couch in liquid amber and shadows stretched long across
the library floor almost, but not quite reaching me.

Come here, a voice from inside the shadows said.

I'm still asleep, I told myself. I'm still dreaming.

Come here!

The voice was harsher now. Gone was the gentle oceanic
murmur of last night. But there was also something
desperate in it. He couldn't reach me in the light. He hadn't
grown that strong.

I will once I feed on you again, the voice whispered.

I shivered – not from fear, but from desire at the memory
of those shadow lips suckling me last night. I could feel

myself going wet already just at the thought of him.

But it wasn't a *him*; it was a thing waiting to feed on me and even if it was only a dream-thing I had to assert myself. Didn't I?

I reached behind me for the lamp, remembering only as I touched it that I hadn't plugged it in yet. The shadows stretched closer. The voice commanded me again. *Come here!* He was getting angry. I swung my legs around and planted my feet in the swath of sunlight. The wood felt warm. Solid. Was I really dreaming?

Yes, only dreaming, the voice said, coaxing now. *But such a lovely dream. Come to me!*

The dreams *were* lovely . . . well, last night's dream had been. But still some shred of consciousness told me that there was a limit. That if I let this thing into the daylight I might never wake up from those dreams.

I stood up and followed the path of sunlight across the floor to the wall switch. I flicked it on.

When I turned back I half expected him to still be there – my shadow man – glowering at me with disapproval for my disobedience. I could feel his anger prickling the hairs at the back of my neck. I spun around but the room, awash with electric light, was empty.

CHAPTER SEVEN

I slept with my light on that night. In the morning I called Brock Olsen to fix the window in my bedroom and he was at my door fifteen minutes later. He was short and broad and bearded. His face would have been handsome, but he must have had a bad case of acne when he was young that had left his skin rough and pitted. When I showed him the broken window he rocked back on his heels and stroked his beard as if he were contemplating the *Mona Lisa*.

"It happened two nights ago when there was all that wind," I said, "This wind chime blew against it and broke it." I retrieved the metal ornament from the desk drawer where I'd stowed it away as if it proved my story. Brock gave me a long considering look as if I was a shelf hung crooked.

"Is that how you cut your hand?" he asked, looking down at my hand.

The scratch had almost healed so I'd taken the bandage off, but it had started to itch. I nodded and he took my hand in his own broad and calloused one. He studied the cut for so long I began to feel uncomfortable, but then he ran the tips of his fingers over the scratch, which should have made me feel even more uncomfortable. It had the opposite effect. As he stroked my hand a wave of comfort and well-being spread throughout my body. I thought of stories I'd read about faith healers, people whose touch could cure suffering. Brock Olsen's hands looked as if they'd suffered a lot themselves; they were nicked and scarred and riddled with burn marks that stood out white against his dark skin. He was missing the top of his left ring finger. Maybe having been through so much pain himself gave him the power to ease the pain in others. When he released my hand the itching in my hand was gone.

"Best be more careful next time," he said, fixing me with his warm brown eyes. He waited until I promised I would and then went to get his tools from his truck.

I spent the morning sorting through Dahlia LaMotte's papers while Brock Olsen worked in the house, re-planing all my doors and windows. I found the background noise of his hammering and sanding oddly companionable. I made a pot of coffee for us and heated up a plate of cinnamon rolls Diana Hart had left on my doorstep with a note saying they were leftovers from last night's guests. The smells of coffee and cinnamon mingled cozily with the piney scent of sawdust. It felt good to have someone else in the house. Maybe Frank Delmarco was right. This was too big a house for one person – although maybe not one person with this many books.

I decided that there were too many boxes to keep in my little turret office, so I hauled them into one of the empty bedrooms. Brock helped me when he saw what I was doing. I unpacked them all and started stacking them in piles on the floor, sorting by category and using the iron mice doorstops as paperweights.

There were notebooks – ledgers from her father's shipping business bound in marbled paper and ruled with narrow horizontal lines and red vertical columns – in which Dahlia had apparently written her rough drafts; piles of typescript and letters. I arranged the letters chronologically, making piles for each decade of her life, and the writing notebooks and typescripts by book.

At some point in the afternoon Brock brought me a plate with cheese, bread and apple slices, and a fresh cup of coffee.

"Oh, Brock!" I cried. "I should have gotten *you* lunch."

"I could see you were wrapped up in what you were doing," he said, blood rising behind his ravaged skin. "Are these Dolly's things?" he asked.

"Dolly?"

"That's what we called her here in Fairwick. To the world she was Dahlia LaMotte."

"There are people who remember her?" I asked, amazed that the town's memory went back that far.

He smiled. "It's a small town and the local families have been here a long time. My people have been here for over a hundred years."

"Really? Did they come from somewhere in Scandinavia?"

"Sort of," he replied. "We made some other stops along the way. Dolly's people, they came later and overland."

"Overland?" I repeated, wondering what on earth he meant. Fairwick was a landlocked village in the Catskill Mountains. How else could anyone approach it? "You mean by train or carriage?"

A vivid red streak rose up on the right side of Brock's face, highlighting a welt on his cheekbone. It looked like he'd been bitten by an insect there.

"Ya, they came by carriage, how else? I only meant some didn't have fine carriages or train fare. My people came on foot, through the woods, through hardship and danger." He rubbed at the welt on his face with the back of his scarred hand. He looked angry, but not at me, or even at the town. He looked angry at himself for not being able to express himself better. I wondered if the marks on his face were the vestiges of some childhood illness – chicken pox? measles? – that had scarred his brain as well as his skin.

"Your ancestors must have struggled hard to find a safe place to live and raise their children," I said gently. "That's something to be proud of."

He nodded, the red streak subsiding. He pointed at the stacks of notebooks. "Dolly understood that. She helped us . . . my great-uncles, I mean, start the gardening shop when there weren't no call for blacksmiths no more and always had them come do what work needed doing in the house. She liked hearing the old stories."

"Really?" I said, looking down at the ledgers. Had she used the stories she'd heard in her books? "That's interesting. Perhaps you can help me by identifying where some of her stories came from."

He smiled. It transformed his face from ugly to handsome. "Ya, I'll be happy to. I am here to help you."

I spent the rest of the afternoon making an inventory of Dahlia LaMotte's notebooks and letters. The letters I found, to my disappointment, were all of a business nature, either to her publisher in New York or her lawyer in Boston. No clandestine love affairs or dark family secrets were likely to be lurking there, but the letters to her publisher could establish a timeline of her writing process. A glimpse of one showed that she reported progress on her novels dutifully. *I finished the handwritten draft of* Dark Destiny *today and will begin typing it tomorrow*, one letter read.

It was curious that she didn't employ a typist. Was she such a hermit that she couldn't stand the human interaction? But then, Brock had said that she enjoyed talking to the locals and hearing their stories. If I could find accounts of those conversations it would be fascinating to compare the references – to boggarts and fairies, witches and demons – that Dahlia sprinkled throughout her books to local folklore.

Only when I had a complete list of all the notebooks – numbered with dates and the titles of which novels she had been working on in each – and a list of typescripts, did I allow myself a peek at one of the notebooks. I chose *The Dark Stranger*, my favorite of her books and her best-known novel. I read the familiar first lines with a frisson of excitement.

The moment I set foot across the threshold of Lion's Keep I knew my fate was sealed. I had been here before, in desperate dreams and fevered fancies , and always I knew it to be the place where he would finally ensnare me – the man of my dreams – the incubus of my nightmares. The dark stranger, my demon lover . . ."

I stopped reading. I didn't recall the word *incubus* from the first paragraph of *The Dark Stranger,* or the phrase *demon lover*. Although Dahlia LaMotte flirted with the supernatural with her use of dreams, portents, creaking stairs, veiled figures, and telepathic voices, she never made overt use of it. At the end of each book the events were tidily explained. Her anti-heroes had all the elements of the rakish Byronic heroes of Gothic Romance, but they were flesh and blood, not incubi, demons or vampires. Perhaps she was just playing with the imagery, but that imagery hadn't made it into her final drafts. When, I wondered, had it been edited out?

I turned to the first page of the typescript of *The Dark Stranger*. On brittle, yellowed paper I read over the first paragraph. It was the same as in the notebook until the last line.

. . . the man of my dreams, the figure in my nightmares.
Interesting.

Between handwritten draft and typescript Dahlia LaMotte had struck the words *incubus* and *demon lover* How many other changes had she made? I flipped through one of the notebooks in which she'd written *The Dark Stranger* and happened upon a scene I remembered well. Violet Gray, timid governess, hears a cry in the night and rushes out onto the landing . . .

. . . so urgently that I didn't stop to cover myself in my dressing gown. When I reached the landing I saw, to my horror, William Dougall standing there chiding the laundry maid for squealing at a mouse. I couldn't bear for haughty William Dougall to think I was spying on him nor to look upon me in my transparent nightgown. To my left was the door to the linen closet, which had been left partly ajar by the careless maid. It was the work of an instant to slip inside and wedge myself between the full shelf of folded linens and the door. I breathed an inaudible sigh of relief and settled myself against the still warm and fragrant cloth. Thankfully the room was not completely dark. A beam of moonlight came through a window at the back of the closet and flowed

through the crack in the door allowing me to watch for Dougall to leave the landing. He was still scolding her.

"You should not be out and about at night. There are things here far worse than a mouse that will make you scream until you have no voice. Go back to your room. Lock your door and close your windows. Draw your drapes to shut out the moonlight. The moonlight plays tricks with one's mind."

Dougall glanced down at the spill of moonlight from the closet. For a moment his eyes seemed to meet mine and I felt a tremor move through me that reached into the pit of my stomach and made my legs go so weak I sank further into the warm sheets. Did he see me?

But then he turned abruptly and stalked away, leaving a very frightened-looking maid who soon scurried back to her room.

As I should have done now. Only my legs were still weak. What had William Dougall meant by the moonlight playing tricks? The moonlight had certainly played tricks on me since I'd come to Lion's Keep. At the memory of those strange dreams my heart raced. Did Dougall know about my moonlight lover who had insinuated himself into my bed . . . and between my legs? At the thought I felt heat spark between my legs. I pressed my thighs together as if I could quench that flame, but instead the heat quickened. I squirmed against the sheets . . . and felt them squirm against me!

I was not alone in the linen closet.

Someone . . . or something had stolen in behind me . . . or had been hiding there when I came in.

Slowly I took a step toward the door . . .

But strong arms wrapped around me and pulled me back.

I started to call out and a hand clamped down over my mouth.

Another hand dropped to my neck, caressed my throat, fondled my breast, lowered to my belly . . . then slipped in between my legs. I struggled but my movements only succeeded in exciting him. I felt something stiff pressing against my back, pressing in between the cleft of my buttocks. The hand lifted my gown and spread my legs just as the hard probing shaft found its way between my legs and thrust into me.

I bit the hand over my mouth and he . . . it . . . returned the bite on my shoulder. He plunged deeper into me, withdrew, plunged again and again, stoking a flame that finally burst inside me. The moonlight seemed to splinter around me, dissolving into a shower of stars . . .

"Miss?"

I jumped at the sound of the voice, guiltily slamming shut the notebook on Violet Gray's orgasm.

I looked up, hoping my cheeks weren't as red as they felt. Brock was standing in the hallway, his coat on and his toolbox in his right hand. "They'll be here when you get back," he said.

"Who? Who's coming back?" I asked.

"The books, I meant," he said, giving me an odd look. "They'll be here when you get back from the faculty reception."

I looked down at my watch. It was a quarter to five; the reception started at six. I'd spent all afternoon in this room sorting through Dahlia's papers, losing track of time, getting lost in an erotic haze.

Dahlia LaMotte had written erotica! And then she had edited it out between manuscript and typescript. What a discovery! What an amazing book it would make! I wanted to go through every single notebook *right now*, but Brock was right. I had to go to the faculty reception.

"Thanks for reminding me." I started to get up and found my legs were cramped from sitting in the same position for so long. Brock held out his hand to help me up. As soon as his broad, rough hand enfolded mine I felt an overwhelming sense of well-being. I looked down at the piles of paper, each watched over by its own cast-iron mouse sentinel, and felt a swelling sense of excitement . . . followed by an almost equally potent sense of dread. Dahlia LaMotte had written of a lover made out of moonlight who ravished her heroines just as the creature in my dreams had ravished me. Either she had dreamed the same dreams as I had . . . or they weren't dreams at all.

CHAPTER EIGHT

I walked briskly across the campus, trying to dispel the ridiculous notion that my dreams were something more than the work of an overheated imagination – mine or Dahlia's. There was a simple explanation. I'd been reading Dahlia LaMotte's books for years. Even in the edited and published versions there was a latent eroticism and plenty of references to moonlight and shadows. Moving to Dahlia's house had simply brought that latent sexuality to life – and into my dreams. That Dahlia had written more graphically in her original manuscripts was an exciting scholarly discovery, I told myself as I entered Briggs Hall, but that was all. It didn't mean my dreams were anything but dreams.

Like Fraser, Briggs was in the Tudor style, only considerably grander. Entering the main parlor I felt as if I might be entering William Dougall's ancestral castle. One whole wall was covered with heavy tapestry drapes. The beamed ceiling must have been at least twelve feet high. Looking up I saw that each beam was decorated in gilt lettering and Celtic designs, which were echoed in painted inserts in the dark oak paneling. Above the stone fireplace at the end of the room hung a huge painting of monumental figures in flowing medieval robes. The room was so impressive that I stood in the doorway for several minutes admiring it – and catching my breath from my hurried walk across campus – before I became aware that I was being watched. Elizabeth Book in a brocade dress and pearls that somehow managed to make her look fashionably chic and Old World elegant at the same time, was pointing me out to a striking, tall woman dressed all in green. The dean caught my eye and waved for me to come forward. I obeyed, feeling as if I'd been summoned by a queen.

As regal as Elizabeth Book was, though, the woman who stood beside her dwarfed her. She must have been at least six feet tall, in a green jersey calf-length dress that clung to her willowy frame. Her loose, waist-length hair was platinum blonde. From across the room I had thought she was young, but as I got closer I saw that her face was creased by fine lines and that her hair was actually silver. Her green eyes were clear and sharp as emeralds and watched me with unnerving focus. I felt as if my progress across the long room were being tracked by a mountain lion.

"Ah, there you are, Callie," Elizabeth Book said, holding out both her hands to me. "You look lovely!"

"Thank you." I had worn my favorite cocktail dress – a vintage peacock blue Dolce & Gabbana that clung just enough to my curves, made my hair glow copper, and brought out the green in my eyes. In the shadow of the regal woman in green, though, I felt suddenly like a scullery maid.

"Cailleach McFay, I'd like you to meet Fiona Eldritch, our Elizabethan scholar."

Fiona Eldritch tilted her sharp chin down in my direction, her green cat eyes narrowing. "Liz has been telling me all about you, Cailleach . . . may I call you Cailleach? I love the old Celtic names. They're so romantic."

"Of course," I said, wondering what the dean had been saying about me. "It's not a particularly romantic one, I'm afraid. It means 'old hag.'"

Fiona shook her head and I heard little bells ringing. The sound must have come from her earrings, which were tiny silver balls suspended from silver chains. I suddenly felt a little tipsy even though I hadn't had anything to drink yet. "That's a corruption of the name," she insisted. "The Cailleachs were revered goddesses among the ancient Celts. Liz tells me you had an interesting encounter in the woods."

"It wasn't anything," I said, surprised that this, and not my academic qualifications, was what they had been discussing. "Just a bird caught in the thicket that I let out. It was nothing."

"I'm sure it was far from nothing," Fiona Eldritch said, shaking her head. "But what it was . . . only time will tell."

As I had no idea how to respond to this enigmatic statement an awkward silence followed, which I finally broke by asking Fiona what Elizabethan authors she was particularly interested in.

"Edmund Spenser, of course," she replied as if it were the most obvious answer in the world. Then she excused herself to get a glass of champagne.

"Don't mind Fiona," Dean Book said, grabbing a champagne flute off a passing tray for me. "If she comes off as haughty it's because of how she was raised. Here, let me introduce you to Casper van der Aart, head of the earth sciences department. I think you'll enjoy him."

I wasn't sure what I would have in common with an earth Sciences professor, but after five minutes with the jovial, short, white-haired man I saw it didn't matter. He complimented my dress, told me I reminded him of a

"Scottish lass" he'd pined for when he spent a semester teaching at the University of Edinburgh, and told me funny stories about his colleagues.

"There's Alice Hubbard from psychology," he said, pointing to a dowdy woman with a poorly cut pageboy hairdo wearing misshapen tweeds. "Last year at a conference in Montreal someone mistook her for Betty Friedan and she gave them a two-hour interview without once letting on who she really was. And the tall Viking next to her is her best friend, Joan Ryan from chemistry." The two women had identical haircuts. I wondered if there was only one salon in Fairwick and decided I'd better go back to the city to get mine cut. "Joan blew up the chem lab two years ago and lost her eyebrows. They've never grown back."

Casper van der Aart wiggled his own bushy eyebrows Groucho Marx-fashion and I laughed so hard I got champagne up my nose.

"Who are those people?" I asked, tilting my glass subtly toward a group of new arrivals – two men, one tall and blond, the other short and bald, and a petite brown-haired woman – in nearly identical dark suits with the same pallor of academics who live in the underground stacks of the library.

"They're from the Eastern European and Russian Institute," Casper said curtly. "They tend to keep to themselves . . . but ah, here's one of my favorite people, Soheila Lilly."

The woman he introduced me to had olive skin and a petite but curvy figure. Her dark hair was beautifully cut (I made a mental note to ask where she had it done). She wore clinging cashmere layers in earth tones that seemed too warm for the mild weather but looked beautiful on her.

"I am always cold," she said when I complimented her on her outfit. "And I feel the damp most severely."

"Soheila is from the Middle East," Casper told me.

"Yes," she said, "I came overland from Iran when the shah was deposed."

There was that term Brock had used before about Dahlia LaMotte's family – *overland*.

"I went to college with a girl from Great Neck whose family came over then, too . . . but why do you say *overland*?"

She shrugged and crossed her arms over her chest; the diamonds on her fingers glittered as she chafed her hands against her upper arms. She and Casper exchanged a look. "It is just an expression we exiles use," she said.

"Here at Fairwick," Casper said, "there is a long tradition of giving asylum to refugees. That's what the painting on the outer doors of the triptych represents. It's called *The Fairies' Farewell*." He nodded toward the large painting at the end of the room. From afar I hadn't noticed that it was a triptych, but when I got closer I saw a seam running down the middle and two small gilt handles, presumably to open the painting to reveal the three interior scenes. I thought it was unusual to display a triptych closed, but then the painting on the outer doors was certainly worth looking at. It depicted a procession of winged fairies and fox-faced elves led by a man and woman on horseback, traveling from left to right across a meadow, heading toward an arched opening in a thick wood. The man was on a white horse. He wore a black cloak, his face in shadow. The woman, on a black horse, wore a long green medieval dress, cinched at the waist with a gold belt decorated with Celtic designs similar to the ones on the painted beams and panels in this room. Her long white hair was entwined with flowers and leaves and, I realized with a start, she looked a lot like Fiona Eldritch. I turned around to glance at Fiona, who was chatting with the dark-garbed Russian studies professors.

"You've noticed the resemblance," Casper said, sounding, I thought, a little nervous for the first time since I'd met him. "Fiona is the grandchild of one of the donors of the painting, who modeled for the Fairy Queen."

"I see," I said, although I thought there was something Casper wasn't telling me. "So if she's the Fairy Queen, who's . . . ?" I was going to ask who the man at her side was, but as I stepped nearer and looked more closely at the shadowed face the words died in my throat. It was he. The man in my dreams.

"Ah, you recognize him," Soheila said.

I tore my eyes away from the painted face and stared at Soheila, aghast.

"What do you mean? Why would I recognize him?"

"Because you've made a study of him," Soheila replied calmly, but giving me a quizzical look. "That is the Ganconer, as he's called in Celtic myth. His name means "love talker." In Sumerian myth he was called Lilu. He's the incubus who rides his horse, the night mare, into the dreams of women whom he seduces. The women he comes to in their sleep fall under his spell and begin to waste away. He sucks them dry like a vampire. He's what you write about in your book – the demon lover." Soheila wrapped her sweater more tightly around her chest and tucked her hands into her long sleeves. She looked like she was freezing. "In my country we have a long history of dealing with demons," she whispered. For a moment I thought I saw her breath condensing into a little puff of smoke, but I must have imagined it; it was warm in the room. "But he is the most dangerous of demons because he is the most beautiful. The others . . ." She tilted her chin to the far right side of the painting – the woods that were the destination of the procession. The dense thicket was inhabited by shadowy figures. While the creatures in the procession were beautiful winged fairies and elves, the creatures lurking amidst the vines were stunted goblins and lizard-skinned dwarves, forked-tongued devils and bat-faced imps. "These creatures are easily recognizable as demons, but the Ganconer assumes the shape of your heart's desire."

"Why is he at the head of this procession?" I asked. "Is he with . . . *her*?" I pointed toward the Fairy Queen, feeling an odd pang of jealousy.

Soheila gave me a long, level stare before replying. "Some say the queen stole him as a young man from the mortals and enchanted him, and that when he seduces a human woman he is trying to make himself human again by drinking her spirit, but always before he can become human he drains his lover dry."

"Oh," I said, "that's . . . sad." And then, trying to assume an air of scholarly detachment: "But interesting. I've never before heard that version of the demon lover tale." I turned back to the painting. "Where are they going?"

"Back to Faerie," Soheila said. "Legend has it that once all the fairies and demons lived with mortals, coming and going between the world of mortals and the world of Faerie freely. But then the mortal world grew more crowded and mortals lost belief in the old gods. The doors between the worlds began to close. The fairies and demons had to choose between worlds. Most went back to Faerie, but some who had fallen in love with humanity remained. The doors closed and then even the doors themselves began to disappear. Only one door remained and it was carefully hidden and most dangerous to pass through. Deep thickets grew up over the last door," Soheila continued, "barring the way between the worlds. They grow thicker every year. Few try to pass anymore, and those who do are often lost between the worlds . . . caught in a bodiless limbo of pain. That is why the doors of the triptych are closed. We open it only four times a year on the solstices and equinoxes, which are the times that tradition tells us the doors between the worlds may open . . ."

As she faltered to a stop I heard the pain in Soheila's voice. Startled I turned away from the painting to look at her. Tears shone in her almond-shaped eyes – and not just in hers. Her story had drawn a small circle. Alice Hubbard and Joan Ryan stood with their arms around each other, dabbing their eyes with cloth hankies. Fiona Eldritch, her face rigid with pain, stood beside Elizabeth Book, who was patting the hand of a tiny Asian woman. The three Russian Studies professors hovered at the edge of the group looking uncomfortable but riveted to the painting. I wondered why this fairy story spoke so strongly to them. Were they all, like Mara Marinca and Soheila Lilly, exiles from war-torn countries?

The somber mood was broken by a familiar voice.

"What are y'all looking at?"

It was Phoenix, in an attention-getting slinky red dress and four-inch high stilettos. She was hanging on the arm of Frank Delmarco, who looked as if he wasn't quite sure how he had acquired this particular piece of arm candy. The circle quickly dispersed, the Russian studies professors, especially, seeming to melt into the far shadows of the room, although I saw one of them glancing back over his shoulder at Phoenix.

"Soheila was telling me the story of this painting," I answered. Frank struck up a conversation with Casper about baseball, using it as an excuse to detach himself from Phoenix. Soheila, who looked exhausted and chilled from her recounting of the fairy story, excused herself to go look for a cup of hot tea.

"I thought y'all were having some kind of séance when I came in, the mood was so gloomy. I'm very empathic, you know."

"It was kind of *odd*," I said, lowering my voice. I recounted the story of the painting and everyone's reaction to it.

"Huh," Phoenix said, squinting up at the dark man on horseback. "If *he* came into my dreams I don't think I'd ever want to wake up."

I nodded, turning away to hide my blush. There had to be an explanation for why he looked like the moonlight lover of my dreams. The painter of the triptych must have also designed the pediment over the door of Honeysuckle House . . . or used the same model . . . and that's how I'd fashioned the face of the man in my dreams.

" . . . and when Frank told me I thought it sounded just perfect. What do you say?"

I realized that I'd been so intent on looking at the man in the painting and explaining his existence to myself that I'd lost the thread of Phoenix's conversation. "I'm sorry, it's so loud in here . . . what did you say?"

"Your spare room. Frank says you're looking for a lodger for it. I was going to stay in an apartment in one of the dorms, but between you, me and the lamppost, I don't think I'm the dorm mother type. I'm sure the two of us together would have much more fun!"

CHAPTER NINE

Trying to sway Phoenix from moving in with me turned out to be about as easy as persuading Hurricane Katrina to make landfall somewhere other than New Orleans. She was so *smitten with the notion* that she followed me home after the reception and swept through Honeysuckle House oohing and aahing over every detail. She thought the face in the carved pediment had "bedroom eyes" and the Greek gods on the mantel and on the dining room frieze "cute butts." My library made her "want to curl up and read 'til doomsday." I thought her ardor would cool when she saw Matilda's spinster apartment, but she deemed it "darlin'" and said it reminded her of the room she had rented in a woman's hotel in St. Louis when she was drying out and writing her memoir.

"This house is the perfect place for me to write!" she said, crushing me to her ample bosom in an impetuous hug. "You see, I sometimes have a teeny problem staying on track. Men are the biggest distraction – don't you think that Frank Delmarco is just hunky? – and then there's—" she extended her pinky and thumb and tilted her hand in front of her mouth in the universal sign for drinking "—the demon rum. But I know that here the two of us will be quiet as church mice and drink hot cocoa in the evenings and get so much work done!"

I wondered what had happened to all the "fun" she'd promised me back at the reception. I was still trying to find a polite way of telling her I didn't want a roommate, but if her moving in was inevitable – as it increasingly seemed to be – then I'd better at least make it clear that I needed lots of undisturbed quiet time in which to write.

"I do have an idea for a new book," I said cautiously as we walked upstairs, hoping I wouldn't jinx the idea by talking about it. "And I'd be working on it most of the time."

"That's perfect!" she cried. "Is this where you're working?"

We'd come to the spare bedroom where I'd laid out all Dahlia LaMotte's papers.

The door was propped open with one of the mice doorstops ("How adorable!" Phoenix squealed at the sight of it). I thought I'd closed it, but maybe Brock, who'd left after me, had left it open for some reason. He'd also hung something in the window – a little bundle of birch twigs and juniper sprigs tied with a red ribbon that I guessed must be some sort of Swedish good luck charm.

I explained to her about Dahlia LaMotte's papers and the unusual terms of her will, but didn't mention that I'd discovered a secret trove of nineteenth-century erotica.

"What serendipity!" Phoenix clapped her hands and then held them out over the piles of paper as though blessing them. "I can *feel* the creative energy here. Oh, I just know I'd get so much work done in this house . . . which would be such a lifesaver. Did I mention that I'm six months overdue on delivery of my next manuscript to my publisher?"

As we walked down the hall to my bedroom, Phoenix told me all the reasons she hadn't been able to *even start* her second book. There were the time constraints of touring, doing interviews, and writing blurbs, plus the pressure of living up to the expectations of her *dear readers* whose lives she had touched. "But most especially," she told me as I opened the door to my bedroom, "you have no idea how hard it is having to use parts of your own life to create. I feel like the bird in that story who plucks feathers out of her own breast to weave silk."

Perhaps it was the reference to one of my favorite folktales, "The Crane Wife" that softened me, or perhaps it was the affinity I felt to Phoenix's struggle to write her second book, but in the end I think it was because I was frightened. I'd begun thinking today that the shadow man in my dreams was real. Surely that was a sign that I was spending too much time on my own. And if anyone were capable of filling up this old house with life, it was Phoenix.

Phoenix was so excited about *getting to be roomies* she insisted we have a drink to celebrate. We opened a bottle of Prosecco that had come as a welcome gift from In Vino Veritas Wines & Fine Liquors.

"Better Prosecco than Prozac, that's my motto!" Phoenix toasted, clinking her glass against mine.

I must have nodded off on the library couch with the light on because the next thing I knew it was eight in the morning and Phoenix was back with a pick-up truck (borrowed from Frank Delmarco, I later learned) full of her belongings. She was moved in by nine and by noon her room looked as if she had lived there for years. There were paisley shawls draped over the iron bed frame, framed photographs of her with various celebrities she had met on tour on the walls, colored glass bottles on the windowsills, and glimmering crystals hanging from the window frames. Even her collection of Franciscan Desert Rose chinaware had made its way into the kitchen cupboards.

"You don't mind, do you?" she asked as she arranged the cream, pink and green teacups on the empty shelves. "They look so pretty in these old-fashioned cupboards. I inherited the set from my mama. You know it's the china Jacqueline Kennedy chose for the White House."

When she took a breath for air I told her I didn't mind at all. And it was true. As I told Paul that night on the phone, the house felt less empty with Phoenix and her things in it. He concurred that it was good for me not to be alone in a big house, unaccustomed as I was to living in the country, and since Phoenix's writer-in-residence term was only for one year I wouldn't be stuck with her forever if she turned out to be a horrible roommate.

I went to bed as soon as I got off the phone with Paul, determined to get a good night's sleep before the first day of classes. I turned out the light, confident that the dream wouldn't come back now that I wasn't alone in the house.

But it did. The room was awash with moonlight, but I knew immediately that *he* was there in the shadows . . . that he *was* the shadow. I couldn't move or breathe. He stood over me, watching me, but not touching me. Was he angry that I'd turned on the lights to banish him from the library? Or that I'd brought someone into the house?

The shadow hovered over me and I saw his face – not angry, but sad . . . and aged somehow. Stark lines were etched around his mouth and deep shadows were carved beneath his eyes. He'd grown weaker in the few nights I'd denied him. Perhaps I could still keep him at bay. As he stretched himself over me, hovering millimeters from my skin, I could feel the static electricity between us. Every hair on my body stood erect; my skin tingled with his nearness. Only his lips touched mine, pressing hard, trying to force my mouth open to inhale my breath.

He sucks them dry like a vampire, Soheila had said.

But what harm could he do me if he was just a dream? Why not enjoy the dream?

I parted my lips. For a moment he hesitated, and then his tongue slid along my upper lip, teasing me, punishing me for my delay. His teeth tugged at my lower lip. I opened my mouth wider and he forced his tongue inside, suddenly hard and urgent as he sucked the breath from me. When he blew his breath into my lungs I could move, but only at his bidding and only to his rhythm.

Which was fine by me.

Tonight he was neither as violent as he'd been the first night or as gentle as the second. Instead he seemed to have learned the particular rhythm that opened all the locked rooms inside of me. He made love to me as though he knew my body as well as his own . . . as if he were inside my body and mind, anticipating my every desire before I even knew what they were. Looking into the face that hovered above mine, his eyes dark shadows, his lips parted over mine, was like looking into my own face . . . only just when I was about to see it fully, just when the moonlight was about to illuminate all of him, the shadows swept across his brow, like clouds passing over the moon, and I felt myself sucked into a deep, endless darkness in which there was nothing but the two of us, making love all night long.

I knew that time was deceptive in dreams and that dreams

of a minute might feel as though they lasted all night, but that's what it felt like – as if we made all love all night. When I awoke I was covered in sweat and my muscles were sore. When I touched myself between my legs I was wet and the insides of my thighs were tender.

I had to drink half a pot of coffee to get myself ready for my first class. I was afraid I wouldn't be up for it, but once I was standing in front of the class I was fine. More than fine. Ignoring my notes, with a reproduction of Fuseli's *Nightmare* projected on the Smartboard behind me, I talked about the demon lover in literature for thirty minutes. As I spoke I found myself often looking toward Mara Marinca, who sat at the back of the class and maintained a steady, interested gaze. I'd discovered on my book tour that certain people had better "listening faces." It might have little or nothing to do with what they were actually thinking – people who'd scowled throughout a reading had come up to me afterward to tell me how much they had enjoyed it – but it was unnerving to focus on someone who looked bored or skeptical. Better to focus on someone whose face expressed polite interest (not the girl next to Mara whose bland moon-shaped face expressed little but the desire to nap) and Mara had the perfect listening face. She looked as if she was drinking in my every word.

My students burst into excited discussion as soon as I opened the floor for questions. Half a dozen came up afterward with more questions – or begging to be let into the class even though it was closed.

Since I'd let in Mara Marinca, I didn't feel like I could turn them down.

Mara herself came up once the crowd had dispersed, with the bored moon-faced girl in tow.

"You see," she was saying to the girl, "I told you Professor McFay was a wonderful teacher. Now you want to take the class, no? Professor McFay, this is my roommate, Nicolette Ballard. She wants to take your class but it is closed."

I looked at Nicolette Ballard. The roundness of her face was accentuated by her unfortunate haircut – the same choppy pageboy that I'd seen on Alice Hubbard and Joan Ryan. There must be some sadistic barber in town. "Are you interested in Gothic literature?" I asked.

Nicolette yawned. "I don't really like all that romance stuff," she said, looking at the floor, the ceiling, and then scowling at Fuseli's *Nightmare* which was still projected on the wall. "But I see you've got *Jane Eyre* on your syllabus and it's my favorite book."

"Nicky is helping me most kindly with my English," Mara said. "It would be so very helpful to me if she were in the class so we could study together." I looked down at my class list. I was already six over the maximum enrollment. I looked back up, into Mara's wide tea-colored eyes, which were glowing gold in the light from the projected image."

"Sure," I said, signing my name to Nicolette Ballard's add slip. "What's one more?"

I sailed home on a rosy cloud of satisfaction and contentment. I should have been exhausted but the talk had given me an idea for the Dahlia LaMotte book. I wrote for four hours until the smell of dinner cooking drew me downstairs. I groggily recalled that sometime last night I'd agreed to exchange part of Phoenix's rent for cooking.

I ate two servings of crawfish etoufée with cornbread and sweet potato pie and then stayed up late, drinking wine with

Phoenix and talking about the students we had in common. ("Did you have that waif-like child from Bosnia?" Phoenix had asked. "You wouldn't believe the things she wrote in her first assignment. I read it aloud and there wasn't a dry eye in the classroom!") I went to bed so exhausted that I was sure I wouldn't have the dream again.

But I did. I had it that night and every night for the next three weeks. Each night I woke – or thought I awoke – to a moonlit room. The shadows reached for me and swelled into the dark lover. I'd feel his weight on my chest and then, just when I thought I'd suffocate, he'd press his lips to mine and blow his breath into my lungs and we'd make love – long, deep, utterly spine-rocking, toe-curling sex that went until the first light of day.

The vivid erotic dreams must come, I decided, from reading Dahlia LaMotte's uncensored manuscripts. Tired as I was each morning, I came home in the afternoon to the empty house (Phoenix's classes were in the afternoon) and immediately started reading the manuscripts, stopping only to eat the elaborate dinner that Phoenix would cook. Then I'd write late into the night until I'd fall asleep . . . and have the dream again. It was as if I'd found a loop of creativity, a closed circuit that could endlessly feed on itself.

It was the same loop that Dahlia LaMotte had found.

Anyone glancing at a bibliography of Dahlia LaMotte could tell she had been prolific, but only by reading her handwritten drafts could you tell she had been *possessed*. She dated each entry so I could tell how much she had written in a day. On average she wrote about forty pages – in a miniscule hand on thin ruled lines – but some days she wrote sixty or more. Sometimes when she came to the end of a notebook she had continued writing in the margins and even between the lines of the filled pages. On the days she wrote the most her usually neat handwriting became nearly indecipherable, as if her pen were skipping across the page like a stone skimming the surface of a pond, barely touching the water.

The content on those days when she wrote the most was different from her other writing. *The Dark Stranger*, the published version, was full of sexuality seething just below the surface. A young woman – penniless, orphaned, friendless Violet Gray – comes to Lion's Keep, a secluded estate on the Cornish coast to work as a governess to the young sister of William Dougall, a brooding man whose behavior becomes increasingly strange and threatening. Accidents befall Violet, from which she is saved by a mysterious figure in a black cloak – the dark stranger of the title. She becomes convinced that Dougall is trying to kill her, although the reasons, involving inheritance, mistaken identities and mislaid letters, are never exactly clear and are the biggest pitfall of the plot. Violet comes to believe that the dark stranger who saves her is the ghost of Dougall's long-lost brother – the good brother who should have inherited Lion's Keep. She begins to dream about him at night and to imagine that he visits her in her room (the castle is full of secret passageways and hidden doors). There's a persistent eroticism in these passages that's heightened by the stranger's ambiguous identity. Sometimes he is masked, sometimes he assumes the face of William Dougall. At the end it is revealed that William Dougall *is* the dark stranger. He has treated Violet brusquely because a curse on all mistresses of Lion's Keep makes him reluctant to fall in love. He has appeared in her room to protect her from the illegitimate son of Dougall's dead brother, who stands to inherit the estate if Dougall dies "childless". Of course it is Dougall whom Violet has loved all along – he is the dark stranger, still potent in his sexual mystery, but reformed enough to make a proper bridegroom by the last page of the book. He is the Beast with the witch's curse lifted, Mr. Rochester redeemed by his attempt to save his mad wife's life from the fire.

The sexual tension in *The Dark Stranger* was powerful, but it was always below the surface. Dougall appears in Violet's room but never touches her.

Not so in Dahlia's handwritten drafts. The scene I'd already read, in which Violet is ravaged by an invisible stranger in the linen closet was one of several in which a "dark stranger" makes love to her. In the manuscript, the dark stranger schtupps Violet Gray in every corner of Lion's Keep, from the linen closet to the butler's pantry, "his thrusts rattling the Wedgewood teacups," to the games-keeper's cottage where he "laid me down on the rough wooden boards and cleaved me with his gleaming shaft." To the modern reader it's clear that the visitations of the dark stranger reflect Violet's sublimated sexual longing for William Dougall, whom she cannot allow herself to love as long as she believes he is evil. But Violet believes that the dark stranger is an incubus. The housekeeper, Mrs. Eaves, reinforces this theory by telling her a local folktale about a youth turned into a demon by the Fairy Queen. Only when William Dougall declares his love for her at the end of the book is Violet able to renounce the incubus – her dark stranger – in order to marry her mortal lover.

The night I finished reading the handwritten draft of *The Dark Stranger,* I lay awake for a long time thinking about Violet's dark stranger and my demon lover, reluctant to give in to sleep. I had tried to tell myself that my dreams had come from reading Dahlia LaMotte's sex scenes combined with the atmosphere of this old house. But the dreams had begun before I started reading Dahlia's rough drafts. I kept going around in circles looking for the answer, but try as I might, I couldn't find a rational explanation for how I'd shared the same erotic dream as a fictional character created a hundred years ago. The effort wore me out. I slipped into sleep at last.

When he arrived I was waiting for him. The shadow branches reached and swelled, the moonlight crested above me, brilliant in its whiteness, but I kept my eyes open against the painfully bright light. I watched him take shape above me. For the first time I realized that he took shape because I watched him, he took his first breath only after he blew into my mouth and drew breath from me . . . Would he move if I didn't move first? I kept myself still even though every cell in my body was pulled to every cell of the dark matter he was made of. His eyes met mine . . . and widened with surprise.

"Who are you?" I asked, shocked that I had the power to speak.

But not as shocked as he was.

I saw the look of amazement spread across his face . . . a face that had never looked so complete or so beautiful before . . . and then he was gone. The moonlight drew back into the shadows with a hoarse rasp like a wave dragging over rough shingle and then the shadows themselves shriveled and shrank and vanished like smoke. I was left gasping like a fish flung onto the shore by an angry retreating tide.

CHAPTER TEN

I woke up the next morning cranky and bad-tempered. I had a headache and felt like I was coming down with the flu. I thought a hot shower would make me feel better but when I turned it on I found that there was nothing but ice cold water; the hot water heater, which the house inspector had certified as sound, must have been broken. Making a mental note to call Brock, I made a pot of coffee, only to discover that the milk had gone sour. When I tried to toast some leftover scones the toaster oven short circuited, caught fire, and burned them to a crisp before I could put the fire out.

I decided to walk to campus hoping the air and exercise would heal my bad mood, but the minute I got outside I realized that the balmy Indian summer weather had come to an abrupt end. It must have been under forty. I persevered, determined not to be a wuss about the cold, but ten minutes from the house it started to rain . . . or sleet, actually. The frozen rain needled my face and the back of my neck. I was soaked and frozen by the time I made it to the college center, where I stopped to buy a bagel and coffee. I was late for class and spent the first ten minutes complaining to a confused group of students about the inferiority of bagels outside the New York metropolitan area and the absurdity of sleet in October.

I'd planned to show *Rebecca* in class but when I slid the D.V.D. into the disk drive, my computer made a grinding noise and then spit the D.V.D. out with a hiss. I swore – and heard a few students giggle at my use of the Anglo-Saxon invective – and pushed the D.V.D. back in. A blue spark flew out of the disk drive and jolted me. My laptop moaned like a sick cat. I felt my eyes pricking with tears at the injustice of the world turning against me. I'm not sure what I would have done next if Nicky Ballard hadn't appeared at my side and gently taken over.

"Here, let me. I've worked at campus tech support for a couple of years and can usually figure this stuff out." Nicky tapped in a few commands on my laptop and within minutes my Mac was purring and playing the movie.

I thanked Nicky and she gave me a rare smile. It was then that I noticed that she had lost weight. Her round face had thinned out, revealing sculpted cheekbones. Her bangs were brushed to the side, showing off a high forehead and wide turquoise eyes. She looked pretty – but I felt a pang of concern. Although it was typical for freshmen to gain weight, I'd also seen some turn anorexic under the academic and social stresses of college. I made a note to talk to her after class and settled in to watch the movie.

The minute of thinking of someone other than myself had put my bad mood in perspective, but as I watched the movie I felt annoyance growing again. I liked to show *Rebecca* because the novel was a classic reworking of Gothic themes and the Hitchcock film was beautiful and moody. But the truth was that the second Mrs. de Winter (the poor woman didn't even rate a first name) was a ninny. It was painful to watch her quailing under the imperious Mrs. Danvers and hiding broken china away like a guilty child.

I dismissed the class after half the movie and told them they should finish reading the book before the next class. "Which ends differently than the movie so don't think you can get away with not reading it." Then, on a sudden impulse, I added: "Ask yourself this: what would you have done in the second Mrs. de Winter's shoes – or in the shoes of any of the heroines we've seen so far this year? Do these women have to be so helpless?"

I caught Mara's eyes on me as I gave this assignment. Instead of her usual reverent gaze she looked puzzled and I realized that I'd asked the question angrily. *Shit,* I really must be losing it.

I had decided to put off talking to Nicky Ballard to another day, but as she walked by me she stopped and said: "I'd fire Mrs. Danvers."

"What?"

"If I was the second Mrs. de Winter. That's the first thing I'd do. Then I'd give all Rebecca's things to the Salvation Army – or whatever the British equivalent was – and redecorate. Then I'd tell Max that if he wanted to make our marriage work he'd better get over his dead wife and start paying attention to me."

"Good girl," I said.

"But what would you do when you found out how Rebecca died?" A voice came from the door. It was Mara, who'd been waiting in the doorway for her roommate.

"I'd say good riddance and make sure no one ever found that boat." There was a sudden hardness in Nicky's eyes that took me by surprise.

"Nicky, could you stay for a moment and show me how

you fixed my computer?" I asked with a disingenuous smile, and then, turning to Mara: "You'd better go on to class. I don't want to make you late."

"But Nicky's in the same class . . ."

"You can tell Phoenix she'll be there in a few minutes."

Mara left reluctantly, giving Nicky a worried glance over her shoulder. I wondered if she'd noticed the change in Nicky as well. While Nicky went though the steps she'd taken to fix my computer, I studied her more closely. I could see that in addition to the lost weight her eyes were feverish and her skin was pale.

"Thanks, Nicky. You were a real lifesaver. Can I call you if I have problems at home with it?"

"Sure. Like I said I've worked in tech support for years . . ."

"But aren't you a freshman?"

"Yeah, but I live here in town and I got the job the summer after my sophomore year in high school. One of my teachers recommended me because I was always fixing the high school's computers. I got to know Dean Book . . ." Nicky smiled and lowered her voice. "For a smart lady she didn't know the first thing about computers. She suggested I apply to college here. I'd been planning to go to the S.U.N.Y. over in Oneonta, but Dean Book told me about the scholarship program and, well . . . here I am."

"And you're liking it so far?"

"Well, it's a little strange. All my life I've watched the college teachers in town and they all seemed like they came from another world. Like that English teacher, Miss Eldritch. Have you ever watched how she walks? She kinda floats. And those creepy Russian professors . . . Do you know that they all live together in a scary old Victorian mansion on top of the hill? It's all shuttered up during the day and you never see any of them except at night. Even their classes are at night. Kids in town say they're part of some kinky sex triangle . . ." Nicky blushed. "Sorry, I don't mean to be disrespectful. It's just weird to have spent all my life on one side and now I'm on the other – like Alice through the looking glass, you know?"

I nodded. I thought I knew what Nicky's problem was now. She was trying to cope with a social class change on top of all the normal adjustments to college. Dean Book had said in my interview that the town and gown relations were cordial, but I bet those relations looked different to the kids who delivered the pizzas and their parents who fixed the plumbing and mopped the dormitory floors.

"How do your parents feel about you going to Fairwick?" I asked.

"Um . . . there's just my mom and my grandmother, who we live with. My grandmother was happy about it and my mom, well, she said as long as she didn't have to pay for anything it was okay by her, but I'd better be sure to study something practical and come out with a paying job and not waste my time with a lot of artsy fartsy nonsense. Sorry . . ." Her voice cracked and I realized that this long breathless speech was a hedge against tears. "You don't want to know all this."

I put my hand on Nicky's arm, which felt alarmingly thin. "Sure I do, Nicky. I lost my parents when I was little and was raised by my grandmother." I guessed by the way her eyes flicked to mine that it must be Nicky's grandmother who was doing most of the raising at her home.

"She made sure I didn't want for anything," I went on. This was what I always said about my grandmother, as if I were afraid she was somewhere nearby, eavesdropping on my assessment of her guardianship. "But of course she was much older and couldn't really relate to a teenager." An image of my grandmother, her mouth squared with disapproval when I showed up for tea at her club in jeans, flashed before my eyes. I shoved it aside. "So I know it's hard being around people with intact families."

Nicky nodded, a tear spilling down her cheek. She batted at it with the sleeve of her sweatshirt which she'd pulled over her hand. "I think that's why Dean Book chose Mara for my roommate. Mara's lost everything. My problems seem really miniscule compared to what she's been through."

"I guess that it's always good to put your problems in perspective," I said, thinking with embarrassment of my own snit this morning. "But as my friend Annie's mother always said, 'When *your* shoe pinches, it hurts *you*.' It's natural that you should feel stressed out in a new environment and need someone to talk to . . . How about your friends from high school, are they still around?"

"Just my boyfriend, Benny. He and I had planned to go to S.U.N.Y. Oneonta together, but when I got the scholarship he decided to stay here and go to the community college. I told him he was being stupid, that we could see each other on weekends and he shouldn't be making sacrifices for me, but then he said someone had to make some sacrifices or we might as well just hang it up. So now he's here in town, miserable at the community college and, of course, blaming me for that."

"I hope you know that's not fair, Nicky. He made that decision, not you." Thank God, I thought, that Paul and I hadn't gone down that road. I understood now why Nicky looked so miserable and fatigued. Between the lack of support from her family, her boyfriend guilt-tripping her about his own lack of ambition and stupid choices, and the academic stress of college it was a wonder she was holding it together at all.

"Look," I said, "if you ever need to talk, don't hesitate to come to me. I live right near campus . . ."

"In the old LaMotte house," Nicky said, brightening a bit. "I used to play in the woods behind there when I was little. I always thought it was the prettiest house in town. I'm glad someone's living there again. No matter what anyone says about it being haunted."

The boost I'd gotten by attending to Nicky's troubles instead of my own was gone by the time I left Fraser Hall, shot down by Nicky's innocent comment about Honeysuckle House being haunted and the conversation after. I tried to dismiss it as harmless local gossip. An old house left empty for many years, once inhabited by an eccentric woman writer – no wonder it had gained the reputation of being haunted. But it was what Nicky said next that had set my teeth on edge. I'd asked her if the townspeople thought that the house was haunted by Dahlia LaMotte.

"No," she'd answered, "they say it's haunted by her lover."

"Her lover? But I thought Dahlia LaMotte was a recluse."

"Yeah, but people say that the reason she locked herself away in that house was because she had a secret lover. There were stories of a man seen standing in the woods behind her house and then a man's silhouette in her bedroom window. Some people say she was engaged to a man who jilted her and that she'd killed him and his ghost was the figure they saw at the window."

I snorted. "I believe William Faulkner wrote a story along those lines. It's called 'A Rose for Emily.'" I tried to laugh off the story as I left Nicky at the door to Phoenix's class and walked briskly across the quad, but I was remembering the man-shaped pillar of mist at the edge of the woods and picturing the face of the man in my dreams – the man who had fled as soon as I confronted him. The truth was that I'd been in a foul mood all morning because the dream had ended before the demon lover made love to me.

I froze on the path – so abruptly that a boy humming to the tune on his iPod bumped into me – at that realization. What was wrong with me? Was my actual sex life so dismal that I'd become addicted to a fantasy?

Because that was all it was, wasn't it? A fantasy.

Only what I'd experienced last night – that moment of recognition and shock in his eyes – hadn't felt like a fantasy or a dream; it had felt as real as the broad-trunked sycamore tree to my right and its yellow leaves drifting down around me, and as solid as the granite towers of the library rising up at the end of the path.

It struck me suddenly as odd that although I'd written about supernatural creatures – vampires, fairies, incubi – I'd never once stopped to think they might be real. Or that the creature who had been making love to me every night was real. He was a fairy tale just like the fairy tales my parents had read me at bedtime, a more sophisticated kind of "bedtime" story. I'd dismissed the phantom figure in my adolescent dreams as a manifestation of grief over the loss of my parents. I'd analyzed his appearance in Dahlia LaMotte's novel as a symbol of Violet Gray's sublimated longing. I'd treated the appearance of the demon lover in literature as a psychological manifestation, a literary trope, a symbol of repressed longing, domination fantasies, or rebellion against the status quo. But what if Dahlia wrote about a demon lover because she'd been visited by one? And what if the same demon lover was the creature who had visited my dreams when I was young and had returned now to consummate our relationship?

What if the demon lover was real?

I stood still for another few minutes, measured by the clock on the library tower, which tolled the hour while I waited for the return of rationality that would dismiss such a notion. Students in sweatshirts and down vests walked around me, leaves fell, squirrels plucked acorns from the ground and swished their tails at me, but the idea that the man who made love to me in my dreams was somehow real didn't go away.

"If he is real," I said to myself out loud, "then I'd better find out all I can about him."

No one stopped to look at the teacher frozen on the path talking to herself. They probably thought I was talking on a cell phone ear set. I wondered how long I could hide my craziness though, if I'd really come to believe in incubi! As long as I could, I'd better use the library to find out all I could about my own personal incubus.

I'd researched demon lovers before but never with an eye to proving they existed. For that, I'd come to the right place. The Fairwick College Library's folklore collection was vast. In fact, there was a whole room dedicated to fairy tales and folklore, named the Angus Fraser Room.

Much I already knew: the incubus was a demon in male form who lay with sleeping women, sometimes to have children (Merlin was the oft-cited example of a child born of an incubus and a human woman), but most often to drain the woman of her vital life force.

Well, I hadn't gotten pregnant and up until this morning I'd felt just fine .. although I had been losing weight . . .

A feeling of pressure on the chest often accompanied the visitation.

Yes, I'd felt that, but there was probably a physiological explanation for that breathless sensation during sleep. Asthma, perhaps, or sleep apnea . . .

The oldest tradition I could find came from ancient Sumeria. Gilgamesh's father was said to be the incubus Lilu (I recalled that Soheila Lilly had mentioned him), but he existed in many cultures by many names: El Trauco in Chile, the alp in Germany, Popo Bawa in Zanzibar, the liderc in Hungary, and the Celtic Ganconer, who was also called a love talker. That, I recalled, was the name of the incubus in the Briggs Hall triptych.

I'd read before that one way to get rid of the incubus was through exorcism, but now I learned that if that didn't work (and apparently it didn't often enough), one could try iron locks on the doors and windows.

Is that why Brock Olson had put new iron locks on my doors and windows and hung that cast-iron dream catcher in my window? I blushed at the thought that he knew about the demon lover and looked around the library, wondering who else might know I was having sex with a demon on a nightly basis, but the only other person in the Angus Fraser room was a ponytailed boy with his head pillowed on an open art history textbook, sound asleep.

I read on in A.E. Forster's *Compendium of Folk-Lore and Demonology* that in Swedish homes virtuous housewives hung up charms made of birch branches and juniper sprigs tied with red ribbon to ward off the advances of the demon lover.

Just like Brock's little air fresheners.

But the best way to send away an incubus was to confront him directly.

"It takes an enormous effort to speak during the incubus's visitation, but if the victim can summon the preternatural will to speak and ask him to identify himself, then the incubus is sure to flee forever."

I raised my head from the book and stared over the head of my sleeping companion out the leaded glass window at red and gold leaves falling in the quad.

Who are you? I had asked.

The lozenges of wavy glass swam before me. I supposed I should feel pleased with myself for summoning "the preternatural will to speak," but all I felt was bereft.

CHAPTER ELEVEN

The demon lover didn't appear that night . . . or the night after that or the night after that.

I should have been grateful, but instead I was restless. I lay awake watching the shadows of branches quivering in the moonlight until the moon passed over my house and the moonlight faded. Then, since I still couldn't sleep, I would pad barefoot into the spare room and take one of Dahlia LaMotte's handwritten manuscripts back to bed with me. I read them quickly and uncritically, devouring the lurid tales of governesses and brooding masters, orphans and mysterious benefactors, with the added bonus material of extended sex scenes.

The demon lover insinuated himself into every one of Dahlia's books just as he insinuated himself between the legs of her heroines . . . and under their skin. In each book the heroine found herself addicted to a demon lover.

I crave him as an opium addict longs for his pipe, India Wilde exclaimed in *The Far Moor*. *He is my opium. I inhale him and he comes to life. I take him inside me and I come to life. He is my life. Without him I would wither and die.*

As I began to fear I would if I couldn't shake off his hold on me.

I would read until the gray shadows of dawn fell where moonlight had fallen before. Then I would go out jogging before classes, choosing the woods again for my route. I ran as far as the honeysuckle thicket where I'd stop and listen for a moment to the thickly intertwined branches rubbing against one another in the breeze. I would listen for birds caught in the underbrush, but the thicket was empty and melancholy. I thought of the painting in Briggs Hall of all those fairies and demons marching out of this world and into another through a thicket like this one and felt a peculiar tug at my heart. What would it feel like to leave one's home and wander for eternity through an ever-tightening maze, the passage back narrower and more twisting with each passing year? It was a strangely evocative metaphor for exile that haunted me on my cool-down walks back to the house with the feeling that I, too, was an exile. Not from my old life in New York City – that I hardly missed at all – but from the demon lover I'd scared away.

Although the long runs and colder weather should have increased my appetite I found myself eating less in those first weeks of October. It was just as well since Phoenix abruptly stopped cooking.

"Do you mind?" she asked, handing me the takeout menus for the local pizzeria and Chinese restaurant. "I'm a little swamped right now reading my students' work. They're really on fire, especially Mara."

"Does she write about her experiences in Bosnia?"

"Sort of. She's writing a parable that *stands* for her real-life experiences, which are too painful for her to face. I'm encouraging her to keep writing the parable with the hope that she'll eventually confront the real facts of her life – as I urge all my students to do – but the parable itself is so vivid and violent, so *disturbing*, I can only begin to imagine how horrendous the truth behind it is."

"Really? Do you think you should show it to anyone . . . professional?" I was thinking of the shooting at Virginia Tech a few years ago and the violently disturbed writing the shooter had submitted to his creative writing classes, which might have, if it had been seen by a mental health professional, given a warning. But Phoenix was appalled by my suggestion.

"Oh no! I'd lose her trust entirely! I've promised her I won't show it to anyone until we've worked on it together. I'm meeting with her every day to go over her drafts." Phoenix held up a two-inch thick purple folder. "So I'm sure I've got the situation under control."

I wondered how well she had it under control. I'd been so absorbed in my own obsession that I hadn't noticed right away how absorbed Phoenix was in hers. She was always reading Mara's work. When I came down at dawn for my runs I'd find her asleep on the library couch with the purple folder lying open on the floor, red-marked pages strewn all over the floor like blood splatter. When I passed her coming into Fraser Hall in the afternoon she was always clutching the purple folder.

Once, delayed in the hall by a student asking for an extension on a paper, I passed by Phoenix's room fifteen minutes into the class and noticed that the teacherless room was full of students texting and playing games on their fancy cell phones. I caught Nicky Ballard's eye and motioned for her to come out into the hall.

"What's going on?" I asked. "Is Phoenix here?"

"So to speak," Nicky said, biting her lip, which I noticed was chapped and peeling. She also looked like she'd lost more weight. Guiltily I recalled that I'd meant to keep an eye on her, but I'd been too deep in my own funk to notice how bad she looked. "She's in her office with Mara having another 'writing conference.'" Nicky made air quotes with her fingers – the nails of which were bitten down to the quick. "We're supposed to be working on our memoirs until she calls us in for conference, but she never gets around to anyone but Mara."

"Uh oh, that must not be going over so well. Has anyone complained to the dean?"

Nicky shrugged. "I don't think anyone wants to. The little bit of Mara's writing that she reads out loud in class is so . . . *painful*. No one wants to complain about the time Phoenix devotes to her."

"But it's not fair for one student to shanghai the whole class . . ." I began, but then, seeing how uncomfortable Nicky looked, changed tack. "How are you doing? Are you adjusting okay to Fairwick?"

She shrugged again – a gesture which I was beginning to see had become a sort of nervous tick for her. "There's a lot of work. I keep trying to explain to Ben that I can't hang out all the time because I have more work than him, but then he just accuses me of lording it over him for being at 'my fancy private college.'" She air quoted again and I wondered how much of Nicky's new life required the ironic distance of finger brackets.

"It's hard on a relationship when one partner – especially the female one – is more successful." I was thinking of how hard Paul tried not to mind when I'd gotten into Columbia and again when my thesis got a big commercial publishing contract and he had to rewrite his at his advisor's request. "But that doesn't mean you should feel guilty or not take full advantage of the opportunities you've earned. If Ben really cares about you he'll understand."

Nicky nodded, but she looked like she was about to cry. "Yeah, but the girls at community college don't have to stay in the library on Saturday night. How long will it be before he figures out it's easier to hang out with one of them?"

I sighed. Of course I'd wondered the same thing with Paul – not that U.C.L.A. was community college – but L.A. was full of leggy blondes and surfer chicks who weren't 3000 miles away. To keep myself from being tortured by jealous fantasies I'd had to shut off a part of my brain – and, I had to admit, a piece of my heart. I worried sometimes that the result was that I didn't love him as much. Lately when we talked at night I found myself impatient to get off the phone. I should have been counting the days until his arrival on Thanksgiving, but instead I was mooning over a phantom lover. Was that why I'd summoned the demon lover – because I wasn't satisfied by Paul?

"If it's meant to work out it will," I said, wishing I could think of less lame advice to offer Nicky. But she nodded as if I'd said something sage.

"Thanks, Professor McFay. It's nice of you to spend the time talking to me. I know you must be busy."

Guiltily I thought about the stack of ungraded papers lying on my desk at home and the ones weighing down the messenger bag strapped across my chest. I'd been feeling so despondent that I'd let myself get behind in my work.

"I do have your last essays to grade," I said, patting my

bag. "I'd better be going . . . but, please, if you need to talk . . ."

"Thanks, Professor. I will."

Nicky went back into class and I headed across campus. Although it was only the last week in October, most of the leaves had fallen from the trees already and it was cold enough for a winter coat – but I hadn't worn one. I was wearing the Armani tweed blazer, turtleneck, skinny jeans and thigh-high boots that were my favorite fall outfit. Back in the city it got me through the season to Christmas, but here I saw I was going to have to put on a down coat and long underwear by Thanksgiving. I was so cold crossing the quad that I decided to pop into the library and do some work there. Every time I tried to grade papers at home I ended up in the spare room reading a Dahlia LaMotte novel. Maybe working in the library would give me the discipline I needed to finish grading these papers.

In the library I set myself to grading essays, managing only marginally better to concentrate on what my students had to say about *The Mysteries of Udolpho* and *Northanger Abbey* than I had at the house. Every few sentences I would look up and stare out the window at the bare trees on the quad and feel a pang of sadness as if someone I'd loved had just died. What was wrong with me? I wondered, forcing myself to stare back down at a paper. I'd never been so unfocused. Was I really going through some kind of withdrawal from the demon lover? Or was I coming down with something? I read the next paper with a head full of imagined ailments: swine flu, Lyme disease, and early-onset Alzheimer's danced through my head. Maybe the demon lover visitations were a symptom of a brain tumor.

As if to confirm my worst fears, when I looked back down at the paper in front of me the print doubled and swam. Blurry vision – wasn't that a symptom of stroke? I closed my eyes and laid my head down on the table. The polished wood felt cool on my forehead. No wonder that student had been sleeping here the last time I came; it was a perfect place to sleep, quiet but for a low, barely audible hum that must have been the ventilation system but sounded like a swarm of insects . . .

I must have fallen asleep. I was in a crowd walking across an endless, rolling meadow. My legs and feet hurt as if I'd been walking for miles. I looked down and saw that my feet were bare in the wet grass. My legs were scratched and bleeding, my dress torn to tatters around my knees. I was alarmed at the sight. I shouldn't be bleeding; my flesh shouldn't tear. I began to fall . . . as if the awareness of my flesh's vulnerability had robbed me of the last vestige of my strength and will. I would lie down right here in the dew-damp grass and sleep. No matter if the horde stampeded over me; let them trample me into the ground until I was dust beneath their feet and I seeped into the earth. As I fell I could hear horses – *The Riders* – and knew I'd be ground to dust all the sooner beneath their hooves. *Fine, let me go back to the earth* . . . But then a shadow fell across me and I looked up. A figure on a white horse was leaning down toward me, reaching out his hands. I took his hands and he pulled me up into the saddle in front of him. He wrapped his arms around me, chafing my bare, cold skin. My dress, drenched and shredded, barely covered me. He pulled me back against him and I felt him harden with desire for me. I knew we had to go . . . that there wasn't time . . . but our desire for each other was too strong. He steered his mount into the woods, deep into a glade that was covered by intertwining branches . . . like a chapel.

"I'd have married you in a church," he whispered in my ear as he pulled me from the horse and laid me on the soft grass, "but this will have to do."

He traced the line of my jaw with one finger and pressed it between my lips. "You are mine," he said, sliding his finger down my throat to my left breast. He drew circles around the nipple, the wetness tingling in the misty air, inscribing a spiral pattern over my heart, all the while keeping his eyes locked on mine.

"Yes," I moaned, arching my hips against him while he hovered a tantalizing inch above me. "We belong to each other. We always have and always will."

Still keeping his eyes locked on mine he pushed the last tatters of my dress up around my hips and pushed himself against me. His face, backlit by the sun-tangled branches glowed gold, his eyes glowing the same green as the deep woods that surrounded us. As he came inside me it was as if the woods were entering me . . . the gold sunlight exploding through the green branches obliterating every-thing else . . . even his flesh and, I saw as I reached for him, my flesh as well. I could see the sun and the branches right through my hand. We were dissolving into each other . . .

I startled awake, my face pressed against a damp patch on the wooden table, and sat up, swiping at my mouth, hoping no one had seen me drooling in my sleep. But that hope was dashed. Elizabeth Book was sitting across from me, her cool elegance making me feel even more bedraggled and embarrassed.

She smiled but her eyes looked sad. "You were dreaming," she said.

"I fell asleep while grading papers." I swept together the pile of papers that were strewn across the table. I must have scattered them as I reached for him . . . Dear God, had Dean Book heard me moan or call out a name? Only I hadn't called his name . . . although I was sure I'd have known it in the dream. I had *known* him. As well as I knew myself. Only how well was that? Who had I been in the dream?

"Have you been having disturbing dreams?" Liz asked.

I looked up from the papers and met her cool blue gaze. I felt the blood surge in my face at the thought that she somehow knew exactly what kind of dreams I'd been having. Dreams in which I made love until my flesh melted. "No," I said. "Not unless you count dreaming about ungraded papers as disturbing. I'm afraid I've fallen a bit behind." I smiled ruefully and hoped she thought my embarrassment was from being caught literally sleeping on the job and not from having a depraved sex life with a demonic being. "But I promise I'll catch up and be more on the ball in the future."

Elizabeth Book reached across the table and laid her hand on mine. "I'm not worried about your performance, dear Callie. I'm worried about you. Not everyone makes the adjustment to Fairwick easily. Being here sometimes brings up . . . issues. And I have to admit I've had concerns with you living all alone in that house . . ."

"I'm not all alone," I interrupted her. "Phoenix is living with me."

"Ah, yes. Phoenix is turning out to be quite a . . . galvanizing addition to our community, but she is perhaps not the most restful of roommates. Nor do I think she would notice if anything were wrong."

"There's nothing wrong, Dean Book. I'm just . . ."

Obsessed with a phantom lover? Sorry I chased him away? "Getting used to the routine. I promise you don't have to worry about me. Now if you don't mind, I'm going to take these home to grade. The library hasn't turned out to be the best work environment after all."

CHAPTER TWELVE

I forced myself to finish grading all my students' papers that night, determined not to give Dean Book any reason to complain of my performance in the future. Although she had seemed sympathetic and concerned, I didn't doubt that if I failed to live up to her expectations I wouldn't last long here at Fairwick College.

I was a diligent and attentive teacher for the next few weeks, with the added incentive of Paul's Thanksgiving visit to work toward. I didn't need a demon lover, I told myself while correcting midterms, I had a human one, one who deserved more of my attention. Even if the demon lover was . . . *not quite imaginary*, it was better that I'd gotten rid of him. The desire I'd felt in the dream I'd had in the library hadn't just been for sex, it had been a desire to *merge* myself with him. And that surely couldn't be healthy.

When I wasn't prepping for classes or grading I threw myself into getting the house in shape for his arrival and planning a Thanksgiving dinner. Since my grandmother had moved to Santa Fe, I'd gone to Annie's in Brooklyn for Thanksgiving Dinner. Before that my grandmother and I would always have Thanksgiving at her club in the pristine formal dining room. I'd never made a turkey myself, and I wouldn't have been able to cook more than a micro-waveable turkey dinner in my apartment. But now I had a beautiful big house that looked like a house in holiday TV ads – the kind with Pachelbel playing in the background. Not only could I give Paul some reasonable facsimile of a Thanksgiving dinner, but I could invite a few of my new colleagues as well. Maybe I could even invite Dean Book (whom I had learned was unmarried and lived alone). That would show her I was adjusting well to Fairwick.

I told Phoenix about my plan, hoping both that she'd help and that the project would distract her from her obsession with Mara Marinca's writing. She was enthusiastic and drew up a menu and shopping list right away. We made a date to go to the farmers' market that weekend to scope out the local produce.

Since she had the food under control I decided to concentrate on nesting. I'd lived in Honeysuckle House for three months now but the place still reverberated like a hollow drum. The sparsely furnished look had felt airy in the warm weather, but with winter bearing down I longed for a cozier environment. I drove to the mall out on the highway and at Pottery Barn I bought a pair of loveseats upholstered in forest green velour for the parlor. Then I bought a rug, throw pillows and velveteen drapes, all in rich shades of ocher, rust and emerald. I picked up glassware and serving platters for the table, and guest towels and a bathmat for the downstairs powder room. On an impulse I bought matching fuzzy bathrobes and slippers for me and Paul.

On the way home I passed a garden and landscaping center called Valhalla and realized that this must be the store Brock and his brother Ike ran. I stopped and soon had a wheelbarrow filled with pots of chrysanthemums and asters, beautiful handmade wreaths woven from maple leaves and bittersweet vines, and a basket of dried flowers I thought would make a pretty centerpiece for the table. I noticed that among the plants and flowers were many decorative cast-iron items – plant hooks, hat racks, small shelves and a menagerie of cast-iron animals like the mice doorstops. Of course, I realized, Brock had said his great-uncles had been blacksmiths before they'd gone into the landscaping business. No wonder all the locks he'd put on at my house were cast-iron. No doubt he'd also made the mice doorstops.

Phoenix was so excited by my purchases that she started outfitting the house herself. Over the next few weeks the downstairs rooms magically filled with embroidered throw pillows, soft alpaca throws, scented candles, dishes of potpourri and crystal bowls brimming with hard candies and chocolate. The house filled with cooking smells again, too, as Phoenix tested out recipes for stuffing, pies, candied yams, puddings, gravies, cranberry sauces, and all the wines to go with them.

"Try this cava," she would say when I came down to dinner. "I thought we'd start with this and then have a nice Pinot Noir with the soup."

By the time I'd finished sampling wines I'd be half-crocked, but Phoenix, who had started drinking earlier than me, would be sparkling with energy. She was still staying up half the night reading Mara's work, but now I'd find empty bottles littered among the red-marked papers – some of those red marks looking suspiciously more like Bordeaux than ink. I remembered what she had said about her "little drinking problem" and wondered if I should say anything.

A week before Thanksgiving I decided to broach the subject by asking if she thought the stress of reading Mara's work was getting to her, but before I could suggest that it might be leading to her drinking more, she interrupted me to ask if it was okay to invite Mara for Thanksgiving.

"She doesn't have any family and Nicky Ballard hasn't invited her to her house. We can't let her be all alone on the holiday."

I thought I knew why Nicky Ballard hadn't invited Mara home. The week before I'd seen Nicky coming out of a decaying Victorian pile – its sagging wraparound porch filled with broken appliances and sprung couches – three blocks over on Elm Street. A shrill female voice had followed Nicky out of the house demanding ". . . and don't forget my Pall Malls!" If that was Nicky's home I didn't blame her for not wanting anyone else to share the holiday with her. Maybe she didn't want to spend it there either.

"Okay," I agreed, "but only if we can invite Nicky, too."

"The more the merrier," Phoenix said, clinking her wine glass full of Puligny-Montrachet against my glass of seltzer.

Although I was still worried about Phoenix's drinking, I had to admit it looked like it would be a merry gathering. I invited Soheila Lilly, Casper van der Aart and his partner, Oliver, who ran an antiques store in town, and, just to show him I wasn't hoarding my big house all to myself, Frank Delmarco, all of whom said yes. Dean Book also accepted and suggested I invite Diana Hart who, she said, was always too busy with her guests to sit down to a real meal. I told her I was happy to find a way to repay Diana for all the care packages of baked goods I'd received.

"Just don't tell her you're 'repaying her.' She's a little

touchy that way. And don't be surprised if she insists on bringing some pies – and don't turn her down! She would be hurt . . . and well, I would imagine you could use the help. You look like you've been working very hard. Are you sleeping well?"

"Oh yes," I lied. "It just took a while to get used to a strange house."

But the truth was that for all my frenetic daytime activity I was barely sleeping at all. Since that day in the library I'd been having dreams – not the erotic visitations of before, these felt . . . even weaker than dreams, more like half-forgotten memories.

Always the same memory. It would start with the march across the desolate heath under a half-lit dawn sky with a crowd of travelers, their faces obscured by mist. In the distance the procession entered through the arch and vanished into the thick brambles. My heart contracted with fear at the sight. Where were they going? Where were *we* going? Those woods were thick and dark and led who knew where. I heard my fears echoed in the whispers around me: the door was narrower than it used to be. No one knew if it still led back to Faerie. It was easy to lose your way among the brambles and then you could wander for eternity *in the Borderlands*. I could tell from the way those words were uttered what a nightmare *that* would be. But if we stayed here any longer we would fade into nothingness.

Then *he* would arrive on his fine white steed, which was already transparent in the morning sun. But I could still make out his face, his wide brow, his almond-shaped eyes, his full lips curving at the sight of me. He reached down for me and swung me up before him and we rode for the woods where he laid me down in the honeysuckle chapel and we sealed our vows to each other just as our flesh began to fade . . .

And I'd awake, my hands grasping handfuls of empty air, my lips forming a name I'd forget at the moment of waking, my body aching with frustrated desire.

Until the morning before Thanksgiving. The dream was the same until the moment he pressed his finger to my lips and drew the spiral pattern on my breast, but this time I felt his touch burning into the flesh, branding me . . .

I startled awake, a fiery pain in my chest. I ran to the mirror and held my nightgown away. There on my left breast was an intricate coiling spiral, like something out of the Book of Kells, *seared* into my skin.

Not only was the demon lover real, he was still here. And he had *branded* me. Like a piece of property.

And part of me had enjoyed it. That was the part that filled me with shame: not all the wild sex I'd enjoyed with this phantom, but the fact that I desired him so much that I was willing to give up everything – my job, friends, Paul, this world, my very flesh – to be with him.

Me, who had based my one adult relationship on the principle of neither of us giving up *anything*.

This just wasn't like me. I had to fight it – and him.

But how? I'd already read all the books on incubi that were in the library. I needed an expert . . . and the person who knew the history of the demon lover – at least the one in the painting called Ganconer – was Soheila Lilly.

After my last class I went looking for Soheila Lilly's office in the maze of narrow hallways on the first floor of Fraser Hall. This part of the building had been the home of Angus Fraser when he taught at the college at the turn of the last century, and retained its labyrinthine floor plan. I wandered for several minutes before finding a door with Soheila Lilly's name above a poster from the British Museum that featured a terracotta plaque of a winged woman standing astride two crouching lions and flanked by two enormous owls. I lifted my hand to knock, but I paused to read the legend under the poster. THE QUEEN OF THE NIGHT, it read, OLD BABYLONIAN 1800-1750 BC. Looking closer at the woman I noticed that her shapely legs ended in curved talons, identical to the talons of the owls standing on either side of her. Something about that detail made me shiver, but I shook off the chill that had passed through me and knocked on the door.

A melodious voice bade me enter. When I opened the door I thought I had been transported to a Near Eastern bazaar. Persian rugs lined the floor and bright multi-colored tapestries hung from the walls and ceiling. Instead of the fluorescent bulbs that wanly lit my office, three glass lanterns – one sapphire blue, one emerald green, one amber yellow – cast warm pools of jeweled light. The polished desk was bare save for an old leather-bound book and a glass tea cup. Soheila, dressed all in shades of caramel from her cashmere shawl to her suede boots to her lipstick, was leaning back in her chair, looking out her window at the last autumn leaves drifting from the nearly bare trees on the quad. Or at least that's what I assumed she was looking at. There was nothing else to see. The campus was nearly deserted. Everyone had cleared out for the holiday.

"Ah, Callie. I thought I might have the pleasure of your company today," she said, turning from the window to look at me. She smiled but her eyes remained distant and sad.

"Would you like a cup of tea?" She gestured to a steaming silver samovar on top of an oak filing cabinet.

"Sure," I said, sitting down in the carved chair in front of her desk. Its back looked too delicate to support the weight of my messenger bag, so I placed it on top of my lap. "If it's no trouble. I want to ask you a few questions about that story you told me at the faculty reception . . . the one about the demon lover who was stolen by the Fairy Queen?"

Soheila sighed as she poured dark toffee-colored tea into a silver-rimmed glass. She held the half-filled glass up to the window, where its color transformed from toffee to gold, and then added a squirt of boiling water from the samovar. She brought me the glass on a silver tray with a crystal bowl of sugar cubes on it and then went through the same process for herself. When she was seated behind her desk with her own cup of tea I took a polite sip of mine. It tasted like cardamom and cloves and some other unnamable spice.

"Delicious," I said, putting down the hot glass. "And so civilized." For the first time since I'd found the spiral brand on my breast I felt warm. "So about this Ganconer . . ."

"I find the ritual of drinking tea puts my students at ease . . ." She tilted her head and narrowed her lovely golden eyes. "But it's not working with you, is it? You are anxious about these questions you have for me."

I laughed, a little too shrilly, and plucked at the neck of my sweater even though I knew the mark was hidden. "Do you have a degree in psychology as well as Middle Eastern studies?" I asked. It came out sounding a little cattier than I meant it to. When I'm nervous I can sound a little . . . well, snooty. Sometimes I think I picked up the habit from my

grandmother who became even more aloof whenever
anything displeased her. But Soheila Lilly was too well-bred
to take offense.

"Yes, actually. I studied with Jung . . ."

She faltered at my surprised expression. She'd have had
to have been in her eighties to have studied with Carl Jung
himself and even though Soheila's eyes looked that old
today, the rest of her certainly did not.

"I mean, of course, that I studied at the Jung Institute in
Zurich."

"How fascinating. I bet Jung had some interesting things
to say about demon lovers."

"He did, but I don't think you came here to talk about
Jung."

"No, I guess not. You see, I've been trying to find a
reference for that story you told about the demon lover who
was kidnapped by the Fairy Queen . . . I think you called
him Ganconer. It's for a book I'm writing. I haven't been
able to find anything on that particular myth on the internet
or in the library, which seems to have just about everything
on folklore ever written. So I was wondering if you could
tell me the source for the story, you told me."

"It was an oral source," she replied. "I don't think
anything's ever been written on it."

"Oh," I said, trying not to sound as disappointed as I felt.
No matter how keen their scholarly interest, academics
usually don't weep over missing sources. "That's too bad
. . . or maybe not . . ." I brightened. "It could be an
opportunity for an article. We could collaborate. Are you
still in contact with the source?"

"No. He died years ago . . ." Her eyes clouded and she
turned toward the window, although I had the feeling she

was no longer seeing the green grass of the quad and the falling autumn leaves.

"I'm sorry," I said. "I didn't mean to bring up painful memories. It's really not important." I started to get up but she turned back to me, pinning me with her suddenly focused stare.

"But it *is* important to you, isn't it? Why do you want to know about this demon in particular?"

I sat back down again and tried to find an answer for her question that didn't involve telling her that I thought the demon lover was real. No matter how sympathetic she seemed, I was sure she'd tell the dean that I needed psychiatric help if I did that. "Well, I've done a lot of research on demon lovers, but I've never come across a story like this one. It provides a history for the incubus – an explanation for why he seduces women. It makes him more . . . well more human. It's like in *Jane Eyre* when we learn how Rochester was tricked into marrying Bertha, or when we find out that the Beast is under a curse. It explains their behavior and makes them . . ." I was going to say *loveable*, but instead I said, "redeemable."

"It seems you have all the fairy tale rationales you need," she said, her voice, for the first time since I'd met her, cold.

Stung, I retreated into the pose of a chilly academic. "But not a genuine folklore source for the phenomenon. Your Ganconer story could be a link between the incubi of folklore and the Byronic heroes of Gothic fiction. But if you don't recall enough about the source . . ."

"I remember *everything*," she said, getting to her feet and shrugging the caramel shawl from her shoulders impatiently. She crossed the few feet to the door beside the filing cabinet and swung it open, revealing a walk-in closet lined with more oak cabinets. "Please," she said, turning to me with a strained smile on her caramel-colored lips. "Drink your tea. This will only take a minute."

I heard her boot heels reverberating against hardwood as she vanished into the closet, which must have been much bigger than my puny office closet. I took a sip of the cooling tea and looked up at the bookshelf next to me. Many of the books were in Farsi, but there were also ones in German, French, Russian, and a few languages I couldn't identify. One that caught my interest, however, was in English. Printed in gold lettering on its red leather binding was a single word: DEMONOLOGY.

I slid it off the shelf, noting that the pages were tipped with gold leaf, and turned to the table of contents. My eyes fell on the title of chapter three: How to Invoke and Banish an Incubus. Exactly what I needed.

I looked toward the closet door, but Soheila was still invisible. I could hear a file drawer opening. I looked back at the book in my lap. It lay on top of my book bag. It only took the slightest motion to slide it inside.

"Here it is," Soheila said, coming out of the closet holding a small blue envelope. "It's my only copy, so please don't lose it."

"I'll take very good care of it," I said, sliding the envelope into my bag in between the pages of the stolen book. I got to my feet, anxious to be gone before Soheila noticed the gap on her bookshelf. "Thank you very much."

"You're very welcome. I hope it helps," she said. "The source paid dearly for the information there. Use it wisely."

CHAPTER THIRTEEN

I walked home quickly, expecting every moment to be stopped by campus security demanding I return Professor Lilly's property. I was relieved when I left the campus, but unhappy to see Diana Hart hailing me from her driveway. She was standing next to a bright yellow Toyota FJ Cruiser, which must belong to a guest. Even if Diana did drive I didn't think she'd ever buy so flashy a vehicle.

"Callie, do you have a minute? I was just telling this young woman from the city about you."

All I could see of the "young woman from the city" was a toned bottom sticking out of the hatchback. *Yoga bum*, Annie would have said appreciatively. The woman undoubtedly did do yoga; she was showing off its fruits in snug leggings emblazoned with the Sanskrit symbol for Namaste. When she turned around I saw that every inch of her was toned and encased in skin-tight Lycra and fleece. Even her long black braid, which she flipped back over her shoulder, looked muscular. Just standing two feet from her made me miss six a.m. Jaivamukti practice and soy chai lattes . . . made me miss the city. I'd only been up here for three months and already I had turned into a crazy wiccan lady casting spells and wearing baggy sweats . . . okay, I wasn't actually wearing baggy sweats, but next to this woman's tights – and after the weight I'd lost – my jeans did feel baggy.

"Cheers," Miss Yoga Bum said in a gravelly Australian accent. "Diana told me you wrote that book on sexy vampires, which I thought was totally brilliant. I do some freelance for the *Times* style section and I thought maybe you could give me an interview. Jen Davies, by the way." She held out a hand and I shook it, not at all surprised to encounter a grip as tight as a Moola Bandha lock. I was already beaming at her, though, as always turned to putty at the thought that a total stranger had read and liked my book.

"Sure," I replied. "Are you up for the holiday visiting family?"

"Nah, my family's all on the other side of the globe. Just thought I'd take some pics of the local flora and fauna." She held up an expensive and complicated-looking camera.

"Jen's planning on hiking in the woods behind your house," Diana said in a strained chipper voice. I noticed now that something about this guest had gotten her wound up. I thought I knew what it was. Diana had counted on all her guests for the holiday having plans for Thanksgiving dinner. She must be worried about abandoning this one to come to my house tomorrow. Maybe I could help out there. While Diana nervously told Jen about how I'd fallen in the woods, I mentally counted out table places. If we scrunched up a bit . . .

". . . and you can get lost in there. Tell her, Callie," Diana concluded, her voice even more high pitched than usual.

"The woods are overgrown," I said mildly to Jen. She was wearing Timberland hiking books and had a small compass attached to the zipper of her fleece vest; she looked like she could take care of herself. "And you can't spend the whole day hiking. Why don't you come have Thanksgiving with us? No family, just colleagues and new friends."

Jen put her hands together in prayer position and bowed her head Namaste-style. "That's very kind of you," she said with a dazzling toothy smile. "I'd love to."

I hurried across the street hoping that news of the extra guest would throw Phoenix into enough of a panic that she'd be too busy to notice me disappearing upstairs. I needn't have worried. Phoenix was passed out on the library couch snoring loudly. In the kitchen I found three punch bowls filled with three different types of punch. I dipped a mug into one and took a sip. It burned my throat going down but spread an agreeable warmth in my belly. I took some more and sat down at the kitchen table with the purloined book. If the spell required anything esoteric – eye of newt, for instance – I'd be out of luck. I almost hoped it would. I'd grabbed the book on impulse and had been too busy worrying I'd get caught to really think about what I was going to do with it until now. Was I really planning to *invoke a demon*? Because the chapter title I'd glimpsed in Soheila's office suggested you had to invoke one before banishing one.

Skimming the chapter I found that the ingredients necessary for casting the spell were all readily available in the house. I gathered them all into one of the decorative baskets Phoenix had bought at Pier 1 and, adding an electric water kettle, and an empty covered sugar bowl, went upstairs to my bedroom.

The demonology book said to summon the demon to a

place "where it was wont to appear." Well, it was *wont* to appear in my bedroom – in my bed, actually, but I didn't want to do this in my bed. Aside from the risk of setting the sheets on fire, I thought it sent the wrong message. Just looking at the bed reminded me of the long nights of lovemaking . . . the way he kissed my breasts, the way he looked at me as he slid inside me . . .

No, I should definitely stay away from the bed. I wasn't invoking the demon lover to have sex, nor was I inviting him to stay. As I arranged a circle of candles on the floor I said aloud what it was I wanted to do. *Set your intention*, my yoga teacher always told us at the beginning of class. If there were ever a time to be clear about my intentions this was it.

"I'm calling him to tell him to go away and leave me alone," I said, plugging the kettle into a wall socket. "Because I don't want him," I said, pouring a circle of salt outside the circle of candles. A pang of longing shot through me. The spiral brand on my breast tingled.

"Okay, maybe I want him, but don't *want* to want him."

I sprinkled cloves, cardamom, and cinnamon into the sugar bowl and set it by the kettle. I needed one more object to take with me into the circle. The demonology book said to have a "gift" for the demon – some object that meant something to the invoker of the spell. I went to my desk and began opening up the little drawers . . . I had put it in one of them . . . . When I found the object I was looking for I slipped it into my pocket along with a book of matches from Sapphire, Paul's favorite restaurant in L.A.

Paul. I hadn't forgotten he was coming. He was the main reason I had to do this now. I had a feeling that Paul might not be safe in the house with the demon lover still lurking about. Once I had banished the incubus, I'd be ready to be with Paul again fully. At least that's what I was hoping.

I looked at my watch. It was 4:20, ten minutes to sunset according to timeanddate.com; 1:20 in California. Paul would still be at home. He was taking the red eye to JFK after his last class tonight and then driving here tomorrow morning. I took out my cell phone and hit his number.

"Hey," he said, "I was just packing. According to my weather app it's in the fifties in Binghamton – that's about the same weather as you, right?"

"Uh, actually we're about ten degrees colder," I told him. In truth, Fairwick was in an oddly cold pocket that was about twenty degrees colder than any of the surrounding upstate cities on any weather map, but I didn't have the heart to tell him that.

"Sheesh, sure you don't want to come here? It's eighty-three and sunny today."

I knew he was only kidding, but for a moment I considered his question seriously. Was I sure that I'd be able to banish the demon lover once I summoned it? If I couldn't, might it feel threatened by Paul? But the idea of the creature I'd encountered in my bed being threatened by Paul was more ridiculous than the notion that he existed in the first place.

"If it's really cold we can just stay in bed the whole time," I said, making my voice sultry.

"Sure," Paul replied coolly, "while your dean is downstairs eating Thanksgiving dinner. Well, at least the weather forecast is clear. No storms in sight. I shouldn't have any trouble flying."

"No," I said, looking out my bedroom window. "Not a cloud in the sky here." The mountains to the east were sharply etched against a clear blue horizon. Not a breeze stirred the tips of the pines or the bare branches of the maples and the oaks. I suddenly found myself wishing for dark rain clouds and gusty winds, rain and sleet and snow – anything to keep Paul from coming. What if I got the invoking part of the spell right, but not the banishing part? Paul could be in danger here. I was about to warn him not to come, but he was saying he had to get to class.

"See you tomorrow morning. I lo—" The connection broke before we could exchange "I love yous." The words might have become commonplaces lately, but I still missed them. I could only hope that after I banished the demon lover forever I'd be able to say them to Paul and mean them again.

The water had come to a rolling boil in the electric kettle. I poured it into the sugar bowl over the spices and then covered it. Then, with the demonology book tucked under my arm, holding the warm bowl in two hands, I stepped into the circle and sat down cross-legged in the center. I placed the sugar bowl in front of me and opened the demonology book to the chapter on invoking and banishing incubi, which I'd marked with the envelope that Soheila had given me. I hesitated for a moment, anxious to start the spell, but if Soheila's "source" had anything useful to tell me about this creature I'd better find out now. I opened the envelope and took out the folded pages. They were the thin blue paper that people used to use for airmail letters in the days before faxes and emails. My mother had had a trove of letters on this stationery – "from the olden days," she had told me when I'd found the ribbon-bound packet of letters. I'd been eleven at the time, an age when most girls gave up fairy tales for teen romances, but I, still bewitched by the fairy tales my parents told me every night, believed she meant from the days of the knights and dragons and fairy princesses, not just the 1970s when she and my father had corresponded the summer after they met at St Andrews College.

"He courted me by letter," I still recalled my mother saying. "Just like in an old romantic novel."

I sometimes wondered if my future love of romantic novels hadn't come from that one chance comment.

The sound of the paper crackling as I opened it reminded me of her, but the contents of the letter soon had my undivided attention.

"My dearest Soheila," it read in a slanting script that leaned toward the right margin of the page as if in a hurry to get to the end of each line.

"I write to tell you one last story – you were always my best listener! – the story of the Ganconer. I came here to this country to find him – to track him down to his roots, so to speak, but I am afraid now that instead of me tracking him down, he has been pursuing me all along – since my childhood.

When I was but a boy of twelve my sister Katy fell ill with a wasting disease that the village doctor could not name or stop. She, who had been a lively, beautiful girl, grew pale and then so weak that she could not leave her bedroom. The village doctor said it must be consumption, although she didn't cough or have fever, and urged my family to take her away to the mountains for a change of air, but when the idea was broached to Katy she grew hysterical and shrieked that she would die if made to leave her bed. My mother said we should carry her out of the house kicking and screaming if need be, but my father, always tender of heart where Katy was concerned, couldn't bear to do it. And so we stayed and Katy grew thinner and paler with each day.

One night I heard her cry out and, thinking she needed something, I crept into her room. When I opened the door I thought I must still be asleep and dreaming. The room was flooded with moonlight, but the moonlight was in the shape of a white horse and on that horse rode a man cloaked in shadow. I stood speechless in the doorway – in shadow myself – as I watched Katy rise from her bed and go to the man. He reached down his hand, and that's when I saw that he was made out of shadow himself. He was no more substantial than the shadow branches that fell across the floor, but I watched my sister take his hand and be pulled up onto the back of the moonlight horse. I watched my sister wrap her arms around the shadow man and rest her head upon his shadow back. Her face was glowing in the moonlight, a smile on her lips, but I saw, too, that she was falling into the shadow, being eaten alive by it. I tried to cry out then, but I couldn't. It was like a hand had reached out – a shadow hand – and squeezed my throat. I felt cold all over and deathly afraid, but I knew that if I didn't cry out I'd lose my sister forever. To this day I don't know how I did it, but somehow I summoned the will to speak.

"Leave her!" I cried.

The shadow man turned to face me then, only he wasn't a shadow man anymore, he was gaining flesh – pale white flesh as though the moonlight was pouring into a mold and making something whole. But his eyes . . . his terrible eyes! . . . were still wells of shadow, and when I looked into them an immense sadness came over me, a sadness that felled me to my knees and dragged me into the dark.

I woke in the morning on the cold floor to the sound of my mother's cries. She was holding the lifeless body of my sister, who lay on the floor beside me.

"What happened?" she demanded when she saw that I was awake.

I told her everything I had seen, never once thinking she might not believe me, and when I had finished I saw that she did believe me.

"Who was he?" I asked.

"That was the Ganconer, the Love Talker, a demon that robs women of their lives. They say that once he was as human as you or me, but he lost his way in the woods one day and fell asleep and the Fairy Queen came with her Riders and found him. He was so beautiful that she had to have him. She took him back with her to Faerie, where he dwells to this day, more fey than human now after all these centuries, a creature of shadow and moonlight. The little spark of human still left in him longs to be human again, but he can only become human if a human girl falls in love with him. And so he enchants girls, hoping to make one love him, but if he fails, the girl perishes."

"But our Katy loved him," I said. "I saw him becoming human. He was turning into flesh – all but his eyes. And then he saw me . . ."

"He would have killed you no doubt, if Katy hadn't

stopped him. There's where her love of him left off. She must've broken free of him and run to save you."

"Then it's because of me she's dead," I said.

My mother – God bless her – looked as stricken then as when she'd been wailing over her dead daughter. She tried to tell me it wasn't so and in time I let her think she'd convinced me.

But I have always known otherwise.

That demon – I have long realized that the creatures we call fairies in my country are indistinguishable from the demons of yours – had killed her, but I had a hand in her death as well. And that is why I've made it my life's mission to track him down and banish him to Hell – or Faerie or whatever dark pit he came from. (Yes, I know my mother's tale says he was once human, but is that any reason to forgive him? On the contrary, I think it is all the more reason to condemn him.) All my studies – the degrees from the University of Edinburgh, Oxford, and Cambridge, the honors, and papers and publications, even the founding of the Royal Order of Folklorists – were all in service to this goal. And now at last I believe I've found the spell to undo him.

I know that if I had told you what I planned to do you would have tried to stop me, but I have no choice: I must confront him. From the moment when I looked into the blackness beyond his eyes a part of me has dwelled in that darkness. I have felt myself, in these last weeks, growing weaker. I believe he is somehow draining me of my life as he once drained Katy. Unless I confront him I will never be whole. And so, before I embark on this last journey I send you the manuscript of my last book for you to dispose of as you see fit. There is no one whom I trust more, *azizam*. Know always that I went into the darkness with your face before me and that if I don't return it was not from want of loving you.

> *Dooset daram,*
>
> *Angus Fraser*

August 29, 1911

The signature and date caught me by surprise. I'd assumed the letter was to Soheila – hadn't she spoken of the writer as a dear friend? – but Angus Fraser had taught at Fairwick a hundred years ago. Perhaps the letter had been written to Soheila's mother – or grandmother even. I opened the book in my lap to the title page and found his name under the title. Angus Fraser, D.Litt Oxon; Ph.D Folklore University of Edinburgh; Ph.D. Archeology Cambridge. The book had been published in 1912.

This must have been the book he'd sent the Sohelia in the letter to publish. Had he come back? I wondered. From what Soheila had told me it didn't sound as if he had. And if he had died using this spell to confront the demon that had killed his sister, was it such a good idea for me to use the same spell to invoke the same demon?

Assuming it was the same demon.

I sat with the book open in my lap and the sugar bowl of boiling water in front of me. Soon it would be too cool to use. The instructions said that once the spellcaster entered the circle she shouldn't step out of it again. So if I was going to do this . . .

What finally made up my mind were two lines from Angus's letter: *From the moment when I looked into the blackness beyond his eyes a part of me has dwelled in that darkness . . . Unless I confront him I will never be whole.*

When I read those lines I felt the spiral coil burning through my flesh.

I knew it was the same for me.

CHAPTER FOURTEEN

I lit the candles while reciting the names listed in Fraser's book. They were the same names Soheila had told me at the reception.

"Lilu, Liderc, Ganconer, hear me.

Lilu, Liderc, Ganconer, I call you.

Lilu, Liderc, Ganconer, come to me."

When I finished lighting all the candles I uncovered the sugar bowl. A plume of spice-scented steam rose into the air. It smelled like pumpkin pie. Comforting and incongruous at the same time.

I took out the object I'd removed from my desk drawer. The offering. It was a stone my father gave me when I was six or seven and I'd been having nightmares. He had told me that he found it on the shore of a lake in Scotland – a loch like the one the Loch Ness monster lived in. It was chalky white and had a hole worn through the middle. He said people called stones like these fairy stones because if you looked through the hole at the break of dawn you could see fairies, but that they also protected their owners from nightmares. I'd slept with it under my pillow every night until I was in my teens and my parents were dead. Then, when I was fifteen, I'd talked Annie into going to Central

Park with me at dawn. I convinced her by playing the dead parents card, as she put it. We smoked pot and sat on the boulders overlooking Sheep Meadow, waiting for the sun to appear through the buildings to the east. When the first rays of light streamed across the meadow I held the stone up to my eye. I hadn't seen any fairies, but I'd heard a buzzing in my ears – like a hive of bees swarming over my head – I'd put it down to the pot and lack of sleep. I stopped sleeping with the stone under my pillow then, but I'd kept it in the same box where I kept my mother's letters.

Now I dropped the stone into the hot water, reciting the three names.

"Lilu, Liderc, Ganconer, accept my offer."

The plume of steam wavered and then thinned into a long tail, as if it had been funneled through the hole in the stone. It coiled in the air – a party streamer tossed on the breeze . . .

There hadn't been a breeze before, had there? At least not when I was talking on the phone with Paul. But now a stiff breeze blew through the open window. The candle flames danced in it, the wicks guttering in the pools of melted wax. Outside I could see treetops tossing in the wind. The steam twisted in the air, coiling like the tail of a kite. I watched it, mesmerized, for several seconds until I realized that it was no longer coming out of the sugar bowl. It had separated from its source and taken on a life of its own.

The next gust blew out the candles.

It's just the wind and water molecules, I said to myself.

But those water molecules were glowing now like phosphorescent plankton – as if they also had a life of their own.

I took a deep breath. The steam eddied toward me as if

borne on my breath. The brand on my breast tingled. I exhaled and the steam moved again. It arranged itself into the shape of a face. His face.

I opened my mouth . . . amazed, yes, but also suddenly stymied. I hadn't really figured out what I was going to say if he showed up. The only thing I could think of was "Who are you?" and that hadn't worked out so well before. Before I could think of what else to say he beat me to the punch.

"Who are *you*?" he asked, as if he'd just thought of a comeback to my previous question.

I laughed out loud, my expelled breath pushing him back in the air. "My name's Cailleach McFay," I said.

"*Cailleach*." The name was a sigh on the wind that caressed my face. I found I liked hearing my name on his lips.

"I know you," the breeze whispered, tugging at my shirt collar. "Don't you remember?"

For a moment I wondered if that's why I had dreamed of him all those years – because a part of me *had* remembered.

The breeze insinuated itself between my breasts and traced the lines of the spiral pattern on my left breast, making the skin tingle and my nipple harden. The coil flamed up as if I'd just been branded. Oh yes, *that* I remembered.

"You don't know a thing about me," I said, batting the breeze away. "And I don't even know your name."

His lips formed a smile, stiffly, as if he wasn't used to moving those muscles – or did he have muscles? This image was different from his earlier visitations. I had a feeling it was just a remote projection. "I have many names," he said. His voice, I realized now, wasn't coming from his mouth. It rode the air, billowing in and out of the window, winding around me like a silk scarf. Outside the trees thrashed. "Those you called me by and many others. You can call me Ganconer."

"Are you the same . . ." I hesitated on what to call him. ". . . *man* as in Angus Fraser's story?"

He frowned at the mention of Angus Fraser's name and the wind coming through the window turned cold. Gooseflesh rose on my skin where it touched me. "Don't believe everything that man says."

"Did you seduce his sister? Did you kill her?"

"*Katy*." The name was a sigh torn from the wind. "I lost her. It was hissss fault."

"I doubt that," I said, beginning to grow impatient with this apparition. Awake and with my eyes wide open he was decidedly less charming than he'd been in my dreams. "Listen," I said. "I called you here to tell you to go . . ."

The mist rippled and the wind roared. It took me a moment to realize he – *it* – was laughing. "*That's* why you called me? I don't think so, Cailleach McFay. I think you called me because you want *more* of me." The mist unfurled through the air and wrapped itself around me. The air had gotten very cold in the room but the mist touching my face was warm. The warmth seeped through me, spreading like a warm liqueur through my bloodstream and coiling into my pelvis and, God help me, landing right between my legs.

I shook my head. "No," I said. "You're a phantom, an incubus. You'd suck me dry and leave me dead . . ."

"Not if you loved me," he whispered, his voice a warm wave that lapped at my ear and filled me with longing.

"That's a big *if*," I replied. "Love comes and goes in my experience. I wouldn't bet my life on it." An image of my parents appeared in my mind, but I quickly banished it.

The coil that had been wrapping itself around me paused. I felt his . . . *its* . . . hesitation. When he spoke again his voice sounded different – less silky, more *real*. It made me realize he'd been acting up until now. "That's been your experience?" he asked. "You poor girl . . ." And then the silky voice was back. "It wouldn't be your experience with me. Perhaps that's how you feel with your *human* lover, but it's not how you'd feel with me."

Maybe it was my loyalty to Paul (I still had some, didn't I?) or maybe it was the disdain in his voice when he said *human*, or maybe it was just the cocky attitude that he knew what I wanted, but I was suddenly disenchanted with this creature.

"You've got a lot to learn about women, pal. There's more to love than being good in the sack," I said, tensing my muscles and trying hard not to think about *how* good he was in bed. "Or maybe it's been too long since you were human to know that."

I thrashed my arms out, breaking the coils of mist into tattered shreds. Then, before he could regroup and whisper his sweet nothings into my ear, I dropped the lid over the sugar bowl and recited the three lines I'd memorized from Angus Fraser's book:

"Begone, incubus!
I send you away, demon!
I cast you into darkness, Ganconer!"

In the strangely quiet pause that followed, the scattered mist tried to reassemble itself into a face. Outside the wind had stopped as if it were waiting for a cue from its master. I suddenly knew I couldn't let him take shape again and speak. I knew what I had to do. It wasn't in Angus Fraser's book, but it had worked at a bar in the Bowery with an obnoxious bond salesman. I picked up the sugar bowl and, just as a face was appearing again in the air, dashed the hot water into it. For a split second the incubus's face had the exact same expression that the bond salesman's had had when I threw my mojito into his face – and then there was no face. The mist was sucked out the window in a gust so strong it knocked me flat on my back. My right hand hit one of the candles, spilling hot wax over my knuckles. I scrambled to my knees and crawled through spilled wax and salt to the window with the idea of closing it, but when I pulled myself up to the windowsill what I saw there froze me in place.

The trees, which had been thrashing a moment ago, were still now, but they weren't upright. They were leaning east, every twig and leaf pulled taut as though by an irresistible magnetic force away from the house. The only movements outside were of animals running across the yard . . . raccoons and squirrels and even deer . . . all of them fleeing the forest as if it were on fire. I felt a tingling on my scalp and, looking down, saw my hair rising in the air, pulling in the same direction. It was perfectly still outside, as if the world were holding its breath . . .

It reminded me of something . . . a description I'd read from a survivor of the Indonesian tsunami several years ago, how the moment before the tidal wave hit all the water was dragged off the beach . . .

I heard it coming before I saw it. A sound like a freight train bearing down on the house. Then I saw it, a tidal wave of air mowing down the forest, snapping hundred-year-old oaks like toothpicks. I ducked a split second before it hit the house. Glass shattered above me and rained down into my hair. I pasted myself on the floor and covered my head with my hands. Something hit my head – one of the candles from the smell of it. For some reason that pissed me off. I raised myself up onto my elbows and shouted at the wind.

"If this is how you act when a girl says no, I'm glad I sent you away. I sure as hell wasn't going to fall in love with you."

A clap of thunder shook the house, followed by a flash of lightning that lit up the room. It occurred to me that I'd better get away from the window and leave the room. I got gingerly to my feet and duck-walked across the floor, glass and salt crackling under my boots. I was afraid I wouldn't be able to get the door open, but the moment I touched the iron doorknob the door swung open. "Thank you, Brock," I whispered under my breath. The minute I stepped through the door it slammed behind me. The sound was echoed by another crash, this one coming from downstairs. *Shit*, I thought. I'd forgotten all about Phoenix.

When I got downstairs I found Phoenix sitting up on the couch, her eyes wide with fright, her hair standing up like an Andy Warhol wig, but otherwise okay. All the windows downstairs had been closed and miraculously they'd all held against the wind. The banging was coming from the front door.

"Shouldn't we get that?" Phoenix asked.

Could a disanimate creature knock at the front door? Maybe, but it was far too polite for my incubus.

I went to the door, wishing it had a peephole. I could have asked who was there, but I doubted I would have been able to hear any response over the lashing wind and rain outside. I opened the door.

The three figures standing in the light of my front porch were so muffled and wrapped in layers of wool, down and

fur that I didn't recognize them at first. They might have
been the three magi – or the three witches in Macbeth. Only
when the middle one turned down the collar of her fur coat
and spoke did I recognize my boss, Elizabeth Book.

"Hello, Callie, dear. Won't you invite us in?"

I looked from her to Diana Hart, zipped up to her wide-
open eyes in a bright red down parka, and then to Soheila
Lilly, muffled in a burgundy wool cloak.

"It's a little early for Thanksgiving dinner," I said.

"We're not here for Thanksgiving, dear," Dean Book
said with a sigh. "We're here for an intervention."

CHAPTER FIFTEEN

"For Phoenix?" I asked in a whisper. "She *has* been drinking a lot."

"No, dear," Dean Book said with another sigh. "For you. Can we please come in? This weather you've raised is quite chilly."

"And likely to get colder as the night goes on," Diana Hart said, shaking the water from her down coat before stepping in. "I do hope it doesn't freeze. We lost so many trees in the last ice storm."

They all came into the foyer. I had to struggle to close the door behind them. "How did you know . . . ?"

"I saw that you took the demonology book from my office," Soheila said, handing me her cloak. "I was at Liz's house telling her when the wind came up."

"And I saw the animals breaking from the forest and then heard the wind," Diana said, handing me her damp down coat. "I called Liz right away and confirmed it was coming from Honeysuckle House."

"We knew then that you must be trying Angus's spell for banishing incubi," Liz said handing me her heavy fur coat which gave off a spark of static electricity.

"I could have told you the spell has its drawbacks,"

Soheila said. "It certainly should never be used by the person possessed by the incubus."

"I am not *possessed*," I said huffily. I was going for righteous, but since I was weighted down by the women's three heavy coats – Elizabeth Book's fur alone must have weighed twenty pounds – I sounded more like an aggrieved housemaid. Or, I realized as the women exchanged pitying looks, a dope addict in denial.

"No one ever *thinks* they're possessed, dearie," Diana said, patting me on the arm. "Now why don't you put those coats away and we'll sit down with some hot tea. I brought homemade donuts." She plucked a fragrant paper bag from her quilted purse.

Of course, I thought grumpily as I wrestled the heavy coats into the hall closet – Elizabeth Book's kept slipping off its hanger as if it didn't want to go – donuts and caffeine, staples of twelve step programs everywhere. And speaking of rehab . . . where was Phoenix? She'd been in the library when I went to the door. Had she passed out?

But when I came into the kitchen I found her opening cabinet doors.

"We have an electric kettle," she was saying, "but I don't know where it's gone to. And I can't find the sugar bowl anywhere . . ."

"Um . . . I borrowed those, Fe. They're up in my room."

"Well, I'll just go get them."

"We can use the kettle on the stove," Diana said. "I think you probably should stay downstairs, isn't that right, Callie? I imagine your bedroom's a little . . . messy right now."

I nodded and sat down at the kitchen table. Diana and Elizabeth exchanged a worried glance behind Phoenix's back.

"I suppose we could try a sleeping spell on her," Elizabeth said.

"Not advisable for bipolars," Soheila said, giving Phoenix an assessing look. "Especially if she's on Depakote."

"Who's bipolar?" Phoenix said, popping her head out of the mugs cabinet. It struck me that that was the word that caught her attention, not *spell*.

"You are, sweetie," Diana said, putting an arm around Phoenix's shoulders. "Which means you don't react well to magic. I'm afraid you're going to have to be around some tonight. I'll give you some herbs for your nerves later."

"What are you three?" I asked, tired of feeling ignored in my own kitchen. "Witches?"

Diana laughed. "Well, Liz is, of course. She's one of the most powerful witches I've ever met." Diana smiled lovingly at the dean and I wondered why it had taken me so long to realize they were a couple. Apparently my gaydar was working about as well as my witch-dar. "But me, I'm just a garden variety fairy."

"Oh my dear, there's nothing garden variety about you." Elizabeth slipped an arm around Diana's narrow shoulders. "Diana is from the ancient line of Sidhe who have tended the fairy deer of the Fairy Queen for time immemorial."

"I see," I said, surprised at how unsurprised I was. "And what about you, Soheila – are you a fairy or a witch?"

"Oh, neither," Soheila said, smiling. "I'm a demon." Seeing the expression on my face she laughed. "Or *daemon*, as the more politically correct of my tribe call themselves now."

"Soheila, you really mustn't be shy about your origins.

Soheila is descended from a great Mesopotamian wind spirit . . ."

"Really, Liz, I don't think it's necessary to go into that right now. The important thing for Callie to know is that most of us are no more dangerous than the fairies – although that's not really saying much. We can discuss genus and species later when we have more time. I'm afraid all you've managed to do with your spell is rile up your incubus. We've got our work cut out for us."

There were a lot of surprises in store for me that night, but the first was how easily Phoenix took to the idea that we'd both landed in a college populated by fairies, witches and demons.

"I always knew I had some fairy blood in me," she crowed once we were all seated around the kitchen table with tea and donuts, the wind howling outside.

"Sorry, dear," Diana said, patting Phoenix's hand. "I'm pretty sure you haven't a drop. But Callie here . . . I had my suspicions from the start, but I wasn't sure until she rescued that bird from the thicket . . ."

"Well, then I can be a witch, right? I've long been a follower of Wicca. Can you train me?"

"That's not a good idea given your mental health profile," Soheila said – a bit too brusquely, I thought. She was clearly the most impatient of the three to get on with banishing the incubus. Maybe it took a demon to know what one was capable of, but I had a bunch of questions of my own.

"Is the whole faculty made up of fairies and witches and—" I still felt a little uncomfortable calling Soheila a demon "—other supernatural creatures?"

"Oh no, not at all!" Elizabeth cried. "Imagine the trouble we'd get in with the M.L.A.! But we do keep an eye out for hires who might have fey ancestry or hidden necromantic talents. Not that we can always tell right away, especially with those who don't know they are descended from witches or the fey. You, for instance. Given your interest in fairy tales and folklore I suspected there might be something there, but I didn't sense any witch's power in you . . ." she paused, a troubled look on her face. "But when you told Diana that you'd released a bird from the thicket, we realized you must have a fey ancestor – and a very particular kind of fairy – one who is able to open and close the door to the world of Faerie. A doorkeeper."

"There's a door to Faerie here—" Diana said, cutting her eyes toward the back of the house "—in the woods. After the fey departed the Old World for Faerie, some found their way through this door back into the human world."

"As far as we know," Soheila added."It's the last door to Faerie."

"The humans we found here," Diana continued, "the Native Americans, were happy to share their land with us. And then the first Colonial settlers who came into the area were witches exiled from Salem and other colonies inhospitable to the old religion."

"You see," Elizabeth said taking up Diana's narrative like picking up a stitch she had dropped, "The Old World witches worshipped the old gods, the horned god . . ."

"Cernunnos," Diana whispered.

"Mithra," Soheila breathed.

"And the Triple Goddess," Elizabeth continued.

"Morrigan," Diana said.

"Anahita," Soheila echoed.

"And so the two groups formed the town," Dean Book continued, "and named it Fairwick to celebrate the union of the fair folk and the witches."

"The witches were helpful to the fey when they came through the door," Diana said. "New arrivals are often weak and confused."

"And the fey taught the witches many secrets of their craft," Elizabeth added, "just as they had in the Old World. The first witches were humans who mingled with the fey and learned how to use the powers of nature from them—"

"But then," Diana interrupted, "during the Middle Ages the Old World witches were persecuted because they worshipped the Old Gods. Some of the witches renounced their connection with the fey . . ."

"But others came here and reestablished their connection with the fey," Elizabeth continued. "It was decided that a college should be formed to store the knowledge that was accumulated. But as more people came to the area it also became important to safeguard the door . . ."

"Because not every being that comes through the door is harmless," Soheila said. "The incubus you've encountered, for instance. He came through more than a century ago and latched on to Dahlia LaMotte. I tried myself to get him to go back . . ."

"A century ago?" I asked. "So you're . . ."

"Older than I look," Soheila finished for me. "By quite a bit. But even I couldn't make this creature go back into Faerie. He's very powerful. It was Angus Fraser who was able finally to drive him into the thicket . . . into the Borderlands, but he couldn't drive him though the door back to Faerie. He died before he could do that . . ." She paused and looked away. Dean Book laid her hand over hers. After a moment Soheila took a deep breath and continued. "After the incubus was driven into the Borderlands we asked Brock—" She saw me about to interrupt and added, "Yes, he's one of the Norse daevas, once blacksmith to the gods. He and his brother have been here for more than a hundred years . . . . We asked Brock to fit the windows and doors with iron locks to keep the incubus out. We believe Dahlia still let him in, though, from time to time."

"But she lived a long life," I said. "I thought the incubi drained their victims until they died."

Soheila and Elizabeth Book exchanged a worried look. The dean nodded to Soheila to go on. "This incubus seems to know how to keep his victims alive for a long time. If the story about him is true he once was mortal and believes that he'll regain his mortality when a human falls in love with him. We think that Dahlia found a way to coexist with him. He fed her creativity – but if she grew too weak she could banish him back to the Borderlands for a little while."

"Sounds a little mean," I said, wondering if it was Dahlia's treatment of him that had left him with such a chip on his shoulder.

Soheila clucked her tongue. "You're thinking he's the way he is because he's been treated badly. But you read Angus's letter. This demon killed his sister. Please don't underestimate him. And don't try to make nice to him. Dahlia may have lived a long life, but she had no energy for anything but her books. She couldn't have a normal relationship, even though I know Brock loved her very much."

I was about to ask what kind of a normal relationship she could have had with an ancient Norse divinity, but Phoenix spoke up. She'd been following the conversation goggle-eyed, sipping eagerly from her teacup (which I suspected from the smell had been spiked with whiskey). "I've been feeling very tired lately. Maybe the incubus has been draining me."

"I don't think so," Diana said, pouring more tea into Phoenix's cup. "You've been sleeping downstairs in Matilda's cast-iron bed. Iron keeps him away."

"Oh." Phoenix looked disappointed, then brightened. "But I sleep on the couch a lot."

"It's Callie he wants!" Elizabeth Book said, slapping the table. The sound was echoed by the wind knocking against the shutters. "But we can't let him have you. You're too important to us. Now I know you probably have lots more questions, but I believe we should leave them till later – after we've banished this demon from your house."

"You can do that?" I asked.

"Yes, together the three of us can – as long as you truly want him gone. Are you sure you're not harboring any hidden . . . um, affection for this creature?"

I considered the question. I'd certainly been infatuated with him – *besotted,* a voice inside my head mocked, *a sex slave* – and I'd felt some sympathy for him after hearing that he'd once been human, but I hadn't liked the high-handed approach he'd taken upstairs. He'd been arrogant and imperious. No way was I going to fall in love with a guy like that.

"Not at all," I said. "Let's show him the door."

Once we had gathered fresh supplies – salt, spices, a new covered dish (an iron blue enamel Le Creuset casserole with a heavy lid), fresh candles, a broom and dustpan – we started up the stairs. Dean Book and I went first, Soheila next, Diana and Phoenix bringing up the rear.

"Is it really such a good idea to include Phoenix?" I lowered my voice even though the wind was so loud I doubted she could have heard me if I shouted.

"We don't have any other choice," she replied. "She's safer *in* the circle than outside of it."

That gave me a little chill, but I told myself that these women knew what they were doing and that I was safer now with company than I'd been alone. When I put my hand on the doorknob and Diana called "Wait" from the end of the hall, though, I half hoped she meant to call the whole thing off. She was standing outside the closed door to the spare bedroom in which I'd been keeping Dahlia LaMotte's papers, her eyes wide.

"We need some iron to keep the circle grounded," she said. "I can tell there's iron in here, but I can't get it. Neither can Soheila." She turned to Phoenix. "Can you?"

Phoenix opened the door and gave a little squeak. "Oh look, it's like they're waiting for us!"

I came down the hall and looked into the room. The five iron doormice, which I was quite sure I'd left weighing down stacks of manuscript pages, were standing in a line, their little paws held out like toddlers' waiting to be picked up.

"Perfect," Diana said. "Phoenix, could you . . . ?"

Phoenix was already kneeling to pick up the doormice. I didn't see how she could carry more than three so I stooped to pick up the last two – including the one with the paint splotch and broken tail.

"My little wounded soldier," I said. "Called back into the fray."

Diana gave me a quizzical look and whispered something in Elizabeth's ear.

"Maybe," the dean said, giving me a curious look.

"What?" I asked, my voice shrill against the moaning wind outside.

"You're part fey so you shouldn't like touching iron, but it doesn't seem to bother you at all," Diana said.

"Your body has found a way to neutralize the iron's power," the dean said. "Which might be why the iron didn't work to keep the incubus out."

"Fascinating," Soheila said. "Casper will want to write a paper on it."

"Well, we can tell him about it in the morning," Elizabeth said with a rueful smile. "If we're all still here."

I thought she must be exaggerating the danger until I opened my bedroom door. In the light from the hallway (all the lightbulbs in the bedroom had been shattered), the room looked as if it had been ravaged by a wild animal. Salt, melted wax, and broken glass were strewn across the floor. The bedsheets had been torn from the bed. The mattress had been ripped to shreds. On the wooden headboard were five long gashes that looked like the mark of a clawed beast.

"You certainly made him angry," Soheila said, examining the claw mark. I thought I detected a hint of admiration in her voice. "What did you say to him?"

I tried to remember our little dialogue, but like most lovers' spats it was hard to unwind its logic, if any. Somehow it had gone rather quickly from him asking my name to me getting pissed off at him. Oh yeah, now I remembered.

"I told him that there was more to love than being good in the sack."

Soheila's eyes widened. Diana clapped a hand over her mouth to stifle a laugh and glanced over toward Elizabeth Book, but the dean was staring at something on the floor.

"I think this is his reply," she said.

I came around the bed and looked at the floor. Written in the salt were two words: *What more?*

"Fascinating," Soheila whispered. I could barely hear her for the wind roaring through the broken window. It swept the salt and glass across the floor erasing the words—as if suddenly embarrassed by them – and I felt a momentary pang of . . . what? Disloyalty? As if I'd exposed him to the ridicule of these four women.

I shook the feeling away. Look at what he'd exposed me to! My boss, neighbor, roommate, and colleague were cleaning up my bedroom, literally picking up the pieces of a supernatural dalliance gone wrong. I hardened my heart to him and pitched in. I held the dustbin for Soheila and dumped the debris into the wastebasket under my desk. He'd pulled out all the little drawers – all but the locked one – and dumped paperclips everywhere. My notes for my book were scattered on the floor. *He* should be embarrassed. What kind of question was that? *What more?*

While collecting the scattered pages, some of which were ripped and water damaged, I found the fairy stone under my desk. I put it into my pocket, and then sat down in the circle between Diana and Elizabeth. Soheila drew a fresh circle of salt around us, intoning something in Farsi that somehow made the salt stick to the floor despite the wind, and then sat down between Diana and Phoenix. There was a candle in front of each of us, each one held now by one of the iron doormice. I was glad to see that I'd gotten the one with the paint splotch and broken tail.

"It would be safer if the mice were *outside* the circle," Soheila said, sounding uncharacteristically irritable. "We would be ironbound."

"But then Diana couldn't be inside it," Liz snapped. "Just because *you've* trained yourself to withstand iron doesn't mean she can. I'm not sure even this is good for her . . ."

"I'm fine," Diana said in a strained imitation of her usual cheerful voice. It was hard to tell in this light, but I thought she looked pale and that she was pressing her lips together as though suppressing a grimace of pain.

Elizabeth Book lit her candle and then passed it to me. When we'd all lit our candles Elizabeth and Diana took my hands, Diana took Soheila's right hand, and Soheila took Phoenix's right hand. When Dean Book took Phoenix's left hand, I felt an electric charge pulse through me.

"The circle is complete," Elizabeth said briskly, as if calling a faculty meeting to order. "Let's keep it that way. Soheila will recite the banishment ritual. The rest of you repeat these words to yourselves: *Begone, incubus. I send you away, demon. I cast you into darkness.* Keep repeating them and don't let any other thought enter your mind . . ."

"Like a yoga mantra," Phoenix said brightly.

Glancing at her, I noticed that she was the only one who didn't look terrified. No doubt because she was the only one who didn't know what was coming.

"Yes, just like a yoga mantra," Elizabeth Book said with brittle humor. "A yoga mantra to save your life."

Soheila began to speak in Farsi. At least I thought it was Farsi. The words blended into a stream of sound that intertwined with the gusting wind outside, like two rivers meeting. I began reciting the lifesaving yoga mantra:

"Begone incubus. I send you away, demon. I cast you into darkness."

The air coming in through the broken window grew colder. There were ice crystals carried on it, settling onto my skin. I opened my eyes and saw there were snowflakes swirling through the air and dusting the floor.

Just like a man, doesn't care what he tracks in on his boot heels.

"Begone incubus. I send you away, demon. I cast you into darkness."

What more? he had asked. That was just like a man, too. Pretending helplessness when anyone would know what more. What about decency and caring and really bothering to see—

"Begone incubus. I send you away, demon. I cast you into—"

—who he was trying to seduce. Anyone who knew me certainly wouldn't mess with my desk or my papers.

"—darkness. Begone incubus I send you—"

And any man worth his salt would know that talking was at least as important as lovemaking. He'd share something of himself, too.

"—into darkness begone incubus I send you away demon I cast you—"

Although maybe that is what he'd been doing by showing me those dreams about the fairies marching. I'd asked him, "Who are you?" and the sex dreams had stopped and the marching dreams had begun. *Is that what you were trying to do? Tell me who you are?*

A particularly fierce gust of wind blew against me, but it wasn't cold. Although snow was now covering the heads and shoulders of my circle mates and ice had formed over the broken glass in the windowpanes, the wind that lapped against my face was as warm as a Caribbean breeze. *Yessss*, it crooned into my ear, sending hot waves down to my toes. *I want to know you and for you to know me. You and I have known each other before.*

I laughed out loud. It was the oldest line in the book: *Don't I know you from somewhere?*

But even as I laughed an image was blooming inside my head – the rolling heath, the long line of travelers, *my companions* fading into mist before we could reach the door . . . because the Riders were going through first . . . and then the one horse coming back. *For me*. He was coming back for me. Then we were in the glade – our wedding chapel – making love. We were vanishing into the mist together, but then his eyes widened into dark shadowy pits. Someone was calling him. "No," I cried out – in my dream and in the bedroom in Honeysuckle House, "don't leave me!" But he was already turning, looking over his shoulder, at *her*. The woman in green on the dark horse who bade him come to her and whom he dared not disobey.

My eyes snapped open.

You left me for that . . .

I couldn't help myself, Cailleach. The warm coil wound itself down the neck of my shirt and caressed my breast. I wrenched my right hand out of Diana's limp hand and slapped it away.

"Get out!" I hissed. "I never want to see you again."

For one moment the warm air turned into a hand and grasped mine, but I let it go – as he had let mine go so long ago – and then the coiled air snapped back like a rubber band and hit the window, shattering what was left of the glass. It whipped against the house like an angry cat's tail and then crashed into the woods. I heard trees snapping and something close by exploded.

I looked down and saw that one of the cast-iron doormice had shattered. The other four were glowing red. Another exploded, sending shards into the air. One hit Phoenix right above her left eye.

"Get down!" I screamed.

Soheila grabbed Diana and knocked her to the floor. I felt Elizabeth's hand on my back, pushing me over just as the third mouse blew, splattering hot molten iron. I heard Diana scream in pain and guessed she must have been burned by one of the drops. As I hit the floor I saw that the tailless doormouse was tottering on its little hind legs. I grabbed it – singeing my fingers on the hot iron – and tossed it away from the circle. I thought I heard the sound of tiny feet scurrying away and one last moan soughing through the woods. Then everything went quiet.

CHAPTER SIXTEEN

Soheila helped Phoenix downstairs while Elizabeth and I helped Diana. Although Phoenix was bleeding and screaming, I was more concerned about Diana. She was barely conscious. Elizabeth and I had to practically carry her to the living room couch.

"I shouldn't have let her get so close to so much iron," Elizabeth said, stroking Diana's limp hair back from her damp forehead. The freckles on her face stood out like spots of blood.

"Is there anything that we can give her . . . an antidote?"

"Do you have any rosemary in the kitchen?"

"I think Phoenix bought some for the stuffing."

"Boil some water, then and steep the rosemary in it along with some black tea and mint. And bring a dishcloth. We can make a compress with the tea until she's able to drink it."

In the kitchen Soheila was cleaning Phoenix's wound and murmuring a steady stream of soothing reassurances. "It's all over. There's nothing to be afraid of. No, you're not going crazy."

"You saw it too, didn't you, Cal?" Phoenix asked when she saw me. "You heard the wind and saw the candles blow out and the mice explode, right?"

"Yes," I answered, putting the kettle on the stove to boil. "It's all over now . . . right?" I tried to catch Soheila's eye. Phoenix wasn't the only one who needed reassurances.

"Yes, it's all over," Soheila said, but she was too busy bandaging Phoenix's forehead to look at me when she said it. At least I hoped that was the reason she wouldn't make eye contact.

When the water boiled I made a pot of the rosemary-mint tea and put it on a tray with a shallow bowl and a checked dishcloth, which I then brought into the living room. Diana was still unconscious. I sat on the opposite loveseat while Elizabeth steeped the cloth in the tea and then swabbed Diana's forehead with it, all the time murmuring soft words of endearment. I felt like I was intruding, but I couldn't budge until I knew Diana was okay. This had all been my fault. If I'd been sterner with the incubus maybe he would have left sooner. Or if I had asked for help sooner . . . The recriminations swirled around in my head, but Elizabeth's soft voice combined with the splash of water and the soothing aroma of mint and rosemary soon lulled me to sleep.

I must have slept for a few hours because when I awoke the first rays of dawn, muted by the ice-coated windows, were spilling across the floor. Elizabeth Book was standing by my chair, her usually immaculate coif a rat's nest, her face in the cold morning light lined and drawn. She was holding a phone in her hand.

"It's your boyfriend, Paul," she said, handing me the phone.

I took the phone from her but covered it with my hand and asked how Diana was.

"I think the worst is over." She glanced at the couch

where Diana lay motionless under Elizabeth's fur coat so that it looked as if a giant bear was snoozing there. I noticed that one of the alpaca throws was over me. Elizabeth must have covered both of us in the night. "But we've got some other problems. Take your call and we'll talk when you're done."

"Paul?" I said into the phone. "Is everything okay? Where are you?"

"I'm in Buffalo!" he cried, his voice more excited than I'd heard it since the Yankees won the Series. "My plane almost crashed! A freak storm came up out of nowhere! The pilot made an emergency landing in a cornfield. Everyone's saying that it's a miracle we all survived!"

"I'm so sorry . . ." A freak storm? Could it be . . . ?

"No, don't be sorry!" Paul started talking so fast and excitedly that I had trouble following what he was saying. I was also distracted by the possibility that I had caused the storm that had almost killed him. When I started focusing I heard him say: "It was the most amazing experience of my life. You should have seen the lightning! They say the wind speed was a hundred and fifty miles per hour. I really thought I was going to die, but then I didn't. It just clarifies things."

"Wow," I said, wondering what exactly Paul's near-death experience had clarified. "That's great, I guess. I can't wait to hear all about it. Can you get a plane from Buffalo? Or maybe drive from there? I think it's about a five hour drive . . ."

"Oh my God! You haven't been outside or watched the news yet, have you? Take a look out your window."

I was staring at my window but the panes were coated with ice. I got up and walked through the kitchen to the back door, not wanting to disturb Diana by opening the front door.

"They're calling Fairwick, New York, the epicenter of the storm," Paul was saying as I opened the door. "The roads are blocked in all directions in a twenty-mile radius of the town. It's the largest ice storm ever recorded. What does it look like there?"

"It looks . . ." I tried to think of a word to describe what I was looking at. A sheet of clear ice, shimmering like melted opals in the first rays of the rising sun, spread across my backyard up to the edge of the woods. As the sun climbed up the trees they too began to glow – every branch, many of which were broken, twig, pine-needle and stray brown leaf had been encased in a sheet of clear ice that burst into fiery brilliance at the touch of the sun. "It looks," I finally said to Paul, "like a fairyland."

Paul told me he was going to the hotel provided by the airline for him and his fellow "survivors," as he called them, to try to catch a few hours of sleep, and then would call me when he found out anything more about his travel options. After I got off the phone, I went back into the kitchen. Elizabeth and Soheila were at the table drinking coffee and watching CNN on my little portable TV. I poured myself a mug from the coffeemaker and sat down to watch.

"The Thanksgiving ice storm came out of nowhere," a female reporter in a heavy fur-trimmed down parka was saying. She stood in front of a line of stalled cars at an exit sign for Fairwick. "Stranding motorists everywhere. Curiously, this is not the first time that the town of Fairwick has been the victim of freak weather. In the summer of 1893 the town was hit by hailstones carrying live frogs . . ."

"One of Caspar's chemistry experiments gone awry," Soheila said, rolling her eyes. "I tell him not to mess with the weather."

"And in 1923 a sandstorm covered the town."

"The Ferrishyn Wars?" Elizabeth asked.

Soheila nodded. "Nasty creatures. I still find sand in my closets sometimes."

"Sources in Fairwick say that the town has been without power since midnight."

I looked at the electric coffee machine and the TV. "How are these working?" I asked.

"Courtesy of Soheila," Elizabeth said. "Didn't I mention last night that she's a wind spirit? She can conduct energy, too. Now shush a moment. I want to hear how far the ice goes."

The screen now showed a map of upstate New York. Fairwick was surrounded by a blue blotch with ragged edges – some graphic artist's attempt to represent ice, I supposed, although it looked more like a malevolent microbe to me – that enclosed all of the state park to the east and north, but didn't quite reach West Thalia to the west or Bovine Corners to the south.

"Oh good," Elizabeth said. "At least it's only our little valley. I think we can manage if it's contained. We'll call Dory to organize a visiting committee to check on the elderly and infirm, to make sure that they have enough firewood – if they don't have generators – and food."

"Brock and Ike can head up the salt truck and plows," Soheila said.

"Thank goodness most of the students have already gone home for the holiday. I'll have Casper and Oliver check for stragglers in the dorms."

"Mara Marinca didn't go home," I volunteered.

A worried look crossed the dean's face. "No, she wouldn't have. I'm sure she's fine, though, and she'll be here later for Thanksgiving dinner."

"I'm not sure Phoenix will be up to cooking," I said, remembering for the first time how many people I had invited over. "She was pretty wigged out by what happened last night."

"I am worried about her," Soheila admitted. "But I got her to bed by two this morning and cooking might take her mind off what happened."

"Plus Dory Browne called to say she'd be by to help," Elizabeth said. "Don't worry about that. Here in Fairwick we all pitch in during an emergency. But there is something I need you to help me with right now. Would you mind taking a little walk with me?"

"Of course not."

"Good. Make sure you wear sturdy non-skid boots. The footing will be rather treacherous where we're going."

Since the entire town was coated with a two-inch layer of ice I thought Elizabeth Book's warning was unnecessary, but when I saw she was heading for the woods I wondered if any warning was sufficient. Before the temperature had dropped the wind had knocked branches and even whole trees down; then the debris had been coated with so much ice that it had all melded together into a glittering, unmovable tangle. I couldn't even see where the path was. While Elizabeth stood uncertainly at the edge of the woods staring at the wreckage, I turned back to look at my house. The shutters over my bedroom window had been completely torn off, and the rest of the shutters were missing slats and hanging crookedly from their hinges. The copper gutter had been wrested from the north eave where it hung limply, twisted like a chewed up swizzle straw. So many slate tiles were missing from the roof that it looked like a checkerboard.

"What a spoiled brat!" I cried. "That demon's little temper tantrum is going to cost me thousands of dollars in repairs."

Elizabeth Book turned around and looked at the back of my house. "Yes, that's the problem with incubi – they're all libido. And he can't use being a demon as an excuse. Soheila's a demon and look how evolved she is! Honestly, though, I'm surprised the damage isn't worse. From the state of these woods I'd say the wind he summoned was moving at a hundred and twenty-five miles per hour. If it had hit your house at that velocity it wouldn't be standing. Something must have lessened the impact . . ." She switched her gaze from the house to me. "Almost as if you'd managed an aversion spell before the wind hit . . ."

"I don't know any spells," I said somewhat petulantly, peeved that the dean wasn't taking my house damage seriously enough. "Should I? You said before that you thought I had fairy blood, not that I was a witch . . . Is being a witch hereditary?" I asked, suddenly overcome with all the unknowns in this new world I'd stumbled into.

"There are witch families that have passed down their craft from generation to generation," Dean Book said as she stepped over a downed pine bough, which the ice had turned into a festive Christmas decoration. "I myself come from a long line of witches. No one is sure how much of being a witch is nature or nurture. Some believe that the original witches interbred with the fey, which is what gave them their power. But the more reactionary anti-fey witches believe that fey blood cancels out a witch's power."

"There are reactionary witches?" I asked, scrambling after her, grasping ice-slick branches to keep from slipping. It felt like we were walking through the ruins of a strange and foreign world. The ice rings of Saturn, perhaps, or Jotunheim, the glacial home of the Norse ice giants. The violence that had caused the wreckage was frightening and yet the effect was oddly beautiful. Giant trees had been snapped in two, but pine cones, acorns, and even the delicate yellow flowers of witch hazel trees had been preserved in ice like sugared treats to put on top of a cake. It seemed an appropriate setting in which to learn about this other strange world that Dean Book was describing.

"I'm afraid so," she told me with a pained look. "There are those who would have us renounce all ties to the fey. But if we did, then the last door to Faerie would close entirely. No one would ever be able to get out again . . ."

She paused as we reached the honeysuckle thicket. The ice-sheathed snarl of vines and branches looked as if it had been spun out of sugar. Jeweled shapes glimmered in the crooks of vine and branch like Christmas lights. Peering closer I made out the shapes of small birds, tiny mice, voles, and chipmunks – all the tiny creatures that had died in the thicket. Elizabeth cupped her gloved hand around a frozen chickadee. Nestled in her palm it looked like an exotic jewel.

"Why do so many creatures die here?" I asked.

"These are the Borderlands," she said. "Small creatures lose their way. Even large creatures – very powerful creatures – lose their way between our world and Faerie. More and more get trapped between the worlds each year.

The door is narrowing and opening for shorter periods. That's why we were so excited when we realized you might be a doorkeeper."

"I still don't know what you mean by that. It sounds like some kind of doorman or janitor . . ."

"That's what the Romans called their doorkeepers. They knew that thresholds were sacred and that certain gods were dedicated to crossing places – Janus, the two-faced god and Hecate, the three-faced goddess of the crossroads – both were doorkeepers, as you are, Cailleach."

"You're saying that I'm descended from gods and goddesses!" I was trying to make a joke of it. "That's even harder to believe than being descended from fairies."

"They're one and the same, Callie. What we call fairies and demons are the last of the race of old gods. They're all from the same ancient race – although the variety within them is great, especially as the old ones began interbreeding with humans . . . as you can see here . . ."

She held back a heavy vine studded with purple berries turned to amethyst by the ice and looked up. I followed her gaze, seeing nothing except tangled ice thicket at first, but then, as the sun appeared and shone through the tangled branches, I began to make out shimmering shapes suspended in the air. It looked as though a giant spider web had been strung between the branches and then frozen – but the pattern in the web revealed faces in its intricate weave: the faces of men and women and animals, and some creatures that seemed to be neither human nor animal. Some had human faces with horns or pointed ears or reptilian skin; some had animal faces with human intelligence glittering in their eyes. All were contorted with pain.

"What are they?" I asked.

"This one's a phouka," she said pointing to a dog-man. "They're related to the Puck of William Shakespeare. "This one—" She pointed to a horse with a fish's tail "—is a kelpie. They like to wait in streams and drag down unsuspecting maidens. Foolish thing. I don't know why it thought it could cross at this time of year when the streams are all frozen. We're probably better off without him. Your incubus raised a storm in both worlds. Generally only one or two creatures cross at a time, but the storm must have driven many into the Borderlands; then, when the ice came, it froze them in the passage.

"Are they all . . . dead?"

Elizabeth stepped close to one – a woman whose slim body ended in a fish's tail. "This one's an undine," she said as if she hadn't heard my question. "Creatures of the water. We've heard that the male undines are dying out, which might be why this one risked coming over in the middle of the winter, although I don't know why she'd come outside of breeding season. Poor thing. She must have been confused. She'll never survive.

She was careful not to touch it, but, when her warm breath reached it, the ice cracked and rained down onto the ground in a tinkling cascade. The rupture in the web spread and soon all the faces were cracking and dissolving.

"Isn't there anything we can do to save them?" I cried.

Elizabeth turned to me, her face so strained it looked like it too might crack and break. "Perhaps. You opened the door for another creature – that bird you let free. It was our first hint that you had some touch of fey blood. Perhaps you can bring one through."

"How? I don't know how to do that . . . don't I need some sort of instruction?"

"No one knows how the doorkeeper does what she does. Just choose one . . . and pull!"

"Choose! How can I choose?" All around me faces were shattering into glittering shards of ice. Soon there wouldn't be any to choose from. I found the first face that was still whole – a tiny creature with a fox-like face, enormous ears, and pointy teeth. I reached out and gingerly touched one finger to its forehead. Instead of ice I felt fur. Quickly I pushed my hand into . . . something that felt like quicksand . . . grabbed it by its furry nape and pulled. The creature came out of the ice snarling, teeth bared, but then instead of biting me, licked my wrist with a long sandpaper tongue. Then it ran into the woods on its two hoofed feet.

"What the hell . . ."

"A satyr!" Elizabeth laughed. "I haven't seen one of those in years. I thought they were extinct in Faerie. Don't worry, he'll find his way to the college and then we'll either offer him a job or relocate him to West Thalia where there's a lovely Greek community." She wiped her eyes and then, much to my surprise, hugged me. "I knew there was a reason you came to us. Now come on. We've got work to do."

CHAPTER SEVENTEEN

On the way back to the house something occurred to me.

"Dean Book . . ."

"Oh, please call me Liz . . . after what we've been through!"

"Um, okay . . . Liz." I was going to have a hard time getting used to that. "I saw a lot of faces in that clearing but I didn't see *him*. The incubus, I mean."

"I know who you mean. Yes, I noticed that too. He might have gone back into Faerie or . . ."

"Or he's still around somewhere?"

Liz sighed. "He's haunted these woods for more than a hundred years. He probably knows where to hide. But I wouldn't worry about it too much. After last night he's not likely to try to get back into your house . . . unless you invite him in, that is." She gave me a sharp look

"Oh, I wouldn't do that. I've learned my lesson."

"I should think so." She patted my shoulder. "You're a smart girl."

Back at the house we found the kitchen bustling with activity. Diana was up eating a bowl of oatmeal at the kitchen table, looking pale but in good spirits. Dory Browne, in ski pants, fur trimmed boots and a sweater appliquéd with turkeys and fall leaves, was washing dishes at my sink, and Casper Van der Aart was stuffing a turkey while listening to Phoenix tell a rather embroidered version of what had happened last night. I wouldn't have thought any embroidering would have been possible, but Phoenix had added spectral apparitions that sounded like the cast from Dickens's *A Christmas Carol*. Except for a hectic gleam in her eyes, she looked none the worse for her brush with the supernatural. She was even enthusiastic about cooking Thanksgiving dinner.

"After all, we have tons of food, a working gas range and electricity. Not everyone in town is so lucky. Honestly, I think we should invite *more* people – anyone who doesn't have power."

Dory Browne and Diana exchanged a look, and Diana nodded. "It's not a bad idea. There are people who have electric stoves who won't be able to cook their dinners."

"And we need to go house to house to check on people to see if they're all right," Dory added. "We could ask anyone who's unable to cook their own dinner."

"No one's asked Callie," Liz broke in. "It's her house. Maybe she doesn't want it filled with strangers."

I looked at the gathering in my kitchen: a witch, a demon, a fairy, a . . . what *was* Casper? He looked, I suddenly realized, a lot like the ceramic gnomes people put in their gardens. The most "normal" person in the kitchen was an alcoholic, bipolar memoir writer. How much stranger could it get?

"Sure," I said. "The more the merrier."

While Diana, Phoenix and Casper started cooking, Dory Browne enlisted me to go house to house with her. "It'll be a good way for you to get to know your neighbors," she said, popping on fuzzy earmuffs over her ears that made her look like a koala bear. She had already spoken on her cell phone to someone named Dulcie and then someone named Davey – her cousins, she explained – to divide up the town by streets.

"Your family is certainly very generous with your time . . ." I began, but Dory started waving her hands in protest, her blue eyes flashing.

"Oh, it's our *job*, you know. We brownies agreed to be the town's caretakers in exchange for asylum two centuries ago."

"Brownies?" I asked, wondering if she could possibly mean the type that grew up to be Girl Scouts.

"My people came from Wales where we were called bwca . . . oh my!" She stopped, noticing my stunned expression. "Diana told me you knew all about the town now, so I thought it was okay to tell. You didn't know I was a brownie?" she asked as if this was the most obvious thing in the world.

"Not only didn't I know, but if you'll pardon me asking, I'm not sure what that means. I mean, I've heard of brownies . . . My mother and father told me stories about brownies who were household spirits who helped with chores in house and field."

"That's basically correct. We like a neat home and will help industrious homeowners, but not lazy ones."

"My father used to leave a bowl of cream or a piece of cake out for the brownies," I told her, "like leaving cookies and milk out for Santa Claus."

"That's perfectly appropriate," Dory said, smiling and nodding her head so vigorously that the fur on her earmuffs trembled. "We appreciate a nice piece of cake, but we don't like being left clothes, because . . . well . . . look at me! Do I look like I need any help dressing myself?"

"Not at all!" I replied, quickly catching the sharp edge to Dory's tone. "I admired your fashion sense the first time I met you."

"And I yours, Callie . . . We also do not like to be criticized."

"Who does?" I asked.

"Exactly! Nor do we like to be thanked."

"I have to admit that I've never understood that part."

Dory looked troubled. "That's a long story . . . perhaps for another day. But we pride ourselves on doing just exactly the right thing at the right time. An appropriate acknowledgement of our labors – like a nice bowl of cream or a plate of cookies – never goes amiss. Of course, I've tried to learn not to get too offended and go all boggart on the poor ignorant thanker . . ."

"Boggart?"

"Boggarts are brownies who become so angry that they begin playing nasty tricks on their humans. My second cousin, Hamm, for instance, has been tormenting a family of dairy farmers in Bovine Corners for years now simply because their great-great-grandfather suggested that his fields had been ploughed crooked. Most of us have grown a bit more civilized, though. The college runs anger management classes for brownies in danger of turning boggart."

It was hard to imagine bright-eyed, pretty Dory Browne needing an anger management class, but I did get to see her temper soon enough. It was at the third house we visited. The first two homeowners we visited – Abby and Russell

Goodnough, a young couple who had recently bought the town's veterinary practice, and Evangeline Sprague, a octogenarian retired librarian – were well prepared for the ice storm. They had woodstoves and Coleman lamps, and not only didn't need invitations to our Thanksgiving dinner (the Goodnoughs had invited Evangeline to their house), but offered to take in any overspill from our dinner.

"Good people," Dory said approvingly when we left the Goodnoughs. "They opened up their practice on a Sunday when my cousin Clyde was hit by a car while still in dog form, and was too hurt to change back."

"Did they know they were treating a . . ."

"A phouka? Oh no! But they couldn't have given Clyde better care if they'd known he was a person and not a cocker spaniel." Dory giggled. "Abby can't figure out why her house never needs dusting and her hardwood floors always polish themselves. Not that they need much help. They're both very neat and share all the work at home and at the clinic, but they're very busy. Not like some who have no excuse for their slovenly ways."

We'd come to the third house, a decaying three story Victorian with paint so faded and peeling it was impossible to tell what color it had originally been painted. I recognized it right away as the house I'd seen Nicky Ballard coming out of. I hoped she wasn't home as I was sure she'd be embarrassed to have me to see her house. The assortment of old couches and broken appliances on the porch alone would embarrass anyone and when I got closer I saw there were crates of empty liquor bottles shoved under the couches.

"It's a shame," Dory said, carefully picking her way across the unpainted and rotting porch floorboards. "The

Ballards were one of the leading families in Fairwick. They used to practically run the town until . . . Oh hey, JayCee, I didn't see you there."

The woman behind the screen door was wearing a faded gray sweatshirt – so big it drooped off one bony shoulder and hung down below her knees – that blended in with the shadows and the blue-gray smoke curling up from the cigarette clamped between her lips. "I didn't want to interrupt your little history lesson, Dor–ee. Go on. Tell the newcomer how the Ballards were once high and mighty, how old Bert Ballard once owned all the railroads from here to New York City and had a big mansion on Fifth Avenue. And now this is all that's left of the great Ballard fortune!" JayCee started to laugh, but the laugh turned into a hacking cough.

"At least your family had this place to come back to. Most of the folks who landed here in Fairwick were grateful for safe harbor in a storm," Dory said, clasping her hands primly together. I had a feeling she was holding them together to resist the urge to pull JayCee's sweatshirt up on her shoulder and pluck the cigarette out of her mouth. "But we're not here to talk about your family. We just wanted to make sure you and Arlette were doing all right after the storm. I see you got the generator going to keep Arlette's oxygen tanks working. Do you need anything?"

"We're not morons," JayCee snapped. The news that the generator was on seemed to take her by surprise, though now that Dory had drawn my attention to it, I could hear the whining thump of its machinery coming from somewhere below us. "Power's out, huh? You say there was a storm?"

Dory let out an exasperated breath that clouded in the cold air. "Yes, JayCee, there's been an ice storm. Why don't you let me come in and have a quick look at Arlette just to wish her a happy Thanksgiving, okay?" Dory was already opening the screen door (which should have been switched out to storm glass as Brock had done for mine the first of November) and edging into the foyer. JayCee shrugged, sending her sweatshirt halfway down her skinny arm, and backed up. There was only room for one person at a time coming in on account of the stacks of newspapers and magazines lining the entranceway. A narrow strip of dirty marble floor led to an ornately carved wooden staircase. I followed Dory, squeezing past JayCee at the foot of the stairs. Feeling uncomfortable invading the woman's house, I smiled and introduced myself.

"Your daughter Nicky's in my class," I told her. "She's a good student and a lovely girl."

JayCee Ballard snorted and rolled her eyes. "I just hope she's learning a trade at that college. She can't just sit on her thumbs and study basket weaving like those rich Fairwick girls."

I couldn't help wondering what trade JayCee plied, but I only smiled and repeated my assertion that Nicky was a bright girl and I was sure she'd do all right for herself. Then I followed Dory up the stairs, exchanging the downstairs smell of menthol cigarettes and cat pee for the medicinal reek of Vick's Vapor Rub and disinfectant. The smell intensified at the end of a dark and crowded hallway.

"Miss Arlette?" Dory called, knocking on a partly ajar door. "Can we come in? It's Dory Browne and Professor McFay from the college."

The door was abruptly swung open by Nicky Ballard, who looked over Dory's shoulder with wide, horrified eyes straight at me. "Professor McFay, what are you doing here?"

I opened my mouth to explain, but a thready, wheezy voice called from inside the room. "Nicolette Josephine Ballard, where are your manners? Invite the good women in and go see if that worthless mother of yours can scare up a cup of tea for them."

"That's really not necessary, Miz Ballard." Dory walked past Nicky into the room. "We're just checking around town to see how everyone's faring after the storm. I see Nicky's got everything under control here."

Following Dory into the warm, steamy room I saw what she meant. Although the room was crowded with large, dark furniture there was order here. The prescription bottles on the night table were neatly aligned. On a lovely old secretary desk decorated with pink porcelain cupids a humidifier pumped warm, mentholated steam into the air. An elderly woman with sharp features and thin but neatly combed hair sat in the middle of a massive four-poster bed with her gnarled hands clasped on the neatly folded sheets, a plastic tube running from her nose to an oxygen tank standing beside the bed. The old woman's keen blue eyes snapped from Dory to me.

"Who's this, did ya say?"

"I'm Callie McFay, Mrs. Ballard," I said loudly and clearly. "Your granddaughter, Nicky, is in my English class. She's an excellent student . . ."

"Well, of course she is," Arlette Ballard interrupted. "All the Ballards start out with good brains until they pickle them in alcohol like my daughter Jacqueline's done. You must be new here." She squinted up at me. "Come closer, but don't shout. My ears are fine. It's my damned worthless lungs that are giving out."

I took a tentative step toward the bed and a bony hand

snaked out and pulled me close enough to smell the old woman's sweetish breath. "Which kind are you?" she hissed. "Fairy, witch, or demon?"

"Grandma!" Nicky covered her grandmother's hand and tried unsuccessfully to pry her fingers off mine. "I told you about Professor McFay. She's been really nice to me."

"Is she that crazy writer woman?"

"No, that's my roommate," I replied.

Arlette cackled at that and squeezed my hand even tighter. "Don't let those witches work my Nicolette so hard. That place can suck the life right out of you. I should know."

I nodded, trying not to wince at the pain in my hand. "I'll keep an eye on her, Mrs. Ballard, I promise."

"I'll hold you to that, young lady," Arlette said with one final bone-crushing squeeze. Then she let my hand go and lay back on her pillow, closed her eyes, and waved a suddenly frail-looking hand to dismiss us from her presence.

We left the Ballards – but the Ballards didn't quite leave *us*. Two blocks away I could still smell cigarette smoke on my clothes and in my hair.

"Ugh, every time!" Dory cried, stooping to pick up a pine branch from one of the many that had come down in last's night's wind. It was frozen solid to the ground, but she knelt and blew a stream of frosted breath on it and the ice disappeared. Then she picked up the branch and proceeded to dust me off head to toe, while repeating three words that sounded like *fyrnsceaoa odoratus epil*. When she was done she repeated the procedure to herself. "There, that's better."

I sniffed the sleeve of my coat, then a lock of my hair; both smelled like pine now instead of cigarette smoke.

"Than –" I began, but stopped at a scowl from Dory. "That's a neat trick," I amended. "Was that Latin I heard and . . . Anglo Saxon?"

Dory smiled as we continued walking down Elm Street. "You've a keen ear for languages. Yes, the language of spells is a mixture of old languages. When the fey first started teaching magic to humans we had no words for spells. We just *thought* a thing and it happened. But to communicate with humans we needed to put things in words and we found that the words, although often imprecise and tricky to use, added power to our magic – a little extra *zing*, if you know what I mean."

I nodded, although I wasn't quite sure I saw how there could be a stronger magic than thinking a thing and having it happen.

"Having something better and bigger happen." Dory answered my unspoken question without missing a beat. "Having something *unexpected* happen. The fey had not been surprised by anything in a millennium. They loved the little extra *umph* that language gave magic. So we taught humans magic in exchange for language and for . . . well . . . for *other things*." Dory blushed pink.

"Other things?" I asked.

Dory turned to me and silently mouthed the letters S-E-X. "It's not something we're proud of, but there it is. The old ones . . . were a bit . . . well, *you know*. To their credit, most of the fairies became quite attached to their human . . . um . . . companions and treated them very well. Better than some of the humans treated them back. But, really, I don't think I'm the one to explain all that. I'm sure Elizabeth will brief you on fairy/human relations, current etiquette, and the sexual harassment laws passed in the nineties once you've had your orientation and received your own spellbook."

"Cool," I said, sufficiently intrigued at the idea of learning how to cast spells to spare Dory the embarrassment of having to explain unsavory interspecies sexual relations. I knew I shouldn't have been shocked. Mythology and folklore was full of randy gods abducting youths and maidens, but somehow the idea that the fey had *traded* for those favors made the whole thing seem more sordid. I decided it was a good time to change the subject. "Is there anything in those spellbooks that could help the Ballards? They seem . . ."

"Cursed?" Dory asked, stopping on the sidewalk. "They are. I'll tell you, but let's first go into the Lindisfarnes' house. They've left to spend the winter in Florida, so I just want to make sure their pipes don't burst."

I followed Dory up a bluestone path bordered by orange chrysanthemums – now encased in ice – to a neat fieldstone and clapboard bungalow. She upended a stone gnome half hidden in the hydrangeas (their tawny globular blooms looking like giant snowballs under their glaze of ice) and retrieved a key. She let us into an immaculate Craftsman bungalow decorated in period Stickley furniture.

"Okay, the Ballards," Dory began as she headed to the kitchen. "Have you ever heard of Bertram Hughes Ballard?"

"Wasn't he a big nineteenth-century robber baron and railroad magnate?

"Uh huh," Dory said from beneath the kitchen sink where she was doing something to the pipes that involved blowing on them and telling them *Ne fyrstig glaciare!* "He was the son of a French trapper – hence all the French names the family's still fond of – who made his fortune in lumber and then, as JayCee said, in railroads. He and his partner, Hiram Scudder, took over the Ulster and Clare in the 1880s and founded the Ballard & Scudder Ironworks here in town to supply the railroad with tracks. At the height of his fortune Ballard built that huge monstrosity we were just in."

Dory emerged from under the sink and cast an appreciative glance around the Lindisfarnes' cheery, neat kitchen. "Ballard and Scudder bought up most of the town between them, but then there was the Great Crash of '93."

"A stock market crash?"

"No, a train crash. The westbound train out of Kingston crashed into the eastbound train out of Binghamton. A hundred and three lives were lost, including a crew of workers whom Ballard had ordered out that morning to remove a section of track that was in poor repair. The crash was blamed on shoddy tracks manufactured by Ballard and Scudder. In the aftermath both the railroad and the iron-works went bankrupt. Scudder's wife, Adele, committed suicide. Ballard lost all his houses but the one here in town. He came back to Fairwick a broken man, but it wasn't until the curse started manifesting itself that we knew he must have done something to get on the wrong side of a powerful witch."

"Curse?"

Dory held up a finger to her lips and cocked her head, listening. The only sound I heard was the ticking of the Stickley grandfather clock in the hall and the drip of melting icicles outside the kitchen window. Dory shook her head. "Sorry, I thought I heard something. Anyway, as I was saying," she continued as she marched briskly into the downstairs powder room, "the curse: the year before the crash Bertram had married a young society girl from New

York. She was pregnant when the crash happened, but lost the baby, a boy, in her sixth month. She got pregnant half a dozen times after that, but they all died at birth – all boys – until she finally gave birth to a live girl and then was told by her doctor that she couldn't have any more children. Bertram was so upset at the idea that the Ballard name would die out that he had a lawyer draw up a will stipulating that his daughter would only inherit the house and the Ballard fortune if she kept the Ballard name and that unless there was a male heir all female Ballards must keep their surnames to inherit."

Finished with the downstairs powder room (she'd given the pipes a good talking to in Spell and set the tap to drip) Dory started up the stairs, continuing her story. "That's when we all guessed that Bertram was under a curse that he couldn't conceive male children. It took a while longer to make out the rest of the curse . . ."

She paused at the top of the stairs, again cocking her head as if to listen. Her face scrunched up, but then she shook her head and went on as she repeated her ministrations on the upstairs plumbing.

"Bert's daughter, Estelle, grew up with every sign of becoming a grand lady. She was beautiful, talented, smart, and witty. What was left of the Ballard fortune went into her debut at the Waldorf Astoria in New York City. I suppose Ballard hoped to recoup his fortunes by marrying her off to money. She had half a dozen rich suitors, but then when she turned eighteen it was like she'd become a different person. She started drinking, she turned down all proposals of marriage, and finally she showed up back in town pregnant. Old Bert locked her up in the house, and when the little girl was born he christened her Nicolette

Josephine Ballard and started all over again, raising her to be a grand lady of society while her mother drank herself to death locked away in that mausoleum of a house."

"And when Nicolette," – I shuddered at the repetition of my student's name – "turned eighteen?"

"The same thing happened all over again . . ." Dory paused at the threshold to the Lindisfarnes' bedroom and sniffed the air. Then she crossed the room toward the bathroom but stopped at the Mission-style slat bed to smooth the rumpled coverlet, her face thoughtful.

"And has it been like that ever since? One girl born each generation who falls apart after her eighteenth birthday?"

Dory looked up, her face distracted as if she were listening to something. Then she shook her head and waved a hand in front of her face as if clearing away a cobweb, although the room was spotless save for the rumpled coverlet and a damp towel lying on the bathroom floor. It looked like the Lindisfarnes might have left in a hurry and hadn't quite lived up to Dory Browne's code of neatness. "Every few generations there's a boy born, but then he runs away from the Ballard house – who could blame him? – before he's old enough to inherit and his sister follows the same pattern again. Arlette went off to Smith College, but came back after her first semester pregnant. Even JayCee finished high school and had a good job at a hotel up in Cooperstown before she came home pregnant and started drinking."

"And Nicky? She's not like that . . . Wait, how old is Nicky?"

Dory smiled sadly. "She turns eighteen on May second. Liz thought if we got her into the college and kept an eye on her maybe we could save her. The witches of Fairwick have been trying for generations to avert the Ballard curse, but the only person who can revoke a curse is a descendant of the witch who cast it. So without knowing who cast the curse . . . Well, I'm afraid it's like trying to cure a disease without a correct diagnosis." Dory wrapped her arms around her chest. "Let's get out of here," she said. "It's freezing."

CHAPTER EIGHTEEN

Dory and I checked in on a dozen more houses – some occupied, some empty. Most of the people we visited were well prepared for the blackout and didn't need our help, and most offered their help to anyone who needed it. The resourcefulness and generosity of my new neighbors would have cheered me if I hadn't been so worried about Nicky Ballard, and missing Paul. I tried him several times on my cell phone and got his voicemail each time. Maybe he was busy calling airlines or rental car companies to find a way to get here.

I remained gloomily preoccupied until we got back to Honeysuckle House in the late afternoon and I saw how it had been transformed in our absence. Brock and Ike Olsen were outside stringing electric lights in the shrubbery, which Brock turned on as we approached. The tiny white lights glittered amid the frozen branches like . . . well, like *fairy lights*. I hugged Brock, making him blush madly, and asked if he and his brother would like to stay for dinner. After a hurried confab in something that sounded like Old Norse, he said yes. When I stepped through the door I was greeted with the smells of roasting turkey and pumpkin pie, and the sounds of a crackling fire and classical music. Diana's city

guest, Jen Davies, was in the living room stoking the fire
and talking to Nicky and Mara. Nicky smiled sheepishly at
me – embarrassed, I guessed, that I'd seen her house and
met her family – but she looked healthy and young in the
firelight. I was damned if I was going to let her succumb to
some stupid old curse!

I squeezed her shoulder and accepted a glass of punch
from her. "I'm giving you the hard stuff," she said. "Mara
and I found some regular cranberry juice."

Mara held up her glass and smiled politely. "Nicky and
Jen have been explaining that here in your country young
people are not allowed to drink alcoholic beverages until
their twenty-first birthdays. Strange that they can vote and
drive and fight in your wars, but not have a glass of wine or
beer."

"Yeah, it's a strange country, all right," Jen said, taking
a generous swig of the spiked punch. "Where did you say
you were from . . . ?"

I left Jen to wield her reportorial skills on Mara and went
into the kitchen. Phoenix and Diana were basting the turkey
while Liz Book, looking like Donna Reed in pearls and a
frilly white apron, lined a pan with sweet potatoes, and
Casper Van der Aart and a slim, dark-skinned, gray-haired
man whom he introduced as Oliver arranged cream-cheese-
stuffed celery sticks and raw vegetables on a tray.

"Oh good, you're back!" Phoenix crowed when she saw
me. "Do you think you could set the table? We're going to
be twelve according to the most recent count . . . Oh, and
your boyfriend called. He says he can't get a plane out of
Buffalo and there aren't any more rental cars. He's going
to stay in Buffalo until tomorrow and see if he can get a car
then."

"So he'll have to have Thanksgiving dinner in a hotel!" I wailed.

"He didn't sound too unhappy," Liz said "Phoenix had him on the speaker phone so we all heard him and it sounded like there was a party going on. He said all the stranded passengers were going to have Thanksgiving dinner together. I imagine after sharing a life-threatening experience like that they all feel very close."

"Well, that's good, I guess . . . but still, I wish he was here. I wanted him to meet everybody." As I looked around the room – at a witch, a manic-depressive, a Mesopotamian wind spirit, a fairy and a gnome – I reflected that maybe it was just as well that I had another day adjusting to my new friends.

I was so busy for the next few hours that I didn't have time to worry about Paul. I set the table with Mara and Nicky's help (adding Brock and Ike to Phoenix's count and wondering who the additional guest was), then ran upstairs to shower and change. I was relieved to see that someone had straightened my room and thrown a shawl over the scarred headboard. The only signs of last night's debacle were the boarded up window and a drop of melted iron on the floor. While I was standing in my closet trying to decide what to wear (casual sweater and corduroys, or dressy velvet mini and satin camisole?) I thought I heard something rustling in my shoeboxes, but I decided it was unlikely that the incubus had taken up residence in among my loafers, pumps, and boots.

I decided on the velvet mini with an emerald green cashmere sweater that brought out the green in my eyes and the red in my hair. I ran downstairs just in time to let Frank

Delmarco in. He was carrying a case of beer and asking Brock and Ike if there was a set to watch the game on. All three men followed me into the kitchen. They were right behind me as I opened the door, surprising my crew of supernatural cooks in some rather surprising maneuvers. Casper van der Aart had levitated the turkey out of the pan and was rotating it in mid-air while basting it. Liz Book was caramelizing the tops of the sweet potatoes with a flame that came from her right fingertip, while Diana was coaxing a bag of potatoes to peel themselves by commanding them *Nudate unmicelettes!* As soon as they all saw Frank they dropped what they were doing – the turkey splattered grease all over the stovetop and two potatoes rolled to the floor – which is how I learned that Frank Delmarco was not in on the whole supernatural thing. (Casper's boyfriend Oliver was, though; he'd been catching the potato skins as they came off and dropping them into the trash.)

I shooed Frank, Brock, and Ike into the library and then, catching Phoenix adding more vodka to the punch, lured her into the living room with the promise of introducing her to a real *New York Times* reporter. I'd just gotten those social niceties worked out when the doorbell rang. Phoenix's count had included one more guest than I knew about, but she hadn't said who it was. I opened the door with a little prayer on my lips. *Please God, let it be a human.* I didn't think I could take any more supernatural beings today.

No such luck.

I knew instantly that the creature standing on my porch had never been human. She must have been hiding her nature before in order for me to miss it. Now, with the sun setting behind her and creating a corona of blazing light around her (I felt sure she had timed her entrance for the lighting effect), she looked unmistakably like what she undoubtedly was.

"Good evening, Professor Eldritch. Or am I supposed to address you as your majesty, Queen of the Fairies?"

"We've dispensed with such formalities since leaving Faerie," Fiona said, casting a gimlet eye on my green sweater. She was wearing a green cloak. I wondered if there was some rule of fairy protocol that only the Fairy Queen could wear green. Too bad. I looked good in green. "I hope you don't mind my inviting myself. I heard about what happened last night and I wanted to have a word with you about my incubus."

"*Your* incubus? You mean . . ." I didn't know why I didn't see this earlier, either. She looked like the Fairy Queen in the triptych – the one riding next to the Ganconer on the white horse. "The story's true? You kidnapped him and made him into a . . . demon?"

Fiona laughed – a high-pitched sound that splintered the icicles hanging from the porch roof. "Kidnapped? I wouldn't quite put it like that. For one thing, he was no kid. For another, he came quite willingly. As for what he became after . . . Well, I'm afraid that's what happens sometimes to humans who spend too much time with the fey. We tend to bring out the best and the worst in our human consorts. You might want to think about that if you plan to spend time in our company – especially with one as volatile as my Ganconer. That's what I wanted to tell you."

She smiled at me and I heard those bells again. I suddenly forgot what I'd been angry about a moment ago – forgot where I was and what day it was. I just wanted to stand here looking at Professor Fiona Eldritch, at the way her pale hair was edged with fire against the sunset, and the way her green eyes glinted like chips of ice in a deep glacial crevasse, one you might fall into and dream away an eternity . . .

"Callie, you're letting in a draft!"

It was Phoenix, shouldering me aside to see who was at the door. "Oh, Professor Eldritch. I see you found the house. Come in, let me take your cloak . . . Oh, and you've brought champagne. What fun!"

I let Phoenix escort Fiona Eldritch into the living room as if it were Phoenix's house and not mine. I was still reeling from the effects of Fiona's smile. I felt as if I'd inhaled some powerful narcotic . . . and that I'd like some more of it, please. If that was the effect of two minutes in her company then what might be the consequences of years spent with her? What good – and bad – might the company of fairies bring out in me?

It soon became clear that Fiona was set on bringing out the best in all of my guests – human and nonhuman. She told Jen Davies that she'd read her *Vogue* article and complimented Phoenix on her earrings. She told Nicky and Mara that they'd both done well on their midterms. She asked Casper to give one of his "lucid" explanations regarding the chemistry term "London dispersion force" – *such a lovely name!* – and complimented Oliver on his holiday display window in his antiques shop. Even gruff Frank Delmarco preened when she handed him the champagne bottle to open, and he and Brock and Ike all jockeyed for the seat next to her when we sat down to dinner.

She was so much the center of attention that it seemed natural that she sit at the head of the table, but she demurred and made me sit in the place of honor. When the champagne had been poured she stood and held up her crystal flute to me. An expectant silence fell over the table.

"To our gracious hostess, Cailleach McFay," she began. "Fairwick has long had a tradition of providing a refuge for the hounded and the weary—" Her green eyes travelled the length of the table, resting on each of my guests in turn. As her gaze fell upon each one their eyes brimmed and shone, as if she'd poured a drop of the sparkling champagne straight into their souls. I heard the sound of distant bells and felt that strange elation I'd felt earlier at the door "—and in opening her home to all of us, Cailleach McFay has shown herself to be truly worthy of Fairwick. May she find a home here. *Slainte!*"

Slainte! A murmur of approbation rose over the sound of bells and I found my eyes filling with tears. I ducked my head to hide my emotion. When had I last really felt like I had a home? I barely remembered the apartments I'd shared with my parents before they died. Archeologists, they were always moving from dig to dig or college to college. When they died I'd been lucky to be taken in by my grandmother, who'd done her best to take care of me – but I'd always felt like a visitor in her apartment. Living in dorm rooms and tiny sublets in college and grad school had felt natural to me. The "home" Paul and I spoke of sharing one day was an elusive mirage.

And what of Paul? A home didn't have to be made out of mortar and wood. I knew couples – my parents, I suspected – who had found their home in each other. When I met Paul in college and we talked about both working as academics I thought we'd have what my parents had: but my parents had always managed to stay together while Paul and I couldn't even manage to spend Thanksgiving dinner in the same house.

I looked up and met Liz Book's eyes. I recalled that she and Soheila and Diana had risked at least their own safety to protect me from the incubus last night. Diana had definitely risked her very life. And Brock had been trying all these months to protect me with his iron locks, dream catchers, and doormice. I looked over at Nicky Ballard, who was holding up a champagne flute of cranberry juice to which had been added a drop of champagne. What did she think of when she heard the word *home*? I'd promised her grandmother today that I would look after her, and I'd promised myself that I'd avert the curse that hung over her. What bound a person more than obligation? I had only been in Fairwick for a few short months and already I felt more at home here than I'd ever felt anywhere else.

I raised my glass and clinked it against Fiona's. The crystal rang clear as a bell, echoed by the chiming of all the glasses as my guests – my new friends and colleagues – clinked their glasses against their neighbor's. It sounded like a hundred tiny crystal bells chiming in a large echoing hall – I could almost see the hall, a vaulted cathedral ribbed with tree branches and paned in brilliant stained glass – a sound that took all the sadness, the *homesickness*, I'd been feeling and made it swell into something else.

"To new friends," I said, holding my glass up to the assembled company. "And absent ones," I added, thinking of Paul.

"Hear! hear!," someone – and then everyone – said. Then there was silence as we all sipped our champagne. A thousand icy bubbles exploded in my mouth. It was so dry I felt as if I were drinking air – delightfully clean mountain air. Only the aftertaste – a strange and subtle combination of oak, crisp apples and honeysuckle – told me that the liquid had gone down my throat.

"Mmm," Phoenix moaned, a hand dramatically splayed over her heart. "It tastes like the first drink I ever had, which was a champagne cocktail at the Plaza on a hot summer night."

"The first drink I ever had," Oliver said while passing a plate of sweet potatoes to me, "was a tequila sunrise at Studio 54. I thought I'd died and gone to heaven."

"Mine was a vodka martini at the Lotus Club," Dean Book volunteered, blushing as she spooned mashed potatoes onto her plate.

We all went around sharing our first drink stories, Mara and Nicky demurely abstaining, as we passed the serving dishes among us. The room filled with the smells of turkey and sweet potatoes, and the clink of china and silverware. The food was delicious – the turkey moist, the sweet potatoes glazed with a delicate carmelized layer of brown sugar. There were roasted chestnuts in the stuffing and tiny translucent pearl onions in the peas. The conversation sailed from first drinks to first kisses to first memorable movies. At first the older – and less human – among us kept their reminiscences somewhat vague or at least confined to the last century. But as we all drank more – although I had seen Fiona arrive with only one bottle of champagne there seemed to be an endless supply – the fairies and other supernatural creatures at the table told stories of parties on Cleopatra's barge and at King Arthur's court. Those who weren't in on the secret of Fairwick seemed undisturbed by these incredible details. Jen Davies was more interested in hearing the details of Phoenix's childhood than in Casper

Van der Aart's tale of sailing on a merchant ship to the West Indies; Nicky Ballard seemed to think that Dory Browne was describing the plot of a historical novel she was writing; and Frank Delmarco was talking sports with Brock and Ike. Only Mara Marinca sat wide-eyed and silent. Perhaps the single drop of champagne she'd drunk hadn't been enough to put her under the same spell as the rest of us – or perhaps she simply mistrusted her English.

I wondered what Paul would have made of all this. I couldn't imagine him falling under any spell or suspending an atom of disbelief. What would he say if I tried to tell him what had happened last night? Would he think I was crazy? Perhaps it was better he hadn't made it. I felt guilty thinking that, but then Fiona refilled my glass and I forgot about everything but the present moment.

After dinner we repaired to the living room where we all rubbed our stomachs and moaned, although in truth I didn't feel uncomfortably full despite all I'd eaten, or drunk despite all I'd had to drink. I just felt content. Brock built up the fire and Casper produced a bottle of very old cognac. We drank it with pumpkin pie and played Trivial Pursuit. Frank Delmarco won twice, which was pretty impressive considering he was playing against a gnome and two ancient Norse divinities.

After the third game, Nicky and Mara said their farewells and left with a pile of leftovers that Dory had packed for them. Phoenix took Jen into the library to show her press clippings. I suddenly realized that Fiona, Soheila, Diana and Liz were all in the kitchen, no doubt doing dishes. Guiltily, I collected the pie plates and headed back, pausing at the door to pick up a fork that had fallen to the floor – which put my ear level with the old-fashioned keyhole.

"Are you sure he's gone?" I heard Fiona ask.

"Diana and I performed the banishment spell while Soheila chanted the . . ."

I missed the next few words in a clatter of dishes. Fiona asked something else in a low, urgent voice and Soheila answered.

"He was moments away from incarnating. I've never seen an incubus gain flesh so quickly. He must be very drawn to her . . ."

"It has nothing to do with her," Fiona spat back. All her lovely graces had fallen away. Even with a wooden door between us I felt waves of cold rolling off her. Even Liz Book, who had managed to remain poised and calm in the face of a demon's tantrum, sounded cowed.

"Of course not, my lady. We were afraid he'd try to find an entrance back through anyone who lived in this house. She is merely a conduit, but perhaps a powerful one. She opened the door on her first day here and today I saw her reach into it and pull a satyr to safety."

Fiona sniffed. "So she's a doorkeeper. Good. We can always use one of those – especially after what happened to the last one. Just be careful whom she lets in. You know as well as I do that there are *things* lurking on the threshold that make my incubus look like a puppy dog."

I stood up then, tired of eavesdropping in my own house. I rattled the dishes in my hand to give them some warning and shouldered open the door. By the time I was across the doorway they were talking about Diana's recipe for pecan pie as if they were on the Food Network.

The last of my guests left by eight, except for Jen Davies who was curled up in the library drinking Casper's cognac and listening wide-eyed to Phoenix's adventures of growing up dysfunctional in the Deep South. I excused myself and went upstairs to call Paul. He was at the hotel bar, eating Buffalo hot wings with Stacy, Mack and Rita, his three new "survivor" friends.

"Stacy and Mack live in Ithaca and Rita's in Binghamton so we're all going to split a car tomorrow. I should be there by one at the latest."

"That's great," I said. "I really missed you today. I've been thinking . . . Well, we really have to try to find some way to spend real time together. I could spend the Christmas break in California . . ."

"I thought you wanted to spend Christmas in your new home," he said.

"That doesn't matter." I gripped the phone hard to give myself the courage to say what I had to say. "What matters is that we spend it together. I want *you* to be my home, Paul, and for me to be yours. If we can't be that for each other . . . Well, then, what are we doing?" I swallowed back the tears – a pause long enough that Paul could have filled it with some reassurance, but he was silent. Maybe he didn't know any better than I the answer to my question. "Because whatever it is we're doing, I'm not sure I can do it any longer." I bit my lip and made myself be quiet to give Paul a chance to answer. I waited . . . and waited. Then I held the phone up and saw that AT&T had dropped the call. I had no way of knowing how long ago.

Fifteen minutes later when I was in the tub, Paul texted me.

Lost u! CU tom. <3 P

I texted back a heart and my initial, but I was beginning to wonder if we hadn't already lost each other.

CHAPTER NINETEEN

Paul never made it to Fairwick that weekend. He made it as far as West Thalia and called to tell me that the road leading into Fairwick (one of only two) was blocked by fallen trees. Suspecting that might be the case I had gotten up early (after a sterile dreamless sleep) and started hiking toward the West Thalia road. When I'd reached the outskirts of town I'd found something that looked like a logjam. Trees lay like pick-up sticks across the highway for miles. When I asked one of the road crew clearing the debris how far the wreckage went he told me more than ten miles.

"The bridge is out here and on the southbound road," he told me. "No one's coming into or getting out of Fairwick until the middle of next week."

I stayed on the edge of town for another hour, talking to Paul on the phone, unable to believe that there wasn't any way to bridge the short gap between us. But Fairwick was wedged into a valley between steep, impassable mountains like some medieval fortress town built to keep out plague and marauding Vikings. After all, its founders – fairy and daemon – probably remembered both threats well enough. Now one of those demons had lifted the drawbridge and flooded the moats, cutting the town off from the world. Had that been his intention? I'd thought at first that the storm and the destruction left in its wake had been the outcome of his temper, but now, looking at this swath of mown down trees, I wondered if the incubus had purposely cut me off from Paul—

And purposely set out to kill him by bringing down his plane.

"I could start walking and maybe I'd be there by tomorrow morning," Paul gallantly offered in our last phone conversation that day.

I imagined Paul alone on the West Thalia road as night fell, the deep woods on either side full of otherworldly creatures, possibly including an insanely jealous incubus.

"That's sweet, Paul, but it's supposed to go down into the teens tonight. You don't have to freeze yourself to see me."

"Yeah, maybe you're right. I did forgot to pack my boots and the shoes I'm wearing are pretty thin. I guess I'll go visit Adam in Binghamton." Adam was a friend of Paul's from high school who was in the graduate writing program at Binghamton University. "Rita's driving there anyway."

"Tell Adam I say hi," I said, and then, glancing down at a particularly savaged tree trunk, added, "And be careful driving there, okay? The weather up here is . . . unpredictable."

It was dusk by the time I got back home, and I was frozen and exhausted. I found Phoenix pacing the house like a caged panther.

"I can't believe we're stuck here," she said when I told her both roads out of town were impassable. "What if there's an emergency?"

"There's a hospital here in town and they could still Medi-Vac any bad cases out to Cooperstown," I pointed out.

"What if there were too many fires for the local fire department to put out . . . or a serial killer struck . . . or gangs started looting? This is just like that Stephen King book where a small town is trapped under an invisible dome. The whole town goes to hell in a hand basket!"

It was my fault Phoenix had read that particular Stephen King book which I'd gleefully devoured a few weeks before. I'd been thinking about it, too, on my walk back through town but Fairwick didn't seem to be going the way of King's small town. Main Street had been bustling with cheerful people strolling on the cleared and salted sidewalks, and congregating at corners to compare storm survival stories. A hot apple cider and donut hut had been set up in a little kiosk in the park. Ice skaters were gliding on the pond. I glimpsed Ike skating with a woman who looked like she was one of Dory Browne's relatives and Nicky Ballard huddled on a bench with a boy in a community college sweatshirt who must have been her boyfriend, Ben. The houses I passed on my way up the hill either had generators on or lanterns in their windows. Many homeowners had put up their Christmas decorations. There were the usual plastic reindeer and inflatable Santas, but also a type of decoration I'd never seen before. Among the branches of the light-trimmed trees hung crystal bells, pinecones, doves and angels. When I got closer I saw that they weren't made of crystal; they were molded out of ice. Trapped within the shapes were tiny objects – natural things like real pinecones and red berries, but also gold charms, children's toys (I saw a pink-haired troll doll and a blue Power Ranger), keys, and tiny scrolls of paper tied with red string.

"Ice gifts," Brock told me when I got home and found him hanging an ice dove from a holly bush near my front door. He showed me the baking mold he was using to make a frozen angel and explained that there was a local tradition of putting small objects inside as offerings to the spirits of the woods. "Where I came from," Brock told me as he poured water into more molds, "it was believed that an object left over winter in the ice would gain power. Humans would leave offerings to the gods inside the ice shapes and the gods, in turn, would leave presents for the humans they loved in them. My father courted my mother Freya so. Each year he made a trinket for her – a pair of earrings, a bracelet, a necklace – and encased it in an ice dove. 'I will wait for you as long as it takes the ice fields of Jotunheim to melt,' he told her each year. In the fifth year he made her a wedding ring. That year Freya built a fire beneath the tree where the ice dove hung. When the dove melted, Freya held out her hand to catch the ring, crying, 'Jotunheim is melted. Come to me now!' When my father arrived the fire leapt up to meet him and it burnt Freya's little finger."

He held out his hand, which, I had noticed before, was missing the tip of his little finger. "My brothers and I were all born missing the tip of our little fingers – testament to the love our human mother felt for our father. Since she was human she died very long ago, but—" Brock looked up at me, his ugly face transformed by tenderness "—I remember her as if she had just left the room, so powerful is the love you humans possess."

I blushed remembering what Dory had told me about the relations between fey and human, but clearly Brock's mother hadn't been trading sex for magic and Brock's father must have loved her for his sons to hold her memory so dear. I dug in my pocket and found the fairy stone I'd been carrying since we'd performed the incubus banishment two nights ago.

"Here," I said, dropping the stone into the water. "My father gave this to me. He told me that it would keep me from having nightmares. Maybe it will do more good out here than in my pocket."

Brock looked at the hollow stone. "It might just," he said. "Sometimes giving something away gives it more power."

After Brock left I tried distracting Phoenix from her doom-laden scenarios by taking her outside and showing her the ice sculptures Brock had hung in the shrubbery – in addition to the dove there were ice deer and ice angels . . . or maybe they were ice fairies – but she only shivered and retreated back inside to a nest she'd made on the library couch of blankets, magazines, and newspapers. She spent the rest of the holiday weekend there, sipping cognac and reading aloud from favorable reviews of her book. Maybe it was her way of coping with the supernatural revelations of the last few days, or maybe her southern blood really was too thin for the cold. I figured she would snap out of it when classes started on Monday.

But classes didn't start on Monday. The roads were finally clear and the bridge on the southbound road was working, but the Trailways bus that ran from New York City was too heavy for that bridge. Dean Book postponed the first day of classes to Wednesday.

I used the time to read up on the history of Fairwick in the archives of the town newspaper, especially on the Ballard family. In addition to what Dory had told me, I learned that Ballard's partner, Hiram Scudder, had left town after his wife had killed herself and gone out west to remake his life.

I read a graphic description of the collision, along with a heroic account of a track worker named Ernesto Fortino who had crawled into a train car hanging off a bridge. He had got all the occupants to safety before the train car crashed into the river, killing him. I looked long at a heartbreaking picture of corpses wrapped in burlap sacks, lined up like cordwood at the side of the mangled train track. I read the lists of the dead and then the lists of people who went bankrupt after the railroad and ironworks went out of business. The number of people who might have wanted to curse Bertram Ballard was vast. No wonder the witches of Fairwick hadn't been able to identify who had cast the curse.

At night in bed I read a Dahlia LaMotte manuscript called *The Viking Raider,* in which a rugged handsome Norseman kidnaps an Irish princess and holds her for ransom. One particular passage caught my eye.

The brute tore my tunic away and fondled my breasts. Because my hands were tied I could do nothing but endure the sensation of his rough, calloused hands squeezing my nipples, cupping my breasts, stroking my belly and pushing his hard blunt fingers between my legs. When I cried out he clamped his hand over my mouth . . . and I sank my teeth into his little finger. I bit so hard I took the tip off. He screamed in pain, but rather than strike me he held up his injured hand and exclaimed, "What spirits you Irish lasses possess! I will treasure this as a keepsake of our courtship for all the years of our long marriage."

I wondered if Dahlia had been thinking of Brock when she wrote this scene – and if so, what it said about her feelings for him.

When I wasn't indulging in Dahlia LaMotte's bodice-ripping tales, I set to work re-organizing my closets. Something was rustling in there and I'd begun to suspect that I had mice. Small holes had been gnawed in my cardboard shoeboxes, and my favorite pair of Christian Louboutin silver patent leather sling-backs had been chewed into Swiss cheese. I went to the dollar store in town and bought plastic shoeboxes and mousetraps – which I couldn't bring myself to set.

Phoenix used the time to drink and make a scrapbook of her reviews. On Wednesday morning, determined to get her up early enough that she'd make it sober to her afternoon class, I made a big pot of coffee and a stack of banana walnut pancakes. I brought it all into the library on a tray along with the *New York Times*.

"Look," I said, brandishing the paper. "Proof we are once again connected to the civilized world! Tiffany ads! Gail Collins! A recipe for vegan banana-chocolate chip cookies! And hey, here's an article by that woman Jen Davies . . ."

"Is it about me?" Phoenix asked in a very small voice, which held no trace of a southern accent.

I sank to the couch onto a pile of cut-up magazines, my eyes riveted to the page. "Um, yes . . . it appears to be . . ." I read the entire article and looked up. Two wide, blood-shot eyes stared out at me from a rat's nest of tangled hair. "It says that you didn't grow up in a dysfunctional family in Alabama. And that your mother didn't abandon you with strangers in a trailer park when you were thirteen . . . and you didn't spend two years at a state mental hospital. It says that your real name is Betsy Ross Middlefield and that you grew up in Darien, Connecticut, with your father, who is an insurance executive and your mother, Mary Ellen, who belongs to the DAR and runs an interior decorating company."

Phoenix shook her head, dislodging a feather that had leaked out of the comforter. "Mother's name is Mary Alice," she said, "not Mary Ellen. She's going to be really pissed when she sees this." She burrowed down under the blankets and covered her head.

I took the tray and the paper back into the kitchen, then sat at the table and reread the article twice. Then I sat staring out the back door at the frozen terrain. I'd had a lot of shocks since I'd come to Fairwick. I'd discovered that the man in my erotic dreams was a real incubus, that my boss was a witch and my next-door neighbor an ancient deer-fairy. My colleagues were demons, witches and fairies. My favorite student was under a curse that was going to ruin her life. I lived in a town that straddled two worlds and apparently I had a hidden talent for opening the door between those worlds. I shouldn't have been thrown by one mendacious memoirist – Phoenix certainly wasn't the first – but I was. Badly thrown. Phoenix had been my roommate for three months. Although she was a little wacky, I'd come to like her. She was funny and generous and cared about her students . . . or at least *one* of them. I'd known her to be careless, silly, and vain, but never mean. I'd enjoyed listening to her crazy stories, but now I knew that they'd all been lies. And it wasn't as if she'd been lying to cover up some secret supernatural identity. She'd been lying because . . . Well, I didn't know why she'd been lying. If she ever got off the couch perhaps I'd ask her.

But right now I had to go or I'd be late for class. I went back into the library and sat down on the couch by Phoenix's feet, moving aside a stack of newspapers and the purple folder that contained Mara Marinca's work.

"Look," I said to the frizz of hair peeking up over the quilt. "I've been meaning to tell you that I've been reading your mem—book, and I think it's really good. Maybe you were meant to be a novelist and not a memoirist. This story will blow over sooner or later. Look at James Frey! He's still publishing."

"I'll have to give back my advance," a small voice moaned from beneath the blankets. "And I'll be fired."

"I don't know about the advance, but if you like I'll talk to Dean Book."

"Would you?" Phoenix's sharp nose and big eyes appeared over the edge of the quilt. She looked like the wolf hiding in the grandmother's bed in Little Red Riding Hood.

"Sure. I'll call her on my way to class. Why don't you get up, take a shower, have breakfast . . ." Sober up, I wanted to add, but didn't. "And whatever you do, don't answer your phone or any emails from reporters."

I was going to tell her to stay in, but then I realized that wouldn't be necessary. She hadn't left the house in days. Honeysuckle House had its second writer recluse.

I called Dean Book on my cell as soon as I was out of earshot of the house. She answered on the first ring.

"I just read the story," she said without preamble. "How's Phoenix?"

"Stricken. She must have realized that minx Jen Davies was on to her because she's been sulking all weekend."

Dean Book called the Australian reporter something rather stronger than "minx."

"Are you going to fire Phoenix?" I asked.

"I have to talk to the board, but I'd like to hear Phoenix's story first. Is she at your house?"

I'd reached the entrance to campus. I turned around before entering the gates and looked back at Honeysuckle House, visible now since Ike had trimmed the hedges back. I thought I saw a shadow move near the back of the house, but it was only a shrub swaying in the wind. "Yes, she's there. I don't think she's going anywhere."

"Good. I'll come by in half an hour to see her. May I use the key under the gnome if she doesn't let me in?"

I told Dean Book she could without bothering to ask how she knew about the hidden key and was about to hang up when she asked me one more question. "There hasn't been any further sign of . . . *him*, has there?"

"No," I answered, making my voice upbeat. "Not a trace. Nada. Zip. Elvis has left the building."

Dean Book took so long to reply I thought AT&T had dropped another call. I half-hoped it had and she'd missed my lame attempt at levity. But after a beat she replied. "Good. One less thing to worry about. Have a good class, Callie."

I did have a good class. I'd asked them to read a Victoria Holt novel over the break, suspecting that a pocket-sized romance novel might be a better travel companion than one of the heavy eighteenth century novels we'd been reading.

"It was great," Jeanine Marfalla, a pretty sophomore from the suburbs of Boston enthused. "I read the whole thing on the train ride home and bought two more of her books at a used bookstore."

Nicky said that her favorite part was when the heroine hears the hero murmuring German endearments at her locked door.

"It gave me chills," she said. Nicky looked better for the break, rested and well fed. Mara, however, wasn't in the class at all. When I asked Nicky after class where Mara was, she blushed and told me that she wasn't sure because she hadn't been back to her dorm room yet. She'd spent the break in town with Ben. I suppressed a jealous pang that she had gotten to spend time with her boyfriend and I hadn't.

I checked my phone and found a text message from Liz Book asking me if I wouldn't mind taking Phoenix's workshop for her. I texted back that I'd be happy to and asked how Phoenix was doing.

Not great, the dean texted back, *come back right after you're done with her class*.

When I walked into the writing workshop the first person I noticed was Mara. She looked embarrassed to see me. "I am so sorry to miss your class, Professor McFay. I got used to sleeping late on the vacation and overslept this morning." She looked awful – exhausted and bone thin – and yet I'd recalled her eating quite heartily at Thanksgiving. I wondered if she was bulimic.

"That's okay, Mara. You can make it up to me by telling me what Phoenix assigned over the break."

"Oh, she never assigns anything," Mara answered. "She just tells us to keep going with our memoirs. To dig down to the bitter roots, as she always says."

"The roots of truth," another student, a boy in leather and piercings, added in a mocking tone.

"Where the real dirt lies," another volunteered.

Clearly Phoenix's students had memorized her adages. Unfortunately they all revolved on the theme of telling the truth. What would these students think when they found out that her entire memoir was fake?

I asked if anyone would be willing to read aloud what they'd written over the break. A few students raised their hands, but when Mara raised hers they put theirs down. Wow, I thought, it's like they've been trained. I called on Nicky.

"Um . . . I actually wrote about why I don't like memoirs," Nicky said sheepishly.

"Well, then," I said, exasperated. "Read that."

So Nicky got up and read something she called "Household Ghosts," a vivid evocation of her house and the people who lived in it.

"Sometimes I think it would be better to forget the past and focus on the future," she concluded. "I suppose that's why I don't really feel comfortable with this assignment. I grew up surrounded by ghosts of the past, ghosts shaped like the silk cotillion dresses rotting inside dusty armoires and like the dead wrapped in burlap sacks beside the railroad tracks. Wouldn't it be better to let those ghosts rest in peace?"

I walked home haunted by the last image in Nicky's piece – the bodies wrapped in burlap sacks that she must have gotten from the photographs of the '93 train crash—a crash possibly caused by her great-great-grandfather's negligence. What must it feel like to grow up in a town with that family history? You wouldn't have to be under a curse to feel like you were.

My musings were cut short by an ear-splitting shriek. It sounded like someone was being torn limb from limb and it came from my house. I broke into a run and nearly fell on the still-slick street. I forced myself into a brisk walk, keeping my eyes on the street for patches of ice. When I reached my house I halted on the front path, as frozen by the tableau on my front porch as the ice doves and angels hanging in the trees. Phoenix – or Betsy Ross Middlefield, as I supposed I should think of her – was standing on the porch in her purple chenille bathrobe, hair wild and loose in the breeze, both arms wrapped around a column.

"I can't go!" Phoenix wailed. "The demon will find me if I go outside. We chased it out of the house, but I saw it before looking in through the kitchen window! It's just waiting for me to leave the house before pouncing on me!"

A sixty-ish woman with impeccably cut and styled ash blonde hair, wearing a slim camel hair coat, stood beside Phoenix, her lips pressed together, one gloved hand resting on Phoenix's back.

"There, there, Betsy," I heard her saying. "There are no demons at McLean. You remember Dr. Cavett, don't you?"

I saw the man she referred to standing in the shadows of the porch with Dean Book. He was a short balding man in a checked blazer and rust-colored turtleneck. He looked frightened of all the females on the porch, perhaps most of all by Dean Book bristling in her heavy fur coat. She came forward when she saw me and the sunlight rippled across the deep brown fur. For a moment the pelt seemed to move on its own, as if a large furry creature held the dean in its grip. I blinked and the illusion faded . . . if it *had* been an illusion.

"Oh, Callie, I'm glad you're here. I've been explaining to Dr. Cavett that some of Phoenix's notions about demons and incubi might have come out of your research."

"Her name is Betsy, not Phoenix," the woman in the camel hair coat insisted. "She was named after her grandmother who was a descendant of Betsy Ross and it's a perfectly good name."

"I hate it, Mother," Phoenix cried – no matter how hard I tried I just couldn't think of her as *Betsy*. "I've told you that a million times. And I hate being named after my crazy grandmother and I hate McLean. I'm a writer – an artist! – and I have an idea for a new book about what I've experienced here at Fairwick, but I need to stay here at Honeysuckle House to write it."

"Where there's a *demon* waiting outside the house to pounce on you?" her mother asked, her voice icily mocking.

Phoenix's bloodshot eyes skittered from her mother to me. If she asked me to corroborate her story, what would I say? I didn't want it on my conscience that Phoenix was dragged off to a mental hospital . . . but neither did I want to be dragged off to one myself. But Phoenix didn't ask me to testify that the house had lately been occupied by a demon.

"Oh Callie, you took over my class, didn't you? Did you see Mara? Did she ask for me? Did she give you any more of her memoir for me to read?" Then turning back to her mother, she said, "You see I can't possibly leave. Mara Marinca is depending on me."

Dean Book glanced nervously at me. I imagined she was thinking the same thing I was – that Phoenix's obsession with Mara was no healthier than her fixation on the demon.

"All your students asked for you," I fibbed. "Nicky Ballard read something . . ."

Phoenix waved away my mention of Nicky. "It's Mara who matters!" she shrieked. "Mara who must learn to tell the truth. She mustn't think I lied. I have to explain."

Dean Book sighed. "Perhaps it's better if you explain everything to your students *after* you've had a nice rest."

Then, turning to Phoenix's mother and doctor, she added, "I can't have her upsetting her students in this state." She turned once again to Phoenix. "But once you're more yourself, we can consider having you come back."

It was an unfortunate choice of words. "I *am* myself! Who else would I be?" Phoenix screamed, and flung herself at the dean. She only meant, I think, to throw herself on the dean's mercy, but she came at Liz with such force that she knocked her back several feet. Liz tottered for a moment, her arms flailing to keep her balance. I stepped forward to help her while the doctor and Mrs. Middlefield tried to restrain Phoenix. They were between Liz and Phoenix, their backs to Liz, so they didn't see what happened next. They didn't see the shadow thrown by Liz rear up on the wall – a huge bear-like creature with claws and an enormous mouth stretched wide in a toothy snarl. But I saw it, and so did Phoenix. She screamed one more time, a scream that sounded so insane that I couldn't blame Dr. Cavett for sticking her with a tranquilizer needle. As Phoenix's screams subsided into soft whimpers, I had half a mind to ask for some of the tranquilizer myself.

CHAPTER TWENTY

With Phoenix gone, Honeysuckle House felt truly empty. I had driven out the incubus – and the incubus had, in turn, driven out my roommate.

Liz Book, after explaining to me that the bear-shaped shadow I'd seen on the wall was her familiar, Ursuline (and promising to tell me more about *that* later), said I shouldn't look at it that way. Phoenix had been clearly troubled to begin with and the real tipping point for her had been the exposure of her fraudulent memoir. But I felt sure it had been the exorcism and its aftermath that had driven Phoenix over the edge. Why else would she have gone on about demons the way she had?

"Besides, we don't know that *he* didn't bring Jen Davies here to expose Phoenix," I pointed out. "After all, he downed a plane two hundred miles to the west and created a ring of ice around a town so my boyfriend couldn't spend Thanksgiving with me."

I knew I sounded paranoid, but I thought I could be excused a little anxiety after what I'd been through. Having failed to gain my love, the incubus had decided that I'd have to be all by myself.

Well, I'd show him. I didn't mind living alone and I

wasn't going to flip out like Phoenix. I was determined to buckle down for what remained of the semester. I had plenty of work because I'd offered to take Phoenix's class until Dean Book could find a replacement, which probably wouldn't be until after the winter break. The first thing I found out from the class was that Phoenix hadn't returned anyone's work since the beginning of the semester. I promised I would rectify that situation right away – and sat myself down to spend the weekend reading the life stories of thirty-four college-age students.

You wouldn't have thought they'd have that much life to write about – but you would have been wrong. I read the story of a girl from central Africa who'd fled her native country to avoid genital mutilation. I read a brief, but poignant, account by Flonia Rugova of how she and her mother had fled Albania. Not all the students came from exotic backgrounds. Richie Esposito from the Bronx had handed in a graphic novel in which rival gangs of rats, roaches and pigeons fought for control of the city after a nuclear apocalypse.

I read Nicky Ballard's work with particular attention, searching for clues to the Ballard curse, but Nicky hadn't written much.

I reread the piece Nicky called "Household Ghosts" that she had read in class. She had written below the last line, "I'd really like to work on poetry this semester."

At the bottom of the page Phoenix had scrawled, "YOU MUST CONFRONT YOUR GHOSTS!!!" But I understood where Nicky was coming from. My grandmother Adelaide had made a fetish of our family's origins, which went back to the Mayflower. She was always going off to some D.A.R. event or to her club – a fusty place called the Grove where all the faded gentry of New York society gathered to compare their family trees. The place had given me the creeps; I was always afraid I was going to use the wrong fork or break the eggshell-thin teacups.

I crossed out Phoenix's comment and wrote: *I love the images in your writing. Why don't you try some poems?*

Then I took out the Xeroxed copy I'd made of the list of the people who had died in the Ulster & Clare Great Crash of '93. I'd start researching each of the names this week. It was one thing to tell Nicky to move on from her ghosts, but until I found the ghost who had cursed her she was going to be trapped in that moldering house.

The one student whose work I didn't get to read was Mara Marinca's. The purple folder containing her memoir in progress was missing. I spoke to Liz about it and she called Phoenix's mother to see if Phoenix had the folder when she checked into McLean, but Mrs. Middlefield insisted that she didn't. "She kept asking us to send for that girl's writing, but of course we told her we couldn't."

I searched the whole house for the folder – or any stray scrap of Mara's writing. I recalled seeing the folder in the library before I went to class the day Phoenix was taken away. Perhaps if she had thought that someone – the *demon*, she'd said – was trying to break in to steal the papers she might have hidden them. But as hard as I looked the only things I found of Phoenix's were half-empty liquor bottles stashed in a dozen clever hiding places.

I saved Mara's conference for last on Monday, dreading the moment when I'd have to tell her that everything she'd written that semester was missing.

"Phoenix spoke very highly of your writing ability," I told her. "If you print out another copy I'll be happy to read it."

"Print out?" Mara asked, her pale, tea-colored eyes staring at me dumbly.

I suppressed a twinge of impatience. Her command of English certainly seemed to come and go randomly.

"Yes, from your computer. If you don't have a printer I believe you can send a file to the campus printing center. Or you could just send me a copy by email."

"But I don't make my writing on the computer. I make it with pen. On paper."

"Oh," I said, my heart sinking. "I don't suppose you made copies."

Mara shook her head. "I never thought that was necessary. These things I wrote . . . they were just . . ." Mara pinched her fingers together and made a series of loops in the air. For a moment I imagined I saw writing in the air – strange runic symbols that hovered like fireflies – but then I blinked and the images faded. "How do you say? Scribbles?"

"Phoenix didn't think they were scribbles," I said, rubbing my eyes. "She was quite taken by what you wrote."

Mara smiled sadly. "I am afraid so taken she was taken away. Maybe it is not so good for me to write about the terrible things I have seen. Perhaps putting them into words makes them more real and does no one good."

"But it won't do you any good to keep those things inside. Perhaps you should talk to someone. Dr. Lilly, for instance."

Mara sniffed. "I have spoken to her, but she doesn't understand."

It seemed to me that Soheila Lilly was exactly the person who would understand the anguish of exile, but like many young people Mara didn't think an older person could understand her experiences. "How about Flonia Rugova?" I asked. "She's from Albania, which is close to your country."

Mara cast her eyes down as she often did when her homeland was alluded to, but when she glanced up her eyes were narrowed with interest. "Hmm . . . perhaps you are right. Flonia and I might have much in common and it would be nice to have someone to talk to. Nicolette is very busy now with her boyfriend, Benjamin. She doesn't even come back to our room at night . . . oh!" Mara clapped her hand to her mouth. "Perhaps I should not have said that. I do not want to get Nicolette in trouble."

"It's okay, Mara. I don't think Fairwick has a curfew. But I can see how that might be lonely for you. Maybe you should try to make some new friends . . . get to know some of the other students better."

Mara gave me the biggest smile I'd ever seen on her – or on anyone else, for that matter. Her mouth was unusually wide . . . and full of really bad teeth. "Yes, that is what I'll do. Starting with Flonia Rugova. And as for the writing class . . . would it be okay if I didn't hand anything in for a while? Just until I decide what I want to write?"

"I suppose that will be all right until Phoenix's replacement arrives," I said uneasily. I didn't like the idea of letting a student off the hook so readily. But then, she had done more than her share already and it would give the other students a chance to get their work read. And besides, I guiltily admitted to myself, at least now I'd be spared reading about the horrors that she'd lived through.

I didn't feel so easy about my conference with Mara afterward. I spent that night restlessly prowling through my empty house, haunted by the feeling that something was really wrong with the girl and determined to find her folder if it was still in the house. The fact that I didn't really want to read it just made me look all the harder to assuage my conscience. I looked everywhere that Phoenix might think to hide papers – through the kitchen cabinets and the china hutches, behind the books in the library, in between the stacks of Dahlia LaMotte's manuscripts, in my own desk (checking again that the one locked drawer was still locked even though it was much too small to hold Mara's folder) and closets, and, finally, in the attic.

I left the attic until last because I didn't like going up there alone. I had a feeling that if the incubus were lurking anywhere in the house that's where he'd be – beneath the steeply pitched roof, among the tea chests and forlorn broken furniture. When I switched on the light and the overhead bulb popped I had to resist the urge to give up, but I made myself go downstairs for one of the battery-operated lanterns Dory Browne had given me in case of any more power outages. I came back holding the lantern over my head, sweeping its light across the dusty floor and into every nook and cranny. I'd covered most of the area when the light swept into the far west eave . . . and a scrap of shadow skittered across the floor.

I nearly dropped the lantern. Instead I swung it in the direction the shadow had sped, sending the shadow-thing scurrying into an open tea chest. My heart hammering, I pounced on the tea chest and slammed the lid. Whatever was inside flung itself up against the lid, making a sickening thump that reverberated inside my own chest.

Shit, what now? Should I lock the chest and bring it to Liz Book?

But then I remembered that the tea chests, built to keep precious tealeaves dry on long ocean voyages, were airtight. If I'd caught something alive in there it would be dead by the time I brought it to Liz's house.

Which shouldn't be a problem. If it was the incubus then he couldn't suffocate . . . right? And if it was an animal that had taken up residence in my attic then I was best rid of it . . . right?

Another thump rattled the box. Whatever was inside, it was mad. Or afraid.

Shit.

I balanced the lantern on top of a nearby broken chair so that its light shone onto the lid of the tea chest. Then, crouching on my toes so that I could move fast, I put a hand on either side of the box and lifted the lid.

Two beady black eyes set in a tiny furry face stared up at me. If the creature had moved a centimeter I would have screamed and run, but the mouse sat perfectly still on its haunches holding its tiny pink paws up in front of the white ruff on its chest as if it were praying for leniency – a posture that struck me as familiar. I peered over at the mouse's tail and saw a short stump instead.

"It's you!" I said. "The tailless doormouse. You didn't explode!"

The mouse cocked its head and twitched its small pink ears. It was, I had to admit, kind of cute.

"I'm glad you survived," I said, feeling a little stupid addressing a mouse, but hey, I'd done stranger things lately. "I'm sorry your little friends didn't."

The mouse squeaked and rubbed a tiny paw across its face, as if washing itself . . . or brushing away a tear.

"Aw, are you crying?" I put my hand into the tea

chest, palm up. "Come here, little guy. I won't hurt you."

The mouse looked at my hand for a few long seconds, then stretched its neck toward it and sniffed at my fingertips, which were still blistered from when I'd grabbed him during the exorcism. What if it bit me? Could magical-iron-doormice-come-to-life carry rabies? But the mouse didn't bite me. Instead he licked my blistered fingertips and crawled into my hand. Then he turned around twice and curled up into a ball, tucked the stub of his tail beneath his haunches, rested his pink nose on top of his paws, and looked up at me.

I laughed. "Okay, you're pretty darn cute. Let's go get you something to eat."

I named him Ralph after the mouse in Beverly Cleary's *The Mouse and the Motorcycle*, one of my favorite books when I was growing up. Ralph the Doormouse – it had a nice ring to it. After I fed him some cheese, lettuce, and carrots, I took him back upstairs in a basket lined with a dishtowel. I put him on my desk while I made my nightly call to Paul. He curled up and listened with one eye open as I told Paul about my conference with Mara.

"It sounds like she's trying to get out of doing any more work for the semester. You can't be so easy on your students, Cal. They'll walk all over you."

We'd had this argument before. Paul had only been teaching for a couple of years, but already he seemed burned out by the emotional demands his students made on him. I had to agree that in this era of email and texting, the self-esteem generation could be demanding and annoying to deal with (I'd actually had students at Columbia who wanted to know why I didn't buy an iPhone or BlackBerry so I could answer their emails immediately), but it was really only a handful of students who acted as if they were entitled to their professor's undivided attention. Paul treated every student as a potential threat to his time and tenure opportunities. Sometimes I wondered if he'd be happier in a line of work that didn't involve teaching.

When I said good night to Paul, I saw that Ralph had fallen asleep. I left his basket on the desk and went to bed. I suppose it was an indicator of how lonely I'd felt since Phoenix left that having a mouse sleeping in my room made me feel better.

I reached for a student paper to read before going to sleep but picked up instead one of Dahlia LaMotte's notebooks. I wasn't sure that reading erotica was what I needed right now, but I just couldn't bear to read another student paper – and I was pretty hooked on *The Viking Raider*. It was the only manuscript I'd read so far in which the sex with a human character was as exciting as the sex with the incubus. I had just gotten to the part where the Viking raider realizes that his captive Irish lass is being visited nightly by a *night-mare*.

"You are mareitt, lass, ridden nightly by the demon mare. I can see it in your eyes and . . ." He reached under my tunic and roughly clasped the tender engorged flesh between my legs. I squeezed my eyes shut and tried to pretend I was elsewhere. "Aye, your sex is swollen with him. Your maidenhood I've been saving for your intended. If he's broken it . . ."

Swearing in his own language he slipped his finger into me and my knees went weak. I bit my lip to keep from moaning and giving him the idea that what he did pleasured me. It was just that I was tender there from the night visitations of this thing he called a night-mare.

"Ah, you're still a maiden, lass, Thank Odin. I'll still have my ransom price off ye – but we've got a wee problem."

He had removed his hand from inside me but now he was stroking my buttocks, squeezing the flesh with his big calloused hands. He pushed himself against me until my back was pressed up against the hard stone ledge of my cell's only window and I could feel the equally stone hard ridge of his manhood straining against my belly. He lifted my hips up onto the ledge, pressing me against the iron bars and spreading my thighs. Now I felt the tip of his manhood prodding against my sex which throbbed in answer to his thrusts. I whimpered with the effort not to moan and clenched my thighs to keep from arching up to enclose him inside of me. Traitor flesh! Even when the night-mare rode me I hadn't longed to be filled as I did now.

I opened my eyes and saw he was studying my face.

"Aye, lass, I want it, too. I want to come inside you and fill you to the brim. I want you to ride my cock as the night-mare rides you." He caressed my face and it was that tenderness that broke me. I wrapped my arms around him and slid my hands down to his iron-hard haunches, which were straining with the effort not to impale me. I pulled him toward me, arching my hips to meet his thrusts. I felt his hot flesh touch mine, the head of his engorged rod grazing my swollen sex .
. . and then I felt the cold slap of air as he stepped back. A mocking smile spread on his lips.

"Not this time, lass. I must protect my investment. But let's see what we can do for ye so you no longer need the night-mare's attentions."

He knelt down on his knees and buried that cruel mocking smile between my legs. His lips met my nether lips in a deep kiss. His tongue probed where his manhood wanted to go and *could not. He sucked on my flesh as a boy sucks a ripe peach down to the pit . . . He reached into the very pit of my dark yearning. His tongue rammed hard against the weir that dammed my deepest, darkest longings and broke it, releasing the sweet wild flood. When I'd spilled myself into his mouth he stood and wiped his face with the back of his hand.*

"I think the night-mare will leave you alone now, lass."
And then he left me, drained and empty as a rind when the fruit has been sucked dry.

I put down Dahlia's notebook and turned out the light. Moonlight spilled into the room as if it had been held back by a dam and was now released, but it was barren cold moonlight and the shadows stood rigid and still, as cold and unmoving as iron bars. I shivered and burrowed deeper under the covers, feeling as discarded as Dahlia's Irish lass.

CHAPTER TWENTY-ONE

The next morning I heard Brock outside shoveling my driveway. I grabbed Ralph and ran downstairs to show him to him, only remembering halfway down the stairs the salacious passage I had read last night. I hesitated, feeling embarrassed. Did Brock have any idea that Dahlia had used him as a model for one of her most passionate heroes? Would he know I'd been reading those scenes? But when I opened the door the look he gave me was so open and innocent I dismissed those thoughts. He was a kind, straightforward man. No wonder Dahlia had liked him. When I showed him Ralph he was amazed and delighted that his creation had come to life.

"When I forged the doormice I added a spark from Muspelheim, the primeval fire from whence came the stars and the planets, so that they would be powerful enough to protect you, but I never dreamed one would actually come to life. You must have sparked his life force some-how . . ." He looked at me with the same admiration with which I'd seen him regard Drew Brees after completing eight passes in a row. "He's devoted to protecting you now."

I was glad to have a loyal companion, but I didn't see

how a mouse was going to be able to do much against most threats.

When I got back inside I sat Ralph in the teacup on my desk and checked my email. I was relieved to see one from Liz Book telling me she'd found a replacement for Phoenix. An Irish poet – Liam Doyle – whose name was vaguely familiar to me. I Googled him and saw that he'd done his undergraduate work at Trinity College in Dublin (where he'd won several poetry awards) and his D.Litt at Oxford (where he'd been awarded a fellowship and honors for his thesis on the Romantic poets). He'd published two books of poetry with a small publisher called Snow Shoe Press. The picture on Snow Shoe's website showed an earnest, bookish-looking man with shaggy dark hair hanging over thick square glasses.

I clicked on a link for the Mistletoe Poetry House in Klamath, Oregon, and found this profile for him:

Liam Doyle, the prominent poet, was the Spring 2001 Zalman Bronsky Writer-in-Residence at the Kelly Writers House at the University of Pennsylvania. Liam has held visiting appointments at Macalaster College in Minnesota and Bates College in Maine. His interests are nineteenth-century Romantic poetry, the poetry of exiles and expatriates, and nature poetry. He spent the last eighteen months teaching poetry in an inner-city high school in Baltimore.

I emailed Liz back that I was happy she'd found a poet for the job because that would be great for Nicky Ballard. Did she still need me to take over today's class?

By the time I'd showered and dressed she'd emailed me

back to say that Professor Doyle planned to be up by the beginning of this afternoon's class ("He was in New York City for a Wordsworth conference, wasn't that lucky?") but would I mind meeting him after class to give him the students' papers.

I emailed back that I'd be happy to, but wouldn't he rather I meet him *before* class to give him the papers and tell him a little about the students?

No, Liz wrote back immediately, *he says that he likes to meet his new students without any preconceptions.*

Pretty idealistic, I typed back to Liz, and then, afraid that I might have come off as cynical, added, *He sounds great.* Still unsure if I sounded snarky, I added a smiley emoticon.

"No preconceptions, huh?" I muttered to Ralph, who was still curled up in his basket. "Who *is* this guy?"

Ralph yawned and stretched, performing a miniature downward facing dog that was just about the cutest thing I'd ever seen. Since Ralph didn't have anything to add, I decided to answer my own question. I still had Liam Doyle's Google results up on the screen and I saw that he had a Facebook page. I clicked it, expecting it would be blocked, but it wasn't. Good. I wouldn't have to friend him to look at his profile. The picture on his wall didn't give me a much better idea of what he looked like than his author photo did. It showed a dark haired man in profile, the corduroy collar of his Barbour raincoat turned up covering the lower part of his face, rain-misted hair covering up most of the other half. He was gazing into the distance at a breathtaking view of mountains and lakes. The Lake Country, I deduced, from the fact that he listed "Hiking in the Lake Country" as one of his interests, along with playing the lute and studying languages.

I scrolled through his profile and discovered that his favorite music ranged from U2, Kate Nash and the Vivian Girls, to Billie Holiday, to Celtic fusion bands like the Pogues, Thin Lizzy, and Ceredwen. His favorite movies were *Beauty and the Beast* (the Cocteau version), *Bringing Up Baby, It Happened One Night,* and, rather surprisingly, *You've Got Mail*.

His relationship status was posted as "It's Complicated."

I was just starting to read the messages on his wall when Ralph leapt onto the keyboard and skittered across the keys. I grabbed him before he hit a key that might inadvertently friend Liam Doyle and reveal that I'd been cyber-stalking him.

"Hey," I said, putting Ralph down on my desk. "Stay off, you're going to get hair all over my keyboard." Ralph shook himself, puffing up his fur until he looked like a miniature tribble, and then began to lick his fur down as if offended that I'd maligned his handsome coat.

"Sorry," I told him, closing my laptop so he wouldn't get into it while I was gone. "Just because you're a magical doormouse doesn't mean you don't shed." Then I glanced at my watch and saw that I was about to be late for class. I'd spent an embarrassing amount of time cruising Liam Doyle's Facebook page. He really ought to block it or else all his students would be doing the same thing.

We were watching *Wuthering Heights* – the classic version with Merle Oberon and Laurence Olivier – in class that day so I used the time to organize the writing workshop folders and attach a Post-it note to each one with a few words about each student. Too bad if I gave Liam Doyle a few preconceptions. After class one of my students – the boy with all the leather and piercings – asked to talk to me about his final paper, so I didn't get a peek at the new writer-in-residence before the workshop started. When I walked by the classroom the door was closed. I heard a deep murmuring voice coming from behind the door and then a ripple of laughter from the class.

Good, I thought, heading across the quad to the library, that class deserved a teacher who would give them all some attention. I just hoped he wouldn't be waylaid by Mara the way Phoenix had been. Maybe I should give him a little warning about the situation when his class was done . . . which was in an hour and twenty minutes. I'd have to cool my heels in the library till then. Of course there was plenty of work for me to do there, but still, it might have occurred to Mr. Doyle that meeting with me after his class wasn't the most convenient plan for *me*. He could have at least asked what worked best for me. Had he even asked Dean Book what my schedule was?

Instead of sitting at my usual table, I sat at a computer desk and logged into my email account. I saw that Liz had responded to my last email – the one I'd signed with a smiley face – after I left the house.

Oh, BTW, Mr. Doyle did ask which time was more convenient for you, but I said that since you often worked in the library either would be fine. I hope that was okay. We are quite lucky to get such a prominent poet (and one with such a good reputation for caring about his students) on such short notice. I was trying to accommodate him, but I do hope I haven't inconvenienced you :)

I sighed. Dean Book was obviously trying to soothe everyone's feathers (a smiley face, for heaven's sake! And what was up with that "BTW"?). I didn't envy her her job

– and she was right: writers-in-residence were notorious for bad behavior and shirking their students. An Oxford fellow who taught in inner-city high schools was a pretty remarkable catch.

I emailed back that I was in the library and had plenty to keep me busy until it was time to go meet Professor Doyle. And I did – I had papers to grade and an article in the latest edition of *Folklore* I wanted to put on my reserve list, and the names on the casualty list from the Ulster & Clare train crash to start looking up. But instead of doing any of these things I Googled Liam Doyle again and read his poetry credits. A couple of the magazines he was in were web journals. I clicked on one called *Per Contra* and found a poem called 'Winter, Liar'.

What came once here will never come again,
no matter monument nor memory;
all sunwarmed green succumbs to winter's wind.
And you, my love, were also my best friend,
and had your life to live. The tragedy
was not just my youth's recklessness, although
I trusted much to impulse, whim, freedom,
a destiny excluding doom. Frankly,
youth can be our insanity. But now I'm cured
of that fever, although the price was high;
and chilly April wind can only sigh
at my regrets, yet sun will brighten wind so,
one knows that soon green stirs, and wild bees hum.
And summer once more will make winter liar,
but I won't warm. You're all I'll ever desire.

Wow, I thought when I had finished reading the poem,

Oxford Fellow, inner city teacher, and he could write, too. But maybe that poem was a fluke. I went back to his Google page and found another poem . . . and then another and another. I read half a dozen. They were all beautiful and all about lost love. Some girl had really done a number on him. I went back to his Facebook page and started to comb through the messages on his wall for any mention of this spectacular girlfriend, but all the messages seemed to be from colleagues or former students. The messages from the students were particularly touching. *Thank you for inspiring me to write poetry, Prof, you really helped me believe in myself!* Ali from Macalaster College had written. *I love the book you recommended, Mr. D, you're right, the Romantics rock!* KickinItKT from Baltimore had written.

No wife or girlfriend mentioned anywhere.

His relationship status was still posted as "It's Complicated." Like he would have changed it during class, I began to chide myself, but then I noticed the digital time read-out on top of the screen and saw that his class had been over for ten minutes.

Yikes! I grabbed my bookbag and hurried out of the library, sprinted across the quad, and arrived at Fraser Hall panting. I paused to catch my breath in the hall outside Phoenix's old classroom and heard voices coming from inside. Peeking in I saw the broad, tweed-covered back of a large dark haired man standing in front and a little to the right of Flonia Rugova. Usually shy – I hadn't ever heard her string more than five words together at a time—Flonia was chattering away, her cheeks glowing pink and her hands waving in the air like songbirds recently freed from a cage. I tried to listen to what she was saying, but quickly realized she wasn't speaking in English. Neither was Professor

Doyle. He said something in what I could only assume was Albanian and Flonia giggled. Then she saw me lurking in the doorway and covered her mouth. Professor Doyle must have realized someone was behind him but before turning around he leaned toward Flonia, touched his hand to her shoulder, and murmured a few soft words. She nodded, serious now, and pressed both her hands together and inclined her head. I didn't know any Albanian, but I could tell she was thanking him for something. Doyle said something else and she laughed again. She gathered up her books and left quickly, walking past me as if I wasn't there.

Wow! One class and shy, sober Flonia Rugova was smitten. What must this guy look like?

I didn't have to wait long to find out. As soon as Flonia was gone he turned around. My first reaction was *Oh. I don't see what the big deal is*. Yeah, he had nice broad shoulders and a generous wide mouth, but his thick black hair was too long for my taste and he was wearing those square-rimmed glasses that guys wore to make themselves look intellectual and that made him look a bit like Clark Kent. And a floppy, collarless shirt that looked like something Errol Flynn had worn in *Captain Blood*. Sure, I could see why a young inexperienced girl like Flonia would find him attractive, but I personally thought he was bit affected.

Then he smiled. A dimple appeared on the left side of his mouth and his brown eyes behind the thick-lensed glasses flashed and turned a mellow tawny gold.

"Ah, you must be Professor McFay," he said in a lilting Irish accent. "My students talked about how generous you've been with your time."

My students? He'd certainly taken possession of them

quickly. Okay, he was good looking, but I was betting he knew it.

"Well, they're a good group," I said. "Nicky Ballard especially . . ."

". . . is a remarkable poet. Yes, I saw that right away. It's odd that Ms. Middlefield was trying to make her write memoir."

I agreed entirely, but I didn't like him kicking Phoenix when she was down – and right now poor Phoenix was probably strapped to a cot in a medicated stupor, which was about as down as a person could get. "Phoenix was under a lot of stress. I'm sure she was only doing what she believed was best for her students. She thought that confronting one's demons was necessary for a writer."

His lips twisted as if I'd said something funny. "Is that what she called it – confronting one's demons? It seems to me she was courting demons. Some of my students said that her breath smelled like alcohol during class and she hadn't returned a paper since September."

"Well, yes, that *is* bad . . ."

"It's worse than that; it's a crime. These young people were willing to bare their souls for that woman and what did they get for it? A drunken teacher who lied her way to fame and fortune." He shook his head sadly. "I only hope I can gain their trust after that."

"You looked like you were well on your way with Flonia Rugova," I snipped, instantly regretting my tone. The man was right. Phoenix's behavior had been abysmal, but still it irked me to have him walk in and pass judgment on someone he'd never met after an hour of listening to her students. He was regarding me curiously, his head tilted to one side, his eyes narrowed.

"Miss Rugova was telling me about how her family got out of Albania. She left a sister there whom she hasn't heard from in three years. I was offering her a contact in Amnesty International to help find her."

"Oh," I said, feeling the blood rise to my face. "That was . . . good of you. Flonia hasn't written much, but what I've read is beautiful. Here." I handed him the stack of student papers. "You're completely right, of course. They all deserve a better teacher than Phoenix was. She got distracted . . . which reminds me, the only student whose papers aren't here is Mara Marinca's. I can't find them anywhere. I guess Phoenix lost them."

I was expecting another diatribe against Phoenix, but instead Doyle sighed. "It doesn't matter," he said. "Mara told me today that she was withdrawing from the class."

"Oh, really? I'm surprised. We talked yesterday and she didn't mention she was dropping."

Liam Doyle shrugged. "I think she was disappointed to see that she wasn't going to be the focus of attention anymore. I'm afraid that too much attention can be just as harmful as too little. At any rate, Ms. Marinca expressed an aversion to writing poetry, which is what I plan to do with the class for the two weeks remaining in the semester."

"It's a shame, though, that she won't get credit for the class after all the work she did. I've looked all over for her papers . . ."

"I'm sure you have . . . which reminds me. I gather you were renting out your spare room to Ms. Middlefield. I'm staying right across the street at the Hart Brake Inn—" he grimaced at the name "—which is fine for a day or two, but if I have to stay there much longer I might go into diabetic shock, from the décor if not the food."

"Diana *does* have a sweet tooth," I concurred, "and a fondness for tchotchkes."

"I didn't mean to insult another of your friends, Professor McFay. Ms. Hart is a gracious innkeeper, but the rooms are . . . well, a tad feminine for my taste and the food *is* a little on the sugary side. What I wondered is . . . well, I don't know if you'd be uncomfortable taking on a male lodger."

"You want to rent Phoenix's room?"

"Yes. Dean Book mentioned it had a separate entrance and access to a kitchen. I like to cook. In fact, I took a course at the Cordon Bleu when I lived in Paris."

I was about to wonder aloud why he didn't list that accomplishment along with lute playing and speaking Albanian on his Facebook page, but caught myself before revealing my cyber-stalking activities. I smiled regretfully instead. "I'd love to help you out, Mr. Doyle, but Phoenix left her things there and I want her to feel welcome to come back."

"That's very loyal of you," he said. "I wouldn't want you to do anything that made you uncomfortable. But if Ms. Middlefield sends for her things . . ."

"Well, then you'll be the first on my prospective lodger list," I replied, confident that Phoenix was in no shape to send for her things. I returned Liam Doyle's brilliant smile, glad that this time I'd had a ready excuse for not taking on an unwanted roommate.

When I left Fraser Hall, though, I felt unsettled. Why, I asked myself, had I taken such an immediate dislike to Liam Doyle? Was I jealous of his easy success with his students when I had spent all weekend reading their papers and all day yesterday conferencing with them? Or his exotic travels and philanthropic activities? Or his Oxford degree? Okay, there was something annoyingly pretentious about the guy. Lute playing, for heaven's sake, and that shirt! I couldn't be the only one to see it, could I?

I turned around and headed back toward Fraser Hall, choosing the back entrance to avoid running into Doyle. If there really was something off about Liam Doyle, Soheila Lilly would be the one to notice it. There were no students waiting outside her office, but there were voices coming from inside. I was going to leave when I heard one of those voices – a deep, rumbly male one – say: "And did you get a good look at his shirt? It looked like he ordered it from the J. Peterman catalog!"

Oh good, I thought spitefully, I am not the only one. I knocked on the half-ajar door and poked my head in. Soheila was behind her desk in a lovely toffee-colored sweater and long amber beads that matched the color of the tea she was drinking. The last person I would have pegged as her tea-drinking partner was Frank Delmarco, but there he was, leaning back precariously on a delicately carved chair, holding a steaming glass of spiced tea.

"Am I interrupting anything?" I asked.

"We were just talking about Phoenix's replacement," Soheila responded, getting up to pour me a glass of tea from the samovar. "Have you met him yet?"

"Yes," I answered, taking the chair next to Frank's. "He seems very . . . dedicated," I ventured cautiously.

"Ha!" Frank snorted, and rocked forward in his chair so roughly I thought the fragile wood would crack. "All you women have been completely bamboozled by him."

"Not at all," I said, annoyed to be lumped in with the infatuated students. "Actually, I thought he was a little presumptuous. He asked if he could have Phoenix's room."

"See!" Frank crowed. "The poor woman's bed isn't even cold and he's trying to take it from her. I hope you told him no."

"I did," I said, then smiling slyly, added, "Although I might regret it. He told me he studied cooking at the Cordon Bleu."

Frank leaned back in his chair again and roared with laughter – as I'd known he would. I felt a little spiteful thrill.

"Maybe he also sews – you could have gotten some curtains out of him! Have you read his poetry yet?"

I wasn't sure if I wanted to admit to that, but Frank didn't wait for my answer. He quoted a line from a poem I'd read in the library in a mocking falsetto. I'd thought the line was lovely when I read it, but now something malicious made me laugh and ask, "Do you think he really believes that nonsense?"

I heard a step behind me.

Soheila cleared her throat and glanced over my head. I looked over my shoulder and there, filling the doorway with his broad shoulders, was Liam Doyle. The late afternoon sun was in his eyes, so I couldn't read his expression, but his voice was cool as ice water.

"Yes, in fact I do," he said. Before I could apologize, he was gone.

CHAPTER TWENTY-TWO

I spent the next week (the last week of classes before finals) trying to avoid Liam Doyle, so embarrassed was I to have been caught talking about him behind his back. Making fun of his poetry, no less! I didn't know what had come over me. Why had I taken such a dislike to the man just because he wore foppish shirts and had gone to Oxford?

Nearly everyone else certainly liked him. Soheila Lilly served me Irish Breakfast tea the next time I was in her office – "a present from that nice Irish writer!" – and confided to me that he reminded her of Angus Fraser. I saw him eating lunch with Elizabeth Book in the student union twice and heard the dean laughing like a schoolgirl. Even Frank Delmarco grudgingly admitted to me that the new hire wasn't all bad – and then he showed me the Jets tickets Doyle had gotten for him for the weekend after Christmas. His students raved about the workshop and told me how he took them on hikes through the woods and recited poetry to them.

Nicky Ballard, especially, had been galvanized by him to write. She was working on a series of poems developing the theme of the ice maiden. When she showed me a few of the poems, I immediately saw that Nicky was working out her fear of being trapped by the legacy of her family history through the poems. I thought it was a good emotional strategy but wondered if it would really help combat a century-old curse. Of course, Nicky didn't know she was under a curse, so it fell to me do what I could to avert it.

I had started the painstaking work of looking up each casualty of the Ulster & Clare train crash, but it was going slowly. Even when I was able to find out something about a victim or their family I had no way of telling whether the person was a witch. There had to some better way of going about this. At the beginning of finals week I decided to go by Liz Book's office to ask if she had any ideas on how to track down the perpetrator of the curse. As soon as I mentioned the curse a pall fell over Liz's face, making her look older and tired. In fact, I noticed that she was looking distinctly untidy. Strands of graying hair had escaped her usually immaculate chignon and her knit St. John's jacket was missing a brass button.

"The Ballard curse has been documented by my pre-decessors for generations. When I took this job ten years ago I made it one of my missions to avert the curse. First I thought that if we could find out the origins of the curse we could undo it, so I asked Anton Volkov to go through the very long list of people who had reason to hate Bertram Ballard."

"Why Anton Volkov?" I asked. She looked confused by the question, so I added, "Isn't he in the Eastern European and Russian Institute?"

"Of course . . . Oh, I see what you mean. I guess I haven't given you your orientation packet to I.M.P. – the Institute of Magical Professionals, that is. Anton's in charge of updating the registry of witches, fairies and daemons. He's computerized the whole thing and named it B.O.G.G.A.R.T. It's really caught on with magical academics and been a real boost to Anton's academic standing since he can't exactly attend most conferences—"

"But was he able to identify the witch who cursed Nicky's family?" I interrupted. I didn't mean to be rude, but I was afraid I could be here all day listening to the dean explain the workings of magical academia which, fascinating as it might have been, wasn't going to help Nicky any.

"Actually he was able to identify at least two witches who would have had cause and opportunity to curse the Ballards, but he hasn't been able to locate the descendants of either witch. I know he's been meaning to go down to the city and look at the Central Registry of Supernatural Beings – or C.R.O.S.B., as we call it – at the Main Branch of the library, but he hasn't had a chance . . ."

"There's a Central Registry of Supernatural Beings at the main branch of the New York Public Library?" I asked, amazed. I'd used the main branch a million times. I'd certainly never come across anything like that.

"Yes, but you need your I.M.P. card to access it. Once you found out all about us I sent in your paperwork in order for you to join I.M.P. I think I have your membership card here somewhere . . ." She sifted through a pile of papers on her usually neat desk. Several sheets drifted to the floor. I picked up a drop/add form and a bill for four cases of champagne and handed them to her. "Ah, here it is!" She produced a laminated card with a symbol of two crescent moons flanking an orb with the letters I.M.P. inscribed in it. "Just present this at the front desk and you'll be shown to the special collections. It also entitles you to use the library during hours when it's normally closed."

"Great. I'll do that the next time I get into the city. Do you have the names of the witches Anton identified?"

"I did . . . somewhere around here . . ." Liz swiveled her chair to face a tall filing cabinet behind her. She pulled open a crowded drawer and fished around in it. She sighed heavily, but then perked up when a book slid off the top of the filing cabinet and into her lap. "Why, here's your spellbook!" She handed me a nondescript book in a green library binding. "But I can't seem to find that list. Perhaps you could just go to Anton and ask him for the names. That might be the easiest thing."

"Sure," I said, "only I don't really know him. I saw him at the faculty party, but I wasn't introduced. Isn't he . . . I mean, Nicky Ballard told me that he and his colleagues live together in town and that there are some strange stories about them . . ." Like the fact that they were never seen before nightfall, I recalled.

Liz waved a limp hand to dismiss my concerns. "You mustn't listen to such gossip. Anton is quite charming. Really, you should go talk to him if you're concerned about Nicky. He's made quite a study of her. His office is in Bates Hall. It's the building up on the hill."

"Okay. I guess I will then."

"Good." The dean looked happy to have something settled – and eager to end the meeting. She looked like she could do with a nap. The end of the semester must be a trying time – especially a semester that had included an incubus invasion, a fraud scandal, and an ice storm. It would age anyone and, it suddenly occurred to me, I had no idea how old Elizabeth Book really was. If her magical powers had been keeping her young, perhaps if those powers waned she would grow old very quickly. The idea made me feel suddenly uncomfortable and sad for her.

I got up to go, clutching my new spellbook. "I'll go see

Professor Volkov right away."

"There is one thing I should warn you about."

"Oh?"

"While I applaud your desire to help Nicky Ballard, you must be careful not to burn yourself out. I was just saying this to Mr. Doyle earlier today. Today's young people – especially the ones we get here at Fairwick – need so much attention. They can suck you dry."

The comment startled me. It was not the kind of thing I'd have expected Dean Book – always so poised and gracious – to say. But looking down at her, at the dryness of her skin, the disarray of her hair and the light tremor in her hand, she looked exactly like someone who had been sucked dry.

I'd never been in Bates Hall, but I'd seen its stone spire in the distance and I knew it housed the Eastern European and Russian Institute—or E.E.R.I. as it was called by the students. It was all by itself on the western edge of campus. I didn't relish the idea of hiking out there, but I felt I owed it to Nicky. Approaching the building up a steeply ascending path I felt a bit like Jonathan Harker approaching Dracula's castle in the Carpathians. Maybe that's why the Eastern European and Russian Institute had chosen it. No one else was on the path. Since it was finals week most of the students were probably holed up in their rooms or in the library studying. The sun was going down behind the western mountains, turning the stone building blood red. With diminishing sunlight the day had turned icy cold, and the gray clouds massing in the north threatened snow. The Weather Channel had been predicting the first snow of the season for days now. I almost turned back, but then I recalled my promise to Nicky's grandmother. The stone building was cold and quiet inside. My steps echoed as I walked down a long hallway, past yellowing maps of countries that no longer existed and glass cases of pottery shards and broken statuary – relics of some ancient Slavic civilization. I stopped to read a list of course offerings in the department. The classes ranged through the Russian language, nineteenth century Russian literature, Balkan folklore, Byzantine and Ottoman history, and Russian guitar poetry. Pretty impressive for a college of Fairwick's size, I thought. Usually it was only the big universities – Harvard, the U. of Chicago – that could devote so many classes to a rather obscure subject area. I wondered if some rich Fairwick alum had endowed the department.

I found Professor Volkov's office but the door was closed and no one answered my knock. Written in a flowing, old-fashioned script on an ivory card were his winter office hours: *Mondays and Wednesdays, six to eight in the evening, or by appointment*. Great, I thought, Dean Book might have told me that Professor Volkov kept eccentric office hours. I saw by his class schedule that he taught at even stranger hours: *8–9:15 on Mondays and Wednesdays*. I was turning to go when I heard a sound coming from behind the closed door. Perhaps Volkov was there after all. I leaned closer to the door and listened. It was a riffling sound – like pages of an old book being flipped, only it went on so long and grew so loud that I began to doubt anyone would flip through a book for so long or so emphatically. No, the longer I listened the more it sounded like wings, as if a large bird had gotten trapped in Professor Volkov's office.

I knocked on the door again and the riffling noise stopped. I waited for someone to respond, but no one came to the door and nothing stirred behind it, although I felt sure now that someone – or *something* – was on the other side of the door. I backed away from the door as quietly as I could and crept back down the hall, with only my own reflection in the glass display cases for company.

I felt better when I got out of the building and felt the cold air on my face, but then I saw how dark the path was. In the few minutes I had been inside Bates Hall the sun had sunk completely behind the horizon and snow had begun to fall, blurring the edges of the path and filling the woods on either side with cold gray shadows. I walked quickly, chiding myself for the rising panic in my chest. The sound I'd heard in Professor Volkov's office had only been loose papers blowing in the draft from an open window, I told myself.

But then why had the sound stopped when I knocked?

And why did Professor Volkov have such strange office hours and only teach at night?

I recalled again the town gossip that Nicky had relayed to me about Professor Volkov and his associates. They never went out before dark, there were lights on at their house at all hours . . . Could they be vampires?

The sound of wings overhead cut short my reasoning – and the next beat of my heart. I looked behind me and saw, silhouetted against the last red streak in the western sky, a black, winged shape bearing down on me.

I turned and ran down the steep path. The sound of wings grew louder and I ran faster. At the bottom of the path was a security light above a red campus emergency phone. I wasn't sure how much good a phone call was going to do me right now, but it was the only goal I had. I made for the light as if it could banish the shadowy thing behind me – a thing that I instinctively felt wasn't just a bird. Stories about vampires turning into bats were running through my mind as I reached for the phone . . . and felt my feet slipping in the slick, freshly fallen snow. As I fell the spellbook slipped from my hands and landed open and face up in the snow inches from my nose.

To halt an attack from above, I read, *pronounce the following words while picturing an empty blue sky and waving a feather*.

Great, I thought, as the sound of wings came closer, where was I going to find a feather on such short notice? But I *was* wearing a down coat, an old one that sometimes leaked . . .

I patted my coat until I felt something prickly . . . and pulled. I waived the tiny feather in my hand while picturing an empty blue sky and pronouncing (correctly I hoped) the three prescribed words:

Vacuefaca naddel nem!

Something thumped my back. So much for having magical talents. I turned over, raising my hands to cover my face for protection . . . and found myself looking up at Liam Doyle.

"Are you all right?" he demanded, his voice hoarse with concern. "I saw you running down the path as if something were after you."

I looked up for the winged creature, but there was nothing but clear blue sky. Snowflakes clung to Liam's dark hair like stars in a night sky, but the sky itself was rinsed clean of the storm clouds that had been there a moment ago.

"I heard something following me." I didn't tell him that the sound had come from the sky. He helped me up and we both turned and looked at the path leading up to Bates Hall. Only one set of footprints stood out in the newly fallen snow. "I suppose it could have been my imagination," I said, feeling foolish.

"Or it could have been someone in the woods," Liam said. "A student smoking pot or drinking beer who didn't want to get caught by a teacher." I had a feeling he was humoring me, but I didn't care. I also didn't care that he was still holding my arm. I was glad to see him.

"I suppose so, or it could have been an animal." As we turned to walk toward the main part of campus, he tucked my arm under his elbow. "I hadn't realized how isolated this part of campus was. What are you doing here?"

"I was heading to Bates Hall to talk to Professor Demisovski about an independent project for Flonia Rugova. Flonia is writing some lovely poetry in Albanian and I thought if she could read some of the poetry of her homeland it would help her find her voice. I hear that Rea Demisovski is one of the world's leading experts in Slavic poetry."

"You're certainly very dedicated to your students," I said.

He glanced at me, his lips quirking up in a sideways smile. "I can't tell if you're making fun of me."

I sighed. "I don't blame you after hearing me mocking your poetry. I can't tell you how sorry I am. I don't know what came over me. I *like* that poem. Especially the last two lines: *And summer once more will make winter liar, but I won't warm. You're all I'll ever desire.*"

He stopped on the path – we had reached the center of the quad where four Japanese maples marked the corners of two diagonally intersecting paths. Their bare branches arched above us, shielding us from the snow. Liam took his glasses off to wipe the snow from the lenses and shook his head, scattering snowflakes from his hair.

"You memorized lines of my poem. I'm flattered. Unless

you memorized them to make fun of it with Frank Delmarco."

"No!" I said, touching his arm. He looked up, surprised at the urgency in my voice, and our eyes met for the first time without the barrier of his glasses. They were dark, but there was a light in them, a white spark that gleamed like one of the snowflakes once again spinning out of the night sky. Looking into them made me feel a little dizzy. "I memorized those lines because when I read them for the first time I had to read it again immediately . . . and then again and again. I couldn't help but learn it by heart."

He didn't say anything for a moment. I supposed he was wondering if he could trust me. I wouldn't have blamed him if he decided I was making fun of him again and walked away in disgust.

"By heart?" he asked, placing his hand over his own heart. "I like that phrase. I suppose that makes more sense than memorizing poetry to make fun of it. Thank you." He reached his hand toward my face and moved a step closer. For a moment I thought he was going to kiss me – I might have leaned a quarter inch closer – but he only brushed some snow from my hair. I shivered as his hand touched my face.

"Come on, you'd better get home before you turn into one of those ice maidens in Nicky Ballard's poems."

We turned and walked briskly to the southeast gate, our arms no longer linked. "I've only read a few of them," I said, desperate to cover my embarrassment at leaning into an imaginary kiss. Had he noticed? "They're quite good, aren't they?"

"They're brilliant! She's invented a whole mythology of these frozen women who live inside the walls of an ice palace. In order for the intrepid heroine to free herself she has to listen to the story of each one of the ice wardens. Telling their stories makes them thaw, but each story forms an ice crystal in the heroine's heart. The question is whether she frees herself before her heart freezes."

"Brrr." I wrapped my arms around myself and shivered. "It makes me cold just thinking about it. Poor Nicky. She shouldn't have to deal with this at her age."

"Deal with what?" Liam asked as we passed through the southeast gate.

Too late I realized I couldn't tell him about the curse but I could, however, tell him about Nicky's family. We stopped in the middle of the road – equidistant between my house and the inn. Glancing behind him at the gaily decorated Hart Brake Inn – Diana had gone all out with colored lights, swags of holly and pine, and an entire team of illuminated reindeer – I felt a pang that I'd condemned him to spending Christmas in Toyland.

"It's a long story. Would you like to come in for a drink?" I asked, trying to make my voice sound casual. "Perhaps something not cocoa – or nog-based?"

He laughed. "Yes, I'd like that very much." And then, leaning close enough that I could feel his warm breath tickling my frozen earlobe, he whispered conspiratorially, "But you have to promise not to serve any cookies or brownies with it. I'm beginning to feel like Hansel being fattened for the oven by the Wicked Witch."

I laughingly promised not to serve any baked goods and then assured him that Diana, at least, was not a witch. I didn't tell him that after my first successful spell I was wondering whether I was.

CHAPTER TWENTY-THREE

Luckily, I still had a bottle of Jack Daniel's left over from Phoenix's stash. I poured us two glasses while Liam lit a fire in the library fireplace.

"What a great room!" he enthused. "I've never lived long enough anywhere to have my books in one place."

"Oh?" I remarked casually, determined not to reveal how much I knew about his peripatetic lifestyle from my internet searches. "I suppose a writer-in-residence must move around a lot."

"Yeah, that's my excuse," he said, smiling ruefully and saluting me with his glass of bourbon. "But sometimes I wonder if I don't use the job as an excuse to move on. Like I'm under a curse that keeps me from staying in any one place for too long. Maybe that's why I'm so touched by Nicky Ballard's poems. They sound like they're written by a girl who thinks she's doomed."

I stared at him, wondering if he did know something about the Ballard curse, but then I realized that he'd just cleverly deflected the subject from his own history to Nicky's. Well, talking about Nicky was the reason I'd asked him in. Wasn't it?

"It *is* almost like she's cursed," I said, carefully

navigating around the couch and sitting down in the armchair by the fire. He took the opposite chair and I proceeded to tell him what I'd heard about the Ballard family, avoiding any supernatural elements and focusing instead on the legacy of dwindling fortunes, disappointed women, teenage pregnancy, and alcoholism.

"Poor Nicky," he said when I'd finished. "I've passed by that house. You can guess the family's blighted from the street. She must feel it's inevitable that she's going to wind up like her mother and grandmother. We have to keep her from making their mistakes."

"We?"

"Don't you know how much Nicky admires you, Cailleach?" It was the first time he'd said my name in full and it caught me by surprise. Most people didn't pronounce it right on the first try.

"I think it's you she admires . . . Liam. Come on, surely you know that every girl in your class has a crush on you."

"Now you're teasing me again, and I'm dead serious. Nicky talks about you all the time. She thinks the sun rises and sets on you. She especially admires how independent you are, you being a woman on her own and all."

"Oh, well . . . actually, you know, I do have a boyfriend."

Liam's mouth twitched and he looked away. The reflection of the firelight flashed across the lenses of his glasses, so I couldn't see his expression. "No, actually I didn't know. Brilliant. What's his name? And where is he?" He looked around the room as if I had a man hiding under the couch.

"Paul. He's finishing up his doctorate in economics at U.C.L.A. I'm going to California to visit him next week.

Hopefully he'll get a job on the East Coast next year."

"And if he doesn't?"

I shrugged. "We'll figure something out. What about you? It must be hard maintaining a relationship with all the traveling you do." I lifted my glass to take another sip of bourbon but found the glass was empty.

Liam picked up the bottle and leaned across to fill my glass. "Yes, I think that may be why I do it. I haven't . . . well, something happened to me in college and I haven't really wanted to 'get involved,' as you Americans say, since then."

"Bad break up?"

He grimaced. "Not exactly," he replied. "It's . . ."

"Complicated?" I suggested when it looked like he wasn't going to finish his sentence. I was only trying to lighten the mood, but when he turned away from the fire and took his glasses off to wipe his eyes I was sorry.

"I suppose you could say that. You see, she . . . Jeannie, my childhood sweetheart . . . she died."

"It was my first year at Trinity," Liam began after I refilled our glasses. "I came from a little town in the west. My father was a horse-trainer and Jeannie's family ran the drapery shop – in Ireland that means a shop that sells just about anything made out of cloth. We'd known each other since we were children. I don't remember a time when I wasn't already planning to spend my life with her. But I also loved reading and writing . . . and I was good at them. I started winning poetry contests when I was ten. Jeannie was so proud of me. It was she who talked me into trying for the scholarship to Trinity . . . and she who told me I had to go when I got it. She told me we'd be together on holidays and when we'd saved up enough money she'd come join me in Dublin."

"It sounds like a reasonable plan," I said. "You were lucky to have a girlfriend who believed in your promise and didn't begrudge you a chance in the world."

"Yes," he replied, downing the last of his bourbon. "I was lucky. I just didn't realize it. And I didn't realize how I'd change. I was so excited to be in the big city, surrounded by brilliant people . . . my professors, sure, but also the other students. Folks who had grown up with books and educated conversation. There was a particular set of Anglo-Irish students who'd gone to boarding school together that I fell in with: Robin Allsworthy and his pal Dugan Scott and Robin's cousin, Moira. I thought they were very glamorous. Everyone in our year looked up to them and talked about them. When they befriended me I couldn't believe my luck. I think I was in love with all three of them, but of course Jeannie didn't see it that way."

"How did she find out about Moira?"

"She came in the last week before Christmas break – this time of year, come to think of it. It was meant to be a surprise. She'd gotten a room at a fancy hotel . . ." He blushed. "We hadn't . . . you know, been together like that and I think she was afraid that's why I'd become distant from her. But when she came I was out in the pubs with Robin, Dugan and Moira celebrating the end of finals. Poor Jeannie went from pub to pub, following our trail. When at last she found us she saw me with Moira. It was only a drunken snog . . . I can't even remember how it happened, but I'll never forget Jeannie's face."

He fell silent, staring into the fire as if he could see his childhood sweetheart's face in the flames.

"Did you try to explain?" I asked after a few moments.

He shook his head. "She ran away. The streets were crowded around the pubs and I lost her. I looked everywhere for her, but finally Robin, Dugan and Moira convinced me I should go back to my room and call the hotel. When the hotel said she'd checked out my friends convinced me that she must have gone home and I could put things right when I went home for the holidays."

He lapsed into silence again, staring now into the empty bottom of his glass. I didn't prompt him this time. I wasn't looking forward to hearing the end of this story.

"But she hadn't gone home. Three days after she disappeared they found her body in the River Liffey," he said at last.

"Do you think she . . . ?"

He looked up before I could finish the question. "I don't know," he said miserably. "Did she kill herself? Did she fall? Did someone push her? I'll never know. But what does it matter? It might as well have been me who pushed her into the river. It was my fault she died."

I shook my head. "You can't blame yourself. It wasn't your fault."

He grimaced. "That's what Moira said. She told me that Jeannie had been weak."

I winced, and he nodded at my reaction. "Yes, I know, how craven was I to listen to her? But I did because I wanted desperately to forget Jeannie. I spent the next three and a half years with Moira, learning to drink and indulge in other inebriants, and acquiring expensive and dangerous tastes. In my worst moments I found myself thinking I'd been lucky that Jeannie had died . . . and then I would drink to forget I'd ever had that thought. It's a miracle I finished college. Somehow I managed to keep writing. I had one teacher who believed in me despite my debauchery and he got me the fellowship to Oxford. I thought Moira would be thrilled. She was always talking about getting out of Ireland, but then it turned out she'd made other plans. She and Dugan were going to Paris together to study painting. She told me not to worry, that we'd see each other on holidays, that we'd figure something out."

It was just what I'd said a moment ago about Paul and me.

"Instead I figured out that I didn't mean anything to her. I'd just been an amusement. I sobered up then – literally and figuratively – and started writing about Jeannie, always hoping, I think, to find her again in my poetry."

"And you haven't . . . been with anyone since?"

He put his empty glass down on the table and leaned forward, his elbows on his knees, and looked up at me. Despite all he'd drunk, his eyes were clear. "Not seriously. I'd had enough of girls like Moira and when I meet someone who reminds me of Jeannie . . . well, I remember what I did to her. I see her face . . . so, my relationships don't usually last too long."

"Has it ever occurred to you that there are more than two kinds of women? That not every woman is an innocent like Jeannie – or a bitch like Moira."

He laughed at that. "You make a good point. Perhaps . . ." He leaned farther forward, his hands braced on his knees.

For the second time tonight I thought he was going to try to kiss me . . . but he was just getting to his feet.

"Perhaps I should consider that when I haven't had quite this much to drink. Thanks for telling me about Nicky Ballard," he said, walking to the door. I followed him. "I think it'll help in dealing with her. Maybe between the two of us we can keep her from going the way of her mother and grandmother."

"That's why you worry so much about your students," I said when we reached the door. "Because of what happened to Jeannie."

"I'd like to think I'd care even if Jeannie were still alive. Look at you. You care about your students and nothing so awful happened. You've still got your Paul."

"Yes, I do," I said, opening the door for him. He rocked forward unsteadily on his heels, but this time I had no illusion that he was going to kiss me. He was just drunk. I gave him a little push out the door. "Think you can make it across the street?" I asked.

"Absolutely," he assured me. "I just hope I can make it upstairs without breaking any ornaments or dragging down the holly swags on the banister."

I wished him good luck as he turned to go. He staggered a bit at the foot of the porch steps, but then I saw that he was just looking at one of the frozen ornaments Brock had made for me – the one with the fairy stone embedded in the ice. After a moment of studying it, he weaved across my front lawn, leaving a meandering trail of footprints in the new snow. I watched until he made it across the street up to the porch. Then he turned and waved as if he'd known all along that I'd been watching him.

I got out my phone to call Paul when I went back in, guilty that I'd missed our midnight call, but I didn't want to call right away. While I was feeding Ralph – he'd stayed hidden when Liam was here – I wondered if I should tell Paul that I'd spent the evening with the new Irish heartthrob writer-in-residence. I'd already told him all the girls had crushes on him. Or maybe I should just tell him I'd been busy grading term papers.

"What do you think, Ralph?" I asked the little mouse as I scooped him up in my hand and carried him upstairs. "A little white lie? Or maybe it wouldn't hurt to make Paul a teensy bit jealous just so he doesn't take me for granted."

Ralph's cheeks were bulging with cheese so he didn't answer. Not that he'd shown any talent for communication so far, magic doormouse or not.

But Paul had spared me the choice between lying and teasing. When I got upstairs and flipped open my phone I saw that there was a text message from him.

Missed your call tonight and have to GT bed early. Change of plans: I'm coming to NYC for interview and have booked room at Ritz-Carlton Battery Park and cancelled your flight to LA. I'll explain when I see you. <3 Paul.

I texted back asking him who the interview was with. It was unusual for a university to interview over the winter break – and even more unusual for Paul to stay at a hotel as pricey as the Ritz-Carlton. But since he didn't reply to my text I'd just have to wait until tomorrow to find out what was going on.

I fell asleep quickly, no doubt aided by all the bourbon I'd drunk, but then woke with a start in the middle of the night. What if Paul had booked the fancy hotel because he was planning to surprise me with the news that he'd finally gotten a job in New York? And what if he was planning to celebrate by asking me to marry him? It had long been understood between us (I couldn't remember who had first broached the subject) that we'd get married as soon as he got a job in New York and we could live together. Why else would he pay for such a fancy hotel? And why, I asked myself with my hand clamped over my left breast, was my heart beating so hard? I sat up in bed and looked toward the window. No moonlight poured in tonight, no shadow branches fell on the floor. I got up and walked to the window, my bare feet cold on the uncarpeted floor, and saw why. It was snowing again – a soft, feathery snow that absorbed the moonlight and cast a hushed pall over the outside world. I sat on the windowsill and looked up at the flakes spinning out of the black sky. They looked like an unwinding spiral staircase. Ralph crawled out of his basket and curled up in my lap. I sat watching the snow for a long time, wondering why I didn't feel happier.

The next few days were consumed with finals, grades and student conferences. I tried calling Paul but my calls always went to voice mail. When I texted him he texted back that he'd explain everything when we saw each other in the city on the 22nd. Paul was lousy at keeping secrets. He probably knew that if we talked I'd get him to tell me where he was interviewing and why he'd booked the room at the Ritz-Carlton. When I found myself hoping that he wouldn't get the job I knew I had a problem, but I pushed the thought away and focused on my last conference of the semester – the one with Nicky Ballard.

Although I hadn't seen Liam Doyle since the night of the first snow, he had emailed me. *I've got an idea about Nicky Ballard*, he had written and then gone on to explain a plan he had for keeping Nicky on the straight and narrow. I was supposed to implement the first part of the plan on the last day of the semester. Most of the students had already left for their homes, but Nicky, since she lived in town, had volunteered for the last conference slot. Since there was a faculty holiday party that started at sunset, I came to our meeting dressed up.

"Wow!" Nicky cried when I took my coat off, "You look great!"

"Thanks, Nicky." I was wearing a silver dress that I'd bought last Christmas at Barney's and the diamond studs my aunt had given me for my 21st birthday. "I do plan to change my shoes." I held up a pair of silver heels over the sheepskin boots I had on.

"It's a good thing you're wearing the boots," Nicky said. "It's supposed to go down into the teens tonight."

I shammed a shiver. "Brrr, do you ever get used to the cold here?"

Nicky laughed. "Truthfully? No. Sometimes I wonder what it would be like to live somewhere warm."

"You should try it sometime. Take your junior year abroad in Spain, or do a semester archeology dig in Mexico, or do your postgraduate work at UT Austin. They have a great writing program."

Nicky's eyes shone at each suggestion I made, but the lights quickly went out. "I couldn't," she said. "My grandmother needs me and I'm pretty sure my scholarship only covers tuition here."

"Hmm . . . I'll ask Dean Book about that. In the meantime, I wanted to talk to you about an idea for an independent study class – actually, it was Professor Doyle's idea."

"Really? You've talked to Professor Doyle about me?"

"Yes, he's very impressed with the poems you've been writing."

"He's been awfully nice about them . . . *he's* awfully nice. Don't you think so?"

"Um, yes, he is very nice, but that isn't the reason he likes your poems. Your poetry is very good—"

"And so handsome! Don't you think he's handsome?" Nicky asked, a dreamy expression on her face.

"I suppose so," I answered as tersely as I could. "But Professor Doyle's looks are not what I want to talk to you about. He – we – had an idea for an independent class that would combine the poetry you're writing with research into the themes of your poetry. For instance, you use the motif of the captive maiden, a motif that appears in fairy tales such as Rapunzel and Sleeping Beauty, and in Gothic fiction . . ."

"Oh, like the way Emily St. Aubert is trapped in the castle of Udolpho," Nicky volunteered. "Or Bertha Rochester is locked up in the attic of Thornfield Hall."

"Exactly," I replied, although I hadn't been thinking of Bertha Rochester, who dies at the end of *Jane Eyre*. The idea was to have Nicky identify with the captive maidens of myth and literature who escape in the end. Liam thought that if Nicky could plot an escape for her fictional alter ego, she might not fall victim to the fate of all the Ballard women before her. Of course, Liam didn't know about the curse, but when I'd run the idea by Soheila she had thought it couldn't hurt. At least it was something to do. I'd read through the spell lexicon looking for ways to avert a curse but they all required knowing who had cast it. Anton Volkov had been away at a conference for the last few days so I hadn't been able to find out the names of the two witches who might have cursed the Ballards. For now, this was the best I could do. "So do you like the idea?"

"Yes. Would I be working with both of you together, or one at a time?"

"Oh, we hadn't discussed that. I suppose we could each

meet individually with you or we could all three meet together. Which would you prefer?"

"I'd like to meet all together," Nicky replied immediately. "I really like Professor Doyle, but whenever I'm alone with him I get so nervous I can hardly speak. It will be better if you're there."

I smiled indulgently at Nicky, as if it had been years since I'd experienced such nerves. "Good, it's settled then. I'll talk to Professor Doyle about a time that will work for all of us when I see him at the party this evening." I looked at my watch. "Which I'd better be getting to."

"Oh yes, you don't want to be late for the holiday party. It's a tradition at Fairwick. Of course, students don't get to go to it. We're all supposed to be off the campus by sunset today. They lock the gates an hour after dusk."

"Do they?" I'd never seen the southeast gate closed, let alone locked. "Well then, you'd best be going. I wouldn't want you to get locked into the campus the whole break." Nicky and I both laughed at the idea, but it occurred to me that it would be just the kind of thing that would happen in the Gothic novels we'd been reading.

CHAPTER TWENTY-FOUR

When I got to Briggs Hall I stopped in the coatroom in the lobby to shuck off my long down coat and swap my boots for party shoes. While I was trying to tighten the buckle on my right shoe I heard whispering coming from the back of the coatroom. I froze, poised awkwardly on one leg, and listened.

"You would tell me if there was something really wrong, wouldn't you?" a woman's plaintive voice pleaded. I hated to be eavesdropping on what sounded like a lover's quarrel, but I was afraid that if I moved I would give away my presence. So I listened, waiting for a response, but none came.

"After all, you've known her longer than I have and I know how much you care for her."

"Hmm . . . not a lovers' quarrel then. Perhaps a ménage a trois? I had to admit I was curious now. I stealthily pushed aside a layer of heavy winter coats . . . and uncovered Diana Hart standing alone beside Liz Book's fur coat.

"Diana?" I asked, too startled to worry about keeping my presence secret. "Are you okay?"

Diana looked up guiltily, her eyes bloodshot and bleary. "I'm fi-ine," she warbled, her chin quivering. "It's Lizzie

I'm worried about. She's fading away and I can't figure out why. I thought I'd ask Ursuline, but she won't tell me."

I glanced at the fur coat, which I had seen move to protect its owner when Phoenix had flown at her. The coat hung still on a padded hanger now, its sheen faded.

"And look!" Diana stroked her hand down the lapel of the coat and then held it up to me. Long brown hairs clung to her palm. "She's shedding in the middle of the winter. She must be sick, too."

"Could that be why Liz is ill? If her familiar is sick, could it make her sick?"

Diana furrowed her freckled brow and pressed her face against the dull fur. "I don't know. A witch and her familiar are interconnected. Usually the familiar grows weak because the witch is sick, but I suppose it could happen the other way around. But then what is making Ursuline sick?"

I touched the fur coat gingerly. I remembered when I had held the coat the night of the ice storm it had bristled with static electricity, but now it lay limp and inert under my hand. Something *was* wrong with it.

"Gosh, I have no idea. Are there vets for familiars? I don't suppose you could take it to the Goodnoughs."

"Oh my no! Abby and Russell have a Humane Society sticker on their car – I'm sure they would disapprove of fur coats! I'd have to coax Ursuline into taking bear-shape." We both looked at the coat dubiously. Diana may have been trying to figure out how to turn the coat back into a bear, but I was remembering how large and fierce the creature on the porch had been, and planning my retreat.

"Well, you let me know how that goes," I said, backing out of the coatroom. "I guess I'll go into the party now."

"You do that, dear," Diana said absently. "I'll be along in

a moment. I'm just going to spend a few more minutes with Ursuline."

I left Diana murmuring to the coat and walked toward the Main Parlor, brushing brown hairs off my silver dress. My head was down looking for stray hairs, so it wasn't until I was in the doorway that I looked up and saw how the room had been transformed. I'd admired the stately hall the last time I'd been in it, but the heavy drapes had been drawn over the windows then. Today the drapes had been pushed back, revealing a wall of glass facing the western mountains. The sun hovered just inches above the highest, turning the sky a brilliant fiery red and the mountains a deep violet. Swaths of russet light poured in through the glass, deepening the colors of the Persian rug and turning the oak beams and panels a rich honey gold. It was the painted triptych, though, that was most affected by the light; it seemed to bring the figures to life. The gilt on the horses' bridles and saddles gleamed like real gold, the grass and leaves sparkled as if freshly dewed, and the faces of the men and women glowed as though blood flowed through their veins – all but the Fairy Queen, whose face, untouched by the sunlight, remained pale and icy. I was so busy looking at the painting that I hardly noticed the human inhabitants of the party until Soheila Lilly appeared at my side with a glass of champagne for me.

"It's beautiful in this light, no? The drapes are drawn open on this day only – or else the light would fade the paint."

"That's a shame. It looks as if it was made to be in this light. I'd love to see the painting inside."

"You'll have a chance. The painting will be opened soon." Soheila glanced out the window where the sun was just slipping behind the peak of the western mountains. "We always wait until a few minutes after sunset to give the night people a chance to join in . . . Ah, here they are now. They must have come in their limo to avoid the sun."

Soheila motioned with her champagne flute toward the doorway. Standing on the threshold were the three Russian Studies professors – tall blond Anton Volkov, back from his conference apparently, petite Rea Demisovski, and short bald Ivan Klitch.

"Are they really . . . ?"

"Shh . . . they don't like the modern terminology. They prefer to be known as night people – or nocturnals."

"But do they . . ." I lowered my voice to a barely audible whisper, "drink blood?"

Anton Volkov's head shot up and snapped in my direction, his cold blue eyes fixed on mine. He was all the way across the room, but I could swear that he'd heard me. He took a step forward, but Rea Demisovski put a restraining hand on his arm and pointed at the floor in front of them where a thin ribbon of red light stretched from the windows to the bottom of the triptych. He took a step back, never taking his eyes off me.

"Damn," I said, turning to Soheila to ask if she thought he had heard me, but Soheila had left my side. She was standing a few feet away with Elizabeth Book, their heads together, whispering. The dean looked upset at something – the worry weighing down her face. When she looked up at me I was alarmed at how much she had aged in the few days since I had seen her last. Her eyes, fastened on me, were bloodshot and one eyelid drooped slightly. For all that, her look was keen when she approached me and I was afraid that she was going to scold me for offending the resident vampires – for surely that's what they were. Glancing back at the doorway where they hovered behind the bar of red sunlight I could practically feel Anton Volkov's bloodlust. He was staring at me as though he'd like to eat me.

"Callie, dear . . ." It was the dean's voice, only so much weaker than her usual tone that I had to look down to check that it was really her . . . and that was another thing. I could have sworn that when I met Dean Book she was my height, but now she was a good two inches shorter than me. Even allowing that I was wearing higher heels, that was still a lot of height to lose to osteoporosis in a few months. "Callie, dear," she repeated in a quavering voice. "I have a favor to ask you."

"I'm sorry if I insulted the Russian studies department, Dean Book. But honestly, how could you have sent me to his office knowing what he is?"

Dean Book looked confused. "Do you mean Professor Volkov? Why, he's a perfect gentleman."

"I think he turned into a bat and chased me!" I hissed.

Dean Book smiled and shook her head. "You must be mistaken, dear. Anton would never . . ."

Soheila interrupted. "We haven't much time, Liz. The door has to be opened before the last sunlight is gone."

"Of course, that's what I'm trying to arrange," the dean replied petulantly. And then, turning to me and straightening herself up to practically her former height, she asked, "We'd like you to do the honors this year, Callie. It seems fitting since you have shown a talent for opening the *real* door. This one is merely a symbol, but still . . . symbols are important."

"You want me to open the triptych?"

"Yes, please. Or rather the right side. Fiona always opens

the left side. I usually open the right side, but I . . . well, I just don't feel quite up to it today."

It was alarming to hear Elizabeth Book admit to such weakness. "Of course," I said. "It would be an honor."

I put down my champagne glass on a nearby table and walked over to the right side of the triptych. Fiona Eldritch, in a stunning green silk dress, already stood on the left side, one hand resting on the gilt handle at the center of the door. She was standing just below the figure of the Fairy Queen, a placement that could not have been accidental. I smiled at her, resisting the urge to curtsey, and placed my hand on the right side handle. I felt a bit like Vanna White on *Wheel of Fortune* gesturing toward a prize.

"You look very nice in that color," Fiona said. "It suits you better than green."

Little dull to wear the same color all the time, I thought to myself – or at least I thought it was to myself. When I saw Fiona's lips thin with displeasure I realized that my thoughts weren't my own in this company. Now I'd pissed off a vampire *and* the fairy queen. I wondered what other supernatural creature I could get on the wrong side of before the end of the night. I glanced around the room. All the guests had formed a semicircle around the triptych – except for the "night people" who still hovered in the doorway. They had all put down their champagne glasses and were holding unlit candles instead – the kind used at candlelight vigils, with paper cones attached to keep wax from dripping on their hands. I looked at the expectant faces – intercepting smiles from Casper Van der Aart and his boyfriend, Oliver – looking for one face in particular. I hadn't seen Liam since I'd arrived. And yet he'd told me I would see him here. I was just about to give up when I spotted him in the doorway, edging past the Russian studies professors. Anton Volkov raised an eyebrow at him as he passed and Rea Demisovski licked her lips.

Yikes! I'd have to warn Liam somehow to stay away from them.

Liam, seemingly unfazed by the attention of the nocturnals, took his place in the semicircle, accepting a candle from Oliver. He caught my eye and winked. I blushed and looked away . . . and caught Fiona Eldritch staring at Liam. While the brunette vampire had looked at Liam as if he'd make an appealing snack, the Fairy Queen was staring at him as if he was the last drop of water in the desert.

"Who *is* that?" Fiona asked without taking her eyes off Liam.

"That's the new writer-in-residence, Liam Doyle. Funny you haven't met him. He's been here two weeks."

Fiona began to say something but was interrupted by Liz Book calling the room to order.

"Friends and colleagues," the dean began, her voice as thin as the last ray of sunlight that quivered across the floor. "We mourn today the dying of the sun and remember those who have passed beyond the light." She paused and gazed around the room. "For who among us has not lost someone to the darkness?"

I looked around at the circle of faces and stopped when I reached Liam. Was he thinking of his childhood sweetheart, Jeannie, right now? He was standing with his back to the window, the last red rays of the sun limning his face, throwing his eyes into shadow so I couldn't see his expression.

"But just as the sun returns, and the days grow longer, so

the memories of our absent loved ones remain and we affirm our faith in love by finding new objects of our affection." Liz looked around the circle until her gaze settled on Diana and she smiled.

"So today we celebrate not the dying of the sun, but its return. We open our hearts to new love just as we open this door." Liz turned to us and I saw Fiona begin to pull the handle on her side. She could have given me a cue, I thought, tugging on my handle. The triptych panel was heavier than I had imagined and the hinges creaked. I had a terrible image of the panel breaking in my hands. That would be just my luck; I could piss off a whole bunch of supernaturals in one fell swoop.

Then I recalled reading the spell for opening in the spellbook. Perhaps it would help the door to open more smoothly.

Ianuam sprengja! I said under my breath.

The panel was suddenly light in my hands. It swung open of its own volition, so swiftly that I was flattened between the panel and the wall. I heard a gasp from the room which I thought might be for my safety, but when I extricated myself I saw that no one was looking at me. They were looking at the painting . . . only when I turned to the place on the wall where the painting had been I found myself looking through a window at another world. Deep green meadows starred with tiny flowers rolled down to a crystal blue lake surrounded by mountains that faded from indigo to violet to the palest rose and lavender. I stepped forward and instead of dissipating, the illusion deepened. I was at the edge of a dark wood, branches arching far over my head, looking out through the trees to the green meadows and the lake beyond. The scene blurred and I realized my eyes were full of tears. A faint buzzing filled my ears, like a million voices whispering or a swarm of flying insects beating their wings together. They grew as they came closer, swelling to almost human size – and *almost* human features. A host of diaphanous glowing figures swarmed around me, their sharp noses sniffing at me, their pointed ears twitching. The buzzing grew louder – the same buzzing I'd heard when I'd fallen asleep in the library . . . then I recognized them. They were the horde I'd traveled with in my dreams. *My companions*.

Our doorkeeper! Their high-pitched voices echoed as they stirred excitedly around me. Those who had wings flexed them now and swooped in the air above my head, their wings brushing my face.

You've come back to us! They cried in unison. *You've come to let us in!*

But already they were fading, just as they had faded in my dream. I reached out to touch one – a young girl with a heart-shaped face and skin mottled like a fawn's – and my hand went right through her. Another face took her place, emerging out of the dark like a skull bobbing up out of black water.

"How did you do that?" With the man's voice, the illusion faded. The lights resolved into candles held by my colleagues, the painting was a bucolic landscape framed by two panels painted to look like trees, their branches meeting over the center of the middle panel. The pale, skeletal man was Anton Volkov, his thin, angular face and ash blond hair turned to white by the candle he held.

"I don't know," I said, stepping closer to the now lifeless painting – and away from the daunting presence of the Russian Studies professor. "I think I may have said an opening spell."

"A spell alone couldn't open the door." He'd lowered his voice to a whisper and stepped closer so only I would hear him. It was like standing next to a block of ice. Waves of cold emanated from him. "But neither could a doorkeeper open a door where there was no door. This triptych is only a symbol of the real door and yet you were able to open the door to Faerie right here. It was only open for a moment, but I suspect that the real door, the one in the forest, is open now and will remain so until New Year's eve. You seem to—" he inclined his head toward my neck and sniffed delicately "—combine the qualities of fairy and witch."

"I don't know about that." I glanced around the room to see if anyone was watching us. What had the rest of the party made of that momentary opening of the door? But if anyone else had seen what Anton Volkov and I had seen they weren't letting on. Most people had been drawn to the buffet, where food and more champagne had been put out. I saw Frank Delmarco talking to Soheila and Liz, Brock and Dory, who were among several townspeople included in the gathering, standing side by side eating mini quiches and gazing at the painting, and, finally, Liam still standing in front of the darkening window talking to a tall woman.

"I've been wanting to speak to you," Professor Volkov said. "I heard you came by my office but left without leaving any message."

"You weren't there," I said, wondering who could have told him I'd been there. The building had seemed deserted. "And I know how busy everyone is during finals week. But yes, I did want to talk to you about Nicky Ballard. Dean Book told me you've identified two witches who might have been responsible for the curse. Have you been able to locate their descendants?"

"No, I haven't had a chance to check the registry in the city. This type of research must be conducted with great sensitivity. If any of their descendants thought their ancestors were being accused of misconduct they could become . . . angry."

"But Nicky will turn eighteen in May."

Although he was already standing too close, he edged an inch closer and reached his hand toward mine. "Ah, your passion is . . . *invigorating*! It makes you glow."

I snorted and made to step back, but his fingertips had come to rest on my hand. It was the lightest of touches, but it released an icy current that swept through my body. Frozen to the spot, my gaze locked on Anton Volkov's blue eyes. They were really a beautiful hue – the color of glacial ice.

"Don't be afraid. I wouldn't dream of injuring a doorkeeper. I do want to help you with Miss Ballard's predicament. I could give you the name of the two witches . . . and I'm sure that someday you would return the favor."

I moved my lips and found that I could talk, although the sound that came out of my numb lips was as faint as ice settling in a water glass. "Return the favor? How?"

"We needn't decide right now." He inhaled deeply, his long patrician nose practically quivering as if I were a glass of very expensive wine. "I wouldn't ask anything that would go against your . . . desires."

I swallowed with difficulty, my throat constricting. Was he asking me to let him drink my blood? "What if this favor . . . is something I don't want to do?"

"If you truly don't want to give what I ask, I won't insist. I trust you."

"Why? You've only just met me."

"You're a doorkeeper. Doorkeepers are always honorable."

I thought about that for a second. It was true I'd never cheated – on an exam or on a man, unless you considered having sex with an incubus *cheating*, which I didn't because I hadn't realized he was real at the time. And it was also true that I had been "lusting in my heart" after Liam Doyle while nearly engaged to Paul. Liam – where was he anyway? Why hadn't he come to rescue me from this vampire? I turned my eyes – they were all I could move – toward the window and found him still talking to a tall woman, who, I saw now, was Fiona Eldritch. He was completely focused on her. That's why he hadn't come to rescue me.

"You promise that if it's something I don't want to do you won't . . . force me."

"I would never force a lady."

"You won't *glamour* me?" I asked, recalling the phrase from a recent vampire book I'd read.

He laughed. "I *do* love that expression! But no, I promise, as a gentleman, no *glamouring*. That wouldn't be sporting."

I remembered that Liz Book had said that he was a gentleman. On the face of it, it seemed like a win-win situation. I got the information I needed to help Nicky and I didn't have to do anything that I didn't *desire*. What could go wrong?

"Okay, it's a deal. I would shake on it, but you seem to have put some immobility spell on me. I can't move."

I was released so suddenly I stumbled into Anton's arms. He grasped my hand in his hand and squeezed, bowing his head to whisper in my ear two names: Hiram Scudder and Abigail Fisk. Then he was gone, vanished in a frigid gust that fanned my face. I looked around to see if anyone had noticed his precipitous exit, but no one was even looking in my direction. Liam and Fiona were no longer standing by the window – or anywhere else in the room.

I didn't feel much in a party mood anymore. I made for the door, dodging past cheerful colleagues bent on wishing me a happy holiday and a good winter break. In the lobby I ran straight into Diana Hart who was standing awkwardly in front of the coatroom, hugging her arms around her thin frame. She started to say something to me, but I cut her off.

"Merry Christmas to you, too, Diana, and a Happy New Year, too."

I put my hand on the coatroom door and she shrieked, "Don't go in there! It's . . . locked."

The door did appear to be locked. But, hell, I'd just opened the door to Faerie. What was a coatroom door in comparison? I turned the handle and pressed my shoulder to the door, muttering, "*Ianuam sprengja!*"

It opened so suddenly that I fell into the dimly lit room, straight onto a pile of fur . . . which moved.

I leapt back, remembering the fierce clawed creature I'd glimpsed on my front porch. The fur billowed and leapt . . . then fell harmlessly to the side. Beneath it lay Fiona and Liam, clothes askew and limbs entangled.

I opened my mouth, but found I had nothing to say. Liam's eyes, full of guilt, met mine, but before he could say anything I grabbed my coat and fled.

I was halfway across the quad before I realized I'd forgotten my boots. I could feel the snow soaking though the thin soles of my delicate party shoes, but I'd rather have ruined all the shoes in my closet than gone back to Briggs to face Liam Doyle.

Not that I had any right to be angry at him, I reminded myself. I had no claim on him. I *had* a boyfriend – one who was winging his way across the country right now, possibly with a diamond ring in his pocket. I wasn't angry with Liam, I told myself as I reached the path to the southeast gate, I was angry with myself.

The path was less well shoveled than the ones on the quad – and darker because of the trees overshadowing it. There should have been a security light at the bottom by the gate, but either the timers hadn't been adjusted to the early twilight yet or it was broken. At least the gate was still open. I could see my street beyond it and even the faint glow of my own porch light. I hurried toward it, wanting nothing more than to be in my own house to nurse my wounds in private. What an idiot! I muttered as I strode down the hill. Not only had I let myself develop a schoolgirl crush on Liam Doyle, I'd made a rather vague deal with a vampire! And all for two names that I could have gotten eventually from Dean Book.

A noise behind me cut short my thoughts. It was the same noise I'd heard coming out of Bates Hall – the sound of wings. Could it be Anton Volkov, changed into a bat, come to collect on our deal? I sprang for the gates. Could iron stop a vampire? Or was it fairies who didn't like iron? Whatever . . . I was running, spurred on by the beat of wings at my back, trying to remember the spell for averting an attack from above. Was it *Vox Faca naddel nem*? Or *va fadir nox nim*? "Oh hell," I shouted within a yard from the gate, "*faca vadum negg!*"

Immediately the ground beneath me lurched and I fell into a pothole that hadn't been there a moment before. My knees and hands slammed onto the broken icy pavement.

Something heavy and feathery struck my head. I crouched and tried to cover my face. Claws dug into my skin . . . then a hand grasped mine. I looked up and found Liam Doyle crouched beside me. The bird – a giant black crow even bigger than the shape I'd seen outside of Bates Hall – beat at his face once and then soared out through the gate, cawing harshly as it disappeared.

"Callie, are you all right?" Liam's hands were all over me, looking for wounds. There was only one cut on my hand. He tore the sleeve of his shirt – he wasn't wearing a coat – and wrapped it around my hand

"I'm okay," I said – but I wasn't. I was shaking uncontrollably. Liam pulled me to him and wrapped his arms around me. I was shaking too hard to resist. I burrowed into his arms like an animal burrows into its nest. Around us the woods were dark and cold. Who knew what other horrifying creatures they held? I looked up at Liam and saw that his cheek was streaked with blood. I touched the scratch that had missed his eye by the merest centimeter.

"It could have taken your eye out!"

"I couldn't let it hurt you," he said fiercely. Then he leaned down and pressed his lips on mine. They were so warm—-with the cold and dark creeping closer around us they were like a candle burning in the vast dark forest. I leaned into that heat, hungry for it. His lips opened mine and I felt his heat pouring into me, flooding me, opening something deep inside me, as if his lips had turned a key at the base of my spine and unlocked a door I hadn't known was locked.

But just as I felt that opening I remembered pushing open the door to the coatroom and finding him with Fiona Eldritch.

I pushed him away.

"Cal—"

"No, don't." I got painfully to my feet, my scraped knees stinging in the cold. When I swayed he reached out for me, but I grabbed the gate and he stopped. "Please, you don't owe me an explanation. I'm practically engaged . . . and I have to go."

I backed away from him, still holding onto the gate. I wasn't sure I could stand without it. I backed through the gate but let it go when I was on the other side. Liam was looking at me, his eyes burning, but he didn't come any closer, didn't try to stop me. Seeing that gave me the strength to stand up on my own. I turned around, and started walking toward my house. I listened for the sound of footsteps – or wings – following but all I heard was the iron clang of the gate closing behind me.

CHAPTER TWENTY-FIVE

I had been planning to leave in the morning to avoid driving at night, but I decided to leave right away.

"Sorry, fellow," I told Ralph as I was getting packed. "If I take you to New York you might get eaten by a rat."

He sat up in his teacup and wiggled his nose. "Don't worry," I said, going to add warmer boots to my suitcase. "Brock is going to look after you and who better to take care of you than the guy who made you?"

When I turned back to the desk Ralph was no longer in the teacup. He wasn't in his basket or in my sheepskin slippers or any of his other favorite places either. He must be sulking that I wasn't taking him with me. Who knew magical doormice were so moody?

I turned off all the lights downstairs, turned the heat down to 65, and wrote a quick note to Brock telling him to give Ralph the rest of the brie in the refrigerator. Then I locked the door of Honeysuckle House behind me and left it to its own devices.

Navigating the dark country roads to the state highway took all my concentration for a while, mercifully giving me no opportunity to dwell on my recent behavior. But when I reached Interstate 17, scenes from the party and afterward began replaying in my head. What had possessed me to make a deal with Anton Volkov? I didn't even know if the names he'd given me would do me any good. I'd never heard of Abigail Fisk, but I recognized Hiram Scudder's name as Ballard's business partner, whose wife had committed suicide after the Great Train Crash of '93 and its resulting shame and bankruptcy. Good enough reason to curse someone, I imagined, but if Scudder's descendants were easy to find then someone at Fairwick would have done it by now. Even if I could find the descendants of Abigail Fisk or Hiram Scudder, what was the likelihood that I could convince them to take the curse off Nicky? So I'd compromised myself for basically useless information – and that wasn't the only way I'd compromised myself. Why had I gotten so upset at finding Liam and Fiona in the coatroom? It was none of my business if they wanted to hook up – they really were perfect for each other . . . both irresistible to the opposite sex . . .

But then why had Liam kissed me by the gate?

At the memory of the kiss my limbs loosened . . . and I nearly swerved into the left lane in front of a tractor trailer. Shaken, I gripped the wheel tighter and glued my eyes to the white lines. The kiss meant nothing, I told myself. Certainly it meant nothing to him. He'd told me a whole long sad story about why he never fell in love, but he hadn't said anything about the occasional dalliance. Clearly Fiona was the Moira-type. And what was I? I didn't really fit the Moira or Jeannie profile. I had suggested to him the possibility of finding someone who wasn't either a Moira or a Jeannie – had he thought I meant myself? Is that why he kissed me? But *had* he really kissed me? Twice I'd thought he'd been about to and I'd been wrong. Maybe *I* had kissed *him*?

The thought was so mortifying that I nearly swerved again. What had come over me lately? First I'd had sex with an incubus – well, I hadn't had much choice about that . . . or had I? There had to be some reason that the incubus had been able to seduce me. After all, Matilda Lindquist had lived in Honeysuckle House for decades without having sex with the incubus. Maybe there was something about me that drew him. Something that was *unsatisfied*.

Well, *duh*, my boyfriend lived three thousand miles away and I only saw him a handful of times a year. No wonder I was unsatisfied. No wonder I was going around seducing incubi and sexy Irish poets and vampires. I was becoming "a woman of loose moral standards," as my grandmother Adelaide, who would never use a common word like slut even when it was perfectly clear that's what she meant, would say. Well, there was one answer to that – I needed to settle down. If Paul really did have a job in New York and he did want to marry me, I couldn't keep up this long-distance nonsense. I had to move back to the city even if it meant taking adjunct jobs until I found something full time. I'd put Honeysuckle House up for sale and use the rest of my trust fund to buy a decent apartment in Brooklyn – or Queens, or Westchester, or even New Jersey – with Paul. By the time I'd reached the George Washington Bridge I'd made up my mind and was confident I was making the right choice. I couldn't wait to tell Paul.

Navigating the West Side Highway down to Battery Park and finding the Ritz-Carlton took up all my brainpower for the rest of the trip. By the time I surrendered my car to the black-coated, fur-hatted valet (he looked like one of the guards of the Wicked Witch of the West) I was exhausted. I nearly wept with gratitude when the bellhop showed me to my club level deluxe room on the 11th floor with a spectacular view of New York Harbor. As soon as I was alone I ran hot water in the capacious tub, adding the lemon-scented bath gel that came with the room, shucked off my clothes, and sank into the hot, soapy water. I gently sponged the grit from my scraped knees. Perversely, the pain brought back the memory of Liam's kiss, the heat of his mouth on mine . . .

No, no, no! I told myself, dunking my head under the hot water. I held my breath until the image dissipated, then washed my hair and scrubbed myself with the comple-mentary loofah and lemon shower gel until I'd banished the image of Liam's face from my head. Then I wrapped myself up in the big lush hotel robe and called the airline to see if Paul's plane had landed on time. It had landed ten minutes ago, so I figured he'd arrive in about an hour.

The plan had been for him to come to the hotel and get some sleep, and for me to arrive in the morning. I hoped that finding me in bed would be a welcome surprise. I called room service and ordered a bottle of champagne (wincing a bit when I saw the price). There was already a com-plementary fruit basket and cheese plate, so I didn't order any food. I dried my hair and changed into a pink silk nightgown that Paul had given me for Valentine's Day last year. I didn't usually wear pink, but I knew Paul liked it on me.

I looked at the clock and saw that I still had at least half an hour until Paul arrived. I tried to arrange myself artfully on the bed, but that just made me feel silly . . . and cold. All those glass windows facing the harbor made the room chilly. I got up to pull the drapes, but then stood instead at the window looking out at the lights of boats flickering on the black water. I sank down into a chair in front of the window, wrapping myself in the terry robe I'd left there, and stared out at the harbor lights. They reminded me of something . . . will o' the wisps floating through a dark wood, candles in a vast hall, snowflakes falling out of a black sky . . . I felt myself drifting with the ebb and flow of the bay's tide . . .

I was standing in a dark wood, the same woods I'd found myself in after I'd opened the triptych in Briggs Hall, but instead of being surrounded by diaphanous creatures only one figure stood before me. It was *him*, the incubus, my demon lover. He glowed as if lit by moonlight, though there was no moon here, nor sun – there was no time at all.

"Only one eternal night", he said stepping toward me, "for us to make love in."

"I sent you away," I said as he raised his hand to my cheek. His flesh was cold but I leaned into the cup of his palm as if leaning toward a warm fire. My skin tingled from head to toe as if a deliciously cool waterfall streamed over me. The hand on my cheek stroked my throat, my breasts . . . My nipples grew hard and I felt a corresponding tug between my legs. He cupped my buttocks with his other hand and pressed me against the cool length of his erection. I wrapped my arms and legs around him, wanting to mold my body to his, to merge with him . . . and that's what was happening. As he entered me I felt cold white light pouring into me. He was filling me up with liquid moonlight . . . and I was vanishing into him . . .

I startled awake, flailing my hands out to grasp

something solid and found myself grasping someone's arm.

"Cal, it's me, Paul."

I looked up at Paul's face and thought, no, that's not him. Then I shook myself fully awake. "I must have fallen asleep," I said. "I was waiting . . ."

"I see that." He sat down in the chair opposite mine. "I thought you were coming tomorrow."

I sat up and wrapped the robe around myself, trying to shake off the bone-chilling cold – a cold I had wanted to draw *inside* of me – and concentrate. "I decided to come down tonight."

"I thought you hated driving in the dark."

"I do, but I wanted to see you . . ." I looked harder at Paul. He was wearing a suit. *That* was weird. He usually flew in jeans and a sweatshirt. Why would he wear a suit on a night flight? He'd cut his hair recently, too, shorter than he usually wore it. He looked thinner; the bit of baby fat that used to fill out his face and around his stomach was gone. He looked good – older, a little edgier, but good. But he wasn't looking at me. He was looking around the room and out the window, but whenever his gaze crossed mine his eyes slid away.

"What's wrong?" I asked, cinching the belt of the robe tighter. "Was your flight okay? It must be scary to fly after—"

"It was fine. It's just . . . I thought we'd talk in the morning . . ." His eyes skittered past me again – to the bottle of champagne cooling in an ice bucket, to the fruit and cheese – then he wrenched them back to me. Not to my face, but to the robe and my bare legs and the bit of pink silk peeking out. For a horrified moment I was afraid he could sense my arousal from the dream.

"Talk about what?" I asked, my stomach clenching.

He leaned forward and covered his face with his hands. "Callie . . . I . . . there's something I have to tell you and it isn't easy. For some time I've wondered if things were really right between us. You've seemed distracted this fall . . ."

"I've been getting used to a new job," I began defensively, but then I stopped. I could see the anguish on Paul's face. He looked as if he were in real physical pain. Oh my God, I thought, he's not here to propose to me, he's here to break up with me! "There's someone else, isn't there?" I asked, immediately hating how timeworn the question felt.

He winced. Swallowed. Ran his hands through his hair as if he meant to pull it out by the roots. "Yes. Rita, the woman I met on the plane last month . . ." It all spilled out then, how they'd held each other's hands when their plane almost crashed, how they'd spent the weekend at her parents' house in Binghamton ("Oh," I said woodenly, "I thought *she* lived in Binghamton." "No, she lives here in the city," Paul replied.), and how she had told him he ought to work in finance instead of just studying it (Rita turned out to be an investment analyst at a major Wall Street firm), and they started talking and emailing and texting and she had arranged an interview out in L.A. for him, and then this interview in New York, which was really only a formality because he'd already been offered the job at the big Wall Street firm, and he and Rita had already talked about him moving into her Tribeca loft.

"So I guess I'm the only detail you had to attend to," I said when he finished.

"Don't make it sound like that, Cal. I didn't want to do

this on the phone. And I couldn't make you come out to California and *then* tell you. I thought it would be easier if you were in the city around friends and family . . ."

I laughed. "Family? Did you forget my grandmother lives in Santa Fe now? Not that I'd be likely to cry on her shoulder anyway."

"I meant Annie," he said. "I didn't know if you were close to anyone up there yet, although I have wondered . . ."

"If I'm sleeping with anyone? I guess that would be easier on you if I were. No, I'm sorry to disappoint you. I'm not sleeping with anyone." I knew what I was saying was technically true and that if I tried to explain about the incubus Paul would have thought I was crazy. Still I felt a little twinge of guilt at the half lie.

"Actually, that's kind of a relief – I know, I know," he said as I spluttered. "I have no right to say that; it's just I've had this feeling that there is something you haven't been telling me."

Although it was painful to realize how serious Paul was about Rita, I couldn't really blame him for feeling I hadn't been entirely honest with him when I'd been hiding a slew of supernatural occurrences – and one very natural kiss. I sighed. "I suppose I might have a crush on the new writing teacher."

"I knew it! That Liam fellow. I Googled him and thought he looked just your type."

"Really? I didn't think so . . . and I don't think it'll go anywhere. We haven't . . . Well, it's not serious."

"Oh," Paul said, looking plainly relieved.

"So you Googled him?" I asked.

"Yeah." He smiled sheepishly. "And looked at his Facebook page. Geez, the guy's like an action hero –

teaching inner city kids, working for Amnesty International, and his poetry's not half bad."

The fact that Paul had actually read Liam's poetry touched me oddly. I looked at him carefully. He'd relaxed enough to sit back in his chair. His hair was ruffled from the strenuous raking he'd been giving it. He looked younger again, like the Paul I'd met in college. I suddenly knew that if I made an effort here I could probably wrest him away from Rita. He'd wanted to talk in the morning because he didn't trust himself not to sleep with me – and if he slept with me he'd feel obliged to tell Rita and they'd fight . . . it wouldn't really be that hard. I could tell Paul my plans for quitting my job at Fairwick and moving back to the city. With his new job on Wall Street we could probably afford an apartment in Manhattan. And I had to admit that Paul would be happier working on Wall Street than he'd been teaching demanding undergraduates. And a happier Paul might be easier to be with . . . as long as I was really happy too.

But I suddenly knew, without a doubt, that my happiness didn't lie with Paul. I got up. "I should leave," I said. "I'll go stay with Annie in Brooklyn."

"No!" he said, jumping to his feet. "I planned to let you keep the room. The firm booked it for five days. I can go stay with . . ." He stumbled over Rita's name and my resolve faltered as well. It was one thing admitting to myself that the relationship was over, and another sending him out to another woman.

But I could only delay that by one night unless I wanted him back.

"I think you'd better go," I said. "But I'm warning you, once this really sinks in I might order a lot of room service."

CHAPTER TWENTY-SIX

In the next two days I *did* order quite a bit of room service and I *did* at first get a rather perverse pleasure out of the outrageous prices – $34 for a pint of Häagen-Dazs ice cream! On the second day I found Ralph eating M&Ms from the mini-bar. I gave him a stern lecture. He could have suffocated in my suitcase! He'd get us kicked out! Did he know how much those M&Ms cost? In truth, he was welcome company during the long nights when the wind shrieked outside the hotel like a banshee.

After a few days of walking along the Battery Park Esplanade through gale-force icy winds and eating expensive ice cream I was tired of feeling sorry for myself. On the 24th I called Annie and asked if I could spend Christmas Eve with her and Maxine.

"If you don't mind delivering bread," she told me.

I'd forgotten that she and Maxine donated bread to homeless shelters on Christmas.

"Sure," I told her. "I can't imagine a better way of spending the holiday."

An hour later Annie picked me up at the hotel. The bakery van was warm and smelled like fresh baked bread. Annie gave me a bone-crunching hug that left me covered with flour and thawed the ice in my heart for the first time in two days. I promptly burst into tears.

"Spill it!" Annie ordered, pulling into traffic.

I told Annie about the break up, about Rita and the Wall Street job and being left alone in a hotel room all by myself. I'd worked myself up into a snit of self-pity by the end of it.

"There's something you're not telling me," she said when I was done.

"About Paul?" I asked, shamming innocence. "I think I told you everything he said . . ."

"No, not about Paul. About what led up to Paul."

"But I told you about the plane and the storm and Rita . . ."

"I don't mean all that," she said impatiently, shaking her head. Her dark curly hair was tied up in a high ponytail that swished angrily. I realized that some of the specks I'd thought were flour were gray hairs. "Paul would never have fallen in love with someone else if you hadn't checked out first."

"Oh, so it's my fault," I said angrily, remembering now how judgmental Annie could be sometimes. "I didn't know you were such a big fan of Paul's."

"I've never said anything against Paul. As I've told you many times, I just didn't think he was the right guy for you. I still don't. If you had broken up with him I'd be saying 'about time,' but for him to break up with you means you haven't been trying. And if you've been as out of it with him as you have been with me since September, I can understand why he went and fell in love with the first girl who held his hand on a bumpy flight."

"Hey, that's not fair!" I said, swiveling around in my seat

to face Annie. "When you first got together with Maxine I barely saw you for six months."

Annie raised one dark eyebrow, but kept her eyes on the road as she turned onto Canal Street. "True," she said. "So is that why I've barely heard from you these last three months? You've been having great sex with someone new?"

I began to splutter a denial, but one cool look from Annie silenced me. With Paul I'd been able to cling to the technicality that sex with an incubus – and one kiss with Liam Doyle – didn't really count as cheating, but I wasn't going to pull the wool over Annie's keen hazel eyes.

"Sort of," I answered. "It depends on how you define sex."

"Well, hello, Bill Clinton!" Annie grinned. "And you've been keeping this from me because I'm so conservative and judgmental?"

"No, I've been keeping this from you because you'll think I'm crazy."

We'd pulled up in front of the Bowery Mission. Annie turned to me and shook her head. "Sweetie, who did I go to when I was thirteen and realized I liked girls better than boys? Who told *me* I wasn't crazy, I was just gay?"

I returned her smile. "I'm afraid this is a bit more complicated, but if you're sure you want to hear it . . ."

Annie crossed her eyes at me. "Complicated, crazy, unbelievable sex? Please honey, start talking."

And so I did. In between delivering fresh bread to more than a dozen shelters and soup kitchens, from the Bowery to Chelsea to Hell's Kitchen and the Upper West Side, I told Annie everything that had happened at Fairwick from the first visitation of the incubus to his banishment and about all the creatures I'd met – the witches, fairies, brownies, dwarves, gnomes, vampires, and magical doormice – and the tantalizing glimpse I'd had of the world of Faerie through the triptych door on the Solstice. She listened in silence, her lips pursed, her eyes focused on the city traffic, opening her mouth only to hurl invectives at an S.U.V. with New Jersey plates that cut her off. I finished just as we reached our last stop, the men's shelter at the Cathedral of St. John the Divine.

She switched the engine off and turned to me. I was expecting her to tell me that I needed to get professional help. Knowing Annie, she'd offer to go with me and support me in any way she could. But all she said was, "Come with me. There's something I need to show you."

She asked two of the helpers at the soup kitchen if they wouldn't mind unloading the bread (they didn't), and took me up a flight of back stairs to the cathedral. While at grad school at Columbia I'd gotten into the habit of visiting the massive, unfinished Episcopalian cathedral. I didn't consider myself religious, but I liked the peace of the hushed, vaulted space and the beauty of the stained-glass windows. I liked, too, the Cathedral's philosophy of inter-action with the modern world. I had learned on a tour that each of the side aisle windows was devoted to an aspect of human endeavor, such as the arts and communication. These windows had secular and often surprisingly modern details – like a panel with Jack Benny playing his violin in front of a microphone in the Communications window. I also liked St. John's mission. First constructed in 1893, the same year as Ellis Island, the cathedral was dedicated to aiding immigrants. There was a sense of inclusion and tolerance – symbolized perhaps most notably by the huge gold menorahs and Shinto vases flanking the altar, but also by the Chapels of the Seven Tongues which circled the apse, each one dedicated to an immigrant group. It was to the Italian chapel – St. Ambrose's – that Annie now took me.

"Did you know I used to come here to pray when we were in high school?" she asked as we entered the ornate, Renaissance-style chapel.

"No," I said, sitting down beside her on a folding chair. "I thought you gave up the Church in the eighth grade."

"The *Catholic* church," she said, folding her hands and looking up at the altar. "I figured why should I keep going to a church that told me I was going to hell because of what I was? But after a while I missed something – a feeling I'd gotten at Mass sometimes, you know?"

She looked at me, an uncharacteristically uncertain look on her face, and I realized she was embarrassed. We talked plenty about our sex lives, but never about religion. "Yeah," I said, "I think I know what you mean. I used to come to the Cathedral between classes – for cultural and art history reasons, I'd tell myself – but also for the feeling I got sitting here."

"Huh, so we're both closet church groupies and we never knew it." She grinned, looking more like the self-assured Annie I knew. "I came to this chapel in particular because it's dedicated to an Italian saint. I figured it was one thing to give up being a Catholic, and another to give up being *Italian*."

"*Dio mio!*" I exclaimed in mock horror. "Perish the thought!" And then, in a more serious voice, I asked, "Did you really think you'd have to give up being Italian because you're gay?"

"I know it sounds stupid, but I didn't know what – or who – I might have to give up. I was relieved that I didn't have to give up my best friend—" she gave my hand a quick squeeze "—but you know I didn't tell my mother until I was sixteen. The day I was going to tell her I came here first. I prayed that my mother wouldn't be too upset, and that I wouldn't lose my temper if she was, and that she wouldn't . . . stop loving me." Annie's voice broke on the last words and I reached over and gave her hand a squeeze. I kept hold of it while she continued. "So I'm sitting here and this old woman comes in and sits down next to me. She looks like your typical Italian *nonna*. Black dress, black kerchief tied over her hair, which was gray – I was sure it was gray when she sat down – a widow's hump the size of a basketball, no teeth. She was muttering something under her breath when she came in. Some prayer, I figured, although it didn't sound like Italian or English or even Latin. Anyway, we're both sitting here and after a couple of minutes she puts her hand on mine, just like you have your hand on mine now, and she says to me, 'There's nothing to be afraid of, Anne Marie. Your mother loves you for who you are and she will always love you.' I started to ask her how she knew what I was afraid of – did she know me? – but when I turned I was blinded by a light behind her, from the window, I thought, only it was an overcast day. I could still see her silhouetted against the light, but she was no longer stooped and old, and her hair was long and shiny white. Then I looked away for a moment and she was gone. Lying in the chair where she'd been was this . . ."

Annie removed from her pocket a small, round, white stone. It was worn away in the center so that one edge formed a slender crescent. "I took it with me and held it in my hand when I told my mother I was gay. You know what she said, right?"

" 'Better you should like women than be a *puta* like your cousin Esta,' " I said, repeating the line that Annie had told me years ago.

"And then she hugged me and scolded me for not telling her sooner. The old woman was right. My mother never loved me any less . . ." Annie wiped her eyes. Sylvana Mastroanni had died of breast cancer when Annie was eighteen. "That old woman gave me the courage to face my mother and if I hadn't – and she had died before I did . . ." Annie stopped, unable to finish the thought. After a few moments she continued. "I've always believed that old woman was some kind of angel . . . or maybe, after hearing what you've told me, a fairy or an ancient goddess. So I believe that you've ended up at a college for witches and fairies." She smiled. "Hell, I'm not even that surprised. You were always a little . . . different."

"Thanks!" I said, swatting her on the arm. "You make me sound like a head case."

"No, I didn't mean it like that. It's just that your background – dead parents, frosty, forbidding grandmother . . ."

"My grandmother wasn't that bad," I interrupted, thinking guiltily that I ought to call her tomorrow. I hadn't spoken with her at all since I'd called to tell her that I'd gotten the job at Fairwick, but then she'd been so snippy that I hadn't wanted to speak to her for a while. "And she did her best for a sixty-year-old woman suddenly saddled with an obnoxious pre-teen."

"Okay, okay, I meant no disrespect to Adelaide. I'm just pointing out that you always had the set-up to turn into the

heroine of one of those gothic romances you're always
reading . . . and now you have."

"I'm not a heroine," I pointed out, trying to hide my
immense relief that Annie believed me behind a façade of
grumpiness. "Merely an assistant professor. I don't even
have tenure yet."

Annie put her arm around my shoulder. "Hey, from what
you told me, you're important to these people . . . uh, fairies
. . . witches . . . whatever they are. You're the doorkeeper!
They'll have to give you tenure!"

CHAPTER TWENTY-SEVEN

Mouse or no mouse, waking up alone in a hotel room on Christmas morning was, I decided, the pits. Ralph's company – he had taken to sleeping in the ice bucket with a shoeshine flannel for a blanket – just gave my solitude that little bit of Victorian piquancy needed to make my situation seem truly pathetic: like Cinderella who has only her little animal friends for company.

I ordered us a big room service breakfast, price be damned, to cheer myself up, and then I did what I'd been thinking I should do last night: I called my grandmother in Santa Fe. I got her voicemail. I wished her a merry Christmas and told her I'd thought of her last night at St. John the Divine. Then I hung up feeling that I'd done my duty without actually having to talk to her. Ten minutes later the phone rang.

"So you're in town," my grandmother said without a hello or seasons's greetings. "Have you come to your senses and left that second-rate college?"

"No, Adelaide." She had dispensed with me calling her *Grandma* when I was ten because she said it made her feel old. "I'm just in town for a few days . . ."

"Good," she cut me off briskly. "So am I. I'm staying at

my club. If you don't have any other plans for the day we could have tea here."

For a moment I considered telling her I was going to Annie's. I hated admitting to her that I was friendless on Christmas Day, but then I realized that *she* was apparently alone – and lonely enough to be checking her home voicemail by remote – and chided myself for my selfishness.

"I'd love to," I told her.

"Come at one," she answered crisply. "And remember, the Grove Club doesn't allow jeans."

I hung up, feeling like a sulky teenager who had to be reminded to dress properly for her college interviews, and remembering why I always tried to keep my interactions with my grandmother brief. I'd meant it when I defended her to Annie last night – she wasn't *that* bad. She could have sent me off to boarding school, but she'd opened her small, tidy two-bedroom apartment to me, giving up her study for me to use as a bedroom (although many of her books and papers remained stored in my closet), and dutifully oversaw my education until I went to college. It had been a little jarring when she retired to Santa Fe the same week I graduated from high school. It meant that I had to spend all my holidays either in the dorm or on a friend's couch. But I couldn't really blame her. At least she'd waited until I graduated high school to move. She'd been complaining about the New York winters and talking about retiring to Santa Fe, where she had a house she'd inherited from an aunt, for years. I was surprised that she'd come back to New York during the winter.

I dressed carefully in a wool skirt and cashmere sweater and put my hair up, recalling that Adelaide always commented on how long it was if I left it down. I left early, figuring the subways would run slowly on Christmas Day. I still had an hour to kill, though, when I reached Midtown. I walked along Fifth Avenue, looking at the Christmas windows in Lord & Taylor, recalling a Christmas my mother had taken me to see the windows.

"Look, fairies!" she had said, pointing to a flock of winged figures crafted out of silk and gauze hovering above a snow-covered diorama of Central Park. "If only they really looked like that."

I'd always thought that she had meant "If only they really existed!" but now I wondered if my mother had known enough about fairies to know they weren't quite so sweet and adorable. Diana Hart had said I had fairy blood, but from whom? My mother or my father? I supposed I could ask my grandmother, but phrasing such a question to Adelaide Danbury was unthinkable.

As I walked past the public library's main branch I realized guiltily that there were other more pressing genealogical questions. I'd meant to use my time in the city to look up the descendants of Hiram Scudder and Abigail Fisk, but I'd been too caught up in my own break-up drama to make it here. Now it was too late. The library was obviously closed on Christmas Day . . . unless . . .

I dug into my wallet, pulled out the I.M.P. card Liz Book had given me, and read the back.

ACCESS TO SPECIAL COLLECTIONS AND EXCLUSIVE HOURS AT PARTICIPATING INSTITUTIONS.

Liz had said the main branch was a participating institution, but did I have to make an appointment? I really should get Liz Book to find my orientation packet and give me some hands-on training in casting spells. My knees were still stinging from the tumble I'd taken when I'd cast the wrong spell on the Solstice . . . but in the meantime, it couldn't hurt to see if the card could get me in the library.

Feeling pretty foolish, I walked up the granite steps, past Patience and Fortitude, the twin lions, resplendent in their Christmas wreaths. When I got to the locked and gated doors I felt even more foolish. What had I thought? That I'd wave my membership card in front of the lock and the great brass doors would swing open?

I did notice, though, that etched amid the swirling acanthus filigree were two crescent moons facing away from each other, just like on the I.M.P. card, which I still had in my hand. Feeling sillier than ever I swiped the card over the moons on the door.

Something clicked.

I stared at the door until another click startled me out of my surprise. I tried the handle. It didn't move. But then, remembering how time sensitive the buzzer on my apartment door was I tried it again. As soon as I heard the click I pulled the door handle. The door opened.

I stood gaping at the open door for several moments until a voice called from inside.

"Are you coming in or not? You're letting in a draft."

I opened the heavy door and stepped into the great marble foyer. The giant marble candelabra and hanging lamps were unlit. The only light came from the clerestory arches. In one of the deepest shadows a slim young man muffled in a heavy wool coat and voluminous scarf sat on a folding chair. He had been reading a book with the aid of a clip-on book light, but was now looking up at me, his bony hand reaching toward me.

"Card, please."

I handed over my I.M.P. card, hoping I wasn't violating

some academic protocol by barging into the library on Christmas Day. The young man held the card up to a weak ray of light and tilted it back and forth. The moons waxed full and waned to slim crescents on the plastic surface.

"Okay," he said, getting to his feet with a sigh and a creak of bones. Although he couldn't be more than thirty, his sandy hair was thinning on top and he acted like an old man – and dressed like one. Underneath the heavy tweed overcoat he wore a plaid vest with pocket watch and tie.

"Justin Plean," he said, holding out a raw-boned hand. "Very Special Collections. What can I help you with today?"

"I'm trying to track down the descendants of two . . . um . . . *persons*."

"What sort of persons?"

"Um . . . I'm not sure . . . do you mean . . . ?"

"Fairies, witches, demons, or miscellaneous?"

"Witches," I replied, wondering what "miscellaneous" covered.

"Very good," he replied, all business. "Come with me."

He took off at a good clip that belied his antiquated clothing, his coattails flapping. I quickly saw why he was so abundantly clothed. The library was freezing.

"They don't leave the heat on for you?" I asked when I caught up with him at the elevator.

"Budget cuts," he said, shaking his head. "You're lucky you found me here today. I.M.P. can't afford to pay overtime, but those of us who take the job seriously wouldn't think of leaving the library unattended."

"That's very conscientious of you," I remarked as we got into the elevator.

Justin Plean shrugged but looked pleased. "It's my job. Do you need help with the genealogical records?"

"I probably will. I've never used them before."

"They're a little . . . *tricky*," he admitted. "You said you wanted to look up two witches? I'll get you started on one and then see what I can find on the other."

Delighted to find someone so helpful, I wrote down both names in a small notebook Justin took out of his coat pocket.

The door opened onto blackness. For a moment I had the dreadful thought that mild-mannered, bookish Justin Plean was a psychotic serial killer who'd lured me to the library's basement to dismember me, but as he strode out the door motion detector lights flicked on revealing row upon row of floor to ceiling bookshelves as far as the eye could see.

"Wow! Are all these about magic and witchcraft?"

Justin turned to flash me a grin. It made him look about twelve. "Cool, isn't it? These are the grimoires." He splayed his long fingers along a row of leather-bound books. "And these are bestiaries. The genealogy records are in the back bay." He walked so quickly I had trouble keeping up with him. I would have loved to stop and explore, but I didn't dare be late for tea with my grandmother.

Justin led me to a small carrel in a dusty corner lit by a flickering fluorescent light. He plucked a large book bound in a standard library binding off a shelf and handed it to me. "R through T of CROSB which stands for . . ."

"The Central Registry of Supernatural Beings," I said quickly, proud to know *something*.

Justin gave me a rather condescending smile. "Just look up your Scudder. The most current descendants should be listed there. I'll go looking for Abigail Fisk."

I thanked him, sat down and opened the books. Puffs of dust rose from its delicate, print-crammed pages. How new could it be? I wondered, peering at the miniscule type. Would it really have the latest descendants of Hiram Scudder?

But as I paged through to "S" I noticed that a more modern type font alternated with the old fashioned print. In fact, there were half a dozen different specimens of type in evidence. I guessed that each time the book was updated a different type was used. My eyes jumped over the uneven type until the lines on the page seemed to be vibrating in the flickering light. I could feel the muscles of my eye contracting and spasming with the effort. By the time I got to "Sc" my eyes stung.

Scales, Scanlon, Scarlett, I read.

Scott, Scott, Scott.

Scu . . .

My finger ran into a black ink splotch that swelled in my bleary vision.

Maybe I needed reading glasses, I thought, leaning back and closing my eyes for a moment.

When I opened them the splotch had grown six inches and sprouted legs.

I screamed and sprang back, knocking the chair to the floor.

The splotch quivered and launched itself through the air directly at my face. I screamed again and ducked. I heard a wet splat behind me and turned, hoping the thing was dead but the gelatinous mass was gathering itself for another leap. As it sprang I grabbed a book from the shelf next to me and swung it like a baseball bat. The splotch squelched like a rotten tomato, but I didn't stop to see if it was dead. I ran, screaming for Justin Plean and pulling down books behind me to impede the splotch's progress. I could hear it chittering wetly at my heels. Not dead. Desperately I tried to remember a spell that would be useful. The thing wasn't attacking me from above, so that one wouldn't work. There was one, I recalled, to prevent bedbugs but then this wasn't a bedbug . . . or – gruesome thought! – what if it was? The city was supposedly overrun with them. What if this was a mutated magical version? Ugh! I recalled the spell as best as I could and turned around to face the creature . . . and wished I hadn't. The splotch had ballooned to the size of an overweight pit bull and it had grown pincers. Horrified, I watched as it gathered itself for one more attack. I raised my hands to shield my face as best as I could and began to recite the spell, but before I could I heard someone else reciting the words: *Pestis sprengja!* Then I heard a shriek that sounded like something's death throes. I lowered my hands and saw Justin Plean standing over a puddle of yellow ooze with an open book in his hands.

"What the hell was that?" I gasped, leaning against a shelf to steady my trembling legs.

Justin took out a handkerchief from his vest pocket and wiped yellow flecks from his glasses.

"A lacuna," he said, his voice trembling. "A biblio-parasite that nests in books and grows when it smells blood. Nasty things." He closed the book in his hands and wiped its cover clean with his handkerchief. It was in a plain library binding like mine, but there were a dozen or so slips of paper sticking out marking pages.

"Geez, do you get a lot of them?"

Justin shook his head. "Almost never. We dust twice a year with repellant and check all new acquisitions for signs of contamination." He slipped the spellbook in his pocket and looked at me. "Where did you find it?"

"In the book you gave me . . . under 'S'. I had just gotten to Scudder when I saw this . . . *spot*." I shuddered recalling that I had touched it. I wiped my hand against my skirt and noticed that I had yellow specks on my sweater.

Justin nodded. "I suspected as much. Someone planted the lacuna there, blotting out the Scudder lineage and discouraging anyone who tried to go looking for it. One of his descendants, I suspect, who doesn't want to be connected to Hiram Scudder."

"That could mean that Hiram Scudder was the witch responsible for the curse."

"Maybe," Justin said, removing his notebook from his pocket, "but I found out something interesting about Abigail Fisk's descendants. One of them teaches at Fairwick."

"Well that's not unusual. Lots of witches teach at Fairwick."

"Yes, but no one knows this one's a witch. He's there under false pretenses." He handed me his notebook. Under Abigail Fisk Justin had written a name I knew. It was Frank Delmarco.

CHAPTER TWENTY-EIGHT

I didn't have a lot of time to digest the news that Frank Delmarco – blunt, proletarian, Jets fan Frank! – was a witch. And a witch descended from a Fairwick witch who had known and been wronged somehow by Bertram Ballard! I was late for tea with my grandmother and I wasn't about to incur her wrath. It was bad enough that my sweater was damp from the Oxi-clean Justin had sprayed on it to remove lacuna-ooze.

I arrived breathless at the Grove Club, which was located in a town house in the East 40s, not far from the Williams Club and the Century Club. Unlike those august New York institutions, though, it had never been clear to me what purpose the Grove Club served. On the few occasions I'd been invited to share tea with Adelaide there, I got only the vaguest impression of the other club members tucked away in the recesses of their high-backed chairs: a glimpse of a thick ankle encased in support hose and a handmade English walking shoe, a charm-braceleted wrist reaching for a china tea-cup, the rare male voice (the membership was strictly female) murmuring in restrained tones, as if afraid he might be thrown out if he rattled the spindly eighteenth century furniture, gilt-framed portraits, and eggshell-thin china cups with his manly bass. Since my grandmother was a well-off, unmarried woman with interests in genealogy, nineteenth-century novels, and American folk art, I assumed the other members must be sedate older women of a similar background with similar interests. But today as I passed the dusty, oak-paneled bar beneath its mural of classically robed women dancing in a forest, I noticed two smartly dressed young women drinking martinis and laughing loudly.

So maybe the current membership was not so old and not so sedate.

One of the women was wearing skinny black slacks tucked into riding boots and a well-cut wool riding jacket. She looked vaguely familiar to me, but her back was to me and she was also wearing an enormous fur hat that masked her hair color. The other woman was blonde, wearing a Missoni knit tunic, leggings and pale suede boots. Models, I decided while climbing the grand curving staircase to the second floor. Maybe the club loaned out its rooms for fashion shoots. You certainly couldn't find a better facsimile of "Ye olde stodgy English club" in the city. The Laurel Parlour looked exactly the same as the first time I had tea there when I was twelve – the same high backed wing chairs upholstered in forest green, the same varnishy oil paintings of elderly gray haired ladies looking down their noses disapprovingly – or so I had felt then in a scratchy lace and velveteen dress from Bergdorf's. I struggled not to feel looked down upon now as I scanned the islands of chairs for my aunt. "No one can make you feel inferior without your consent," Adelaide would say, quoting from Eleanor Roosevelt, when I complained of feeling uncomfortable in some environment. The effect of the admonition, though, was often to make me feel worse, as if I were somehow complicit in my degradation, but today it made me lift my chin and square my shoulders. I was twenty-six, not twelve, I had a Ph.D and a good job. Just because Adelaide had sniffed when I told her I'd taken the job at Fairwick meant nothing. What did she know about the academic job market . . . ?

"Miss McFay?" An Asian man in a dove gray suit had appeared soundlessly beside me on the thick Persian rug. "Miss Danbury is waiting for you over here." He waved a white-gloved hand, like a magician performing a conjuring trick, toward the grouping of chairs nearest the fireplace. I followed him across the room, keenly aware of eyes following me from the dim recesses of the deep, plush chairs. Was it my imagination or had the hum of conversation ceased as I crossed the room? I had the unnerving feeling that I was being tracked by raptors hidden in their arboreal roosts and found myself nervously listening for the rustle of feathers. When we reached the chair by the fire, my escort bowed to me and backed away, his shoe soles sliding on the carpet as deftly as Michael Jackson moonwalking in the "Thriller" video.

"Adelaide?" I asked, addressing the back of the chair.

A gnarled hand grasped the wooden chair arm, which was carved like a bird's talons, and began pulling her up.

"Don't get up," I said, edging around in front of the chair and leaning down to plant a kiss on my grandmother's cheek. The feel of her cool skin and the familiar scent of Chanel No. 5 instantly brought me back to my childhood, but when I moved back and got a good look at my grandmother for the first time I really thought I had time-traveled back to my twelfth birthday. I hadn't seen Adelaide since she'd come to my college graduation five years before, and so I'd been preparing myself for her to look older. After all, she was in her eighties and the hand I'd clasped was an old woman's hand. But except for her hands, which remained crabbed around the carved talons, she didn't look any older than the sixty-something woman who had taken me in. Same thick blue-black hair (maintained by weekly appointments at the hairdresser), worn in the same neat, but dated, chin-length pageboy, same keen close-set gray eyes and sharp hawk-like nose. Even her outfit – a cherry red wool suit, cream silk blouse, and pearls – was one I felt sure I'd seen before. Albert Nipon, I thought. The black onyx intaglio brooch she wore was the same one she'd always worn.

"You look great," I said truthfully. "The southwestern climate must suit you."

She waved her hand, the fingers remaining curled, to dismiss the compliment. "The dry air is good for my arthritis, but the minute I set foot in this city it flares up. Sit down. You're making me nervous hovering there."

I sat down in the chair across from her, perching on the edge rather than settling back in its recessed depths. The Asian man reappeared with a tray, which he placed on the table in front of us, containing a hobnailed iron teapot and two china cups decorated in a branch pattern that when I was little I'd thought looked like skeleton hands. He placed a silver strainer over my cup and poured a stream of fragrant jasmine tea from the squat iron pot into my cup, repeated the procedure with my grandmother's cup, and then bowed himself away. All through this ritual my grandmother's gunmetal gray eyes remained fixed on me.

"You're looking well," she admitted grudgingly.

"Although I don't see how that damp, cold upstate climate can agree with anyone."

"I don't mind it," I said. "The campus is very pretty in the snow . . ." Unbidden an image of Liam kissing me on the snowy path above the southeast gate flashed before my eyes. "And I have a lovely Victorian house. You should come visit . . ."

"I can't abide those drafty old Victorian houses," she said, ignoring my invitation. "And those small college towns . . ." She shuddered, a movement that made her collar-bones stand out against her neck. Her skin, I noticed, although unwrinkled, looked thin where it stretched over her bones, like a fine silk gone threadbare at the seams. "It must be like living in a fishbowl, everybody knowing your business."

My grandmother, I recalled, had always maintained a meticulous layer of privacy between the compartments of her life. She never socialized with the neighbors in our building or invited guests home. She lunched at her club, attended meetings of the various boards she belonged to, and went to the annual parties of arts institutions she supported, but I never heard her refer to anyone as a friend.

"I like that part," I said. "People look out for one another. During the ice storm I went house to house with Dory Browne to make sure everyone was okay—"

"Dory Browne? Is that one of your colleagues at the college?"

"No," I said, lifting the teacup to my lips, "she's the realtor who sold me Honeysuckle House and she's friends with the dean, Liz Book . . ."

"Elizabeth Book? Is she still there? She must be ancient. How do you get on with her?"

I looked up from my teacup, surprised. "How do you know Liz Book? You didn't mention it when I told you I got the job." *A second-tier college with a second-rate staff*, is what she had said then.

"Our paths have crossed. I always found her a bit . . . *diffuse*. And perilously naïve. That whole philosophy the school practices of recruiting students from all over when there are plenty of qualified young people right *here*." She tapped the arm of her chair as if she literally meant *right here*, and I looked around the muted parlor as if candidates for admission were going to pop out of the recessed chairs.

"I had no idea you were so well acquainted with Fairwick." I put my teacup down on the table and leaned forward. "Just *how* well acquainted are you anyway, Adelaide?"

Her gray eyes widened at the direct question and she retreated even further into the shelter of her wing-backed chair, but then she smiled, her thin lipstick-red lips parting over yellowed teeth. "Quite well acquainted. I see you've been initiated into their little cult. Tell me, did they promise to train you to be a witch?"

"You know about that?" I asked, my voice shrill in the hushed room. Normally I would have struggled to remain composed in front of my grandmother, but I'd just been chased by a blood-sucking parasite and found out my most normal colleague was secretly a witch.

Adelaide looked surprisingly pleased at my reaction. "Of course I know, dear. What do you think the Grove is?" She waved a crooked hand to indicate the gloomy room.

"You're . . . witches?" I whispered.

"The Grove is an old name for a coven, from when our ancestors met in the forest. But just because our ancestors had to lurk around dark cold forests doesn't mean *we* do.

The membership of the Grove practices a more refined version of the Craft."

I thought about the rite Soheila, Liz, and Diana had held to cast out the incubus from my house. It hadn't been refined, but it had worked. But then they hadn't all been witches . . .

"Do you know about the fairies, too?"

Adelaide clucked her tongue disapprovingly. "The Grove does not admit fairies, gnomes, elves, or dwarves. We consider dependence on such creatures a sign of poor discipline in the Craft. Besides, those creatures can be so . . . disruptive. And dangerous. I do hope you haven't gotten involved with any up there at Fairwick. It's what I was afraid of when you took the job."

"So it wasn't Fairwick's academic standing you disapproved of?"

"Well, there's that, too. They didn't even make the *U.S. News & World Report* top one hundred colleges, which I attribute to their liberal admissions policy, letting in refugees from all over the world . . . and *off world*. I mean, would you want *your* daughter to sit in class next to a hobgoblin . . . or room with a phouka?"

"I really like my students," I said, shocked by the venom in Adelaide's voice. "And I haven't seen any hobgoblins . . ."

"That you know of. What we at the Grove hear is that Elizabeth Book allows otherworlders to attend – and *teach* – in human guise. Who knows what sort of creatures you've got in your classes! It's irresponsible not to let people at least know what they're dealing with. I wanted to warn you when you took the job, but you've never listened to me."

"But you never even told me I had fairy blood!"

Adelaide leaned forward and grabbed my hand so quickly I gasped aloud. Her crabbed fingers dug into mine like pincers. "Of course I didn't tell you that you had the taint of the fey. Your mother, although she never chose to practice the Craft, was descended from a long line of distinguished witches. She disgraced her heritage by marrying a man with fairy blood."

"What heritage?" I asked, ignoring the slight to my father. I'd always known my grandmother didn't like him, but I'd thought it was because he was Scottish.

"The heritage of the Grove. One of its tenets is that we do not associate with fairies."

I snorted. "But witches have been the victims of prejudice and persecution for centuries. Why would you be intolerant of fairies?"

"It was the association of witches with demons – which is just another name for what you call fairies – that brought about that persecution. It is also well known that fey blood neutralizes a witch's power, which is why I assumed you showed no signs of any talent for witchcraft. Your mother assured me she saw no sign of it." She narrowed her eyes at me. "Though perhaps we were both hasty in that judgment . . . at any rate, now that you do know the true nature of Fairwick College it would be best if you resigned."

I sat back in my chair, yanking my hand out of Adelaide's claw-like grasp, and stared at my grandmother. Small white lines had appeared around the corners of her mouth where she clenched the muscles to control her expression. I could feel the anger rising off her, though, like heat waves, except that her anger was a cold thing. I noticed, too, now that neither of us were speaking that the Laurel Parlour was deadly silent. Tucked away in their deep cavernous chairs the members of the Grove were listening.

"And if I don't resign from Fairwick?" I asked, pitching my voice loud enough to be heard throughout the hushed room. "What will your club do to me?"

"You always were so dramatic, Callie." She shook her head and smiled, almost fondly, as though at a small pet's misbehavior. "The Grove won't do anything to you, but . . ." Her smile vanished. "Neither will we help you if you are in danger there. And trust me, sooner or later, you *will* be in danger there."

I thought of the incubus who had nearly wrecked my house and the vampire who had gotten me to agree to an ambiguous deal. I thought about Frank Delmarco, who was hiding the fact he was a witch. What I had always hated about fighting with my grandmother was that she often made a good point. And that she often turned out to be right.

But she wasn't *always* right. She had discouraged my friendship with Annie (*that little Italian girl*) and told me not to write a book about vampires, "because vampires had gone out after Anne Rice." I had to hope she was wrong about Fairwick, because even though I had seriously considered resigning on the drive down to the city, I knew now that it was the last thing I wanted to do. In fact, I couldn't wait to get back.

"You always told me to rely on myself," I said, rising to my feet. "So that's what I'm going to do. Rely on myself and the good friends and neighbors I've found at Fairwick. And if you – or any of your club – should change your minds about Fairwick, I'm sure you'll find that the door is open."

I had only meant to extend a message of tolerance (one I

was very far from feeling at the moment), but when I uttered the last four words Adelaide's face turned ashen.

"The door is open?" she repeated hoarsely.

So there was one thing she didn't know. "Yes," I said, smiling. "I opened it." Then I turned and walked away across the soft carpet, past the plush upholstered chairs, feeling like a small naked field mouse making its way through a forest populated with sharp-clawed owls watching me from their roosts.

CHAPTER TWENTY-NINE

"Who would have believed it?" I complained to Ralph as I threw my clothes into my suitcase. "My grandmother is a witch and so is Frank Delmarco – gruff, beer-swilling, football-watching Frank Delmarco!"

Ralph, perched on top of the flat-screen TV to keep from being trampled during my frenzied packing, squeaked.

"And clearly Frank's hiding something because no one at the college knows he's a witch. Maybe he's there to watch poor Nicky succumb to his curse."

Ralph stood up on his hind legs and squeaked again.

"Yes, I know it's not certain that he's the one who placed the curse on the Ballards. It could be the Scudder descendant who sneaked that lacuna in that book, but then what is Frank Delmarco doing at the college incognito? I say it's too much of a coincidence."

I started to close my suitcase but Ralph jumped into it – an impressive four foot leap that made him look like a flying squirrel.

"I wasn't forgetting you, but you don't have to ride in a suitcase." I held open a Century 21 bag that still had the tissue paper from the last-minute Christmas shopping I'd done two days ago. "Jump in here for now, then you can sit up in the front seat."

Ralph looked at the bag dubiously, then he made another impressive leap onto my laptop, which lay open on the desk.

"Hey, no, fellow! I told you to stay off that." I scooped up Ralph, who was chittering loudly now, and dropped him in the shopping bag. "Or were you just reminding me not to forget it? Thanks, little guy."

I slid the laptop into its case and shouldered it along with my purse. I took one look around the room to make sure I wasn't forgetting anything. It occurred to me that if I *did* forget something the hotel would call Paul because the room was registered under his name, and then he would have to call me . . .

I checked the back of the bathroom door, found my nightgown hanging there, and stuffed it the Century 21 bag with Ralph. "I think we're done here," I told Ralph and then closed the door behind me.

I had to wait another twenty minutes for the valet to bring my car around. I tipped everyone handsomely and then promptly got lost in the maze of one-way streets around Ground Zero. It was after four by the time I was headed up the West Side Highway, the sun hanging low above New Jersey on the other side of the river. Another night drive, then.

"That's okay," I told Ralph, who had curled up in my scarf on the front passenger seat. "I did okay coming down here."

I hadn't counted on the snow. I was too preoccupied by the surprising revelations of the day to listen to the weather and traffic reports on the radio. If I had, I would have stayed on the highway instead of taking the shortcut over the mountain. I was only twenty miles from Fairwick when the snow began. It started out as light flurries, but within minutes it was coming down so heavily I had trouble making out the yellow dividing line. I considered pulling over, but the fields on either side of the road stretched off emptily into the dark shadows of the woods – shadows that seemed to move when I glanced at them out of the corner of my eye. I had the feeling that if I stopped here the snow would cover the car and I'd freeze to death, or worse, that one of those shadows might detach itself from the woods and come loping across the fields. I was on the edge of the forest that surrounded Fairwick now, the same forest that contained the door to another world. I had bragged that I opened the door – and Anton Volkov had said it would remain open until the last day of the year. That meant that it was still open. Who knew what creatures might have come through the door and even now be prowling through the woods and fields for prey?

So I drove on . . . crawled on, rather, at fifteen miles per hour, gripping the wheel so hard my knuckles were white and leaning forward to make out the yellow dividing line. Even with the defrost running full blast, the windshield kept fogging up. Ralph jumped up on the dash and whisked a space clear with his paws, then remained on the dashboard peering worriedly into the snow and shaking his head so often that he looked like one of those bobble-head dashboard ornaments. I was glad to have him there.

When we drove through Bovine Corners I looked for an open gas station or diner where I could stop, but the white clapboard houses and farms were strangely dark. I wondered why everyone would be asleep so early, but when

I stopped at the town's one traffic light I saw that all the shutters had been closed over all the windows. For the storm, maybe? Or because the residents of Bovine Corners were afraid of the creatures that came through the door at this time of the year? As I drove, slowly through the town, I noticed, too, that hung on every door was a round wreath – or what I at first took for wreaths. On closer inspection I realized they were hex signs. I supposed that wasn't so odd in an agricultural area with lots of Dutch settlers, but although these hex signs superficially resembled those of the Pennsylvania Dutch, there were subtle differences. Instead of birds and tulips these signs were painted with large eyes and gargoyle faces – apotropaic symbols to ward off evil. On the last barn on the town's edge, just as the road began to climb toward Fairwick, a huge hex sign had been painted with a grinning gorgon's face, its menacing eyes staring into the woods between the two towns. What were they afraid of? I wondered, as I shifted my car into second gear to climb the long slippery hill. What had they seen come out of these woods?

Well, the residents of Bovine Corners weren't the only ones with access to magic. There was one spell I remembered from the spellbook – a spell for safe homecoming. It simply involved repeating the word for home in three different languages: *Casa, heima, teg*. That should be easy enough. Even if I had *shown no talent for witchcraft*, as Adelaide had said, and I was *tainted with fey blood*. I repeated the words while concentrating on keeping a steady pressure on the gas pedal. If I had to stop here I'd never get the traction to start up again. The trees came close to the shoulder now, tall pines that grew in serried ranks that hemmed in the narrow route. If I ran off the road I'd plow straight into one of them. When I reached the top of the hill I let out a long breath that fogged the window.

"Pshew! Ralph, that was scary. At least it's all downhill from here."

Ralph gave me a quick nervous look and pressed his nose against the windshield. I looked ahead and saw what he was worried about. The road curved downward at a steep grade and it was slick with unplowed snow. I took a deep breath and slowly edged the car over the precipice, keeping one foot on the brake. As I picked up speed I realized that if I braked too quickly I'd skid. Although there were still trees on the left side of the road, on the right the mountainside fell away in a sheer drop to the valley. I could see the lights of Fairwick down below, beckoning like a safe harbor. Home, I thought, *Casa, heima, teg.* Suddenly the rear wheels fishtailed and I went into a skid. For one horrible moment I saw the lights of Fairwick gleaming out of the falling snow. Had my spell backfired? Maybe Adelaide was right about my lack of magic talent? Was it trying to take me back to Fairwick by the most direct route? I heard Ralph excitedly squeaking . . . and then somehow the car straightened itself at the last minute and we sailed down the last slope onto Main Street.

I was shaking so badly that I had to pull over. I peeled my fingers off the steering wheel, closed my eyes, and said a little prayer of thanks. When I opened my eyes I saw that I was in front of the Fair Grounds café. "What say we treat ourselves to some hot chocolate?" I said to Ralph. But when I got out, I saw that the café was dark. A cheery sign with snowflakes and pinecones announced: CLOSED FOR THE HOLIDAYS! SEE YOU IN THE NEW YEAR!

Looking up the street I noticed that all the shops, at least some of which usually stayed open late for students, were closed. I supposed it made sense since the students were all gone, but I was disappointed at how dreary the town looked. Well, I thought, getting back in the car, Diana will be home at the inn . . . and Liam would be there. At least he hadn't said anything about going away for the holidays, but then our last encounter had ended rather abruptly. It was probably going to be awkward the first few times I ran into him . . . Better if he had gone away for the holidays. But if he hadn't, I'd just act like nothing had happened.

I started the car and drove to the end of Main Street, peering at all the shops with their CLOSED FOR THE HOLIDAYS! signs. It looked like the whole town had cleared out for the period between Christmas and New Year's.

I turned right up the hill that climbed to my house and saw that most of the houses on my street were dark, too. Oddly, though, the woods to my right weren't completely dark. Lights flickered through the trees as if someone had strung Christmas lights through their branches. I was staring into the woods when an enormous antlered buck bolted right in front of my wheels. I slammed on the brakes and went into my second skid of the night. This time I wasn't able to come out of it. The car spun completely around, ploughed into the woods and pitched down into a gully. I ended up at a tilt, my headlights tearing a crooked path through the snowy woods. I stared dumbly into it, too rattled to move, watching the snow fall through my high beams. Then I looked for Ralph.

He was on the floor of the backseat, puffed up like a dandelion seed head, a crumpled Post-it note sticking to his right hind leg, but otherwise he looked okay.

"Thank goodness we weren't hurt," I said, "but I think we're going to have to walk from here."

I turned off the engine and the lights. Darkness enveloped the car. I was tempted to turn the lights back on, but then I'd have to add a drained battery to the list of repairs on the car. I checked the glove compartment for a flashlight, but there wasn't one. Then I put Ralph in my pocket and got out.

The dome light briefly showed how close I'd come to hitting a tree; then I closed the door and found myself in the dark again. Not total darkness though. The falling snow seemed to carry its own soft silvery light, but it didn't really illuminate anything. There *was* light coming from some-where, though, probably from the street, I guessed, but the gully I'd landed in was so deep I couldn't see streetlights. Nor could I climb back up the way I had come because the slope was too steep on that side. I'd have to walk parallel to the street until the slope leveled. Sooner or later I would run into my house, which was at the top of the hill on this side of the road.

I locked the car and started trudging uphill, bending my head down against the blowing snow. I was wearing a warm pair of sheepskin boots, so I didn't feel the cold right away, but after about ten minutes I discovered that my expensive and stylish sheepskin boots weren't even the least bit waterproof. Once the snow seeped through my whole body felt cold. I considered going back to the car for a pair of rubber boots that I'd thrown in the trunk a month ago, but decided that was silly – I must be almost home.

I lifted my head and squinted through the driving snow. Yes, I could see small twinkling lights up ahead. Had I left the Christmas lights on? Or maybe Brock had come by to check on the house and left them on to welcome me home. *Casa, heima, teg*.

I quickened my pace, stamping my feet with every step to shake some warmth into them and keeping my eyes on the twinkling lights. They weren't as close as they looked, though. In fact they seemed to recede as I approached, floating through the swirling snow . . . I stopped and looked around me. The lights *were* moving. They were swaying with the wind in the branches all around me. I peered closer and saw that hanging from the branches were the frozen ornaments that the townspeople had made during the ice storm – ice angels, partridges, elves and reindeer. I could see the little charms that had been embedded inside the ice because the ice was glowing. As the wind moved them they clinked against each other like crystal chandelier drops, making a shivery chime that filled the woods. I had never actually *felt* magic before, but I knew it when I felt it and I could feel it now, stirring all around me, the power of all the wishes, hopes and dreams contained within the charmed ornaments straining to break through their ice shells. It was a feeling of anticipation, as keen as the bite of the icy wind, swelling to the breaking point. Just as the feeling became unbearable something crashed out of the brush directly behind me. I whirled around, nearly losing my balance in the deep snow, and found myself facing an enormous buck – no doubt the same one that had run in front of my car earlier. It looked at me with wide sentient eyes. Its antlers cast wide branching shadows across the snow. It huffed, its breath frosting in the cold air, and then lowered its head slowly to the ground. I noticed then that its antlers were tipped with silver and it wore a leather and silver collar around its broad neck.

"Are you from . . . the other side?" I asked.

But the buck only pawed the ground. Then it lifted its head, sniffed the air, its ears twitching, and leapt away as suddenly as it had appeared. I listened for what had frightened it, but all I heard was the chiming of the ice ornaments.

I turned and went on, soon coming out into a clearing that I recognized as my own front yard. Honeysuckle House was twenty yards away, my front porch light shining through the snow. I struck out for it, breaking into a clumsy run through the ankle-deep snow, but then something hit my head. I turned and met the yellow eyes of an enormous black bird, its talons stretched out. I ducked and flung my arm up to protect my face. The bird screeched horribly when I hit it and beat the air with its huge black wings, like a swimmer treading water. Its yellow eyes latched on to me, their hatred piercing the snow better than my high beams had.

Then it gathered itself for another dive.

I crouched and covered my face, sure it meant to pluck out my eyes, steeling myself for its talons and beak tearing into my flesh. But instead I heard a hollow *thwack* followed by the bird's outraged scream and then the heavy beat of its wings. I uncovered my face and looked up at the figure towering above me, his back to me. Black feathers clung to his shoulders like a capelet. When he turned, the black feathers drifted down in front of me and landed in the snow, staining the white with splatters of blood. I looked up again, half expecting, half fearing that those yellow eyes would still be there. That the bird had transformed itself into this bloodied, feathered man, but the eyes regarding me were the soft brown eyes of Liam Doyle.

"Bloody hell, Callie!" he said, crouching down in front of me, "What did you do to piss off that bird?" His voice was shaking. I saw he still clutched the stick he'd used to fend off the bird. It was matted with blood and feathers.

"Liam, how did you know . . .? What are you doing here?"

"I was sitting in my room at the window, watching the snow fall, and then I saw someone in the woods. When you came out onto the lawn I saw it was you – and then I saw that crazy crow come out of the woods behind you. You know, I think it was the same one that attacked you the day you left . . . only it looks like it's grown . . ."

He faltered and I wondered if he, too, was remembering what had happened the last time he'd rescued me from the bird – how we'd kissed and I'd pulled away. He reached out and touched my face, and I started to shake.

"You're half frozen," he cried, grabbing my hand and pulling me up. "We've got to get you inside. Do you have your key?"

I patted my pockets and realized that not only was the key gone but so was Ralph.

"Oh no!" I cried, scanning the blood-speckled snow. When had he fallen out? Had the monster crow gotten him?

"Don't worry, you've probably got one stashed away. Most people hereabouts do, I've found. Let me guess – under this wee gnome perhaps?"

He'd helped me up to the front of the house and sat me down on the porch steps while he tilted back the stone gnome that had come with the house. "Ha! I knew it!" He cried, holding up a key. "Come on now, don't cry. It's just the shock of being attacked by that nasty bird."

I wasn't crying from shock – or at least not just from

shock – but because I'd lost Ralph in the attack. Even if the bird hadn't gotten him he'd freeze to death if he didn't get inside soon. I had to look for him.

I got up and started to walk back across the snow, but I only got a few feet before a wave of dizziness overcame me and I sank to the ground. I heard Liam's feet coming down the porch steps and felt his arms hauling me back to my feet. "Where do you think you're going, Callie?"

"Um . . . I forgot something in the car . . . I have to go back."

"You're delirious, girl, which is one of the signs of hyperthermia. You're going inside now."

Liam half carried me up the steps and into the house. I began to explain about Ralph, not caring anymore if he thought I was nuts.

"A pet mouse? What a strange woman you are, Cailleach McFay. But don't you worry. Wild animals know how to take care of themselves. He'll go to ground until the snow stops and then he'll come home."

He sat me down on the library couch and crouched beside the hearth where logs lay ready for a fire. He set a match to the logs as he talked, his voice a soothing patter – like raindrops falling on a tin roof – but I couldn't stop crying. It wasn't just Ralph anymore; it was everything that had happened: Paul breaking up with me, my grandmother turning out to be a witch, finding out about Frank Delmarco, crashing my car in the woods, getting attacked by a giant bird . . . It all bubbled up inside me now and spilled out in long wrenching sobs. I told Liam some of it – about Paul and the car . . . and somehow I managed to throw in finding him on the cloakroom floor with Fiona.

"That hussy," he said, wrapping a knit throw around my

shoulders. "She asked me to get something off a high shelf for her and then was all over me. Don't worry about her . . . or your *eejit* ex-boyfriend. You're home now." He knelt in front of me and pulled off my sodden boots and socks and rubbed my feet, his hands incredibly warm against my chilled flesh.

"It's okay," he whispered, his voice as warm as his hands. "You've had a bad time of it, but it's okay now, you're home now."

He slipped his hands up under my jeans and chafed my calves, bringing the blood back into my legs. I'd never noticed how large and strong his hands were. He could span the width of my calf with one. I felt the warmth of them stealing up my legs.

He let go of my calves and sat on the couch beside me. He stroked my matted hair back from my forehead and brushed the tears away from my face. His eyes were the color of warm brandy, a tawny brown with floating specks of gold. Staring into them I felt myself growing dizzy, as I had when I'd stared into the swirling snow. He leaned forward and pressed his lips to my cheekbone. When he leaned back his lips were wet with my tears. He leaned in again and touched his lips against my earlobe, and then to the top of my jaw. I stayed perfectly still, feeling his breath moving over my face, then down my throat and along my collar bone, the warmth of his lips and breath spreading heat throughout my body. He unbuttoned the top two buttons of my blouse and grazed his lips across the top of my breasts. I started to tremble. He lifted his head and looked into my eyes.

"It's okay," he said, stroking my face. "You're home now."

He pressed his mouth against mine, opening my lips with his. I felt his tongue inside me, then his breath, then the heat of this body pressing me down into the couch, his legs moving mine apart as deftly as his lips had opened my lips. That's what his kiss felt like – an *opening*. His hands moved up inside my shirt and down below the waistband of my jeans, his fingers moving between my legs.

"Liam," I moaned.

He shifted his weight to the inside of the couch and withdrew his hand, but left it resting flat on my belly. "Yes, Callie?" he said, as if we'd been in the middle of a conversation, as if we'd known each other all our lives.

"I'm afraid . . ." My voice came out breathless and husky. "We're . . . going . . . too fast."

"Too fast?" he asked, tilting his head, one side of his mouth quirking up into a crooked smile. "I'm sorry. I'll go slower. How's this?"

He dipped his head to my clavicle and ran his tongue along my throat and up to the lobe of my ear at exactly the same excruciatingly slow pace as he drew his fingers down from my naval to the inside of my thighs. Then he exhaled on the wetness on my ear at the same time as he slipped his fingers between my legs, so that it felt exactly as if his lips were where his fingers were. He pulled the lobe of my ear between his lips, grazing the flesh with his teeth, and sucked on it as his fingers slid inside me.

"How's that?" he breathed into my ear. "Still too fast?"

"No," I admitted, turning to him and twining my hands around his hips to pull him to me. "That was exactly right."

CHAPTER THIRTY

True to his promise, that first time we made love was long and deliciously – almost maddeningly – slow. By the end I felt he had touched every millimeter of my body with his mouth or fingers – and I often couldn't tell which had touched me where. But what I remember best about that night was waking up in my bed and finding him watching me, his body carved marble in the moonlight, his eyes silver. As soon as my eyes opened he slid inside me and came immediately, as if he'd been carrying that excess sum of desire from the first time we'd made love and had to spend it now.

He never did that again. He was always the most thoughtful and generous of lovers, always giving me pleasure first, always holding himself back until I came. But whenever I recalled that swift second coupling, wherever I was – standing in front of a class or walking down a grocery aisle – my knees went watery at the memory of his desire for me. It was the moment that sealed us, and the only time he acted without putting my pleasure first.

When we awoke the next morning he was already thinking of ways to please me. He'd sneaked into the Hart Brake Inn – where he was staying alone since Diana had gone to Liz's house to take care of her – and brought back supplies to make a huge breakfast of banana pancakes, fresh fruit, eggs and coffee. He brought it all to me on a tray with a single rose.

"Did you steal the rose, too?" I asked.

"Ah, that I found in an enchanted wood, the last rose growing in the garden of a ruined castle."

"Hmm," I said, sniffing the rose. It didn't smell like a hothouse flower – it smelled of summer. "Just like in *Beauty and the Beast*. I love that Cocteau version, too . . ." I stopped, embarrassed that I'd finally given away my internet sleuthing.

He grinned. "I *know* you do – it's listed on your favorites, too. Let's watch it later."

I'd been afraid to mention "later," not wanting to assume we'd be spending our *later* together, but Liam made no pretense about wanting to spend every minute he could with me. We spent that first day in bed, letting the still raging blizzard serve as our excuse for not budging, although in truth I think that even if the sun had been shining we would have found an excuse to stay in bed that first day. But the next day I awoke to a bed empty except for long swaths of cold sunlight twisted in the sheets. I felt a pang of loss as sharp as the crystalline light reflected off the icicles hanging from my bedroom windows, and for a moment I wondered if I'd dreamed the last day and a half. It felt like a dream, more incredible than the nights I'd spent with the incubus. Maybe the incubus had been real and Liam was the dream . . .

But then I heard a scraping noise coming from the front of the house. I went to one of the front bedrooms and, looking out the window, found Liam shoveling the front path. He looked up at the sound of the sash opening and waved, his cheeks glowing pink from the cold and exercise, a puff of condensed air hanging above his head. How could I have thought he was a dream? He looked more real than anything I could ever imagine.

I made breakfast that day and later we put on heavy boots and hiked down the hill to meet Triple A at my car. It turned out that the tow truck was owned by Brock's cousin, Alf, and that when he heard I had made a service call, Brock had insisted on coming along to help. He looked a little surprised to see Liam there, but Liam explained that he'd seen me walking down the hill to the car and offered to stay with me while I waited for the tow truck. Brock squinted suspiciously at Liam, and kept looking back and forth between us, as if he suspected that Liam was holding me captive.

"I thought he was going to tackle me," Liam admitted after the car had been winched out of the gully and towed away.

"He's just being protective," I told him. But I too wondered why Brock had seemed so wary of Liam.

Since we didn't have a car we hiked to the Stop & Shop, the only store open in town, and bought groceries. Later we borrowed two pairs of cross-country skis from the inn and skied through the woods, making new tracks in the deep virgin snow. The woods still scared me a little after being attacked by the giant crow, but with Liam blazing the trail ahead of me I told myself that nothing bad would happen – and nothing did. The woods were silent, hushed by the deep mantle of snow. Whatever creatures had stirred free through the door between the worlds, they had all gone to ground now.

As did we. For the next few days – in the still time between Christmas and New Year's – we marooned ourselves in Honeysuckle House. Outside the snow fell steadily, dropping a thick white curtain between us and the rest of the world. The heat we made steamed the bedroom windows and then the steam froze, sealing us in.

"It feels like the ice age has come and we're the only two people left in the world," I said one night as we lay in bed, my head pillowed on his chest, watching the snow fall through the almost opaque windows.

"Would that be so bad?" Liam asked.

I laughed and looked up to see whether he was serious, but he was looking toward the window and his face, a white profile against the shadows had no more emotion than a bust carved out of marble. "We can't go on like this forever," I said, trying to make my voice light but hearing a tremor in it.

He turned to me, his eyes twin dark wells in his face. "I could," he said fiercely. He shifted his hips and pinned me beneath him in one quick fluid movement that made me gasp. We'd made love less than an hour ago, but he was hard again. But he didn't come inside me. He stretched both of my arms over my head and wrapped my hands around the bedpost.

"Hold on," he whispered, kissing my hands. His breath was a silken sash that bound my wrists to the bedpost. He pressed his mouth to the inside of my wrist and ran his tongue down my arm.

"I could tie you to this bed and make love to you forever," he whispered into my clavicle. He pressed a line of kisses down my chest that seemed to seal me to the bed. I felt myself sink deeper into the mattress and clutched the bedpost harder to keep from sinking. He tongued my naval and my back arched as if pulled by a thread connected to his mouth. He was spinning a web around me with his lips, each word and kiss binding me.

"I could *devour* you," he said, breathing into the cleft between my legs.

He really means it, I thought, arching my hips to meet his mouth. He *could* devour me. But as his tongue slipped inside me I understood that I didn't care. He could tie me to this bed, lick me dry and pound my bones into dust and I'd still cry out for more – as I was now, crying out in the empty house where the snow muffled the sounds and locked us in together, snow bound.

I woke the next morning with aching arms and that prickly sensation of having done something I should be embarrassed about but couldn't remember – a feeling I recalled from drunken nights in college. Liam lay asleep beside me, his face angelic in sleep – an angel who'd told me last night that he wanted to tie me up and eat me.

It wasn't really bondage, I thought, rubbing my wrists. And even if it had been – well, there wasn't anything wrong with that. Plenty of consenting adults engaged in far wilder games. But I never had, and something about the abandon I'd felt – the willingness to give myself over – made my stomach feel hollow now. I slipped out of bed quietly, so as not to wake Liam, and stole downstairs. I felt like I had to reconnect to the world somehow, so I opened my laptop and checked my email while I started the coffee machine.

I had 283 unread emails.

"Shit," I swore, scrolling through my inbox. When was the last time I had gone this long without checking my email? How long had it been? What day was it anyway?

I looked at the date on the most recent email and was shocked to see that it December 31st.

Most of the messages were easily disposable but there was one from Paul. I poured my coffee before opening it.

Just wanted to make sure you're okay, he'd written, *and wish you a Happy New Year. <3 Paul*.

"What's that symbol mean?"

I jumped at the sound of Liam's voice. He was standing right behind me.

"You scared me!" I yelped. "I didn't hear you come down."

"You were pretty engrossed," he replied, tilting his chin toward the screen. "What does it mean? Is it a math symbol? Paul was a math person, right?"

"You know it's not polite to read other people's emails," I said, more testily than I'd meant to.

Liam flinched. "I didn't think we had secrets from each other. I thought . . ." He looked again at the screen and a look of understanding crossed his face. His jaw muscle clenched. "I see now. It's supposed to represent a heart. Is that his idea of romance? Sending you a heart cobbled together of signs and numbers?"

"He just wanted to make sure I was okay," I said, ignoring his critique of Paul's heart. Truth was, I'd always thought the heart emoticon was a little goofy, but I didn't like the idea of laughing at Paul with Liam. It seemed disloyal – and petty of Liam.

"And are you?" Liam asked, narrowing his eyes at me. "Okay?"

"Of course I'm okay," I replied. "I guess maybe I just need a little . . . space."

Liam blanched and looked away. "Space? I see. Well, I can give you that."

He left the room so quickly it was as if he'd vanished. I could hear him pounding up the stairs, though. If only he'd made that much noise when he'd come down before – but I shouldn't have to hide an email from an ex-boyfriend. He was being ridiculous, I told myself as I heard him thumping down the stairs. And if he was this possessive after a week together, what would he be like in a long-term relationship?

The sound of the front door opening made something hurt inside my chest. Was he really going to storm out without saying good bye?

What a baby, I told myself, gripping the seat of my chair with my hands to keep from running to the door.

I was still listening for the door to close when he appeared at the kitchen door. I let out my breath and unclenched my hands to wipe away a tear before he saw it, but he was at my side, kneeling and kissing the tear away, telling me he was sorry, before my hand could reach my face.

"I am such an idiot," he said, lifting me from the chair and pushing me onto the kitchen table – and closing the laptop on Paul's suddenly inadequate heart cobbled together of signs and numbers.

Liam was penitent all that day. He disappeared for a while, telling me that he was giving me my "space." When he got back, just before dusk, he said he had a surprise for New Year's Eve. He got out our borrowed skis and told me to follow him. Instead of taking one of the trails we had skied before, he set off down the path that led to the honeysuckle thicket. We hadn't gone this way – and neither had anyone else. The snow was undisturbed, crusted on top with a sugary glaze that crackled as Liam broke the surface with his skis. I followed in his tracks, glancing nervously into the thicket on either side. Somewhere in this thicket was the door to Faerie and it was still open – if only a crack – until midnight tonight. Wouldn't the creatures who had come through on the Solstice be going back tonight? What if we got between them and the door? What if, somehow, we went through the door?

"Hey," I called to Liam, "it's getting dark. Don't you think we should head back? We could get lost."

"We can't get lost," he called back over his shoulder without stopping. "We just have to follow our tracks back."

We skied on, Liam going so fast that I broke a sweat keeping up with him. The last thing I wanted was to lose sight of him and find myself alone in these woods in the dark. But as the light began to fade from the sky, turning first clear lavender tinged with mauve, I was distracted by how beautiful the woods were at this time of day. The snow, reflecting the fading light, took on an opalescent sheen. The last light caught in the net of tangled honeysuckle and hung there heavy as dusky grapes in a net. I could feel the weight of that purple light, hanging on the verge of night and then spilling over, casting violet shadows on the frozen crust. Just as the last light faded, the narrow path ended and we came into a clearing. Liam had moved to one side, side stepping with his skis so that I could stop at the edge of the clearing without disturbing the surface of the snow.

It was a perfect circle. Branches of the sprawling shrubs arched overhead, forming a ribbed vault. At the opposite side from where we stood, two trees leaned together forming a narrow arch. Like a doorway.

"I found this place before the blizzard and thought it would look perfect in the snow. Look . . ."

He pointed toward the opening in the trees and for a moment I thought, *Something is coming.*

Something *was* coming through the door. The gap between the trees filled with white light, cold and pure as the moonlight that had carried the incubus across my bedroom floor to me. I suddenly felt afraid, but more for Liam than myself. I turned to him. His face was so still and white that for a moment I had a presentiment of his death. This is what he'd look like dead, I thought, and felt a pain that seemed to cleave me in two. I reached for him . . . and saw that my hands were white, too.

I turned back and saw that something *had* come through the door. The full moon was rising directly in the gap between the trees, spilling its light into the clearing and turning the circle of snow into a silver disk – a mirror into which the moon gazed and fell in love with its own reflection.

"It's beautiful . . ." I said, turning back to Liam, but fell silent when I saw his face. "Liam, what is it?"

"I wanted to bring you here because I knew how beautiful it would be tonight with the snow and the full moon . . . that it would be perfect, just as this last week has been . . . or at least until I acted so stupidly today. But I know it's all going to change once the new year starts and we go back to work and everyone comes back to Fairwick. It won't be the same."

I started to tell him that it would, that nothing had to change, but I knew he was right. "I've been afraid of that, too," I said instead.

He took my hand. "You have?"

I nodded and he put his arm around me – as best as he could with both of us standing still in our skis.

"This sucks," he said.

I laughed . . . and was startled at how the sound echoed in the round glade. "Yeah, poor us. We've had amazing sex for a week and now we have to go back to the real world. How will we survive?"

I'd meant it as a joke, but he answered gravely, "By remembering. That's why I wanted to bring you here. So we'd have something perfect to picture when we thought about this week."

I looked at the glade. The moon had risen to the center of the gap now, so large and full that it looked as if it would burst through the trees and come rolling toward us. I had a sense of other things – strange and unfriendly things – waiting on the other side of that door for their chance to come through. I recalled my vision of Faerie and the diaphanous host who had pleaded with me to release them. Were they there waiting for me now? Would they pull me through the door if I strayed too close to it?

"It *is* beautiful," I said, wanting now to go, but not wanting to alarm Liam. How could I explain what I was afraid of? "But it's also frigging cold. Let's go home."

"Home?" he asked, the light of the moon in his eyes.

I understood that he was asking if it was his home too, and in that moment I realized I wanted it to be, that Honeysuckle House had never felt so much like my home as it had this week with Liam there. Should I ask him to move in right now? But when I remembered the way he'd acted earlier about Paul's email, I hesitated. A shadow fell across Liam's face. He looked away and then he started turning his skis around, pleating the once perfect snow into a wide fan. We fitted our skis back into our own tracks, which the cold air had turned icy in the few minutes we had stood in the clearing. Liam went first, his skis shooting away on the slicked tracks. Although I didn't like the idea of being left behind, I took one look back over my shoulder. The clearing was still empty, but the moon had risen high enough now that it cast the shadows of the trees onto the white snow. I thought I saw other shapes among the shadow branches – shapes with horns and wings and spiked tails. Creatures from the other side of the door trying to come through. *Otherworlders*, my grandmother had called them. She had also said there wasn't any difference between a fairy and a demon. These shadow creatures certainly looked more like demons than fairies.

I turned and followed Liam, skiing as fast as I could in the iced tracks. As the moon rose higher the shadows stretched out longer in the woods on either side of the narrow track. I had the impression that the shadows were chasing us back to the house and if they overtook us we'd never make it back. I skied faster, trying not to look to either side, but unable to resist. Out of the corner of my eye I thought I saw one of the shadows break free and skitter across the snow, scuttling sideways like a crab, its claws scraping against the crusted snow. I pushed my skis faster in their grooves. The shadows fell across the path now, like leaves tossed by the wind, but there was no wind. One shadow landed right in front of me, fat as a toad. Without thinking twice I speared it with my ski pole while reciting the anti-pest spell that I'd heard Justin Plean use.

Pestis sprengja!

It popped like a swollen blister and then turned into *two*

shadow crabs. *Shit*, maybe Justin's spell didn't work on these creatures or maybe my grandmother was right about my lack of magical talent. One landed in my left track. I lifted my ski up, slammed down hard, and heard it splatter. Something sticky dragged at my left ski and I nearly stumbled, but then I was back in the icy groove moving faster than ever. I could see Liam up ahead, standing beyond the path in the yard behind Honeysuckle House. Should I call out to him? What would he see if he looked back? Me batting at shadows? Would he be able to help me – or would the shadow-crabs turn on him?

I felt a sudden conviction that the latter would happen. I whacked one of the shadow-crabs with my right pole and raced to reach Liam and the open shadowless lawn he stood in. Just as I reached the end of the path, a prickly ball launched itself at my feet and latched onto my ankle. I lifted my leg to shake it off – and froze in my tracks. There was nothing on my ankle . . . because I had no right ankle. Where the *thing* had attached itself there was a blank hole where my ankle should have been, as if the shadow had swallowed my flesh.

I could feel myself falling, but I knew that if I did the shadow crabs would devour me. I used the right pole to balance myself and the left to pry the shadow thing off my ankle before it ate my whole leg. But before I could accomplish that rather complicated maneuver, something else flew out of the woods. I thought it was another shadow crab, but then I noticed that this one looked more like a flying squirrel.

"Ralph!" I screamed.

He landed on the shadow crab attached to my ankle and sank his teeth into it. The thing squealed and fell off, my ankle taking shape again, and the two of them rolled onto the snow and into a snowdrift.

"Callie?" I heard Liam calling me. I couldn't let him come back into the woods for me – and I couldn't leave Ralph.

"I'll be right there," I called.

I released my boots from the skis and knelt down, plunging my hands into the drift, knowing full well that I might pull out stumps. But instead I pulled out Ralph. He was limp in my hand. I didn't have time to see if he was breathing. I stuck him in my pocket and ran for the moonlight, out of the shadows, stumbling straight into Liam's arms.

"What are you doing?"

I looked around us. The shadows didn't reach to where we were standing. In fact, they seemed to be shrinking back into the woods.

"I saw Ralph," I said, pulling him out of my pocket. "He was attacked by . . . an owl."

"Poor little guy." Liam peered closer at him, but didn't touch him. "He seems to be breathing. Let's get him inside – and you, too. You're limping."

"I think I twisted my ankle," I said, leaning on Liam's arm.

"Should I go back and get your skis?"

"No!" I said much too loudly. "I'll get them tomorrow. Let's get in before poor Ralph freezes to death."

I put Ralph in his old basket, wrapped up in a blanket, and put the basket near the fireplace in the library. He was breathing but still unconscious. Maybe the shadow-crab had done something to him. My ankle was swollen and bruised.

It didn't hurt, though; it felt completely numb, as if it wasn't even there. Liam propped it up on a pile of pillows on the couch and put an ice pack on it.

"Some New Year's Eve," he said. "I guess we'll have to cancel the dancing. At least we've got champagne."

He produced a bottle of Moët et Chandon and two glasses and then, even more magically, a picnic of bread, cheese and fruit which he fed me as if my hands were injured and not just my ankle. I downed two glasses of champagne before I could stop shivering – from the cold, Liam thought, but I knew it was from the fear of fending off those nasty shadow-crabs. My grandmother had been right when she said that sooner or later I'd be in danger in Fairwick. I hated when my grandmother was right.

I drank another glass of champagne and let Liam feed me strawberries and whipped cream. Somehow a dab of the whipped cream ended up on my nose. Liam leaned forward and licked it off. I laughed and drew a mustache over his mouth with two swipes of cream. He retaliated by burying his damp, whipped-cream covered mouth between my breasts. Then he unbuttoned my shirt and drew a line of whipped cream from my solar plexus to the waistband of my ski pants. When his tongue reached my navel I conceded defeat with a long moan. I tried to pull him to me, but instead he gathered me in his arms and picked me up. He rolled his eyes toward Ralph's basket on the hearth

"Sorry," he said, "I'd feel like your friend was watching." He carried me to the stairs.

"You know, I *can* walk," I said hoarsely.

"Nope, sorry, I don't believe you can. In fact, I believe you're utterly and completely helpless. At my mercy, to do with what I please."

"And what do you please?" I asked when he laid me down on the bed.

He showed me.

Hours later I startled out of a delicious post-coital languor. "Hey, did we miss New Year's?" I asked.

But Liam was already asleep. I got up and limped to my desk to reach the clock. It was 11:58. I should wake him for a New Year's kiss, but he looked so peaceful that I didn't want to disturb him. And he certainly had kissed me plenty in the last few hours. Yes, indeedy, I felt pretty thoroughly kissed.

I sat down at my desk and leaned forward to see out the window. The moon had crossed over the top of my house and was in the western half of the sky, throwing all the shadows east, back toward the woods. I thought I could see some of those shadows moving through the woods, skulking between the trees, flitting through the branches, scurrying back before the door closed at midnight. Would they all make it? Or would some be stranded on this side? I shuddered thinking of those shadow-crabs and hoped that they, at least, had made it back. Fairwick already had enough monsters, I thought, climbing back into bed beside Liam. I spooned myself against his back, burrowing into the warmth of his body, but it was a long time before I stopped shaking.

CHAPTER THIRTY-ONE

Liam was right that things were different in the New Year. Even though classes didn't start until the second week of January, the town started coming back to life in that first week. I heard it in the scrape of shovels and the cheery shouts of "Happy New Year" as my vacationing neighbors returned to find their driveways blocked by snow. I saw it in the CLOSED FOR THE HOLIDAYS! signs removed and replaced with NEW YEAR'S SPECIALS! signs in the stores downtown. Our idyll was coming to an end.

I also sensed a change in Liam. At first I thought he was trying to make up for his display of possessiveness by giving me the space I'd asked for, but then I saw that he was the one who'd become restless and in need of that space. Seemingly whole woods full of it. He went out for long walks by himself in the morning – searching, he told me, for the inspiration to write a poem – but he came back looking more agitated than when he'd left. Once when I watched him from my desk window crossing the yard, I saw him look back over his shoulder with a scowl as if he were angry at the woods for failing to give him the material for a poem. And another time I greeted him when he came into the kitchen and he looked up at me with the startled eyes of a fox caught snatching a chicken. It occurred to me that he probably needed a little time to himself. I started spending more time at my desk and in the "Dahlia LaMotte room," trying to get back on track with my own writing, but I found myself too distracted. Maybe it was because Ralph was still unconscious and I'd begun to fear that he'd never wake up. I'd shown him to Brock when he brought my car back from his cousin's repair shop.

"If he was still made of iron I could solder him back together," Brock told me regretfully. "I'm not so good with things made of flesh and bone. You should take him to Soheila. She's better with things of the spirit."

I promised Brock I would.

Toward the end of that first week I got emails from both Soheila Lilly and Frank Delmarco announcing that they were holding office hours on Friday. I decided to take Ralph to Soheila and then go confront Frank with what I had learned and find out somehow if Abigail Fisk was responsible for the curse. After breakfast on Friday I told Liam I had to go pick up some papers from my office. I was afraid that he'd offer to go with me, but he said he felt like doing some writing. Did I mind if he used my desk? He liked the view from the window and he'd be careful not to disturb any of my things. I said of course I didn't mind and he gave me a kiss before going upstairs, but the exchange left me feeling uneasy. It seemed silly that he should have to ask to use a corner of space in a huge house – and silly that he always had to go back to the inn for a change of clothes when there were three or four empty closets upstairs. But if I told him to move some of his things over, would he think I was asking him to move in? Did he want to move in? Did I want him to? I promised myself that we'd at least talk about the issue that night and left the house.

My ankle was still sore, but it felt good to be out in the air and moving. I went through the southeast gate, which stood wide open now, and up the path to the quad. I saw a couple of students who must have been back early for campus jobs or to get a head start on the semester. One of them was Mara Marinca.

"Good morning, Professor McFay," she said in her formal English. "Merry New Year. I see you are walking with a . . . gimp? Have you injured yourself?"

"A limp. Yes, I got caught in a wild New Year's Eve rave." Mara's blank, wide-eyed stare made me sorry I'd resorted to sarcasm. "Just kidding, Mara. I twisted it cross-country skiing. How was your vacation?"

"It was very productive, thank you. I worked in the admissions office, sorting through applications. You would be amazed at how many students want to come here to Fairwick. And such interesting, accomplished young people! It made me feel very lucky to be here."

I'd thought waking up in an empty hotel room on Christmas morning was pathetic, but Mara's holiday sounded even more bereft. "I hope you didn't work the whole vacation."

"Oh no! Dean Book was very kind and invited me to her house for . . . what did she call it? Wassailing?"

"Really? What did that entail?"

"We drank eggnog and decorated her Christmas tree and then sang Christmas carols. It was fun. Dean Book is very kind and Miss Hart makes the most delicious cakes and cookies." Mara rubbed her stomach. "I am afraid that I gained weight over the holiday."

"That's okay, Mara, you needed it. You look good."

Mara did, in fact, look a little plump, bloated even, her skin a shiny pink as if it had been stretched a little too far, too fast. The poor girl had probably never had enough to eat in her whole life. It was little wonder that Diana's cooking had been an invitation to splurge.

"You, too, are looking well, Professor McFay," Mara said, leaning in closer as if trying to get a better look at me. Perhaps the girl needed glasses; she often stood a little too close. Or perhaps the people in her country had a different sense of personal space. "You are glowing. You must have had a very satisfying holiday."

I blushed thinking of just how *satisfying* my holiday had been and where that well-rested glow came from – and also because something in the way Mara was staring at me made me think that she knew, too. Could word have already gotten around campus that Liam and I were seeing each other? Was Mara deliberately teasing me? But then I dismissed the idea as paranoid. It was just Mara's awkward English that made her comments sound suggestive. I took a step back. "Well, I have to get something from my office . . ."

"Do you need help?" Mara asked, stepping forward and closing the space between us again. "It won't be easy for you to carry anything with your injury. Dean Book won't mind if I'm a little late for work . . ."

"No, Mara," I said firmly and perhaps a bit too brusquely. "I'm not picking up anything heavy. I'll be fine. Go to work. I'm sure the dean needs you more than I do."

"Yes, you're probably right. She hasn't been feeling very well. But if you ever do need anything . . ."

"Thank you, Mara. I'll remember that."

I turned and continued on my way to Fraser Hall, disturbed to hear that Liz still wasn't feeling well. I should drop by later to see if there was anything I could do for her – or for Diana, who must be worried sick about her. Right after I saw Soheila and Frank.

Although I'd planned to go to Soheila first, I changed my mind when I got to Fraser. If I saw Soheila first I'd be tempted to tell her what I'd learned about Frank and then I would lose the only bargaining tool I had: the advantage of being the only person who knew his secret.

I would have liked the advantage of surprise as well, but my limping progress up the four flights of stairs announced me way before I got to Frank's office.

"What'd you do, McFay?" I heard him yell as I limped into his office. "Get into a fight down in the mean old city?"

I stood in the doorway for a moment, looking at him. He had his feet up on his desk, a Jets cap pulled low over his eyes, and a *New York Times* opened in front of his face so I couldn't make out his expression. "No," I answered, "but I was attacked by a lacuna while doing some genealogy research at the public library."

Frank lowered the paper and looked up, eyes narrowed. He might have been calculating whether he could get away with pretending not to know what I was talking about, but after a moment he asked, "Are you okay? Those things are nasty."

I sank down in a chair, my knees suddenly weak. Part of me had been hoping that he'd deny being part of this world. After all the shocks I'd absorbed this fall learning that witches and fairies existed, I had counted on this brusque but utterly familiar man being simply what he appeared to be.

"I survived," I said, "and learned that you're a descendant of one Abigail Fisk."

"My nonna," he said fondly. "Abbie Fortino."

"She was a witch."

"Among other things – a superb cook, a loving mother and grandmother, a wicked bridge player." He grinned, but sobered when I didn't return his smile. "But yes, she was a witch."

"And you? Are you a witch?"

He shrugged. "'Magic Professional' is the politically correct term in fashion currently, but I think 'wizard' has more panache. Just please don't ever call me a Wiccan."

"Does Dean Book know you're a witch?" I asked.

"Nope. I was hired on my academic standing alone – just as you were. I bet the dean was surprised to learn you were a doorkeeper."

"I have a feeling she'd be more surprised to learn that you're a witch," I snapped back, not wanting to give Frank the satisfaction of showing surprise that he knew what I was. "But she hasn't, has she? You've kept your identity secret. Was that so you could secretly watch Nicky Ballard succumb to your grandmother's curse?"

"My grandmother's curse?" Frank's voice boomed through the empty building. He got up and closed the office door and turned to face me, leaning against the closed door, his face red. Although he had often yelled at me I'd never seen him look this angry before. "You think my nonna cursed the Ballards? She wouldn't have cursed a fly. Not that she didn't have cause. Did you get far enough in your research to find out who she was?"

"No, I had to go . . ."

"Well, if you had you would have learned that she was

married to the foreman of the safety crew. My grandfather, Ernesto Fortino, told Bertram Ballard that the tracks were unsafe because the iron that had been used – the iron made by Ballard & Scudder Ironworks – was inferior. But Ballard let the trains run on it anyway. The day of the crash my grandfather was trying to warn the conductor of the Kingston train to stop. When the trains crashed, he died trying to rescue the victims."

"I read about that," I said. "He went into a train car suspended over the bridge and rescued everyone in it before dying when it finally fell. He was a hero. It sounds like your grandmother had every reason to curse the family."

Frank smiled. "Except for the fact that Ballard's wife was my grandmother's sister. It would have been cursing her own family."

"Oh," I said, sitting down. "Then why *are* you here?"

He crossed the room and yanked open a filing cabinet drawer, took out a thick file, and flung it on the desk in front of me. "These are complaints lodged against Fairwick with I.M.P. They range from unauthorized tampering with the weather to harassment of civilians by supernatural creatures. For instance, I noticed you in a rather close clinch with Anton Volkov during the Holiday Party. If he asked you to give blood in exchange for information, or if he's glamouring you, he's violated your rights and should be brought up on charges."

"I didn't know . . ."

"But you should have known. Once you became aware of the true nature of Fairwick, Elizabeth Book should have debriefed you and informed you of your rights."

"She did give me some forms and brochures a few weeks ago," I lied. In truth she hadn't been able to find them and

I'd told her not to bother. I didn't mention the spellbook because given my recent experiences with using it I was beginning to suspect I shouldn't have been given it without more guidance. All my spells seemed to backfire. "I just didn't get around to reading them."

"It was her responsibility to review the material with you."

"She hasn't been feeling well," I countered. Somehow my showdown with Frank Delmarco had turned into an interrogation – of *me*. I had to think of a way to turn things around. "Which is probably why she didn't realize you're a witch. Awfully convenient for you . . ."

"*Not feeling well* is the understatement of the year. She's *fading*. For a witch who has used her magic to augment her lifespan that's fatal. Somebody – or something – is sucking the life out of her. I thought at first that it was the vampires, but she doesn't have any bite marks. I'm looking into other possibilities now, but it's crucial for my investigation that I remain undercover."

"Investigation? Undercover?"

Frank sighed and pulled his wallet out of his back pocket. It was made of old worn leather and had acquired a curve that no doubt matched the curve of his butt. He took out a laminated card and handed it to me. I recognized the insignia of I.M.P. – two crescent moons flanking an orb – but under the logo were printed the initials I.M.P.I.A.

"I.M.P.I.A.?" I asked.

"Institute of Magical Professionals Internal Affairs," he said.

"You mean you're a . . ."

"Undercover investigator. And one of the matters I'm investigating is the Ballard curse. I'm trying to track down the descendants of Hiram Scudder, Ballard's partner. My grandmother said he was an extremely powerful wizard."

I nodded. "I was looking up Scudder's genealogy when I was attacked by the lacuna."

"Figures. His descendants have been very clever in hiding themselves. I suggest you leave the investigation to me. If the Scudders planted a lacuna to hide their identity – which is strictly against I.M.P. regulations – there's no telling what else they might do to someone getting too close to finding them out."

"I can take care of myself," I snapped, resenting his paternalistic tone.

He shrugged. "Suit yourself. Just promise not to blow my cover. If you do, I can't keep looking for the Scudder witch or trying to find out what's making Liz Book sick."

"Okay," I agreed. "As long as you promise to let me know what you find out."

"Sure," he said, sticking out his hand. "You'll be the first to know."

I wasn't sure if he was being sarcastic or not, but I shook his hand anyway. As deals went it wasn't as bad as the one I'd made with Anton Volkov.

As I walked downstairs to Soheila's office I wondered if it was naïve to trust Frank. I had no real way of knowing whether he was telling the truth – especially since I couldn't talk to anyone about his real identity, but my gut told me to trust him. Frank was brusque, opinionated, and sometimes downright obnoxious, but I instinctively felt that he was a good man. Of course, my instincts had been wrong before.

Soheila greeted me warmly with a kiss on the cheek and an offer of tea and almond cookies. "From my grandmother in Long Island. I visited her over the vacation."

"That must have been nice."

Soheila shrugged, pulling her bright red cardigan across her chest. "I love seeing my grandmother, but my aunts spent the whole time asking me when I was going to get married. My cousins spend all their days getting their hair done and shopping. I was ready to come back."

"I had a rather surprising visit with my grandmother, too." I told her about my visit to the Grove.

"Oh my, they are rather intolerant there. One of my cousins was exorcised by one of their members in the 1890s."

"You'd think that after all the persecution witches have suffered they would be more tolerant."

Soheila shook her head. "Often it is just the opposite. Once a persecuted group finds its own place in a culture, their members draw a line around themselves to keep their own places secure. Witches were persecuted in the Middle Ages for their connection with nature spirits and old divinities such as myself – what the Church called demons. While the witches who founded Fairwick continued to embrace their connection to the Old Gods, the witches of the Grove chose to distance themselves and repudiate demons and fairies. The rift goes very deep. There was a battle in the 1600s called The Great Division that divided the witches into two opposing groups. Many faded and died. I imagine your grandmother was upset to learn you were teaching here."

"I think in a way she always expected something like this from me. Apparently it was a big disappointment that my

mother married a man with fairy blood. She said it might
have compromised my power as a witch."

Soheila frowned. "I've heard that theory before but I'm
not sure if there's any truth in it. It might be an apocryphal
tale meant to discourage such unions. A witch and a fairy
marrying always causes quite a stir. Even outside of the
Grove. My aunts, for instance, would be appalled if I dated
a witch. They were upset enough when I fell in love with a
mortal."

"Angus Fraser?" I asked.

"Yes, Angus." Her voice softened when she said his
name and her toffee-colored eyes gleamed like polished
amber. "Mind you they often marry mortals, but to fall in
love with one . . . Well, they said that was foolish for one of
our kind."

"*Our kind*? I'm sorry, Soheila, I don't mean to pry, but
I'm not actually sure what your kind is. I remember
Elizabeth said something about you being a Babylonian
wind spirit . . ."

Soheila smiled. "That was rather a euphemism, I'm
afraid, although it's true that my kind are descended from
Babylonian wind spirits. Under the circumstances,
Elizabeth and I agreed that it might be best if you didn't
know my more common name. You see, I am a descendant
of Lilith, one of the lilitu, or as we are more commonly
known, a succubus."

"A succubus! You mean like a female version of the
incubus who invaded my house? But I thought they were
always . . ."

"Selfish? Destructive? Evil? Yes, certainly that's how
they have been characterized in myth and Western religion
and, to tell you the truth, most of my sisters and cousins are

rather . . . shall we say, opportunistic? A bit mercenary, even? It's not entirely their fault. When my kind first came into contact with mankind we were barely conscious and certainly not flesh. We rode the wind . . . We *were* the wind. Sometimes we briefly possessed a winged creature. The owls were our favorite hosts, hence our identification with them." She nodded toward the poster on her office door. "But when we encountered men our interaction with them caused us to *incarnate*. We took on the shape they dreamed for us. And as we became flesh so we craved flesh . . . needed it in order to sustain ourselves." She shivered and drew her sweater around herself. I recalled what Dory had told me about how the fairies had traded their magic for sex, but what Soheila had described sounded like a different sort of bargain – sex in exchange for fleshly existence. And yet it was hard for me to imagine someone of Soheila's refinement engaging in that sort of sordid deal.

"So in order to stay . . . like you are . . . you have to . . ."

She smiled at my embarrassment. "I no longer have to feed on men that way. But that is only because I was loved."

"Angus?"

"Yes, even after he learned what I was . . . learned that I was of the same race that had devoured his sister, he loved me. And I loved him. I thought that because I didn't have to feed on him we could be together. I didn't realize he was growing weak from our . . . contact . . . until it was too late. He hid his sickness from me until he was too far gone . . . and then when he went up against the Ganconer he was too weak to fight properly. He died in my arms. Since then I have sworn never to take a human lover." She shivered again. "No matter how much I might crave the warmth of a human touch, I could never take that risk again."

No wonder she always looked like she was freezing.

"I'm sorry," I said, feeling how inadequate the phrase was. "That must be very hard. Especially if you like someone . . ."

"I can't afford to give into those feelings," she said so quickly that I knew at once that she must, in fact, like someone very much. "But enough about me. You came to ask me something, didn't you?"

"Yes," I said, relieved in spite of myself to change the subject. I put my hand in my coat pocket and brought out Ralph. I held him out to Soheila. "He attacked some kind of shadow creature on New Year's Eve and he's been in a sort of coma ever since. Can you do anything to help him?"

Soheila held out both hands and I passed Ralph to her. She cupped him gently in her hands and tilted her head to angle her ear above his chest. Then she laid him on her desk and angled her desk lamp so that it shone directly on him. "See," she said, tapping the wood next to Ralph. "No shadow. That means he's travelling in the shadows of the Borderland. Do you have your spellbook with you?"

"Yes," I said taking the book out of my bag. I'd started taking it with me everywhere. "But I'm afraid I haven't had a lot of luck using it."

"It takes practice – and guidance. I'll talk to Liz about enrolling you in an Introduction to Witchcraft and Magic class this summer. But for now, look up 'Shadow Travel – how to call a traveler back from.'"

I thumbed through the S's, past Sand Shifting, Séance Summoning and Shadow Repelling (which would have been useful on New Year's Eve) until I found the spell Soheila had asked for. "It says that to keep him safe on his travels I should draw his shadow on a piece of paper and then burn it while repeating the words, *intra scath hiw . . .*"

"*Hiwcuolic*," Soheila pronounced the difficult word. "Old Icelandic for 'familiar.' You see, that's why you had to look up the spell in your spellbook. The book intuited that the creature you're trying to help is your familiar."

"You mean the book changes the spell depending on who is using it?"

"Yes, and the more you use your spellbook the better it gets to know you and the more useful it becomes. I bet you didn't even realize that Ralph was your familiar."

"No," I admitted, stroking Ralph with my hand. "I just thought he was my friend. The book says that to bring him back I have to catch the shadow that dragged him into the Borderlands. But how? That creature probably went back through the door New Year's Eve."

"I doubt it. It's probably lurking around your house waiting for a chance to get the rest of the spark out of your little friend. Take it from someone who fed on the human life force for centuries. Once you get a taste of it, it's hard to do without. You'll have to keep an eye out for it and when you see it . . . well, here, I'd better give you something to catch it with. You can draw his shadow while I'm doing that."

While Soheila went into her closet I took a piece of paper out of Soheila's printer and laid it next to Ralph. I sketched in a little Ralph-shadow as best I could and then using the box of matches Soheila kept by her samovar, I burnt the paper in a copper tea saucer while repeating the spell. The smoke coiled up into the air in the shape of a mouse and then vanished. When it was gone I noticed a familiar-looking figure out on the quad through Soheila's window.

I got up and walked to the window, but the figure was gone. It had looked like Liam . . . but Liam hadn't said he was coming to campus.

A chime drew my attention to Soheila's desk behind me and I turned and looked at her laptop before I realized that I was snooping. An instant message box was in the corner of the screen, an icon of a bobbing Jets logo beside a scroll of text. *How 'bout lunch?* was all it said, but I had a sudden inkling of what mortal Soheila liked. Only he wasn't just a mortal – he was a witch and because of that the last person her family would approve of. But Soheila didn't know that. I heard Soheila coming out of the closet and I quickly scurried back around her desk so that she wouldn't see I'd been reading her I.M.s.

"It's a little old and out-of-date, I haven't used it since capturing a kelpie on a fishing trip fifty years ago, but I think it will still work." The wicker fishing creel she handed me looked like it was meant to hold trout, not demons, but I thanked her for it and put its worn leather strap over my shoulder. Then she told me how to destroy the shadow-crab once I'd caught it. I started to leave, but turned back to ask another question. She was looking at her computer screen with such a winsome smile that I couldn't bear to disturb her.

Walking home slowly through the damp, chill air I thought about Soheila's story. Angus Fraser had been dead for nearly a hundred years. What would it feel like to live alone for that long? And what would it feel like to love someone but know that if you gave into the desire to be with him you would endanger his life? It made my dilemma about whether Liam and I were moving too fast seem pretty insignificant.

When I opened the door to Honeysuckle House I was greeted with the smell of cinnamon and bergamot. Liam was in the kitchen making a pot of Earl Grey tea and fresh cinnamon rolls, which he knew was my favorite afternoon snack. With the tea kettle still in his hands, he leaned forward to kiss me. His skin was warm and there was a dusting of flour in his dark hair. He smelled like yeast and butter. I must have been mistaken about seeing him on the campus; clearly he'd been here all day.

"I've just got to run across the street to get a change of clothes," he said. "I've gotten flour all over these."

"Why don't you get all your things," I said impulsively. "I mean, it's silly for you to keep going back and forth . . . The house is so big and . . ." I looked up and saw he was staring at me, his brown eyes widening. "What I mean to say is, if you want to live here, I'd like you to."

Liam put down the kettle on the stovetop and wrapped his arms around me. I could feel the heat of his skin through his flannel shirt enfolding me, taking away the chill of my slow walk home. "Yes," he murmured into my neck. "I'd like that very much."

CHAPTER THIRTY-TWO

I'd never lived with a man before. Paul and I had both lived in dorms with roommates when we met, and by the time I got an apartment he'd moved to California. We'd spent long vacations together, but we'd never mixed our *stuff* in one place.

Liam didn't have much stuff—he'd been traveling light for years, he told me – but his presence immediately pervaded the house, a clean salty smell like the sea, a peaty tang from the Irish whiskey he sipped watching the sunset from the front porch when he'd finished writing for the day, and something sweet and evasive, like a breath of honey-suckle on a summer breeze. The ledges of the windowsills and the empty bowls and baskets filled with things he brought back from his walks – a twisted piece of honey-suckle vine that looked like driftwood, round gray riverstones, a bird's nest – things a twelve-year-old boy or a nineteenth-century naturalist might collect . . . or, I sometimes thought, the things a wild animal might bring back to its lair.

I didn't want him to feel as if he were squatting in the house rather than really living in it, though, so on the weekend before classes were to begin we borrowed Brock's pick-up truck and drove out into the country to comb antique shops to turn one of the spare bedrooms into his study. We found a Stickley Morris chair and a Victorian roll-top desk in an antiques barn in Bovine Corners. The town still creeped me out a bit after my night drive though it, but they did have some great antiques and a general store that sold artisan cheeses, fresh-baked bread, and homemade chutneys and jams. We probably could have bought everything he needed there, but it was a sunny day, the temperature above freezing for the first time in weeks, and the hills beyond Bovine Corners seemed to beckon.

We drove further east into Delaware County, across snow covered fields and sun-burnished mountains that Liam said reminded him of his home, and through farmland and small lonely villages whose once grand Victorian and Greek Revival houses were sadly faded and dilapidated. Many of the farms outside these villages had clearly been deserted. The long ridgepoles of their barns sloped like the backs of horses that had been ridden too long and hard. Some had collapsed completely and lay like great mastodon skeletons rotting in the fields.

We stopped at another antiques store on the way back.

"That's pretty," Liam said when he saw me looking at a lovely old fashioned emerald and diamond engagement ring. The old woman who ran the shop seized the opportunity to open the case.

"Ah, the gentleman has a good eye. That's my best piece – got it from the Trask estate over by Glenburnie. Victorian, platinum setting, one carat emerald flanked by two half-carat diamonds." She took the ring out of its velvet case and handed it to Liam instead of me. He held the ring up in the weak wintry sunlight, turning it back and forth to release a spray of fiery sparks in the dull, dusty shop. Then he took my hand and slipped the ring onto my ring finger. It fit perfectly.

"It's lovely," I said, holding my hand up in the light. The old stones glittered as if they held a spark of forgotten life inside of them. Then I turned my hand over and read the price tag. "But expensive." I started to take the ring off but Liam had already had a quick whispered confab with the shop owner, who was smiling like a schoolgirl at something Liam had said. He grabbed my hand and pushed the ring back on my finger.

"It belongs to you," he said. "I want you to have it."

I looked down at my hand. It was my right hand, not my left, so *not* an engagement ring. Still, it was a diamond ring. "Oh, Liam, it's beautiful, but I don't know . . ."

He held my hand up in the light again. A bit of the spark from the diamonds lit up his eyes. "The diamonds remind me of the snow in the moonlight New Year's Eve," he said, and then leaning down to whisper in my ear, "and the emerald is the color of your eyes when we make love."

I felt the warmth of his breath on my ear travel straight down my spine.

"Well, I'd better keep it then," I said, my voice wobbly with desire. "I can't have anyone else wearing those memories."

That night when we made love I twined my hands around the bedpost as I had on the night before New Year's Eve. The moonlight caught the ring and cast a spray of diamond and emerald starlight across Liam's face. It made him look insubstantial – as if he might dissolve into a zillion atoms and blow away. I unwound my hands from the bedpost and gripped his arms instead, his hard, solid biceps, and remembered what he'd told me that night.

Hold on, he'd said.

And so I did.

Of course it was the ring that my students noticed first.

"Oooh, Professor McFay, did you get engaged over the break?" Flonia and Nicky asked simultaneously.

"It's the wrong hand," Mara said, pressing in between Flonia and Nicky and reaching out to touch my hand. "She'd be wearing it on her left hand if she were engaged, right Professor McFay?"

"Yes," I admitted, surprised Mara knew such a thing. Apparently Nicky thought so too.

"How do you know that, Mara?" she asked.

"I read it in one of Dean Book's magazines. *Your left hand says you're taken*." Mara moved her hand to touch my left hand, and then back to my right where she left it. "*Your right hand says you can take over*." I recognized the slogan from an ad campaign that had run a few years ago. It had annoyed me at the time because even though the ads seemed to promote an image of women as independent and capable, it had also suggested that the woman who couldn't afford to go out and buy an expensive ring for herself was somehow lacking in those qualities. It had also made me want to go out and buy a ring and I could still remember another line from the ad: *Your left hand believes in shining armor. Your right hand thinks knights are for fairy tales*. "So she must have bought it for herself, right, Professor McFay?"

I should have been glad for a graceful evasion to my students' prying questions, but when I saw the disappointed looks in their eyes I smiled enigmatically and, removing my hand from under Mara's, wiggled my fingers so that the diamonds and emerald caught the light.

"Maybe," I sang, "or maybe not." My students oohed as I waved them back to their seats with a flourish that made the ring flash again. "Now let's get to work. You were supposed to have read *Dracula* over the vacation."

The oohs were soon replaced by groans as my students complained about Lucy Westenra's passivity in the book. I'd hoped that they'd have exactly that reaction. I wanted them to be impatient with the helplessness of the heroines of Gothic novels so that they could fully appreciate the Buffys and Sookies of the modern vampire genre. I also wanted them to stop wondering who gave me the ring, but in that I failed, sabotaged by Liam showing up at the end of the class with a book I'd forgotten *at home*.

I believe it took about five minutes after that for the news that I was "shacking up with" and "nearly engaged to" Liam Doyle to spread throughout the campus.

"I didn't know you wanted to keep it a secret," Liam said later when I confronted him at home. "I don't. I want to shout it from the rooftops. Why do you want to keep it a secret?"

I had no good answer for that and I didn't want to fight. I felt tired suddenly from the stress and excitement of being back at work after a long break.

"Maybe you're right," I said, letting my head drop and rubbing my neck. I felt *achy* as well as tired. Maybe I was acting so cranky with Liam because I was coming down with something.

"What's right is *us* – you and me. We fit together perfectly. How could anyone begrudge us our happiness when they see how good we are together?" He massaged the back of my neck. "Your muscles are really tight. Why don't you take a nice long bath while I make dinner?"

That sounded like such a good idea that I followed Liam's advice. I think he still felt bad about the argument, though, because he came upstairs while I was in the tub and offered to shampoo my hair. He sat on the rim of the tub and rubbed the lavender-scented shampoo into my scalp, kneading the muscles in the back of my neck and shoulders. Then he picked up the soap and lathered my back. "Hmm . . . I could do this better if I were *in* the tub . . ."

I heard his clothes slipping to the floor and then he was climbing into the tub behind me, sliding his legs around either side of me. He massaged my scalp and neck, his fingers whisking the tension away as though by magic. He soaped my back, stroking wide arcs along my shoulder blades.

"Ummm," I moaned, leaning back against his chest, the soap from my back making his skin slick. He reached around me and lathered my breasts, pinching my nipples lightly. I moaned and scooched my behind back between his legs and felt him go hard. He lifted my hips, tilting me forward, and came into me from behind, sliding inside me so fast and so *far* that I felt a part of me that had never been touched before leap into life. I cried out with a sound that startled both of us.

"Did I hurt you?" he panted in my ear.

"No," I said, although in truth I wasn't sure if what I was feeling was pleasure or pain. I only knew I wanted more.

I got up early the next day to go by the dean's office before class to make sure that she heard the news that Liam and I were living together from me and not from one of the students.

"That's nice, dear," she said smiling vaguely while accepting a cup of tea from Mara who was there helping her sort admission forms. "He seems like a nice young man. We were so lucky that he happened to have sent in his application just when we lost poor Phoenix." She shivered and drew a shawl up around her shoulders. The shawl made her look old – she'd lost weight over the break and her hair was so thin I could see patches of her scalp. *She's fading*, Frank had said. She did look as if she were dissolving into the muted wallpaper of her office. "I guess it was lucky for you, too."

"Lucky?" I asked.

"Yes, if Phoenix hadn't left you wouldn't have met your new young man."

I stared at her, aghast that she was suggesting I was lucky that poor Phoenix had had a nervous breakdown.

"I'm sure what the dean means," Mara said, laying her hand on the dean's frail shoulder, "is that we were all lucky to get a very competent teacher to replace poor Miss Phoenix while she is getting a chance to rest and get better."

"Yes, that's just what I meant. Thank you, Mara dear," the dean said, patting Mara's hand. "And I am lucky that you were here to help with the next year's applications over the break. Usually I read each and every one myself and then hand them over to admissions with my recommendations, but this year I just didn't feel quite up to it so Mara has read them to me. She has a very soothing voice."

I tried not to look incredulous, but I couldn't help wondering what Mara's fractured English had done to those applications – nor be somewhat shocked to see Mara's hand still lying on the dean's shoulder. Maybe in Mara's country such physical contact between young and old people was more common – maybe Mara thought of the dean as a surrogate grandmother – but I had been brought up in the sexual harassment era and the easy physical contact made me uncomfortable.

"We're almost done with all the applications, aren't we?" Liz looked up hopefully, like a child asking if she had to take any more distasteful medicine.

"Almost, Dean Book. We have a handful left that I think we can finish today."

"Excellent, Mara. But I'm afraid I won't have enough work to keep you busy then. Perhaps someone else needs an assistant . . ."

"What about you, Professor McFay, aren't you writing a book? That must be hard to do with your teaching responsibilities?"

"That's right, Callie, you're working on a book about Dahlia LaMotte, aren't you? How's that coming?"

"Oh, it's coming along fine," I lied. The truth was that I hadn't done any work on it in weeks. "There's a lot of material to organize."

"Well, then, why don't you take Mara? I'll assign her to you as a research assistant." The dean beamed at me and at Mara – the first really animated expression I'd seen on her face since I'd come into the office. Clearly she was pleased with herself for solving two dilemmas at once. And honestly, I could use the help. It was only the second day of the semester and already the essays I'd asked my students to write in class yesterday were weighing down my bag. Maybe I could get Mara to grade them. Although her spoken English was awkward, her written command of the language was impressive and she was a punctilious stickler for grammar and spelling. I could also have her catalog the Dahlia LaMotte manuscripts.

"That would actually be great," I told Liz. "If it's okay with Mara," I added, glancing worriedly at the girl. We'd been talking about her as if she were a piece of chattel to be traded between us. But Mara looked almost as pleased as Dean Book.

"It will be an honor to work for you," she said in her stilted, formal English. "I'm happy to be of use."

I was still a little worried that some of my students – especially the ones who had crushes on Liam – would be jealous of my new relationship, but I couldn't detect anything like that in class. After class that day, Nicky Ballard came up to tell me that she was glad I wasn't all alone in "that house" anymore and that she thought Professor Doyle was perfect for me.

"You've both been so nice to me. I'm really looking forward to doing the independent study with both of you. I wrote a lot over Christmas." Nicky, looking well-rested and happy from her break, didn't betray any sign of jealousy even though I knew she had a crush on Liam.

The only person who did begrudge my new romantic liaison was Frank Delmarco, who cornered me in the department office later that week.

"I hear you and Mr. Poetry are shacking up. That was pretty quick. Didn't you just break up with some other guy? Do you think it's such a good idea to move in with another man so soon – especially one you don't really know anything about?"

"Who are you, my mother?" I snapped angrily – partly to cover up my inability to answer his questions.

I knew it was too soon, that Liam and I were moving too fast. At times I felt like I'd stepped on one of those conveyor belts that moved tired travelers through airports. How exactly did I get here? I would wonder, coming home at night to find Liam lighting a fire in the library and handing me a glass of wine to drink while he finished dinner. (I knew I should offer to cook sometimes, but I'd started working with Mara in the afternoons and I always felt so tired when I came home.) After dinner we'd curl up on the couch in front of the fire and I'd think, Who cares? Why question happiness? And when, later in bed, I watched Liam's face above me, pale in the moonlight that struggled through the opaque ice-coated windows, I'd think: All we ever have is *now* – this moment – so how can it ever be too soon to be happy?

CHAPTER THIRTY-THREE

It was an unusually cold January all over, with record low temperatures from New York to Florida – where the citrus crops were destroyed, nesting sea turtles were brought into hotel rooms to keep from freezing, and manatees huddled around the warm currents coming from electrical plant pipes – but in Fairwick it was arctic. For most of the month the temperature stayed in the single digits. Who wouldn't choose to hibernate? Each day I drew Ralph's shadow and burnt it while repeating the spell for safe travel, but he remained soundly asleep. When I put him back in his basket I'd find myself wanting to crawl back into bed instead of tromping through the snow to lecture a class full of sleepy college students in an overheated classroom.

It was perfectly normal, I told myself, that I'd want to crawl back into bed when I came home from campus and that I'd want to spend all weekend curled up on the library couch with Liam. It's not as if we made love *all* the time. Sometimes we'd read and Liam would make tea and cinnamon toast at 4a.m. Sometimes we'd watch old movies. Liam, as I'd guessed from this Facebook page, loved the same romantic comedies I did – the old classics like *Bringing Up Baby*, *It Happened One Night* and *The*

Philadelphia Story and also their modern counterparts, like *Annie Hall*, *Sleepless in Seattle*, and *You've Got Mail*. He knew them all practically line for line, and yet they still seemed to surprise him.

"They start out not liking each other, but then they fall in love. They keep fighting even while they are falling in love. Why is that? Do they have to start out not liking each other to fall in love?"

"It makes a better story," I told him. "It would be too easy if they liked each other from the beginning and the things that irk them about each other . . . Well, maybe those are things they really are looking for but are afraid to believe exists."

"Is that why they're always with other people in the beginning? Because they've given up on finding the right person and settled for the wrong one?"

"Maybe," I said, wondering if he was thinking of me and Paul – or him and Moira. When we got to the part in *You've Got Mail* just before Tom Hanks appears in Riverside Park and Meg Ryan finds out that her secret pen pal is really the man who put her out of business, Liam asked, "If I lied to you about something that big – like pretending to be someone I wasn't – would you be able to forgive me?" he asked.

"Uh oh, don't tell me, you're a spy from the Dahlia LaMotte Society and you've been having wild, passionate sex with me just to gain access to her papers."

I hoped the reference to "wild, passionate sex" would divert him – perhaps toward some more of the same – but instead he became even more agitated. He got up and started pacing back and forth in front of the bookcases.

"All these books you read and write about, your *romances*, do you think they really tell the truth about love?" He plucked a copy of *Evelina* from the shelf. "Could a person read them and learn how to be in love?"

"They're not operating manuals," I snipped, growing irritated now. I didn't have the energy for a philosophical debate on the nature of love. Or maybe he'd hit a nerve. I sometimes wondered if the reason I read romances was to figure out what it meant to be in love. "There's no such thing. People learn to love from experience. It takes time. You can't study it like studying the piano or economics . . ."

Perhaps it was my choice of economics with its reminder of Paul that teed him off.

"Then what good are they?" he asked, lobbing *Evelina* across the room and then stomping out of the library.

"Hey! That's a 1906 edition!" I called after him. I considered following him, but I suddenly felt too tired – tired of Liam's outbursts and just plain *tired*. I burrowed into the couch, covering myself with the fluffy alpaca throw that Phoenix had bought. It still smelled like Jack Daniel's and Shalimar. The thought of Phoenix made me feel sorry for myself. Everybody left. Phoenix. Paul. Now Liam. I'd worked myself up to a good cry when Liam came back, repentant and smelling like the outdoors. His forehead was cool when he pressed it against mine.

"I'm sorry," he said. "Do you want to watch the rest of the movie?"

"No," I said, wrapping my arms around his neck. "I think we ought to get you some more experience in the art of love."

"Oh," he said, scooping me up in his arms and heading for the stairs. "Like this?"

"Rhett Butler one-oh-one – yes, exactly like this."

*

As January slid into February, I had to admit that my constant fatigue was more than the effects of lots of sex. Something was wrong with me. Since I didn't have a family doctor in the area yet, I went to the school infirmary before my class. After walking through a light snow I found a crowded waiting room full of sniffling, bleary-eyed students and a harassed nurse.

"What's going on?" I asked when I signed in – I recognized some of my students' names on the sign-up sheet: Flonia Rugova and Nicky Ballard and also Richie Esposito whom I remembered from the creative writing class. "Is it swine flu?"

The nurse, whose I.D. badge identified as Lesley Wayman, held up a finger for me to wait while she sneezed. "No," she said. "That's mostly passed. There's something else going around. Dr. Mondello thinks it's mono, although so far the tests have all come back negative."

"What were their symptoms?" I asked.

"Fatigue, night sweats, anemia."

"Huh. I have the fatigue, but I haven't noticed any night sweats . . ." I said, but then I realized, blushing, that I did sweat a lot at night, but that was because of what I was *doing* at night. And I had no idea whether I was anemic or not, although I never had been before.

"Have a seat," Nurse Wayman said. "The doctor will be with you as soon as she can."

I sat in an uncomfortable plastic chair – the only seat left – and took out a pile of papers to grade. The room was certainly quiet enough to get some work done. The only noise was the hiss of the steam heaters and the muted whisper of MP3 players plugged into many of the students' ears. I graded two papers – adding the scratch of my red pen to the hushed atmosphere – before noticing something peculiar. I was sitting in a room full of college students and no one was talking. Shouldn't a group of eighteen to twenty-two-year-olds, all attending the same small college, have something to say to one another?

I looked up and scanned the room's occupants. Directly across from me, sprawled in a too small chair, was a shaggy-haired boy with a goatee and silver nose ring. I recognized him from Liam's class, but didn't recall his name. Wes? Will? Waylon? Something with a W. Or maybe I thought that because a flying W – the trademark of the band Weezer – was tattooed on his neck. His eyes were closed, his head bobbing to the music leaking tinnily out of his plastic ear buds . . . or no, actually, his head was nodding because he was asleep. Each time his head fell heavily forward he snapped it up again and made a strangled gurgle. It was painful to watch but also a teeny bit funny. I looked around to see if anyone else was noticing his nodding-out performance, but everyone else was either asleep or staring vacantly into space or out the windows at the now heavily falling snow. Not only wasn't anyone talking, no one was even reading, writing, or sketching. The only person who even had a book in her lap was Flonia Rugova, who I noticed now curled up in the one comfortable looking sofa. I got up and went over to her. She flinched when I put my hand on her shoulder.

"Professor McFay, where did you come from? I didn't see you there."

"I've been sitting here for fifteen minutes, but I didn't notice you either. I was grading papers. I'd say you didn't see me because you were so engrossed in your book, but although I'm not an expert on Czech, I'm pretty sure you don't read it upside down."

Flonia glanced down at the book in her lap – Czeslaw Milosz's *Collected Poems* in the original. "Oh," she said. "I'm reading it for the independent study I'm doing with Mr. Doyle and Dr. Demisovski. It's really great but somehow I read two lines and then find myself staring into space." She yawned. "I don't know what's wrong with me. I seem to sleep all the time and I have such strange dreams . . ."

"Flonia Rugova?"

I thought that Flonia had stopped mid-sentence because Nurse Wayman had called her name, but she hadn't made any move to get up or acknowledge the sound of her name and when I looked down I saw that she had actually fallen asleep.

"Flonia?" I laid my hand on her bare forearm. Her skin was cold to the touch. "I think it's your turn."

"Oh!" she cried, startling awake. The color in her cheeks darkened and she stared at me as if she didn't know who I was.

"Miss Rugova?" The nurse was standing over us. "Dr. Mondello will see you now."

Flonia smiled at me and got up. The book of poems fell to the floor. I picked it up and handed it to her. "Czeslaw Milosz!" she exclaimed, as if she'd never seen the book before. "I love him. Thanks!"

Dr. Kathy Mondello, a tall woman with closely cropped gray hair and large serious eyes, listened as attentively to my symptoms as she did to my heart and lungs. She peered into my throat and ears, palpitated my glands, and took my blood. She asked me the standard questions.

"Any shortness of breath?"

"No," I answered, recalling the gasps I made while making love to Liam.

"Heart palpitations?"

"I don't think so." My heart felt like it was racing right then as I thought about Liam.

"Dizziness?"

"Not really." I didn't think the swoony feeling I got when I looked into Liam's eyes counted.

"Weight loss?"

"I wish! I've been eating like a truck driver."

"Really? Because I noticed your pants are loose. Have you weighed yourself lately?"

I admitted I hadn't and she asked me to step on the scale. I was five pounds lighter than when I'd weighed myself last, which was just before Christmas.

"Do you eat at the cafeteria?" she asked.

"No," I said. "Why? Do you think this is some kind of food poisoning?"

"No, there's been no stomach involvement, but I am seeing a lot of anemia. I wondered if there was some food at the cafeteria that leached iron from the blood. Certain foods are iron absorption inhibitors – red wine, coffee, tea, spinach, chard, sweet potatoes, whole grains, and soy. Have you been eating large quantities of any of those foods?"

"No, I don't think so," I answered.

She sighed. "Neither have any of the others who have anemia. I'm afraid it was a bit of a screwball idea." She laughed good-naturedly at herself. "But not as screwball as my first thought."

"And what was that?" I asked.

"Vampires," she said, wiggling her eyebrows in mock horror. "Honestly, when I started seeing all this anemia my first thought was it's like all these kids are being drained of their blood."

CHAPTER THIRTY-FOUR

I left the infirmary feeling worse than when I came. Although Dr. Mondello had been joking – clearly she was not in on the Fairwick secret – I couldn't help wondering if she was on to something. Were the Russian Studies professors preying on the student body? Draining them of blood? It seemed improbable. Surely they wouldn't be allowed here on the campus if they couldn't be trusted with the students, but then Frank had said that there'd been similar complaints against the college in the past. I had to tell someone what I suspected . . . but who? Liz Book was in no shape to take action. Maybe the vampires had felt free to prey on the students because they thought the dean was too weakened to do anything about it. Or maybe they were the ones who were making her so weak.

I was so distracted in class that I could barely pay attention. Fortunately I was showing a film: the original 1931 *Dracula* with Bela Lugosi. It was not the best choice for a dreary snowy morning. By the time the Count made his way to England, half the class was asleep and I didn't have the heart to nudge them awake. Instead of watching the film I studied the somnolent faces of my students, who looked, in the flickering reflection of the black and white film, as wan and lifeless as poor silly Lucy Westenra as she lay in her big Victorian bed drained by the Count. I couldn't see any bite marks on their necks, but then plenty of them were wearing turtlenecks or scarves. Besides, I'd read enough vampire books to know the neck wasn't the only place that could be bitten.

Five minutes before the end of class – just before Van Helsing and Jonathan Harker save Mina – I stopped the film and turned on the lights. My students blinked and covered their eyes like a pack of young vampires exposed to the sunlight, but instead of burning to a crisp they yawned and surreptitiously checked their laptops and cell phones for messages.

"So, do you think they're able to save Mina?" I asked the class, hoping that at least those who had read the book would have an answer.

But instead Nicky Ballard – who I was sure *had* read the book, answered, "What difference would it make? She's already been contaminated by Dracula. She'll never be the same."

I was so startled by the note of despair in Nicky's voice that I asked her to stay after class. I'd seen her name on the infirmary sign-in sheet and noticed that she seemed pale and tired, but it wasn't until I saw her close up that I realized how bad she really looked. Her skin was the blueish-white of skimmed milk, her eyes circled with purple rings, and her dark hair hung in oily strings around her face. Just a couple of weeks ago she'd looked happy and well-rested.

"Nicky, what's wrong? Are you sick?"

She shrugged. "They did a bunch of tests at the infirmary, but they couldn't really find anything except a B-12 deficiency. I'm going for shots, but they're not really helping." She yawned.

"Are you sleeping okay?"

She shook her head. "No. I've been staying in the dorm again." A faint flush of pink rose in her cheeks, but the blush didn't bring any life to her face; it merely made her look feverish and drew attention to the rash on her forehead and around her mouth. "Our suite is kind of crowded because Mara asked Flonia to move in last term because I was always with Ben, but then Ben and I had a big fight last week and broke up and I had to move back into the dorm."

"I'm sorry, Nicky. I know how rough that is."

"You broke up with your boyfriend, too, didn't you?"

I didn't really like to talk about my private life with my students, but Nicky was looking at me with such naked desperation that I didn't have the heart not to answer her question.

"Yes. It was painful, but then I realized we probably weren't really meant to be together."

Nicky nodded and bit her lip. "Then you got together with Professor Doyle. So it was really all for the best. Flonia says a new man is the best cure for a broken heart."

"Well, it's a bit more complicated than that . . ." I began, but then seeing the look on Nicky's face I paused. Here was a seventeen-year-old girl – almost eighteen – asking for my advice. So far I'd provided a model of a woman who'd leapt from one relationship right into another with barely a pause for breath. Is that what I wanted Nicky to do? I imagined her jumping into bed with the next available boy. Who knew? That might be how she would get pregnant and ruin her life. Instead of averting the curse, my example would lead to its fulfillment.

"It's not such a good idea to rush into another relationship so soon when you're still hurting from the last. You're not in the best frame of mind for making decisions and you may wind up hurting yourself and the other person."

"But you and Professor Doyle . . ."

"Are older and our circumstances were different . . . Still, who knows how things will work out for us. At least we're mature enough to deal with the consequences of our mistakes. You should be concentrating on school right now and working on your own dreams . . ."

"But that's just it!" Nicky cried, her face flushing red now. "I have these *awful* dreams. I'm lost in a frozen forest and I see these icicles hanging from the trees. They're like the ornaments people make around here, but in each one of these is a dream I once had – to be a writer, to be loved, to travel, to find my place in the world. And they're all melting. I run from one to another, trying to catch my dreams before they melt and drip to the forest floor but they all run through my fingers. When I wake up I know that I'll never realize any of my dreams. I'll be like my mother and my grandmother. I'll live alone in that old house until I die."

"We all wonder at some point if we'll ever realize our dreams," I told Nicky, remembering moments in college when I thought my grandmother was probably right about me and I'd never amount to anything. "But that's just fear talking. It sneaks up on you when you're tired and sad and whispers bad stories in your ears."

Nicky startled and looked up at me. "That's *exactly* what it feels like, Professor McFay. I wake up in the morning and I feel like someone's been whispering awful things in my ear all night long. That's why I'm so tired all that time. That whispering is keeping me up."

"Maybe you should sleep with earplugs," I suggested, only half kidding. "And lock your door at night," I added, wondering if Nicky's night-whisperer might be one of the vampires stealing into her room.

Nicky wiped her eyes and managed a weak smile. "The earplugs are actually a good idea. Mara and Flonia stay up late talking and it's hard to sleep hearing their voices." Nicky looked down at her watch. "Uh oh, I'm late for Mr. Doyle's class. I'd better go. Thank you so much for listening to my silly little problems, Professor McFay. It means a lot to me to have someone I can talk to."

"Anytime, Nicky. Really. If there's anything else you're worried about . . . anything that frightens you . . ."

"Thanks. And Professor McFay? One more thing. I'll take your advice about not jumping into bed with another guy right away, but I don't think you made a mistake hooking up with Mr. Doyle. I think you guys are perfect for each other."

After Nicky left I stood in my empty classroom for a few minutes trying to decide what to do next. Normally, I went to the library for an hour and then met Mara in my office to go over the papers she had graded. Lately, though, I'd brought her back to Honeysuckle House in the afternoon to work on cataloging the Dahlia LaMotte papers. Mara had turned out to be an industrious and organized research assistant and had come up with a system for indexing the LaMotte letters and manuscripts. Because the papers couldn't leave Honeysuckle House I'd invited her to work in the house. Instinctively, I'd shied away from having her come when Liam was there. There seemed to be some antipathy between the two of them that I attributed to Mara's disappointment over losing Phoenix's attention and her unfortunate way of expressing that disappointment when Liam took over the creative writing class. I'd chosen the hours when Liam was teaching his afternoon classes – and conducting the independent class with Nicky, which I'd left to him to do himself most days, to have her come over, but it was becoming exhausting keeping them apart. And it meant I wouldn't have a minute to myself for the rest of the afternoon. If I wanted to talk to Frank Delmarco about the rash of student illnesses, I'd better do it now.

I took the back stairs so I wouldn't pass Liam's classroom. I knew it was silly – even if Liam saw me going up the stairs he'd just think I was going to my office, but I did it because I knew Liam would be jealous if he thought I was going to see Frank. I don't know why I knew that. It had been Frank who'd acted jealous of Liam, not the other way around, but I guiltily remembered that first afternoon I'd met Liam (was it really only two and a half months ago?) and he'd caught me trading condescending jokes at his expense with Frank. I'd told him once that I was sorry about that, but he'd only laughed and told me rather formally that he'd forgiven me. But he hadn't said anything about forgiving Frank.

Frank was in his office in his usual pose; feet up, newspaper spread in front of his face. The Jets paraphernalia was gone, though, since the defeat of the Jets in the AFC championship game several weeks ago.

"I'm sorry about the Jets losing," I said, hoping to soften him up before presenting my theory to him.

He shrugged. "I didn't really expect any other outcome. It's the jinx. One of these days I'm going to find out who's jinxing them and then watch out – they'll win three Super Bowls in a row."

"Really? Sports jinxes are . . ."

"Don't even say it!" He dropped his newspaper and held up his hands, palms out. "Every time someone doubts the jinx it's strengthened. What? You think Bill Belichick being the Jet's head coach for only an hour was by chance?"

"Huh." I had to admit that made sense, but I hadn't come to talk about sports jinxes. "Have you noticed that a lot of students are out sick?"

Frank took his feet off the desk and leaned forward. "Yes, I have, but colleges are hotbeds of germs. The infirmaries are probably full at most colleges in the Northeast right now."

"Are they full of cases of unexplained fatigue, anemia and weight loss?"

"Truthfully, those symptoms could be caused by pulling all nighters, living on bad cafeteria food and dealing with negative body image . . . but wait." He looked me up and down in a way that made me blush. "You've lost weight, too, haven't you? And you look tired."

"I *am* tired, even though I sleep all the time. Could . . ." I blushed again. "Could a person be bitten by a vampire and not know it?"

Frank got up from his chair and came around his desk. He brushed aside my hair and peered down at my neck before I had a chance to object to the examination. He swore, his breath tickling the skin behind my ear. "I can't see in this light . . ." He grabbed me by the forearm, pulled me from the chair, sat me on the edge of his desk, and aimed his desk lamp at my neck. He tilted my head right, then left, his blunt calloused fingertips methodically palpating my skin, his voice crisp and business-like as he gave me a run-down on the vampire modus operandi.

"It *is* possible for a vampire to drink a victim's blood without him or her knowing. They would come at night, of course, but they must have previously been invited in. Have any of the Russian studies professors been to your house?"

"No," I answered, and then yelped as Frank slid his hand under my shirt.

"Sorry, just trying to be thorough. I don't see anything, but I'm afraid you'll have to check the femoral artery. Do you know where the femoral artery is?"

"Yes," I said, blushing even more.

"Do you sleep alone?" he asked.

"Uh . . . no . . ." I could feel the blood heating my whole chest now. I hoped Frank didn't think it was a reaction to his touch. Because it wasn't.

"Then it's probably not a vampire attack. Still, I'll look into it."

The only think he was looking into right now was my cleavage.

"Hey, I don't think vampires bite *there*."

Franks mouth quirked into a crooked grin. "No?" he asked, straightening the collar of my shirt. He was just stepping away when I heard a step behind him. I looked up, over Frank's shoulder, and saw Liam standing in the hall, his face white, his eyes wide.

I opened my mouth to call his name, but he was already gone, vanished so quickly I almost thought I'd imagined him. But that was just wishful thinking.

I pushed Frank away – or tried to. Frank's chest was a

solid obstacle. "Liam?" he asked, pursing his lips to keep from grinning. "Uh oh. That probably didn't look so good from his angle."

"I've got to catch him." I tried pushing Frank again and this time he stepped aside.

"I'm sure you'll come up with a very reasonable explanation for why I had my hand down your shirt." He was grinning now, not trying to hide his amusement. "Let me know what you come up with. I'll be happy to back you up."

I opened my mouth to reply but realized I didn't have time to spar with Delmarco. "Just look into why all our students are getting sick," I snapped as I left the room. "I'll take care of Liam."

I didn't look back but I could hear Frank's laughter echoing in the stairwell as I ran down the four flights. I was hoping Liam had gone back to his classroom as there were twenty minutes left to his class period—what had he been doing upstairs anyway? Maybe he'd come up to get a book from his office? – but I found his classroom empty except for a tow-headed boy sleeping with his head pillowed on his arms.

"Hey." I shook the boy's shoulder. When he looked up at me blearily I recognized him from his tattoo as the Weezer fan who'd been snoozing in the infirmary earlier. "What happened to the creative writing class that meets in here?"

"Yeah, that's my class, man. I'm here. I made it to class."

"Uh huh, good for you. So where are the rest of the students and where's Mr. Doyle?"

"Liam? Hey, he's cool . . ." The boy rubbed his eyes and looked around the empty classroom. "Hey, where'd everybody go?"

I sighed with frustration and turned to go but the boy grabbed my hand and pointed at the chalkboard. "Look, they left me a note. How cool is that?"

Written in Liam's elegant old-fashioned script were the words: *Wilder, I cancelled class due to low attendance. Go back to your room and get some sleep.*

I felt a lump in my throat reading the cheerful, bantering note. Liam must have written it minutes before he went upstairs and saw me with Frank. "How long ago . . . ?" I started to ask Wilder, but when I turned around I saw he'd already fallen back to sleep.

I left Fraser Hall and crossed the quad, scanning the paths for Liam, but it was hard to make out the faces of the muffled pedestrians bowed under the heavily falling snow. I stopped in the library to see if he'd gone there, but the rooms where he usually sat were empty save for studying – or napping – students. His independent study with Nicky wasn't for another hour. There was no place else to look but home.

I started off fast down the path to the southeast gate, but slowed when I went through it. I could see footsteps in the snow leading up to the porch steps, but none leading away. There was a light on in the front bedroom Liam had made into a study. So he *was* home. I clasped my hand to my chest, conscious for the first time of how hard my heart was beating, how afraid I'd been that he'd be gone. But my relief was quickly replaced by uncertainty. What was I going to say to him? How could I explain what he'd seen in Frank's office? I could try telling him that Frank had been looking for a tick in my hair – but down my shirt? No, I'd never be able to tell that lie with a straight face.

Or I could tell him the truth. That I'd gone to Frank

because I suspected the college's resident (and tenured!) vampires were helping themselves to student blood – and maybe mine, too. Why not? I thought defiantly, marching across the street. No one had told me I had to keep the college's secret. I could take him to Liz and Soheila to back-up my story . . .

I stopped halfway across the street. Even if I managed to convince Liam that Fairwick was populated by witches and fairies, I could only explain what happened in Frank's office by blowing Frank's cover – first to Liam and then potentially to anyone I asked to confirm my story. If Frank's cover was blown he wouldn't be able to investigate what was making so many students – and myself – sick. And while I might find Frank annoying and arrogant, I also suspected that he was the most competent and efficient man to get that job done. I couldn't compromise his ability to do it.

I walked the rest of the way across the street and up the porch steps more slowly. I opened the door, still without the slightest idea of what to say to Liam, and tripped over something in the foyer. Looking down I saw that it was a bird's nest with a cracked blue egg inside. I stared at it, trying to figure out how it had come to be in the foyer, and then remembered that it was one of the "finds" that Liam had brought back from his poetry walks and left on the table in the foyer. I glanced at the table and saw that all the other objects that were usually there – the wooden bowl where we left our keys, the pile of spare change, the basket full of takeout menus – had been swept onto the floor. Clutching the house key in my hand because I didn't know where to put it in all this chaos, I followed the debris up the stairs, my feet crunching on shards of blue glass from a bottle that had once stood on the windowsill on the landing, to the doorway to Liam's study. He was at his desk, which was empty save for the round gray riverstones he collected and used as paperweights, gazing vacantly out at the falling snow. The cold gray light had washed his face of all color, blanching his skin as white as the cotton shirt I myself had washed and bleached and ironed. His black hair and eyes – sunken deep in their sockets – looked like part of the gathering afternoon shadows, as did the loose folds of his dark wool coat. He looked, in the pitiless winter light, as if he might vanish if I blinked my eyes.

"Liam . . ." I said.

He raised his hand without turning to me. "Don't," he said. "You don't have to explain. I understand."

"You do?" I stepped softly into the room and perched on the edge of the chair we'd bought in Bovine Corners a few weeks ago.

"Yes. I know we've gone too fast . . . that I never gave you time to get over breaking up with Paul. It's natural you should have second thoughts."

"But I don't!" I cried, getting to my feet. "What you saw . . . It's not what you think. Frank . . . ."

He winced at Frank's name and held up his hand again. I noticed this time that it was trembling. "It doesn't matter. I don't care about what you may or may not have done with Frank Delmarco. It's what you said to Nicky Ballard that upset me."

"What I said to Nicky?" I sank down into the chair, searching my mind for what he could mean. "I talked to Nicky about her break up with her boyfriend . . ." And then I remembered. "She thought that finding a new boyfriend was the best cure for heartbreak because she thought that's what I had done."

"And is it?" He turned now. His eyes were rimmed with red, the only color in his face. "Is that why you're with me? As a cure for heartbreak?"

"No," I said. "I know that's how it might look from the outside, but you and me coming together . . . I know that had nothing to do with Paul."

"But you said we might be a mistake."

"Nicky said that to you?"

"She wrote about it in the journal she turned in today."

"Oh," I said, trying to recall exactly what I'd said to Nicky. "I think what I actually said is that you and I are old enough to deal with the consequences of our mistakes. I didn't mean that us being together *was* a mistake."

Liam tilted his head and narrowed his eyes. "From what I saw in Frank's office today you seem to be having second thoughts."

"Hey, a minute ago you said you didn't care about that! Anyway, it wasn't what it looked like."

Liam laughed. The sound startled me. "That's exactly what the unfaithful lover always says in the movies when he or she gets caught."

"Oh, Liam, please. This isn't a movie!" I was beginning to get exasperated. "Sometimes I think you've learned everything you know about love from the movies."

The minute the words were out I remembered Jeannie and the things Liam had learned from his time with Moira, but it was too late to take it back. Liam was already getting up and reaching for the duffel bag at his feet, which I'd missed seeing until now.

"Liam," I cried, reaching for him, "I didn't mean . . ." But when I laid my hand on him he jerked his arm away as if my touch had burned him. He held his hand up in front of his face, fingers clenched into a fist, his eyes dark and wild in his pale face. Then he turned and left, so quickly that I felt the air stir from his coat as he whipped around. I stood staring after him until a sharp pain in my hand drew my attention. I looked down and saw that I'd slipped the toothed end of the house key between my fingers the way Annie had once shown me to do if I was afraid someone was following me. Part of my brain had been so frightened by Liam's reaction to my touch that I'd been ready to attack him.

CHAPTER THIRTY-FIVE

I didn't get much chance to dwell on the fight – or on that surprising flash of violence I'd seen in Liam's eyes – because fifteen minutes after Liam left Mara showed up for her work-study assignment. Most college freshmen would have taken my failure to show up at my office as an opportunity to take the afternoon off, but not Mara.

"I was sure you'd want to get some more work done on the Dahlia LaMotte papers. They are so very fascinating."

Normally I would agree, but the last thing I wanted to do that afternoon was catalog the romantic fantasies of a reclusive spinster – especially with Mara, who had a way of zeroing in on the most erotic passages of LaMotte's fiction. I hadn't really intended for Mara to read the more salacious material in the handwritten manuscripts; I'd only asked her to make a record of how many pages LaMotte wrote each day. I wanted to see if LaMotte wrote more as the book progressed, if she was sometimes blocked, and how much time she took off between books. But it was impossible to keep Mara from reading the material and she often picked the raciest scenes to read aloud, asking for embarrassing explanations of sexual terms. Whenever she came across a word she didn't know she would come sit beside me – quite *close* – and point to the word. I wondered sometimes if she wasn't deliberately trying to make me uncomfortable, or if she might even be trying to make a sexual advance. It made for some long, awkward afternoons, but on this afternoon she did make an interesting discovery.

"I've noticed," she said, looking up from the yellow legal pad on which she kept her page tallies, "that there's a correlation between Miss LaMotte's output and the sex scenes in the book."

"Really?" I asked, intrigued.

"Yes, look . . ."

Mara came over to where I was sitting on the floor and knelt beside me. She put the yellow legal pad in my lap and reached across me, her arm brushing against my shoulder. "I've put asterisks wherever a romantic interaction occurs, one for a meaningful glance, two for a kiss, and three for actual intercourse . . ."

"I think I get the idea. What exactly is the correlation you see?"

"Well, look at the page tallies. In between the meaningful glance and the kissing scenes Miss LaMotte writes an average of ten to fifteen pages a day. For every book, see, I've cataloged them all this way." She flipped the pages of the notepad and I saw scores of asterisks dotting the pages. So many kisses, I thought trying to remember the last time Liam had kissed me. Would it be the *last* time? "Then between the first kiss and the intercourse, she writes an average of twenty to thirty pages a day, the number escalating sometimes to as many as sixty pages a day as she gets closer to the intercourse scene."

"Really?" I asked, distracted from my memories of

Liam's kisses by Mara's discovery. I picked up the pad and shifted my weight so that Mara wasn't quite so close. "That *is* interesting."

"What's really interesting is that after the intercourse scene the page tallies decrease again. Sometimes she doesn't even write anything for a few days. It's as if she's worn out."

I flipped through the pages, each one representing one of Dahlia LaMotte's novels. Mara was right. There was a definite pattern. It was as if Dahlia LaMotte became increasingly excited as the sexual tension between her characters mounted and then suffered a sort of sympathetic post-coital slump after they finally made love.

"Mara, that's a really important discovery. Thank you very much."

Mara smiled a rare smile and her cheeks glowed pink. She looked almost pretty. The poor girl, I thought, she gets so little encouragement, I really should make more of an effort with her . . . invite her over with some of the other students for dinner sometime . . . But not tonight, I thought, yawning, I just wanted to crawl into bed and go to sleep tonight.

"I want to go through these and think about what you've found," I said, getting to my feet. "Why don't we call it a day?"

Mara looked disappointed but then brightened. "Can we work again tomorrow?" she asked.

"Sure," I said, even though tomorrow wasn't one of our scheduled days. I might as well throw myself into my work to distract myself from replaying in my head the fight I'd had with Liam.

After Mara left I made myself a cup of soup and took it

upstairs to my bedroom to eat in bed. The house felt hollow and empty without Liam there. I went into his study and looked out the window across the street to the inn to see if there was a light on in his old room. There wasn't. Had he gone somewhere else? Or taken a different room? Or was he there and sleeping soundly, undisturbed by our fight?

Before I left the room, I noticed that he'd piled the gray riverstones into a small pillar – as if he'd been fashioning a grave cairn. They looked so eerie like that I unpiled them. I carried one of the stories into my bedroom, its cool, round, weight somehow soothing in my palm.

As tired as I was I still couldn't sleep that night. Even the racy Dahlia LaMotte manuscript of *The Viking Raider* failed to distract me. I'd come to the part where the heroine is finally to be ransomed back to her royal fiancé. Her Viking captor unlocks her room one last time the night before she is to leave and sweeps in . . .

. . . like a storm at sea come to capsize my resolve. "Will your young lord do this to you?" he growled, sinking his bristly face to my breasts and licking my nipples until they hardened. "Or this?" grasping my hips and grinding his manhood against me, but then pulling back, teasing me as I thrust upward, hungry to feel the length of him inside me at last. Always he had held back this one last intimacy between us, preserving my maidenhood for my intended. But I no longer cared what my husband might think on our wedding night. I wrapped my legs around his hips and pulled him to me, begging him to come inside me. "Ah lass," he moaned as he finally entered me. "You have conquered me. It is I who am your captive."

And even though I knew full well that by the logic of these books the Viking and the Irish lass would end up together by the last page my eyes filled with tears when he gave her the key to her cell as a final parting gift and she read the note tied to it with a scarlet ribbon.

"I give ye the key to your freedom, lass, but can you give me back the key to my heart?"

When I turned out the lights Liam's side of the bed – how had we ended up with sides so quickly? – yawned like an icy crevasse I might fall into if I relaxed a muscle. I lay tensed, replaying our argument over and over, trying to come up with some other way I could make it come out differently, but instead I kept coming up with the same interlocking loops. I'd doubted that we were right together and told Nicky that we might be a mistake, and then I ended up in Frank's office letting him put his hand down my shirt. I could try to explain that I was only trying to discover what was making me so tired and thin, but then mightn't the reason I couldn't sleep and I was losing weight be that I had made a mistake? Maybe Liam and I *had* moved too fast. What did I really know about him? There was always a piece of himself that he kept to himself – I'd thought at first it was the sadness over Jeannie's death, or the part of him that wrote poetry, but when he'd drawn his arm back today I'd thought he was going to hit me. Had I sensed that potential for violence all along? Was I looking for a way out of the relationship? Was *that* was the reason I'd gone to Frank with the idea about the vampires because really, I could have looked down my own shirt to check for fang marks.

I kicked at the sheets, which had become as tangled as my thoughts, and they fell to the floor and lay in the moonlight like snowdrifts. Was it still snowing? I wondered. I got up and walked to the window. No. The snow had stopped and the moon had come out, turning the snow-covered trees into gaunt skeletons, their shadows thrown across the clean white expanse of the backyard, reaching toward the house.

One of those shadows detached itself from the edge of the woods and scuttled across the lawn. The shadow-crab. I ran downstairs, threw a coat over my nightgown, and pulled on shearling boots over my bare feet. The fishing creel that Soheila had given me was in the kitchen, hanging from a hook by the back door.

I opened the door slowly, watching for any movement in the shadows. It might be lurking by the door, trying to find a way in to do away with Ralph. It could be hiding in the wedge-shaped shadow of the door that widened across the kitchen floor as I opened it. I waved the wicker creel over the darkened wedge and, when I was sure that I hadn't let anything in, stepped out into the moonlit night, closing the door behind me.

The backyard was covered with a pure expanse of virgin snow, frozen on top with an icy crust that sparkled in the moonlight – everywhere but in the shadows. There were the shadows of the trees at the edge of the lawn, one thrown by the birdbath in the middle of the yard, a long oblong shadow in the lee of an old stone wall a few feet from the kitchen door, and a delicate tangle of shadows cast by an old lilac bush at the edge of the wall. I studied each shadow carefully, comparing it to the object that made it for any suspicious lumps or movement. There was nothing.

Then a wind moved through the yard, sifting loose snow across the icy crust and stirring the branches. One of the shadow branches cast by the old lilac seemed to swell. I stepped toward it, stepping across the shadow of the stone wall, and felt something brush against my ankle.

I looked down and saw the shadow-crab scuttling toward the back door. I dove for it with the creel open in my hands . . . and missed. The shadow-crab dodged and headed back toward the woods. I scrambled to my feet and chased after it, stumbling in the snow. The shadow-crab was light enough to move across the surface, but my feet crashed clumsily through the crust. If it made it to the woods I'd never catch it – and Ralph would pine away and die in the Shadow Land. It was nearly at the edge of the woods . . . about to merge with a large man-shaped shadow . . .

I reared back as the larger shadow stepped toward me and dropped the creel to the ground.

I looked up, fearing some horrible shadow-monster, but instead I saw Liam's face, pale and dim in the shadows.

"Liam! What are you doing here?"

"I couldn't sleep without you, so I went for a walk in the woods. Then I heard a noise from the house and thought somebody might be trying to break in. What were *you* doing?"

"You couldn't sleep without me?" I asked, ignoring his question. "I couldn't sleep without you either."

He took another step forward to the edge of the shadows. The moonlight touched the top of his hair and the shoulders of his cream knit sweater, but his face was still in shadow and somehow wavery, as if he were underwater or dissolving – but then I realized that was because my eyes had filled with tears.

"Oh Liam, I'm so sorry, I don't think we're a mistake, and I don't want Frank Delmarco or anyone else. I want *you*."

He stepped toward me, full into the moonlight, his body

taking shape in the light, and pulled me into his arms, which were icy cold, but when I slid my hands under his sweater and found his mouth I felt a spark of heat leap up to meet me. He moaned and slid his hands down my back and under my coat. When his hands found bare skin he gasped and lifted me off my feet. I wrapped my legs around his hips. He stumbled, but then he pushed me up against a pine tree, hard enough that the tree moved, feathery branches releasing a spray of snow and casting shadows across Liam's face. When he pushed himself inside of me I smelled the sharp scent of bruised pine. The tree swayed in rhythm with us, joining our gasps and moans, as if the tree, the forest, and the whole shadowy night were party to our lovemaking.

After, Liam carried me upstairs to our bed and we lay side by side. I found I couldn't keep my hands or eyes off him – as if I had to convince myself that he was real. When I closed my eyes I saw him dissolving into the shadows and I would startle awake as though I was the one falling backward into darkness.

I woke up sore *everywhere*, but when Liam ground his hips into my back I turned eagerly to him and we made love again – making me late for class and so sore I'm pretty sure I walked funny.

"Did you and Poetry Man make up?" Frank asked me as I hobbled past his office.

I looked anxiously up and down the hall to make sure Liam wasn't anywhere nearby – I certainly didn't want him to see me with Frank again so soon – before answering.

"We're fine. He just had a jealous moment, but I explained that there was absolutely nothing to be jealous about and we made up." I smiled brightly, hiding a wince.

Even my lips felt sore and chapped from Liam's kisses.

"Great," Frank said. "Then he won't mind if you come in here and sit down for a moment. I have something important to discuss with you."

I glanced behind me again and noticed Frank smiling when I turned back. Then I strode firmly into his office and plopped myself down in the chair in front of his desk, wishing I'd finessed my landing a little more gently.

Frank got up and shut the door.

"I don't think that's a good idea," I objected.

Frank sat down on the edge of his desk. "We can't risk anyone overhearing this. There's more than your boyfriend's delicate feelings at stake here."

I opened my mouth to object again but realized I'd get out of there quicker if I didn't argue. "What is it?"

"I checked in with our resident vampires last night and I don't think they're the ones who are preying on the students."

"Why? Because they told you they weren't?"

"No, because I watched them all night and the only blood they drank was imported."

"Imported?"

"As in not local. Three people arrived at their house last night – all over twenty-one, none glamoured – to volunteer their services."

"Ew. Why would anyone do that?"

"One was a middle-aged woman from Woodstock who's writing a paranormal romance and considers herself the luckiest person on the planet to have found real live – or real *undead* – vampires who are such *gentlemen*. That's what she told me when I stopped her leaving their house near dawn. The other two were a couple from Manhattan who are trying to spice up their marriage . . ."

"Okay, maybe I don't want to know any more."

Frank smiled. "Good call. There are some images I'd rather not have in my head either."

"But just because the vampires weren't stalking students last night doesn't mean they don't ever."

"No, but I also went by the infirmary and had a little chat with the night nurse. There are no bite marks on any of the students and when I spoke to Flonia Rugova she had no memory – conscious or unconscious – of a vampire attack."

"How is Flonia?" I asked.

"She's very weak and appears to have suffered some short-term memory loss, but seems to be recovering. I told the nurse she shouldn't have any visitors."

"But if it's not the vampires draining the students . . ."

"I don't know. I'm going to track Flonia's progress. How do you feel?"

"I feel fine. I think it was just a virus, but I'm over it now." I got to my feet and gave Frank a wide smile to keep from wincing at the soreness in my legs. "I've never felt better."

But I couldn't help thinking: if not a vampire, then who – or what – was draining the students. What else could it be but a succubus?

CHAPTER THIRTY-SIX

I considered telling Frank my suspicions, but if I did I'd
have to also tell him that Soheila was a succubus. Somehow
I couldn't bear to betray her secret, knowing how Soheila
felt about him. Unless, of course, it was Soheila who was
draining the students.

I started keeping track of the students who got sick and
then seeing whether they had any contact with Soheila. Both
Nicky and Flonia were in Soheila's Introduction to Middle
Eastern Mythology class. So was Scott Wilder, who got so
sick he had to take a leave of absence. And of course the
dean had had ample contact with Soheila. But when I went
to see Liz to share my concerns with her I found her
completely recovered.

Her eyes were sharp again, her skin smooth and pink, her
silver hair coiled into a gleaming chignon. She was wearing
a kelly green tweed suit and pink blouse to celebrate the
approach of spring, but her fur coat lay across the back of
the couch where she sat and occasionally she reached out to
stroke its glossy pelt.

"Is Ursuline better?" I asked, eyeing the coat uneasily.

"Oh yes! She pretended to be a dog and we took her to
the Goodnoughs' clinic. She enjoyed being a dog so much

I've agreed that she can spend a few hours each week at the dog park so she can see Abby and Russell with their Rottweiler Roxy – as long as she *behaves*." She injected a note of sternness into her voice but patted the coat fondly. I wondered how Ursuline liked the hours she spent as a coat but thought it might be rude to ask. Instead I told her my suspicion that the "flu" that was going around might be caused by a succubus.

"I suppose that's possible, but the only succubus on campus is . . . Oh! You can't mean Soheila? She would never do such a thing! And especially not to students!"

I felt instantly guilty for even suggesting the possibility, but I persevered. "If not Soheila, then is it possible that there's a succubus – or incubus – on campus we don't know about? I mean, you don't always know who is and who isn't a supernatural creature, do you?"

Liz frowned. "No, I'm afraid it's not always possible to tell. With you, we suspected something when you told us about letting the bird out of the thicket. But if someone really wanted to hide their true nature . . . Oh my, it would be awful if I hired a succubus or incubus who was draining the students. I'd never forgive myself!" She looked stricken. "I'm going to do a thorough background check on all recent hires. I'll ask Mara Marinca to help me . . . if you can spare her."

"Sure," I said a little too readily. As useful as Mara had been I'd found our sessions awkward and exhausting – especially now that she was focusing on the erotic passages in Dahlia LaMotte's books. I wouldn't mind having my afternoons free again. I was actually disappointed when Mara volunteered to do both jobs but told myself that I was being ungenerous. Clearly the girl needed all the money she could get from her work-study jobs.

As the semester went on fewer students got sick and many who had been sick recovered. The exceptions were Nicky who became so sick she had to move back into her grandmother's house, and Mara, who missed class the last day before spring break. She texted me from the infirmary saying she was sorry she had missed class and that she wouldn't be able to come by that day to work on the Dahlia LaMotte manuscripts. My first reaction was relief. I could go home and take a nap instead. But then I felt so guilty at that thought that I went by the infirmary after class to visit her. Lesley Wayman was in her room, fluffing her pillows and straightening her blankets.

"Poor dear," Nurse Wayman said, laying a motherly hand on Mara's pale forehead. "She was weak as a kitten when she came in last night. She should have come sooner."

"I hated to miss class and work," Mara said through blueish lips. "I could lose my scholarship and get deported."

Nurse Wayman clucked her tongue. "Nonsense, dear, I'm sure no one's going to take away your scholarship because you're sick. Isn't that right, Professor McFay?"

"Of course not," I answered, patting Mara's hand.

"But we were making so much progress on cataloging Dahlia LaMotte's books. I could still come to your house over break to work on them . . ."

"Don't be silly, Mara. Those manuscripts will still be there after break and you should really use the time to rest."

"That's what I intend to do with my break," Lesley Wayman said, bustling me out of the room. "I'm going to spend the whole week in my hot tub."

"I bet this has been rough on you, having so many sick students at once."

Nurse Wayman yawned and arched her back, kneading her sacrum with one hand, a gesture which made me feel the ache in my own back.

"At least it wasn't stomach flu. Most of them get better with a little rest. I hear Nicky Ballard's still pretty bad, though. I'm afraid that fool mother of hers has got her running around taking care of old Miz Ballard instead of resting."

"Hmm. Maybe I should drop by and see how she's doing," I said, seeing the possibility of an afternoon nap slipping away.

"If you do, could you take these iron supplements with you? I ordered them for Nicky and called JayCee to pick them up, but she said she was too busy." She snorted. "Can you imagine? Too busy to pick up her sick daughter's vitamins? I went to school with JayCee and she was a nice enough girl back then so I hate to say anything bad about her, but . . ." Lesley Wayman shook her head and folded her lips together as if to suppress her criticisms of JayCee Ballard. I offered to take the vitamins and wished her a good break.

"You, too," she said. "Get some rest and put some meat on your bones. You're still looking peaked."

Before I left the campus I texted Liam to tell him I'd meet him at home later. He texted me back to say he had an appointment with the dean and would be back around five. I walked out the southeast gate, passed my house with a longing look, and turned down Elm Street. The Ballard house looked more decrepit than ever in the sunshine, although there were some cheerful crocuses peeking up through the sooty snow on the front lawn. I wondered who had planted them. Someone had cared once about making the house look more cheerful. I noticed, too, that stacks of newspapers, tied off neatly with twine, had been left for the recycle pick-up. Maybe Nicky had been cleaning up while she was home – an admirable endeavor, but probably not the best way to recuperate.

I knocked on the door and waited. I could hear a radio playing inside – W.F.A.I., the college station – and an occasional thump. I knocked again and heard some muttered curses. Then the door was yanked open. JayCee Ballard, in the middle of lighting a cigarette, scowled when she saw it was me.

"Let me guess, you're here to check up on Nicky. Don't you people have any other students to worry about up at the college of ours?"

"Why, has someone else been to visit?"

JayCee squinted through her cigarette smoke and then smiled slyly. She folded her arms across a faded Phish logo on her tight ribbed tank top. "So you didn't know your boyfriend came here this morning. Inner-resting . . . He even brought muffins! Can you feature that? A man baking! If he hadn't stared at my tits so hard I'd have said he was a homo."

"Oh, Liam was here?" I said, trying not to sound surprised. "He *did* say he was going to drop by sometime. I didn't realize he'd gotten around to it. I'd like to see Nicky, too. I've got some vitamins for her." I took the bottle out of my pocket and JayCee snatched them out of my hand.

"I'll give 'em to her. She's asleep. Your boyfriend's visit tired her out. If I find out there's any funny business going on between them I'll sue that college for sex harassment."

"Liam would never take advantage of a student," I sputtered. "He cares about them too much . . ."

"'Too much' is right. He was holed up in Nicky's room for half an hour. Nicky said they were talking about her poetry, but I saw his eyes. Bedroom eyes, if you know what I mean."

To my horror, I blushed.

"I guess you do know what I mean." JayCee snickered. "My advice to you, honey, is keep your man satisfied so he don't go prowling around here looking for younger meat."

With that sage advice delivered, JayCee slammed the door in my face. I almost knocked again but decided it wasn't worth the effort. I retreated down the steps and along the unshoveled front path which, I noticed now, did have large footprints that matched Liam's size 13 L.L. Bean snow boots. So JayCee hadn't been lying about him visiting. Which was no big deal. It was just the kind of considerate thing Liam would do – even the baking part. So why did I feel funny about it? Surely I wasn't taking JayCee's obscene hints seriously. Liam would never take advantage of a student that way. But still there was something about Liam visiting Nicky that bothered me . . .

"Yoo hoo! Yoo hoo!"

The call, which might have belonged to a migratory waterfowl, pierced my consciousness as I was stomping up Elm Street. I turned and found a petite middle-aged woman in a bright red sweater and jeans waving at me from the front porch of a Craftsman bungalow. I recognized the house as the one I'd gone into on Thanksgiving Day with Dory to check the pipes for its owners who wintered in Florida. A glance at the R.V. in the driveway suggested they were back.

"Hello?" I answered back, holding my hand over my eyes to shade the glare. "Are you talking to me?"

The woman came down her steps and then looked at the snow on her unshoveled path and the red slippers on her feet with dismay. "Oh dear," she said as she began to pick her way gingerly through the snow. "We came back early and forgot to tell Brock to shovel our paths. Or to turn up our heat. And now we've found that we've been broken into! Harald's on the phone with the sheriff. Can you believe it? Here in Fairwick? I'm Cheryl Lindisfarne, by the way, but everyone calls me Cherry." She held out her hand when we reached each other on the middle of the path.

"Callie McFay. I'm at the college. And actually I came by your house with Dory Browne after the Thanksgiving ice storm to check on your pipes. Everything looked fine then."

"Oh my, I hate to tell you this but from the dates on the fraudulent credit card charges the home invader was already in the house on Thanksgiving Day! We noticed some unusual charges on the AmEx in December and we cancelled all our cards. But who knows what other information he might have taken! He might have stolen our identities!"

She glanced nervously up and down the street as if clones of Cheryl and Harald Lindisfarne might be strolling brazenly in broad daylight along Elm Street.

"Well, that *is* upsetting," I agreed, unsure what the woman wanted me to do about her problem. "But if you haven't seen any more fraudulent charges maybe it was just a vagrant trying to get warm . . ."

"Do you think?" she asked, laying her hand on my arm. "He ate an entire Hormel ham and all the peaches I'd put up last summer, but he was very neat. He washed out the peach jars and put back all the D.V.D.s from Harald's collection. Harald is a bit of a movie buff . . ."

"He put back the D.V.D.s?" I asked. "Then how do you know he took them out?"

"Oh, because they're out of alphabetical order . . . Oh dear, maybe he was an *illiterate* vagrant! Maybe he turned to a life of crime because he never had a proper education. I'm a literacy volunteer, you know," she added. "I work with newly arrived immigrants in Florida and migrant workers up here in the summer. Gosh, do you think it could have been one of the men I tutor?"

Thankfully the new conjecture was cut short by the appearance on the porch of a short, bald, rotund man in khaki shorts, a T-shirt that proclaimed the owner was a Retired Snowbird and Proud of It!, and red suspenders.

"The sheriff's on his way, Cherrybaby," the man called as he picked his way across the snow toward us. "He says we need to make a list of everything that's missing. You'll have to do the pantry."

"Oh," Cherry said, squeezing my arm, "I'd best go in. Thank you for being such a good listener. I just had to tell *someone*! And I'm glad to meet you. Dory told me we had a nice new woman professor at the college. You'll have to join our book club and Harald's Friday night movie club. We watch classics and new movies. My favorites are the romantic comedies . . ."

I'd been trying to come up with a polite way to get away from Cherry Lindisfarne when the words *romantic comedies* brought me up short.

"Which movies did the thief watch?" I asked,

interrupting Cherry's personal review of the new Nancy Meyers film.

Cherry Lindisfarne blinked at my rudeness, but recovered herself quickly and turned to her husband. "Do you remember, Harald?"

"I made a list for the police," he said taking a folded piece of paper out of this shorts pocket. "Let's see . . ." While he adjusted a pair of bifocals on his sunburned nose I suppressed an urge to throttle him. "*Beauty and the Beast* – the French one, not Disney – *It Happened One Night, The Philadelphia Story, You've Got Mail* and *When Harry Met Sally*."

"He was apparently quite the fan of romantic comedy!" Cherry exclaimed. "I bet he'd been disappointed in love and was trying to figure out how to get back with his girlfriend. Those movies are practically primers on the art of love!"

"Yes, a person could learn a lot from those movies." Like how to lie to your girlfriend, I reflected bitterly. "And those credit card charges. Do you recall what companies they were from?"

"Oh yes," Cherry said. "L.L. Bean, Land's End, and J. Peterman. All Harald's favorites so we didn't notice at first. But then we looked closer at the orders and saw that the pants were a narrower waist size and longer inseam and the shoes were way bigger . . ."

"What size shoes?" I asked.

"Thirteen!"

"Oh," I said, feeling my heart grow heavy in my chest. "That's . . . big. I guess there aren't too many men with that size shoe."

"No! It will be a good clue for the police. But you poor thing, you look pale! I can imagine realizing he was in the house when you came by is upsetting. I don't blame you for feeling shocked. It makes you feel *violated* somehow."

"Yes," I told Cherry in perfect honesty. "It does. I think . . . I think I'd better go home now."

"You do that, dear. Make yourself a cup of tea with plenty of sugar in it for the shock. And make sure you lock your doors. Who knows? Our home invader might still be lurking around."

I walked back to the house going over what I'd learned from the Lindisfarnes. The day after I'd banished the incubus someone had broken into the Lindisfarnes' house and used their credit card to buy clothes from the same catalog companies that Liam favored, and then less than two weeks later Liam Doyle showed up in Fairwick.

When I turned the corner onto my street I saw three women sitting on my porch. Two of the women were the same as the ones who had arrived on the night of the ice storm: Diana Hart and Soheila Lilly. The third was Fiona Eldritch.

As I walked up my porch steps my legs felt heavy. I *had* been feeling tired lately, hadn't I?

"You don't have to do an intervention," I said. "I know what you're here to tell me. Liam Doyle is the incubus."

CHAPTER THIRTY-SEVEN

"Aren't you the clever one!" Fiona said. "It took you long enough to realize."

"That's not fair," Diana pointed out. "You didn't know either."

"Well," Fiona huffed, "He wouldn't let me get close to him and he was so very *solid* I thought he couldn't really be my incubus. You made him incarnate, Callie. It's very impressive, actually. In order for an incubus to become flesh his love object has to have a strong mind and strong desires. You must have wanted him to become flesh."

I shook my head. "I tried to vanquish him. You saw me do it!" I turned to Soheila and Diana. Soheila, who hadn't spoken a work yet looked stricken, but remained silent. Diana looked unhappy, too, but she answered me. "We saw you go through with the ceremony, Callie, and I'm sure you *meant* well, but we couldn't see what was in your heart. No one can see that . . ." She glanced at Fiona with a nervous but determined look. "No one is saying you brought him to life intentionally."

Fiona glared at Diana, but reluctantly agreed. "No, I suppose not intentionally."

"But," Diana continued, turning so pale under Fiona's

disapproval that her freckles stood out, "if you had just the teensiest bit of hesitation when you performed the rite . . . if just a little bit of you wanted the incubus to stay, then it might have been enough to allow him to become flesh."

I stared at Diana, remembering the night before Thanksgiving when we'd vanquished the incubus. Had I harbored a small desire to keep him with me? "But," I said, noticing a look of triumph pass over Fiona's face and one of even greater sadness over Soheila's. "How did he do it? Liam has professional credentials . . . degrees from Trinity and Oxford, publications in magazines . . . a Facebook page, for goodness' sake. I Googled him!"

Diana and Soheila exchanged looks. Fiona just laughed.

"Yes, I have, too!" Fiona crowed. "It's all quite cleverly done, isn't it? The degrees and the residencies at writers' conferences . . . Did anyone think to call any of them? And the poetry – it's lovely, isn't it? He always did have a way with words."

"He created a virtual web using the Lindisfarnes' computer," Diana added, "much like an identity thief would . . ."

"But his whole identity couldn't have just been *virtual*!" I cried.

"Did you ever find any of the actual print magazines that carried one of his poems?" Fiona asked smugly. "No, I didn't think so. Neither did Dean Book, I'm afraid."

"She was ill," Diana said defensively. "He bewitched her and compromised her judgment so that she didn't look into his credentials thoroughly."

"You're telling me she didn't call any of his references?" I asked.

Diana sighed. "She read his resumé, his letters of recommendation, and then met with him. She emailed with a professor at one of the colleges where he taught and tried to call another professor, but couldn't get through. In hindsight, she says that all his credentials were digital and therefore could have been faked. She should have realized that, of course, but she was charmed by him and happy to get a replacement for Phoenix so she didn't investigate as much as she should have."

"And you . . ." I said, turning to Fiona. "You seem to be suggesting that Liam is the incubus you knew hundreds of years ago. Didn't you recognize him?"

"I suspected it was him, but I couldn't be sure. I have to have actual physical contact in order to tell and when I lured him into the cloakroom to kiss him you interrupted us."

"But he didn't want to kiss you, did he?"

"No . . . he probably knew that it would give him away."

"Or he just didn't want to kiss you because he liked me better."

Fiona's eyes blazed and she seemed to grow three inches taller.

"Remember she's still under his power," Diana told Fiona in a small voice. "She's not responsible for what she says."

"I know exactly what I'm saying. You have no proof that Liam is your incubus, do you?"

Fiona and Diana remained silent at my outburst, but Soheila finally spoke. "No, Callie, we don't. But we do have proof that there is an incubus-like creature sucking the life force out of students on campus. All his victims – Dean Book, Flonia Rugova, Scott Wilder, Nicky Ballard, and Mara Marinca – had the same symptoms: fatigue, troubling dreams, and anemia. I should have seen it earlier, but I never like to think that one of my kind would behave so . . . so indiscriminately. Preying on young people!" She made a face. "Even my sisters are more principled. But when I visited Nicky Ballard and held her hand. I could feel the signature of the incubus."

"Before you said incubus-*like*," I pointed out.

"There are a number of creatures who prey on the life force of humans – incubi, succubi, love talkers, lamias, lideres, undines. They're all related. I can feel the presence of a creature feeding off the life force . . ." She reached out her hand to grasp mine and I took a step backward . . . right into Fiona. It was like stepping into a wall of ice.

Soheila reached for my hand. I tried to pull it away, but Fiona held me steady with a touch on my arm that was light but compelling. I was powerless to move away. Soheila took my hand in both of hers. She closed her eyes and stroked my skin. Her eyes moved rapidly back and forth beneath her eyelids as if she were dreaming . . . then flicked open, releasing a tear that slid down her cheek.

"I can feel him, Callie. His presence is strong in you. I can feel his love . . ."

"An incubus is incapable of love," Fiona hissed. "And if he did love her why would he prey on all those students? Does he love them, too?"

I turned away from Soheila's grief-stricken eyes to face Fiona. "I can believe that Liam is an incubus – that he preyed on me – but I can't believe he preyed on his students."

"He'd have to if you weren't enough to satisfy him."

My hand was in the air headed toward Fiona's mocking smile before I knew I meant to slap her, but Soheila and Diana grabbed me before I could make contact. A wind knocked the three of us back against the wall of the house and a white light blinded me. I heard Fiona's voice inside my brain, piercing my head like an ice pick. *Don't you ever defy me again, little doorkeeper, or I will turn you into dust. I spare you now only so you can send your demon back to the Borderlands. I want him to know what it feels like to be rejected by the one he desires.*

A high-pitched screech filled my brain – I felt sure my head was going to explode – and then it was gone, leaving an ache, a ringing in my ears and a coppery taste in my mouth. I fell to my knees and threw up. Dimly I felt Diana holding back my hair and Soheila murmuring.

"It's okay, she's gone. She's angry because he's chosen you over her, but she knows she can't destroy you. Even the Queen of the Fairies needs a doorkeeper to open the door to Faerie."

"She said she spared me so I'd send him back, so he'd know what it felt like to be rejected by someone he loved . . . but she herself said that an incubus couldn't love . . . and if Liam's really the incubus . . ." Another wave of nausea rose from my stomach as the reality finally penetrated. Liam, whose body I knew so intimately, was not made of flesh and blood, but was a creature of shadow and moonlight, a golem fashioned from the clay of my own lust. "If he's an incubus . . . if he's lied to me and fed off his students . . . then he doesn't love me. He can't love anyone."

Soheila winced but said nothing. Diana smoothed my hair back from my damp forehead.

"I think he must love you as best as he can," Diana said. "But it doesn't matter. You have to send him back. He'll suck you dry if you don't."

Soheila nodded. "Diana's right. He can't help it. It's how he's made."

"But then how am I supposed to make him leave?"

Soheila and Diana looked at one another and for a moment I thought – hoped? – they would throw up their hands and tell me they had no idea. *Oops, sorry, once an incubus is made flesh there's no way to disincarnate him. You're stuck. You'll just have to make the best of the situation.* But instead, at a nod from Soheila, Diana took out her cell phone and punched in a number.

"She's ready," she said without greeting, and then hung up without a good bye.

Across the street the front door of the Hart Brake Inn opened and Brock came out carrying a box. He crossed the street with the box held out in front of him, like a waiter carrying a tea-caddy to a customer in a restaurant.

"Neither Soheila nor I can help you with this part, Callie, because we can't handle iron. Brock will explain what to do."

"Wait a minute," I said as both women got to their feet. "If an incubus doesn't like iron, then why are all his victims *drained* of iron?"

Diana bobbed her head up and down. "Good question. It's not fully understood, but apparently there's a sort of symbiotic relationship that develops between the incubus and his victim that makes his victim shed iron so that the incubus can continue feeding. We think it's why the victim eventually weakens and dies. If we understood it better then the incubi – and succubi—" she glanced at Soheila "—could have normal relationships with humans."

Soheila smiled at Diana but shook her head. "Casper Van der Aart has been working on the problem for decades. I'm afraid there's little hope for a solution. Meanwhile . . ." She glanced behind her at Brock, who had stopped midway up my front path. "We have to go. The iron that Brock has forged is especially powerful. Diana and I can't be near it." She took my hand in hers. "Good luck, Callie, and remember, he can't help what he is, but if he truly loves you he doesn't want to destroy you. He'll be better in the long run banished to the Borderlands than living with your death." She gave my hand one final squeeze and got up to go. Diana patted my shoulder and followed her. I got up, too – mostly to move away from the place where I had thrown up – and met Brock on the steps.

"I'm so sorry, Callie. I should have protected you better. I should have recognized him. I just never thought that he could become flesh – he never did all the years he haunted Dahlia."

"I think she kept him at bay with her writing," I said, thinking of the pattern that Mara had discerned in Dahlia's handwritten drafts. "She gave him flesh – of a sort – in her fiction when he grew too strong and then she was free of him for a while. She must have had a strong incentive to keep him at a distance. She had a man in the flesh who was enough for her."

Brock's eyes widened and brightened with unshed tears. "That's a generous thought, Callie. Thank you. I think Dolly believed that he was her muse, that he enabled her to write. But I think she was wrong there. It was her writing that drew him to her. I don't think he loved her, though, not the way he loves you. Still . . ." He opened the box. Lying on a piece of embroidered white linen were two bracelets made of cast-iron braided into intricate knot designs. At the center of each knot was a keyhole. An iron key attached to a chain lay between the two bracelets.

"You'll have to slip these on his wrists." He showed me

how they opened and clicked shut. "And then you'll have to turn the key in each lock. Keep the key around your neck and he won't be able to touch you."

"And you think he'll stand still for that?"

"Once the iron's on his wrists he won't be able to move. Just make sure you turn the key to the right. If you turn it to the left, you'll unlock the bracelets and he'll be free. Then . . . Well, he's sure to be angry and you saw what he did the last time he was angry."

I shuddered, recalling the destruction of the ice storm – the acres of ravaged forest, Paul's plane downed. Could that really have been Liam? Could I really believe that of him? A part of my brain – and my heart – still resisted the idea, but the evidence was overwhelming. My own doubts . . . Well, as Diana had said I was still under his power. I couldn't trust my instincts.

"Where is he?" I asked.

"The dean agreed to keep him in her office until she got a call from me. If you're ready I'll call now."

"Wait. There's one other thing. If I do this . . . if I put these things on him, what happens to him?"

"He's banished to the Borderlands between this world and Faerie. The iron will keep him from materializing in this world, but it will also keep him from being able to enter Faerie since nothing iron can pass through the door."

"Does it . . . hurt?" I asked.

Brock didn't answer at first. I could tell he was considering whether he could lie, but I held his gaze and he finally nodded. "Yes, it will hurt him. He'll be bound in pain for all eternity, imprisoned with all the other tortured souls who have lost their way between the worlds. My people call this place Niflheim, or Fog World, where dwells a goddess whose house is called Rain-Damp; her plate, Hunger; her knife, Starving; her threshold, Stumbling-Block; her bed, Sickbed; her bed hangings, Misfortune. From her name, Hel, comes your hell. But there's no other choice. He'll drain you dry if you don't banish him." He placed the box in my hands and then turned around and left without another word, leaving me with the means of torturing my lover for all eternity.

CHAPTER THIRTY-EIGHT

I took the box inside and put it on the kitchen table. Then, after a moment's thought, I stuck it in the pantry on a shelf with the cleaning supplies and the mousetraps I'd bought and never had the heart to use. Great, I thought, I couldn't use a mousetrap. What were the chances I was going to use an incubus trap on the man I . . .

Loved?

Did I love Liam? I'd never said it to him. I'd told him that I wanted him, but I'd never said *I love you*.

Did I?

I opened the pantry again and took out a bucket, rubber gloves and a bottle of ammonia. I filled the bucket with hot soapy water and went out onto the porch. It was measure of how much I didn't want to think that cleaning up vomit seemed a preferable activity.

I scrubbed until the paint started coming off the porch boards and I'd mixed a pint of my tears in with the dirty water. Then I brought the bucket and sponge back into the kitchen, washed them out in the kitchen sink and put them back into the pantry. I took the box Brock had given me out, put it on the kitchen table, and opened it. I squeezed the two iron bracelets into the two front pockets of my jeans and slipped the chain with the key over my head, sliding the key under my shirt where it lay against my breast bone, cold and heavy as my heart. Then I sat down on the couch in the living room – not in the library where Liam and I had watched movies and made love – and waited for Liam to come home.

The minute I wasn't moving, my mind became active again. What if it was all a mistake? a desperate voice whined inside my head. Even if there was an incubus on the loose there was no conclusive proof that it was Liam. It could be some other size-thirteen shoe, J. Peterman shirt wearing old movie buff, *not* my Liam.

I heard the key click in the lock. *There!* It was an iron lock and an iron key. If Liam was an incubus he couldn't use it, could he? I was so excited by the discovery that I leapt to my feet and ran to meet him at the door. He was in the foyer, his head bowed, a lock of dark hair falling over his eyes as he closed the door behind him. He slid the key back into his wallet – a leather wallet with Eddie Bauer stamped on the outside flap – and he took off his leather cashmere-lined (Land's End) gloves, folded them carefully and put them in his (L.L. Bean) coat pocket. His fingers never touched the iron key or the doorknob.

He looked up. The lock of hair still lay over his eyes, like the wing of black bird shadowing them. The late afternoon sunlight streaming through the stained-glass fanlight above the door threw a streak of red across his cheek, like a smear of blood. As if he'd been devouring something bloody and wiped the blood from his mouth.

"Callie! I didn't see you there. What's wrong? You look like you've seen a ghost."

He took a step forward and I stepped back. "Hey," he

said, his voice husky. "Are you upset I'm late? Didn't you get my text?"

"Yes," I answered, sliding my hands in my pockets. "What did the dean want?"

"Damned if I know. Honestly, I think she might be going senile . . . or she's not entirely over her illness. First she wanted to talk to me about starting a poetry reading series. She had a list of poets and she wanted to see what I thought of their work and their 'characters.' I explained I didn't know a lot of American poets personally. Then she got a call and kept me waiting while she took it and then she wanted me to call some of these poets with her. It was strange . . . but not as strange as how you're looking at me right now." He took another step forward – into a swath of blue light from the fanlight that cast a deathly pall over his features – and reached for me. I knew that if I let him touch me it would be all over. Already I could feel myself melting in his eyes. I'd let him kiss me and make love to me right there on the foyer floor. So what if he was an incubus? He was *my* incubus.

I pulled my hands out of my pockets and, as he reached for me, desire and concern mixed in his eyes, I clamped the iron bracelets around his wrists.

The effect was instantaneous. He fell to his knees like a puppet whose strings had been cut, his iron-bound wrists clanking loudly on the wooden floor. My name in his throat came out a scream of agony.

"Good," I said, making my voice cold. "You can still talk. I wasn't sure if you'd be able to, and I think you owe me an explanation."

He lifted his head – slowly, painfully – and looked at me out of the hollow shadowy pits that his eyes had become.

His skin, always pale, had gone nearly translucent. The only color in his face came from the play of light from the fanlight which spread itself on the floor around him like stage lights.

"You know . . . what I am . . . what more . . . do you want to know?" he gasped through gritted teeth.

I knelt down so I could look straight into his eyes. "I want to know why you picked me and what you intended to do with me. When you drained me dry would you have gone on to another victim?"

He shook his head slowly, like an injured animal. "I didn't . . . pick you. You . . . picked me. You wanted . . . me." He took a long shuddering breath and then his words seemed to come easier. "You wanted me enough to give me flesh . . . even as you were telling me to leave, I felt your pity for what had happened to me. And I heard you answering my question . . ."

"What question?"

"I asked you what more you wanted and you told me . . . in between the words of the banishment . . . You told me you wanted decency and caring and a man who really bothered to see who he was trying to seduce." He looked up at me. "Haven't I given you those things, Callie? I care about you. I've spent three months getting to know you . . . *really* know you . . . and falling in love with you"

I shook my head. "You *lied* to me. All the facts of your life that you told me were lies. The whole story about Jeannie and Moira . . . it was all a lie!"

"I had to pretend to be someone else to get the chance to know you better. As for the story about Jeannie . . . that was what happened to me with only the details changed to modern times. I did love a girl from my village who had a touch of the fey about her and could open the door to Faerie, but I was seduced away by a fairy temptress. You've met her. You've seen how powerful she is."

"Fiona? The Fairy Queen?"

"Yesss." He hissed the word. "She stole me away from my village. I was her captive. She kept me in Faerie so long I lost my humanity . . . I faded into a shadow . . . Only a human's desire can give me flesh, and only a human's love can give me a soul. But still I broke away . . . When the fairies were exiled from the old country, when we were on the march to the door, I broke away and came for *you*, Cailleach . . ."

The dream rose up inside me again: the long march, my comrades fading around me, the dark figure on the white horse coming toward me, his hands reaching for me . . . I looked up at Liam. The dark eyes were the same, the hands reaching for me were the same. I felt the iron key, hot now, burning against my bare skin. *Turn right to send him to the Borderlands, left to free him.*

"So you're saying that I'm . . . what? The reincarnation of the girl you loved centuries ago? Is that why you want me? Because I remind you of her?"

He shook his head. "Her spirit lives inside you . . . and yes, at first, that's why I was drawn to you, but then I got to know *you* . . . who you are now . . . Callie McFay. You've got a piece of the ancient Cailleach inside you, but you're *more*. I love who you are now . . . If you loved me, I could be mortal again."

"Then I must not love you," I said, pointing at his iron-cuffed hands. "Or those wouldn't be bothering you.

A tear slid down his face. "No. You don't love me . . . yet . . . but you are close to loving me. I can feel it." He lifted one hand. It was a struggle, I could see, but still he lifted it and brought his hand to my face.

He won't be able to move, Brock had said. So if he was moving it meant the iron only had some effect on him . . . and maybe that was because I *almost* loved him. How hard would it be to *really* love him? And then he would become fully human and we could be together.

He pulled me toward him, his hand shaking with the effort. His lips when they touched mine were on fire. They seared my skin like a hot brand, but I didn't care. I opened my lips for him and felt the heat of him flooding me. He was peeling me open, the way a boy peels back the petals on a honeysuckle blossom and sucks the nectar off the stamen. He was sucking the life force out of me . . .

I pushed him back. "No!" I cried, "You lied to me. I could hear the indecision in my voice, feel my resolve wavering. "How can I trust anything you say?"

"Is a lie really the worst thing if it's told out of love?"

I smiled sadly and touched his hand. I saw where the iron had burned through his skin. There was no bone there, only darkness—the shadow he came out of and would return to if I didn't do something soon. I pulled the key out from under my shirt. If I released him we could still be together and when I loved him he'd become mortal. We could be together without him draining me dry . . .

I had already fitted the key into the keyhole of the left bracelet, but I stopped and looked into the shadowy pits that had been his eyes. "The students," I said. "And Liz. You were feeding on them."

He flinched. "No!" he cried. "I would never . . ."

"Then why have they been getting sick? Flonia, who you see every day? Nicky, who you went to visit? Even poor

Scott Wilder . . ." I froze, recalling that day I sat in the infirmary. "*All* the students who were sick were in *your* class. You had private conferences with them. You were feeding on them." My stomach clenched, nausea rising in me again. I tried to find something in his eyes to convince me that I was wrong, but there was nothing in his eyes but darkness and his voice when he tried to protest was the merest creaking of dry branches in the wind.

"I didn't, Callie, I swear. I didn't feed on my students."

But how could I trust him? He'd lied about too much already.

I turned the key right. He screamed. The sound tore through me, but I made myself move the key to the bracelet on his right hand. Before I reached it, though, he grabbed my hand and wrapped his fingers around my wrist. I felt them digging into my skin with the same cold bite as when the shadow-crab had attacked me. They were made of the same thing, weren't they? I looked up into his face and saw that the shadows where spreading out from his eyes, eating into his flesh. He was dissolving right in front of me, turning back into the darkness he was made of. How could I love that darkness?

But I knew even as I saw him dissolving in front of me that it was the darkness in him that called to me. I still wanted him. I looked down at my hand, where his fingers gripped my wrist. My own skin was dissolving under his touch, merging with him. I felt the pull of him, like an undertow dragging me out to sea. I might not love him, but I wanted him more than I'd ever wanted anyone or anything. That might not be enough for us to stay together in the light, but maybe it was enough for us to stay together in the dark.

And all I had to do was . . . nothing. As long as I didn't

turn the key in the second lock I would dissolve with him.

I lowered my hand . . . and waited, my eyes locked on his. He saw what decision I'd made. In what was left of his eyes I saw surprise and I heard a gasp from what was left of his mouth. I felt his grip loosen on my wrist. He held out his arms to me. I closed my eyes and dropped the key to hold him . . . As we embraced I felt the darkness rush around me with a sound like wings. I opened my eyes and saw a wasteland of shadows – no color, no light, no heat. Ghost-like shapes flitted around me like bats but each one had a human – or nearly human – face. I recognized them as my comrades from the long march. This is where they had faded before reaching the door to Faerie. They had counted on me, their doorkeeper, to let them into Faerie, but I had failed them. Instead of going with them I had gone into the woods with my demon lover. Now I had come back to join them. It seemed only right.

A tug brought me back into the real world, into the foyer of Honeysuckle House crouched beside Liam, who had all but dissolved into the shadows. He was holding the key to the lock on the right hand bracelet. He inserted the key in the lock . . . and turned it to the right.

"Why?" I screamed.

"I couldn't let you destroy yourself for me."

They were the last words that he spoke before his lips dissolved. I reached for him, but he was already gone – a shadow that melted into the colored light pooling on the floor beneath me.

CHAPTER THIRTY-NINE

I don't know how long I would have lain there watching the last vestiges of colored light drain into the shadows on the wooden floor if Brock and Dory hadn't come for me. I dimly heard the sound of Brock's key in the lock, but it seemed to come from a long way away. I thought for a moment that it was an echo of the key turning in the iron bracelet on Liam's wrist and I reached out my hand into the shadows to stay his hand.

"He might still be there," I explained to Brock and Dory when they found me creeping along the wall. "In the shadows."

Brock waved his hand through the shadows to show me there was nothing there. Dory turned on the overhead light. The shadows scurried into the corners. I screamed at her to turn it off. I screamed again when Brock tried to carry me to my room upstairs.

"Not there," I begged. "I can't sleep in that bed."

They put me in the back bedroom on the first floor – Phoenix's old room and Matilda's before her. Liam had never gone in there, not even the one time I'd asked him to fetch an extra blanket from Phoenix's bed. Now I knew why. The room was filled with the smell of iron from the iron bed frame. I felt the cold of it on my wrist where Liam's fingerprints were seared into my skin—five ice splinters lodged in my flesh. Brock made me a salve for the wound while Dory got me undressed and into bed. "Don't worry, dear," she said over and over, "you'll be all right now." But after Brock had bandaged my arm and spooned some bitter tasting tea down my throat I heard them whispering in the kitchen.

"I'm afraid the shadows got in under her skin," Brock said.

"Will it spread?" Dory asked.

"There's no telling," he answered. "We'll have to watch her."

So that was the creeping I felt under my skin, like a drug moving through my veins. I drifted off then into the darkness beneath my eyelids. I could feel it rushing up to drown me, pull me under. When I was little my parents had taken me to a beach out in Montauk and I'd been pulled under by a wave, tossed and tumbled like a sock in a washing machine until I couldn't tell which way was up. The darkness I went into now was like that, just deeper than the ocean. Was Liam somewhere in this darkness, waiting to drown me for sending him away? I swam deeper and deeper, passing the phosphorescent faces of drowned swimmers – half-eaten faces with crabs crawling out of eye sockets and eels wriggling where their tongues used to be – but no Liam.

Then I would surface, into Phoenix's room, the shadows lapping around the great iron bed like a retreating tide. Dory would be there, trying to get me to drink some tea or broth. Liz Book came and told me that everyone who had been sick was getting better now – Flonia and Nicky and all the other students from Liam's class, proof that it had been Liam making them sick. The only one who was still recuperating was Mara.

"He must have drained her when she came here to work on the LaMotte papers," she said. "Poor girl. After all she's been through. I feel so responsible – to be taken in by a love talker at my age!" She patted my hand and bent down to whisper in my ear, even though we were alone in the room; maybe she sensed the shadows listening. "He was a very charming one, my dear. No one could blame you for falling for him. No one blames you at all."

But she was wrong. The shadows blamed me. I could hear them whispering, their voices growing louder as the day lengthened their tongues, their briny breath lapping at my ears, rough as cats' tongues, flaying my skin from the bone. *You brought him to life,* they whispered. *You are a thing of darkness. That's where you belong. With us.*

"No," I whimpered back, but I was already sinking back under the black water beneath my eyelids, where the rotting corpses of the drowned waited to embrace me. *We're your demon lovers now,* they whispered. They latched themselves to me with their suckered tentacles and hungry mouths and I gave myself to them, glad to feel the pull and suck of their hunger.

Once, though, instead of slipping into the dark I found myself standing in a green meadow, the dew on each blade of grass new-touched by the rising sun. I was wearing a long dress, the hem of which was soaked by the dew. Ahead of me, where the sun had not yet penetrated the mist, was a young man, his slim legs rising out of the mist like reeds rising out of water, his loose white shirt a swan's wing cleaving the fog. He turned to me, his faced blurred in the mist, but then the rising sun reached him and drew Liam's face on the white mist. He held his arms open for me and I ran into his embrace. For a moment I felt the strength of his arms encircling me and the heat of his lips on mine, but then he was gone, vanished into the mist. I woke up, grasping the knotted bed sheets and weeping. I got up out of bed for the first time and ran out into the backyard, my bare feet sinking into the melting slush. The yard and woods beyond were filled with a white mist rising off the melting snow, as if the earth was exhaling a long-held breath into the cold. Liam was out there in the woods, I knew now, not in the darkness, but wandering somewhere in the Borderlands. I would have run into the woods, but Brock caught me and dragged me back. I wasn't strong enough to put up much of a fight. I'd have to wait until I got my strength back.

I began drinking the tea and broth that Dory brought and nibbling on the bread and scones that Diana baked for me. I could see that the iron bed made Diana uncomfortable, so I asked to sit in the kitchen with her . . . and then the living room. Once I was able to sit in the living room I had more visitors. Soheila came on the first warm day of the year, which happened to be the first day of spring, with almond and rosewater cookies for the Persian New Year. I was glad she had come because I had some questions for her.

"Liam told me that if I loved him he would become human," I told her after Dory left us alone. "Was that true?"

Soheila exhaled a long breath – a sigh that sounded a little like an owl's song and reminded me that she had once been made of wind. "Yes, that part was true. That is how I became as I am now – not quite human, but not quite all succubus. But what he didn't tell you is that loving him would drain the life out of you the way it drained Angus. I didn't know that I was killing him until it was too late, but Li—the incubus knows what happened to Angus. He was there. He finished him off. So if he really loved you he wouldn't ask you to sacrifice your life for his."

I thought about that for a moment while Soheila sipped her tea and nibbled on a cookie. I looked out the window where the icicles were melting from the eaves with a steady drip that sounded like rain.

"But he took the key from me and turned the lock on the bracelet on his own hand. He turned it *right*. If he had turned it left he would have freed himself." *Or I would have been sucked into the shadows with him*, I thought, but didn't say. I was too embarrassed to admit that I'd been ready to destroy myself. "Why did he do that?"

"I don't know," Soheila said, brushing crumbs from her fingertips. She looked uncomfortable suddenly. "Perhaps he made a mistake. Most of my kind have a poor sense of direction. Without GPS my cousins couldn't find their way to their hairdressers or tennis lessons."

I frowned. "But you're descended from wind spirits . . ."

"Do you think the wind knows which way it's blowing?" she demanded, her eyes flashing. "Or cares what tree it blows down? Or what destruction it leaves in its wake? Have you forgotten that the incubus raised a storm that knocked Paul's plane out of the sky?"

I looked away guiltily. I *had* forgotten that.

"Trust me, Callie, you're lucky to have escaped from him whole. Look at what he did to those students. Could you love a creature who fed off children?"

"Who's feeding off children?" The voice came from the foyer. Frank Delmarco, followed by a flustered Dory

Browne, came into the room, tugged a Yankees cap off his head and sprawled out on the couch. "I'm pretty sure that's been outlawed since Swift's time."

"Frank." Soheila smiled nervously. "I thought you'd gone to the city for the break."

"I had, but then I heard about an outbreak of child cannibalism and came hurrying back. What's wrong, McFay? You look like someone sucker-punched you in the gut."

"Poor Callie," Dory answered in a loud stage whisper for me. "Liam Doyle was deported back to Ireland for tax evasion."

"Really?" Frank asked, cocking his head at me. "I wouldn't have pegged him for financial fraud, but then many a man has been led down the road of financial ruin by his love of foppish clothes."

"Frank, that's unkind!" Soheila scolded. "It's been a shock to Callie."

"I'm right here," I pointed out, tired of people talking about me as though I were an invalid. Maybe I was getting a little tired of *being* an invalid.

"Yes, you are," Frank said, beaming at me. "I'm glad to see that you didn't abscond to Ireland, too. You're better off without him, McFay. You're worth a dozen Liam Doyles."

"Yes, that's exactly right," Soheila said, looking back and forth between Frank and me with curiosity. Getting to her feet, she said, "I can see you're in good hands, Callie, and I have other houses to visit. It's a Persian tradition to visit all one's good friends on the New Year." She smiled a bit too brightly at Frank, as if she were posing for a picture, and then asked Dory if she'd run over to Diana's for a few minutes with her. Frank watched her go with a puzzled expression on his face.

"I can never quite figure her out. She runs hot and cold like a broken faucet. What *is* she?"

"You don't know?" I asked, surprised that Frank's intelligence had failed to discern Soheila's nature.

"No. My bosses think she's an ancient divinity of sorts, but her exact designation has been carefully veiled. It's one reason I'm investigating Fairwick. Supernatural beings should be clearly labeled so you know what you're dealing with. Look at what happens when you're not. What did Liam turn out to be? A vampire? A werewolf? He always looked a little shaggy to me."

"An incubus," I answered, embarrassed, but at least I could distract him from asking more questions about Soheila. Poor Soheila – clearly she thought Frank was interested in me and had graciously stepped aside since she couldn't have him. I'd have to let her know that there was nothing between us – but I didn't have to let *him* know that she was a succubus.

"Ooooh, an incubus. That's rough. No wonder you looked so tired all the time. And his students . . . ouch! That must smart, knowing he was going after them."

"If you came here to gloat . . ."

"No, actually I came here because I came across something in researching Hiram Scudder that I thought you would find interesting. That is, if you're still interested in averting Nicky's curse."

"Of course I am!" I replied angrily, although in truth I'd spared very little thought for Nicky Ballard since the day I'd gone to her house.

"After Hiram Scudder's wife killed herself he went out

west. He changed his name several times and moved around a lot, which is why it's hard to track him down. But I think I found him in Colorado under the name Stoddard. I'm trying to track him down after he left Colorado."

"Oh, that's smart. I'm sure you'll find something. If anyone can find a way to stop the curse, you can."

"Does that mean that you're giving up?" he asked, leaning forward and squinting at me. "That doesn't sound like you."

I shrugged. "It's just that I may have to go away for a while. Maybe go somewhere warm. I may not be cut out for . . . this climate." My voice wobbled and I realized to my embarrassment that I was dangerously close to tears.

"Yeah, you do look like you're freezing to death," he said.

I looked down and saw that I'd pulled the sleeves of my sweatshirt over my hands to hide the bruises there.

"Why don't I make us some hot tea?" he said, getting up. "And we can talk some more about your plans."

Before I could object he'd gone into the kitchen. I heard the water running and the refrigerator door opening and guessed that Frank was also giving me some time to compose myself. Which would have been great if the front door hadn't opened at the same time.

"Hello? Professor McFay?" Mara's voice came haltingly from the foyer.

"In here, Mara," I called, getting to my feet and hurrying to the front door. I was hoping to head her off at the pass and suggest I was too ill for a visit. She was standing on the front porch, a bouquet of anemic-looking pink carnations cradled in her arms. Instantly I felt guilty for begrudging her visit when she'd gone to the trouble of buying me flowers. Still . . . if I let her in she might stay for an hour.

I stepped out onto the porch to greet her. "These are lovely, Mara," I said, and then, taking a big breath of air, "Why, it's like spring out here! Let's sit on the glider for a moment before I go back to bed. I've been cooped up inside for days."

I gestured to the porch glider and Mara sat down right in the middle, placing the flowers to her right and leaving me almost no room. Rather than crowd in with her I leaned against the porch railing. "It's very considerate of you to visit me, Mara, but I heard you were still in the infirmary. Shouldn't you be resting?" Mara looked, in truth, pretty awful. She was pale but for two blotches of color in her cheeks, which were the same calamine pink as the carnations she'd brought. She sat on the edge of the glider, tensed against its rocking motion as if afraid she might become seasick.

"I am doing much better," she said stiffly. "I heard that you were unwell . . . and that Mr. Doyle had to leave the country suddenly. I thought you must be sad."

The idea of being pitied – by Mara Marinca of all people – was almost too much for me. A sharp pain twinged behind my right eye. I raised my hand to massage my temple. "That's sweet of you, Mara, but really I'm quite all right . . ."

But Mara wasn't listening. Her eyes were fastened on my wrist, where my sleeve had fallen back from the black bruises Liam had left. She was on her feet, inches from me, her hand on my wrist. I shrunk away from her touch but the porch railing cut into my back.

"Did he do this?" she asked, her voice a low hiss, her breath hot and copper-tinged in my face.

"It's nothing, Mara; it was an accident."

She shook her head, her eyes still glued to my wrist. One by one she placed her fingertips over the marks Liam had left. The pads of her fingers were damp and strangely spongy and clung to my skin like suction cups. "No," she said, the tip of her tongue appearing between her crooked yellow teeth. "This was no accident. He was trying to pull you into the Borderlands with him. And you . . ." She looked up. Her eyes had turned a strange sulfurous yellow. They looked oddly familiar. "You were ready to go with him. Such devotion! I can still smell it." She sniffed and then to my utter horror and disgust her pink leathery tongue darted out of her mouth an impossible distance and licked my wrist.

I screamed and tried to push her away, but it was like pushing against foam rubber. My left hand sunk into spongy flesh. She was lifting my hand to her mouth, which was gaping wider and wider, her lips opening like rubbery flaps, revealing a second row of sharp yellow teeth behind the first row. Black feathers were sprouting from her skin. Her tongue was covered with suction cups that latched onto my skin and started to pull.

"What are you?" I cried, but already I recognized her. The great black crow that had tried to attack me. This was its true face: a feathered monstrosity that sucked the life force out of its victims . . . just as it had fed on Nicky and Flonia and Liz Book.

I had to get away from it before it sucked me dry. Already I could feel the life draining out of me. I couldn't push against it, so instead I braced my feet on the lower porch railing, hoisted my hips up onto the upper railing, and tipped myself backward. I fell six feet onto my back. If the snow hadn't cushioned my fall I might have broken my spine. As it was the fall knocked the wind out of me. Above me Mara was spreading her arms – wings now, sprouting black feathers – opening her mouth into an angry caw, and preparing to swoop down on me.

I rolled to the side just before she landed. I scrambled to my feet and pushed off the ground, my fingers grabbing handfuls of slushy snow as I came up . . . and something else. A stone with a hole in it. The fairy stone that I'd put in the ice ornament back in November had fallen to the ground and now it was in my hand. As the creature wheeled around to attack me I fleetingly wondered if there was some way to use it against her, but I didn't have time to figure it out. Nor could I recall a single spell – not even the one for defending against attacks from above. The creature was flapping its wings, getting ready to attack me.

I turned and ran blindly, my slippered feet sliding in the snow. I could hear the sound of wings behind me – *huge* wings. The creature she'd transformed into was far larger than the bird I'd seen before. Maybe the size she transformed into was governed by her hunger, in which case she was starving! I had felt the force of her need when she sucked at my wrist. I didn't think she would stop once she caught me. But how could I escape her? I could see the inn across the street, but if I ran there Mara would catch me in the middle of the open road. I pictured her pecking at me like a vulture stripping meat from a piece of road kill. To my right stood the line of pine trees at the edge of the woods. If I made it in there she'd follow me, but it wouldn't be easy to fly through the narrow gaps between the trees. At least it would slow her down.

My decision made, I flung myself to the right, in between

two trees, scraping my shoulder on the rough bark. I heard the creature's angry caw behind me and turned just in time to see her crash into the trees, black feathers flying everywhere. She hit the snow and for a brief moment I thought she might be stunned senseless, but then she gathered herself up and, tucking her ragged wings to the side, dove through the trees.

I ran. Further into the woods, leaving the path so she wouldn't be able to spread those huge wings. Geez, its wingspan must be six feet wide! I was sure the bird hadn't been this big when she attacked me on Christmas Day . . . and she'd been bigger then than when she'd attacked me on the Solstice . . . and way bigger than she'd been when she'd swooped down on the path outside of Bates Hall the first time I'd seen her . . . but *had* that been the first time I'd seen her? Those yellow eyes, that plaintive *caw* – they were the same as the small bird I'd found trapped in the thicket . . . and released. I had let this monster loose on Fairwick! I had to do away with it.

I glanced behind me, hoping I'd lost it in the maze of trees, but it was right behind me, soaring above the tree line, so big now that it blotted out the sun. It was looking for a clear path to dive down at me. I had to lead it into the thicket, where the overgrown shrubs and vines were so thick that it would be trapped. I had to trap it in the Borderlands where it came from.

I blundered on through the trees, not even sure I was going in the right direction since I'd left the path. When I'd last looked up the sun had been behind me. If I veered to the left I'd be going north – the direction I'd gone the first time I'd found the thicket. I dodged around a tree to correct my direction . . . and heard the flap of wings overhead.

Something sharp grazed my cheek – talons stretched out to grab me. Ahead of me I saw the beginning of the thicket, the bare branches of the honeysuckle shrub twisting together in an arch. I dove under a low-hanging branch and heard the bird crash into the shrubs with an angry shriek. Black feathers filled the air around me like soot from an infernal explosion. I looked back and saw it stumble to its feet dragging one broken wing behind it, its awful yellow beak snapping at my heels. I ducked my head and crawled deeper into the thicket, pushing vines out of my way to block the thing's approach.

I had found the thicket all right, but my plan had been a little short-sighted. So long as I was bigger than the creature I couldn't lead it into a space small enough to trap it. Instead I would soon be snared in the vines like a fly trapped in a web and then the creature would be able to pick my bones at leisure. Still I blundered into the underbrush, digging myself deeper and deeper into what I was beginning to suspect would be my tomb. It had been the tomb for other creatures – the small birds and mice I'd seen before – but, as I dug myself in deeper, I also found larger and stranger creatures: an animal that looked like a rabbit but had long fangs, bat skeletons with tiny human skulls, and a long sinuous fish tail that led, horribly, to a human torso. A mermaid? How had a mermaid gotten trapped in these woods? There must be a body of water on the other side of the door, which meant that I was close to the door. Perhaps if I could lead Mara to the door I could make her go through it. Today was the Equinox. If the door opened on the Solstice mightn't it also open on the Equinox? And I was a doorkeeper . . . with a fairy stone in my pocket. It was worth a try. It might be my only chance to escape being killed by Mara.

But first I had to find the door.

I paused for a moment to listen and realized it had been some time since I'd heard the creature behind me. Had I lost it? Or had she circled around to cut me off? The thicket was full of tiny sounds: the rustle of twigs, the drip of melting snow, and, faint and distant, the rumble of surf – the sound of the ocean in a landlocked woods trapped in the thicket as if trapped in the whorls of a seashell. I crawled toward it, drawn by the strange mystery of it as much as by the slight chance of escape. As I crawled I noticed that the snow grew thinner and the ground softer, and my hands sank into sand. Around me, threaded in the vines were seashells and fish bones that swayed and clanked like wind chimes. And then I was out in the open in a round glade.

I stood up and looked around me. It was the glade I'd come to with Liam on New Year's Eve. Across from me was the arched doorway only now, instead of being filled by the moon, it was filled with a milky blue-green mist – the color of sea glass. I stepped toward it . . . and heard a corresponding step behind me.

I wheeled around and found myself facing a creature out of my worst nightmares. The bird-thing had begun to change back into human form but had gotten stuck in between. It stood on two legs, but those legs ended in scaly talons. Its body was stippled with black feathers. One arm hung fleshy and broken, the other – feathered – flapped angrily at its side. Her face was just recognizable as the girl I'd known as Mara, but for an ugly yellow beak and that horribly gaping mouth that opened now to scream at me. The long sucker-covered tongue lashed out like an angry cat's tail.

"Mara," I said, willing my voice to be steady. "This

world isn't the right place for you. Wouldn't you rather go back?"

She squawked and beat her wing in the air. "What do you know?" she croaked. "We are starving in that world. There is nothing there to eat. Here . . ." The awful tongue snaked out of her mouth and writhed over her beaky lips as she took a step toward me. "Here there is such abundance that you waste it. These young people take drugs that deplete their life force. They drive in their fast cars half blind from alcohol. They have sex for entertainment and stay up all night pretending to study. Why shouldn't I drink of their life force when they treat their lives so cheaply?"

"They're not all like that," I said, taking a step back toward the door. I could smell salt air mingled with honeysuckle. Was it always summer in Faerie? I wondered. I wanted to turn and look, but I couldn't risk taking my eyes off Mara. "And I'm certainly not like that. I don't take drugs or drive drunk . . ."

"Ha! You're the worst of all! You were willing to let that incubus suck you dry. You were even willing to go with him. I can smell it on you." Her tongue lashed out and grazed the bruises on my right hand, which I'd stuck in my pocket. "Those marks were made because your flesh was dissolving with his – and that could only happen if you were willing to go with him. I'll tell you what." She stretched her beaky lips wide in what I realized was supposed to be a smile. "After I suck you dry I'll leave what's left of you in the Borderlands. You can spend eternity in that hellhole with your boyfriend."

"Is it really that bad there?" I asked, turning slightly to look behind me through the door. The minute I turned Mara launched herself at me – as I knew she would. I drew my hand out of my pocket, slipping the fairy stone onto my finger, and shouted the opening spell: *ianuam sprengja!*

A cold wind rushed through the arched doorway and shadows stretched out toward me, sniffing at me, hungry for my warmth, my solid flesh . . . my very life. Was *he* there? I wondered, leaning toward the door, but then I heard the flap of wings at my back and I dodged to the right . . . just as Mara's right wing brushed my face. She should have gone through the door, but instead a flash of light split the air above us, accompanied by a cracking noise and a shout that sounded like *bucky frakking dent*, and Mara crumpled to the ground at my feet.

Confused, I looked up and found Frank standing over the crumpled body wielding a baseball bat.

"Jesus, Frank, what are you doing here?"

"Trying to save your life, McFay. You're welcome." He stepped over the body, reaching for me, but Mara's wing struck him square in the chest and threw him back against a tree with a sickening crack of bone. Then she launched herself at me.

I didn't have time to dodge this time. She landed on me inches from the open door. She crouched over me, one hand around my throat, one wing beating the air above me. The awful mouth opened wide, the yellow beak stretching like Silly Putty, revealing rows of razor-sharp teeth gnashing together. Drops of putrid saliva fell on my face. I closed my eyes and prayed that it would be over soon.

The pressure of the creature's weight lifted so suddenly that I felt lightness in my chest. Was this what death felt like? I opened my eyes and saw Mara hovering in the air above me. She was wrapped up in a tangled skein of shadows . . . and then she was spinning, head over heels, toward the door. I rolled over just in time to see her crash through the door. The shadow hovered on the threshold, coiling back.

"Quick, close it!" Frank was next to me, screaming in my ear. I looked down at the fairy stone on my hand . . . and pulled it off.

A wind blew threw the glade, sucking all the air through the door. Frank grabbed me and held on to a tree trunk to keep us from being sucked through. A whirlpool churned just in front of the door. The coil of shadow that had banished Mara writhed in the air and then took a shape. For just a moment I saw Liam's face hovering above me. I felt a brush of lips against mine, caught the scent of honeysuckle in the air . . . and then the coil of shadow melted and, with a loud crack and sucking *whoosh*, the door slammed shut.

CHAPTER FORTY

It took a long time to get out of the woods that day. Frank couldn't put any weight on his right leg (it would turn out to be broken in two places) and he wouldn't leave his baseball bat behind.

"Are you kidding? It's signed by Bucky Dent!"

"Okay," I said, lifting the bat in my left hand while using the right to support his weight. "How did you get it anyway?"

I meant how did he happen to get it before chasing Mara and me into the woods, but he responded by telling me a long story about how the bat had been signed by Bucky Dent outside Fenway Park after he hit his famous three-run home run to beat the Red Sox in a one game playoff to end the 1978 season.

"Jeez, Frank, you being a witch and all, couldn't you have brought something *magic* to save me?"

"Magic? Weren't you listening, woman? The bat's signed by Bucky fucking Dent. It *is* magic!"

He continued to splutter about the magical properties of sports memorabilia, distracting himself (as I'd hoped) from the pain. Only when we were in sight of the house and Brock, Dory and Diana were running toward us did he add:

"The Bucky Dent bat was in my trunk. I carry it in case I run into any crazies on the road. I grabbed it when I saw that giant bird chase you into the woods."

His remark was loud enough to be overheard by the others and he repeated it as Diana drove us to the hospital. Frank repeated it so many times that I thought he might be going into shock, but then I realized he was just trying to preserve his cover by adamantly denying that he'd witnessed anything supernatural. When he was wheeled into surgery he winked at me and made me promise I'd make sure his Bucky Dent bat was safe.

I stayed at the hospital until Soheila showed up. "Tell Frank I went back to make sure Bucky Dent was safe," I said, getting up to leave.

She looked at me strangely but settled in to wait for Frank to regain consciousness.

Everyone looked at me strangely for the next few days. I think they were afraid I was in shock and would soon lapse into the depression I'd wallowed in after I'd banished Liam. When I told Liz and Diana what had happened they both looked guilty. "So it wasn't Liam who was feeding on the students," Diana said. "Or on Liz."

"I should have realized that I was always more tired after Mara had been with me," Liz said. "I *should* have realized what she was."

Soheila especially felt bad that she'd failed to recognize Mara.

"What exactly was she?" I asked when I paid a visit to her office after the break.

"A liderc," she told me, taking down Fraser's *Demonology* from the shelf and opening it to an illustration of a chicken with a woman's head. "It's a sort of Hungarian succubus, distantly related to us lilitu. They shape shift into birds – chickens, usually, but sometimes crows – in order to hunt their prey and then feed on the life force of their victims through close contact. Not through sex, as a rule."

"Well, that's a relief." I hadn't liked the idea of Mara having sex with all her victims. "So she could have been the one making me weak, not Liam."

"That could be, but the fact remains that Liam was an incubus and you were having sex with him. Sooner or later he would have drained you."

How much later? I wondered, but didn't ask aloud. I knew Soheila – as well as Diana, Brock, Dory and Liz – were afraid I'd have some sort of breakdown if I thought that I'd banished Liam for nothing. But I wasn't going to have a breakdown. In fact, I felt better than I had in months.

As the days grew longer and warmer I subjected Honeysuckle House to an orgy of spring cleaning. I packed up Liam's clothes and books and stored them in the attic. I dusted and scrubbed and washed all the windows. While dusting my desk I found a key that fit the locked drawer. Inside was another key – an iron key identical to the one Brock had made for me to send Liam back to the Borderlands. So he'd been sent there before – and then released. I wondered why and when.

While cleaning out the pantry I dislodged a shadowy lump with the mop and quickly recognized it as the shadow crab. I poured a bucket of bleach over it and it shriveled up into a gray film that I briskly mopped up. Then I ran upstairs and found Ralph sitting up in his basket, cleaning himself.

"You're back!" I ran down and got a whole mini Bonbel for him to eat. While I was gone he found his way onto my laptop and typed, *Is the incubus gone?*

So Ralph had known all along. *And* he knew how to type! No wonder he'd always been trying to hop on my laptop. I told him the whole story while he ate enough cheese to bloat his stomach. Then he typed a single word on the screen.

Sorry!

I rubbed his little bloated belly. "It's okay, fellow, at least I've got you back. I don't suppose you would have liked sharing the house with an incubus." But Ralph was already asleep, snoring loudly enough to reassure me that he hadn't lapsed into another coma.

After I scoured the house and made a list of more substantial outdoor repairs that I would need to tackle in the summer, I turned my attention to my students. I'd taken over the creative writing class again, so I had plenty to keep me busy. I was afraid they'd spend all their time bemoaning Liam's absence, but the first time Scott Wilder (back from his medical leave looking drowsy as ever) mentioned Liam's name, Nicky shot him an icy stare and no one ever brought him up again. Still, I saw Liam's influence in their writing – in a new openness and sensitivity to language I hadn't seen when I'd taught the class in the fall. He'd given them the confidence to experiment and find their own voices. Especially Nicky.

She had written a beautiful series of poems on the theme of a young girl trapped in an ice palace populated by frozen guardians. Each one had a story to tell. I recognized in each story a bit of Nicky's family history, a bit of the Romantic heroines we'd read about in class, and more than a bit of Nicky's fears about her future.

When I see how their dreams have gone awry, she wrote, *I wonder how I will my fate mollify*.

May 2nd, Nicky's birthday, was fast approaching and I

was no closer to averting the Ballard curse. To keep her close to me I hired her to take Mara's place as my assistant. I showed her the charts that Mara had been keeping on Dahlia's notebooks and she laughed when I explained Mara's asterisk system.

"She was a strange one," Nicky said, shaking her head. "Kind of a prude. She was always so shocked when I stayed at Ben's, but then she'd always sit too close – you know what I mean? – and ask the most embarrassing questions. I figured she was trying to understand our culture, but sometimes it felt like she was trying to suck up all my experiences. Anyway, it's too bad her visa expired. Do you think she'll come back?"

"No," I told her, hoping it was true. "I think she got all she could out of Fairwick."

Nicky completed Mara's charts, but she also made her own discovery from the notebooks.

"I think Dahlia LaMotte based one of her books on my family," she told me in the last week of April. "It's not one she ever published. It's called *The Curse of the Bellefleurs*."

When I read it I thought I saw why it hadn't been published. It had little of the romantic tension that LaMotte was known for and it didn't have a happy ending. It told the story of two ambitious men who join forces to gain control of the railroads in a small upstate town. Andre Bellefleur proves the more ruthless of the two and drives out his partner, Arthur Rosedale, and Rosedale's wife kills herself. Before Rosedale leaves for the west he curses the Bellefleur women with an urge to kill themselves after they've given birth to a successor.

"It's just like my family," Nicky told me. "Except for the suicides. We Ballards prefer to decay slowly. My grandmother once told me when I was little that there was a curse and that's why my mother acted the way she did. I never believed it . . . but lately . . . Well, there are a lot of strange things that go on in this town. A curse would be one of the *less* strange things. I just wish I knew how to make it go away."

Nicky also noticed a marked number of correlations between the Bellefleurs and the Ballards – a wolf's head cane sported by Andre Bellefleur that she said was identical to one that had been in her family until her grandmother had pawned it, the antique pink Sevres *secretaire* with its pattern of frolicking cupids that still stood in her grandmother's room, and the same brown freckle in their light blue eyes. I, too, found a family heirloom in the manuscript. Arthur Rosedale sported a black onyx intaglio watch fob inscribed with a tree which sounded remarkably like the brooch my grandmother wore. Once I'd thought of my grandmother I noticed some other similarities between Hiram Scudder's story and my own family history. Hiram Scudder had gone out west to seek his fortune – so had my grandmother's grandfather. Frank had told me that one of the aliases Scudder had used was Stoddard. I looked through my old copies of Dahlia LaMotte books and found the name Emmeline Stoddard written on their flyleaves.

It didn't take a genius to make the next deduction. My grandmother was descended from the witch who had cursed the Ballards. Which meant she could uncurse them. If only I could convince her to after telling her off the last time I saw her. The last person I felt like talking to right now was my grandmother. If her informants had told her about the incubus invasion on campus she wouldn't spare me an embarrassing interrogation – or a gloating "I told you so."

But what choice did I have? Fate was offering me an opportunity to lift the Ballard curse, something Fairwick witches had been trying to do for decades. I'd just have to swallow my pride.

I recalled that my grandmother usually came into the city around the first of May for a board meeting at the Grove. I emailed her and asked if I could meet with her when she was in the city. She took so long replying that I thought I wasn't going to get an answer, but then, a few days before the end of the month, I received a formal invitation in the mail inviting me to attend cocktails at the Grove on the evening of April 30. Overnight accommodations and all meals to be provided by the Grove at the request of Adelaide Danbury. My grandmother had written a note at the bottom. "I'll be free to meet with you half an hour before cocktails in the library." Staying overnight at the Grove was the last thing I wanted to do, but I understood that refusing wasn't an option. Not if I wanted my grandmother to lift the Ballard curse.

On the drive down to the city I wondered what else Adelaide might ask in return for lifting the curse and how much I would be willing to give. The "request" Adelaide was most likely to make would be for me to leave Fairwick.

Fine, I thought, passing the big hex sign outside of Bovine Corners, I could live with that. In fact, it would probably be for the best. Although I'd finally gotten to the stage where I didn't weep at every reminder of Liam (his favorite coffee mug, the last drop of Irish whiskey, the smell of honeysuckle) I was still sleeping in the downstairs bedroom and I still woke in the middle of the night reaching for him. I still hadn't gotten up the courage to go into his study and clear it out. Just driving past the general store where we'd bought cheese, or the antiques store in Glenburnie where he'd bought me my ring, made me almost drive off the side of the road. Wouldn't it be better to get far away from all reminders of him, away from any temptation to go out into the woods, to the threshold between worlds, and release him? And wouldn't it be better to teach at a college that didn't attract life-sucking creatures? Although I'd told Liz Book she shouldn't blame herself for failing to realize that Mara Marinca was a liderc – or that Liam was an incubus – shouldn't the school monitor its faculty and student body better? Adelaide had been right; it *was* irresponsible not to let people know what they were dealing with. So, I decided by the time I got onto Interstate 17, if my grandmother asked me to leave Fairwick as a condition of lifting Nicky's curse, I would agree. No matter how much I would miss it.

Having made my decision I popped in an audiobook of the new Charlaine Harris novel and didn't think of anything but Sookie Stackhouse's troubles until I reached Manhattan. (At least I hadn't fallen for a vampire! I congratulated myself, realizing that it had been four months since I'd made my deal with Anton Volkov and he'd never bothered me once.) Then rush hour midtown traffic occupied all my attention until I pulled into a parking garage on Forty-third Street.

I wheeled my suitcase into the lobby, checked in, and was escorted upstairs by an elderly bellhop to a small, but elegant room papered in blue toile and upholstered in a watery blue moiré. The mirrors were old and spotted, tarnished to faded silver. My reflected self looked like a stranger in them – a person I only half remembered. Was that pale thin woman with rust colored hair hanging loose like a drowning victim, really me? I looked like an old photograph of myself that had faded in the sunlight. When had that happened? And when was the last time I had looked at myself in the mirror? I had been avoiding meeting my own gaze for so long it was as though my reflection had faded with disuse.

I looked at my watch and saw that I had a few hours before I was due to meet Adelaide. Then I called my old hairstylist, Elan, and asked if there were any way she could fit me in even though I knew that she was always booked solid months in advance.

"Oh," she said, "but someone just called to make you an appointment. A Miss Danbury. I told her there were no openings, but she left word to call you if there were any cancellations and we just had one . . . I was just about to call."

I could hear the confusion in Elan's voice – a common side effect of talking to Adelaide. I bristled at the idea of my grandmother arranging my life – how did she know I needed a haircut? – but what was the point of acting proud and looking horrible?

"What time is the appointment?" I asked.

"In half an hour," she told me.

"I'll be there," I told her.

Two and a half hours later I was back at the Grove with a cut that brought the life back to my hair and a couple of shopping bags from Bergdorf's. I had just enough time to slip into the lilac Jil Sander sheath and Christian Louboutin pumps I'd bought and freshen my make-up before joining Adelaide in the library – or rather just enough time to be five minutes late so I didn't feel as if I were hopping to Adelaide's orders.

Adelaide defeated that little rebellion by arriving exactly *six* minutes late and found me gawking at the three stories of bookshelves that lined the library walls. The only other library I'd seen half this impressive was J.P. Morgan's.

"I was unavoidably detained by the initiation committee," she told me, presenting her cheek for me to kiss. "The new generation can't make any decisions for themselves."

Out of habit I touched my lips to her cool cheek before remembering I'd promised myself not to. She smiled and sank into a silk-upholstered chair beside a crackling fire. Adelaide's cream woolen suit, with the onyx intaglio pinned to its lapel, looked exactly right in the setting, while my lilac dress, which had looked fabulous at Bergdorf's, suddenly seemed a bit showy.

"Have you been ill?" she asked, pouring tea from a china pot into my cup. "You look like you've lost weight."

"I had a . . . bug," I said, taking a sip of the strong smoky tea. "But I'm fine now. And there's something I need to discuss . . ."

"I do hope you're taking care of yourself up there," she continued as if she hadn't heard my reply. "Schools can be such a breeding ground of germs, especially with all the *foreigners* Liz Book lets in. I hear you had a bit of a run-in with one of the immigrants."

I wondered if she meant Liam or Mara – and I also wondered who her informant was – but I wasn't about to take the bait. "I would think you would have more sympathy with people who were forced to leave their homes. Your grandfather, Hiram Scudder, had to leave Fairwick."

Adelaide smiled. "Good girl. I wondered how long it would take you to find out. But please, don't confuse your great-great-great-grandfather Hiram to the flotsam and jetsam that wind up on our shores and expect a free handout. Hiram rebuilt the family fortune in a single generation. But look at those pathetic Ballards! Still moldering away in their big old mansion."

"Because Hiram cursed them. And you've allowed the curse to continue. Poor Nicky had nothing to do with what her great-great grandfather did to Hiram Scudder."

"Did you discover in your research what happened to Hiram's wife, Adele? Your great-great-grandmother."

"Yes," I said, chastened. "She killed herself. I'm sure that was awful . . ."

"Her daughter, my mother, found her hanging from the chandelier in the front parlor. She was never a . . . happy woman after that. And it was all Bertram Ballard's fault."

"But it wasn't Nicky's fault. She's an innocent girl, just as your mother was an innocent victim."

A flicker of emotion passed across Adelaide's face. The fine lines around her eyes creased, her lower lip trembled. Was she about to cry? I'd never seen my grandmother shed a tear. But if she had been close to tears she quickly gained control of herself.

"It's not up to me to remove the curse. Only the youngest of the family can do that."

"You mean I could remove the curse?"

Adelaide smiled. "Only if you accepted your rightful place here at the Grove."

"You want me to join the Grove?"

Adelaide laughed, all trace of the sentiment she'd been on the verge of displaying a moment ago gone. "You needn't make it sound like I'm asking you to join the Mafia! The Grove is an honorable and venerable institution. Look around you . . ." She waved a diamond-bejeweled hand at the three stories of leather-bound books, the brass railings shining in the firelight. "Membership comes with many amenities: a lovely place to stay when you're in the city, connections to well-placed women in business and academia – and men; we've just aligned with a very elite men's club in London which has most impressive accommodations and membership – *and*, best of all, access to this library. You'd be amazed what knowledge you can find among these books."

I looked up at the leather-bound tomes. The gilt on their spines seemed to wink at me with promises of secrets held within their covers. "I wouldn't have to do anything harmful to join – like sacrifice anyone?"

Adelaide laughed. "We haven't even sacrificed animals since the eighteenth century."

"Good to know," I said. "But what exactly would my membership obligations entail?"

"Dues are one thousand dollars a year," she said briskly. "You have to attend quarterly Council meetings on Samhain, Winter Solstice, Beltane and Summer Solstice which will be held this year in Fairwick so it'll be convenient for you. Oh . . . and you do have to perform some community service."

"What kind of community service?" I asked suspiciously. I had a feeling it wasn't going to be visiting nursing homes or reading to the blind.

"It differs with each member. As your nominating member I decide what's appropriate. I've come up with the perfect job for you."

I shuddered to think what that could be, but I braced myself and asked.

"I'd like you to be the Grove's confidential intelligence provider at Fairwick College."

"You mean a spy."

"Call it what you like. You've seen how poorly supervised the campus is and what dangers can ensue with the college's proximity to the door to Faerie. There's long been a feeling here at the Grove that we need to take a more active hand in monitoring the traffic between worlds. Someone has to. That's why the Council meeting is to be held there this year."

"Don't you already have spies there?"

"Yes, but we're no longer sure how reliable that intelligence is. Agents tend to go . . . *native* at Fairwick. Of course it's arguable that you already have, but my proposal to the board was that you've had first-hand experience with 'hostile foreigners.' I think you'll provide an honest report of what occurs at Fairwick."

"And the Council accepted your proposal?"

"The Council has *never* turned down a member I nominated."

"How would the information I provided be used?" I asked. "I couldn't allow anyone to come to harm because of my say-so."

"No one would come to harm who hadn't harmed a human. You'll find we're quite fair at the Grove. So what do you say?"

I considered. I hated the idea of spying on my friends and colleagues but I hated more the prospect of Nicky Ballard falling victim to an ancient curse. Besides, Adelaide did have a point. Things were out of control at Fairwick. Maybe the college needed a guiding hand. If my decision was at all swayed by the fact that now I'd get to stay at Fairwick close to where Liam still lingered, well, I couldn't help that, could I?

"Okay," I said, "I'll do it. As long as you promise to tell me how to lift the curse."

"Certainly. I just need you to lay your hand on this book and repeat after me."

She indicated a slim volume that lay on the table. I laid my hand on it. The worn leather was warm to the touch.

"I hereby avow that I, Cailleach McFay, will abide by the rules and regulations of the Grove. In exchange I will be given the secret of the Ballard curse."

I repeated the words. The leather grew warmer as I spoke and the gilt on the cover began to glow. The branches of the gold tree appeared to sway and the leaves crinkled up and flew away – a shower of sparks – into the fire. One of those sparks landed on my wrist. I drew my hand away and batted at the burning cinder but it had already sunk into my skin, leaving a mark in the shape of a tree.

"Hey, you didn't tell me it would leave a mark?"

"It'll fade," she said dismissively. "But its power won't. Now come. The Council is waiting. Everyone is so excited to meet you."

True to Adelaide's word, the mark on my wrist faded and my initiation involved no slain animals or satanic rites. Rather, it involved a short swearing-in ceremony during which I was given a grimoire of novice spells including a family curse reversal. Afterward there was a good deal of champagne and pleasant chatter with a group of lovely, sophisticated women – some of whom I recognized as prominent figures in publishing, television, and journalism – and a few men – all tall, good-looking blonds who came from the London club now aligned with the Grove. One of the women was Jen Davies. She was, I realized, the dark haired woman I'd glimpsed at the Oak Bar the last time I'd been to the club. Toward the end of the cocktail hour she managed to get me aside for a word.

"I wanted you to know that I'm sorry about outing your friend to the press. It was my initiation community service and I thought, fine, why not expose a lying upper-class prat. But since I've gotten to know her . . ."

"Know her?" I asked.

"I've been visiting her at McLean. She's doing very well and attending a writing workshop there. Working on a 'novel' now – a fantasy novel about witches and fairies. She just got a brilliant contract. Irony is, every word is true, but it'll sell as fiction."

I knew I had to visit Phoenix. She was owed an explanation. It hadn't been my incubus who had driven her over the edge, it had been Mara, feeding on her until she was weakened. And the demon that Phoenix had seen outside the day she was taken away to McLean – well, that was probably Mara, too.

"Anyway," Jen continued, "I wasn't happy about being made an instrument of torture. A lot of the younger members aren't happy with the old ways here: the knee-jerk prejudice against fairies and demons, the whole anti-immigration stance. We've formed a small ad hoc group to affect change. If you're interest in joining . . ."

By the end of the evening I'd agreed to attend an informal (and secret) meeting of the group Jen called "Sapling." As I made my way unsteadily up the stairs to my room my head was spinning with champagne and the multitudinous warring allegiances I'd have to balance in the coming months. My life was going to be very complicated. When I opened the door to my room I realized just *how* complicated. Sitting in the blue moiré chair by the window, sipping a glass of champagne, was Anton Volkov.

I opened my mouth to scream, but then closed it. Who would come to my aid here at the Grove? Then I noticed that Anton Volkov was wearing a tie clip embossed with the insignia of the Grove.

"You're a member?" I asked coming into the room. "But I thought the Grove didn't admit supernatural creatures?"

"They don't admit fairies and demons. We nocturnals were among those who remained neutral during the Great Division. As a result we've been able to provide many useful services for both groups. But I'm not a member, I'm merely an *associate*."

"You're the informant!" I said, sinking down onto the foot of the bed.

"I prefer to think of myself as a *liaison* between the Grove and Fairwick."

"Uh huh. Then what are you doing here? Have you come to collect on our deal?" I asked, trying to keep my voice from shaking. Anton was close enough that I could feel the magnetism of his presence. And he was close enough that it would be the work of a minute for him to attack and drain me dry. I realized that I didn't want to be attacked and drained dry. I wanted to live. Whatever despair and nihilism that had come over me after I'd banished Liam, it was gone.

"Look," I said, "you told me you wouldn't do anything I didn't agree to and I don't want to . . . get bitten . . . or become a vampire."

Anton smiled and leaned forward in his chair. He touched

one finger to my throat, just below my ear and traced a line down to my collarbone. I shivered.

"Pity . . . but that's not what I was going to ask for. What I want . . . what we, the nocturnals of Fairwick, want is a spokesperson at the Grove. An ally who will attest to our 'good behavior.' You'll be reporting to the Grove on the activities at Fairwick. We merely want to be sure you report that we are behaving according to the guidelines of The Grove. That we only drink from adult, willing non-glamoured volunteers and that we're not turning anyone into vampires."

"But if you *are* obeying all those rules, why do you need to make a special deal with me to report the truth?"

He shrugged and put down his empty champagne glass. I noticed that there were red lip marks on the brim of the glass as if left by lipstick, but I didn't think they came from lipstick.

"Let's just say that an extra word in our favor from a doorkeeper might come in handy in the future. We suspect that relations between the Grove and Fairwick are heading for a crisis. We *fear* that the Grove's power is growing, while Fairwick's is waning. We don't want to get caught in the crossfire."

He got to his feet and extended his hand. "What do you say? Do we have a deal?"

I took his hand, which was icy to the touch. I considered whether this was something I desired. And then I realized how much it would piss off my grandmother.

"Yes," I told him. "We've got a deal."

Driving back to Fairwick the next day through the pouring rain I thought about all the secrets I would have to keep in the coming months: Frank's cover, Soheila's succubus nature, my membership at the Grove, the deal I'd made with the vampires . . . For a girl who'd always valued the truth I'd be telling a lot of lies.

But at least I got to tell one truth. I'd spent half the night reading my new grimoire, paying special attention to the section on reversing a family curse. I'd been surprised and relieved to find out that it didn't involve any bloody sacrifices or burnt offerings. It required only that I speak one sentence to Nicky and mean it:

I forgive the pain your family gave to my family and release you from the pain we've given you.

Pretty simple. Nicky would probably think I'd gone off my rocker when I said it.

I pulled up in front of Honeysuckle House, thinking about the power of forgiveness and the pain we unknowingly cause others. In my head I heard the last question Liam had asked me.

Is a lie really the worst thing if it's told out of love?

I looked at my house for a few moments before getting out of the car. It was a little worse for wear after the long winter – there were tiles missing from the roof and the trim around the eaves could do with a fresh coat of paint. And I really should replace the shutters. But there were also daffodils coming up in the front beds and the honeysuckle shrubs were filling out with tender green buds. This was my home now – for better or worse. My great-great-grandfather had set out from here a bitter and broken man, but somehow I'd found my way back and somehow, against all odds, I'd landed on my feet.

I got out, but instead of going inside I cut across the lawn and walked though a gap in the trees onto the path. The ground was damp from the rain, but at least the snow was gone. I followed the trail to the glade in the middle of the honeysuckle thicket. The twisted branches were stained dark by rain. Against the new trembling green they looked like stained glass windows.

Like a cathedral, Dahlia LaMotte had written at the end of *The Dark Stranger* when Violet Grey and William Dougall find each other in a secluded glade in the forest. In the published book the scene ends with Violet accepting Dougall's offer of marriage. In the handwritten manuscript there were a few additional lines.

I turned from my earthly lover and watched my demon lover rise in the mist beyond the trees. I could see longing in his face, a longing matched in my own sinews and veins. If he called to me, I would follow. But he didn't call to me. He lifted a hand – in parting or benediction I'd never know – and then he vanished into the shadows from which he came.

A fine mist rose from the ground, filling the arched doorway. I stepped closer and the mist parted for me, curled around me, and caressed my face. I felt it linger on the iron key I wore around my neck. I closed my eyes and breathed in the scent of sea air and honeysuckle.

"No," I said, answering the last question Liam had asked me. "A lie told out of love isn't the worst thing."

Then, my face damp from the mist, I turned around and went home.

Turn the page for an interview with
author Carol Goodman:

EBURY
PRESS

You've written a number of critically acclaimed literary thrillers and* Incubus *seems to mark a real change of direction for you as a writer; where did the inspiration for the novel come from?

I was possessed by a demon lover . . . okay, not actually possessed, but it felt like that. I had been walking in a nearby woods that was overgrown with honeysuckle shrubs and I began to think about a house on the edge of such a woods that was possessed by an incubus. Once I started writing the book, I did feel as if I were possessed. I wrote it in half the time I usually take to write a book. Also, I'd like to point out that I've always written about fairy tales . . . it's just that in *Incubus* the fairies are real.

Are you a fan of paranormal fiction? Who do you like to read?

Yes, I was a fan of paranormal fiction before it was called that. Growing up I was obsessed with the TV series *Dark Shadows* and read anything that had a vampire in it, from *Dracula* to the early Anne Rice novels, back when there weren't so many books with vampires. I fell in love with urban fantasy when I read Emma Bull's *The War For The*

Oaks and *Neverwhere* by Neil Gaiman. The contemporary paranormal writers I like best are Charlaine Harris, Karen Marie Moning and, most recently, Deborah Harkness.

True Blood or Twilight?
I liked them both, but if I had to choose: *True Blood*. I think it's one of the best urban fantasy series out there.

So, Eric or Bill?
Eric.

And Edward or Jacob?
Edward.

Fairwick is such a wonderfully imagined town; is it based on a real place (albeit peopled by supernaturals) or did it spring entirely from your imagination?
Like most of the places I create it's an amalgam of real places and my imagination. Fairwick started with a walk I took on an estate in Long Island that was overrun with honeysuckle shrubs. Then I added a Victorian house I'd seen on a trip to a town in upstate New York, added a bit of another town I'd visited . . . and a couple of the college campuses I was visiting with my daughter who was applying to college at the time. Now it mostly resides in my imagination, but I'll recognise bits of it in the outside world and incorporate those bits into my internal geography. There's a house nearby that I now refer to as "Lura's House" (Lura's a character in the next Fairwick book: *The Water Witch*.) I'd been writing about it flooding and then I drove by and saw that the water in the creek behind it was actually rising and threatening to flood the house and I had

this very strange sensation of my real and fictional worlds colliding.

If you could choose to be a 'supernatural' would you? And what form would you take?

I think the lesson we learn through thinking about the alternatives to being human is that no matter how alluring those alternatives there's always a catch. In the long run I think I'd prefer to hold onto my humanity.

Incubus is an incredibly erotic novel. Do you find sex scenes difficult to write?

At first, yes, because it feels like I'm invading my characters' privacy. But then once I'm imagining the moment . . . no.

Dream casting time: who would play Liam in a movie of Incubus? And, who would play Callie?

Enver Gjokaj for Liam, he's a young actor from Joss Whedon's TV series *Dollhouse*.

For Callie, also from the Whedon-verse, Amy Acker. She played Fred in the spin-off *Buffy the Vampire Slayer* series *Angel* (My daughter just insisted I watch all of *Buffy* and *Angel* so I've become immersed in the world of Joss Whedon.)

Which begs the question: Angel or Spike?

Spike!

What comes first, plot or character?

Character. Then something happens to them.

The book interweaves fragments of wonderfully Gothic romance novels – published and unpublished from Dahlia La Motte? Do you have any aspirations to write 'romance'?

I can't imagine a novel in which romance isn't a major element. The books I love – and the books I want to write – are a mixture of genres. If you would call *Jane Eyre* – which combines elements of fairy tale, romance, and mystery – a romance, then yes, I aspire to write romance.

Do you have a favourite time of day to write? A favourite place?

My brain tends to work best in the morning, at least once I've had a cup or two of tea, so I always start out in the morning, at my desk, which has a window over it so I can sit and stare out of it. Usually, most of my writing gets done by the afternoon, but when I was writing *Incubus* I found it hard to stop writing. I'd wake up in the middle of the night and want to write, I'd be standing on line at the supermarket and need to jot something down, I'd take long train rides and write for the whole trip . . . did I mention before that I was a bit possessed?

Which book are you reading at the moment?

I'm reading three: a biography of Daphne du Maurier by Margaret Forster, a soon to be published boarding school thriller called *The Twisted Thread* by Charlotte Bacon, and a book on fairies called *At the Bottom of the Garden* by Diane Purkiss.

Who are your favourite authors?

Charlotte Brontë is my all-time favorite. I love the great

nineteenth-century writers: Dickens, Hardy, the Brontës, and George Eliot. In contemporary fiction: Alice Hoffman, Margaret Atwood, Margaret Drabble, Val McDermid . . . oh, and a British mystery writer I recently started reading, Elly Griffiths.

Which classic have you always meant to read and never got round to it?
Sentimental Education by Flaubert.

Which fictional character would you most like to have met?
Mr. Rochester.